A Killing
in
Zion

A Killing
in
Zion

Andrew Hunt

Minotaur Books

A Thomas Dunne Book
New York

A THOMAS DUNNE BOOK FOR MINOTAUR BOOKS.
An imprint of St. Martin's Publishing Group.

A KILLING IN ZION. Copyright © 2015 by Andrew Hunt. All rights reserved. Printed in the United States of America. For information, address St. Martin's Press, 175 Fifth Avenue, New York, N.Y. 10010.

www.thomasdunnebooks.com
www.minotaurbooks.com

Library of Congress Cataloging-in-Publication Data

Hunt, Andrew E., 1968–
    A killing in Zion: a mystery / Andrew Hunt. — First edition.
        pages cm.
    ISBN 978-1-250-06462-2 (hardcover)
    ISBN 978-1-4668-7082-6 (e-book)
    1. Police—Utah—Salt Lake City—Fiction.   2. Murder—Investigation—Fiction.   3. Mormons—Fiction.   4. Polygamy—Fiction.   I. Title.
    PR9199.4.H858K55 2015
    813'.6—dc23   2015022088

Our books may be purchased in bulk for promotional, educational, or business use. Please contact your local bookseller or the Macmillan Corporate and Premium Sales Department at (800) 221-7945, extension 5442, or by e-mail at MacmillanSprecialMarkets@macmillan.com.

First Edition: September 2015

10 9 8 7 6 5 4 3 2 1

In Memory of
Minerva Colemere
(1917–2013)

Acknowledgments

It is impossible to thank everybody who has enriched my life during the writing of *A Killing in Zion,* but I shall do my best.

I reserve my strongest thanks for my agent, Steve Ross. There is not a better literary agent on earth. Steve promptly answered my email queries with kind and detailed responses. He represented me at all times with a firm professionalism that left me in awe. He is the type of agent who makes you feel like you're his only client, even though that's far from the case. Thank you, Steve.

Thank you to the lovely people at Minotaur/St. Martin's Press. What a pleasure to work with this fantastic publisher a second time. In particular, Bethany Reis was an outstanding copy editor who offered suggestions that greatly enhanced the finished product, while always maintaining a careful eye for even the smallest of historical details. The book you're holding in your hands would not have been possible without the invaluable help and support of Peter Joseph, who also guided me through my first book, *City of Saints,* when it won the Tony Hillerman Prize in 2011. Editors simply do not come any better than Peter. His feedback—always constructive and meaningful, yet also rigorous and challenging—shaped *A Killing in Zion* in profound ways. I am forever indebted to him, as well as the patient and helpful staff at St. Martin's Press that had to deal with me. Thank you.

To my family here in Canada: Madeline and Aidan, no words can express the extent of my love for you, and no father was ever prouder of his children. You've given me endless amounts of joy and laughter and happy times. Bless you, and thank you. Welcome, Marissa, to our family. It is great having you on board!

Thank you to my companion, Luisa, for your love, patience, support, superb cooking, and willingness to listen to my problems and hear me read passages from the book. I love you truly, madly, deeply and I count my blessings each day that you're in my life. Moreover, I consider myself beyond fortunate to have Ruth and Tony in my immediate family.

Anne Hillerman, thank you! You always inspire me, and I loved *Spider Woman's Daughter.* Your father, Tony Hillerman, remains a central figure in my life. I reread and revisit his works often, and with great delight.

To my Utah family: Kay Hunt, I have within me a bottomless sea of gratitude for all of the love, support, and kindness you've shown me over the decades. You've always been my role model as a dad and as a man. Thank you. Linda Hunt, for being a magical and rewarding presence in my life. I am eternally grateful for all of the guidance and love and friendship you've given to me all of these many years. Love and thanks to the world's finest brother, Jeff Hunt, and his wife, Stephanie, and their wonderful children, Charlene, Emily, and Spencer. And I would never forget Adam, whose mighty spirit will never die. Jodie Hunt, I love you, and I am elated you've been such a crucial part of my life for nearly thirty years now. Heartfelt love to all of my fabulous extended relatives—cousins, aunts, uncles, you know who you are—and to the magnificent Bona clan, who will always be my kin.

Finally, I dedicate this book to Minerva Colemere (1917–2013). Grandma Minnie, your beautiful home on Milton Avenue was always a haven of joy and laughter and comfort, a place where each member of your big family felt a sense of belonging, and a Rock of Gibraltar in good times and bad. You showed me the noblest side of humanity, through your words and your deeds. I will miss you until the day I die. I keep the afghan blanket you made for me by my side, and it reminds me of a time and place in my past that I will always cherish.

*This was fairy-land to us, to all intents and purposes—a land
of enchantment, and goblins, and awful mystery.*

—MARK TWAIN ON HIS TRAVELS
THROUGH SALT LAKE CITY, IN *ROUGHING IT*, 1872

A Killing
in
Zion

One

"Crime does not pay!"

The deep voice belonged to a slick gent in a tuxedo, who seconds earlier had slunk up to a radio microphone on a stand. A blinking light above the stage cued musicians in a cramped orchestra pit. The house lights dimmed as the music swelled. The theme song relied heavily on violins, with a few horns sprinkled in for sinister effect. The packed studio audience included my wife, Clara, and my two children, Sarah Jane, age eleven, and Hyrum, five. Earlier in the afternoon, the show's producer had asked me to sit on a stool by the stage so I could get a choice view of the actors. The show, he informed me, was being "transcribed" (a word radio big shots used for "recorded") for nighttime broadcast coast to coast on the NBC radio network. He asked if I'd be willing to answer a couple of questions at the microphone at the close of the broadcast. I said I'd be happy to do it, but stage fright ate away at my stomach something fierce, and I don't think I ever stopped squirming on that hard wooden surface under my behind.

A technician in a glass booth pointed at the widow's-peaked announcer, who responded with a nod and read from a script in his hands. When he spoke, his voice came out more resonant than I expected, especially for such a lean man.

"Welcome to *Crime Does Not Pay*, a copyrighted program, transcribed in Hollywood, USA, presented to you by Bromo-Seltzer, for quick, pleasant relief of upset stomach, nervous tension, and headaches."

I could use some of that, I thought.

Music thundered in the background as he continued: "Each week, *Crime Does Not Pay* brings you a dramatic reenactment of real-life police cases from across America. Tonight, we are proud to present, from the files of the Salt Lake City Police Department, the Case of the Running Board Bandit."

The actor playing me, Lyle Talbot, walked out from behind the curtains and the flashing APPLAUSE light nudged the audience into action. The handsome Talbot bore no resemblance to me— no hint of my gangly frame, ruddy complexion, or unruly auburn hair—but I suppose it didn't matter, this being radio and all. Debonair, in a three-piece suit, with slick dark hair, Talbot held a script and mouthed "thank you" repeatedly. As the applause and music quieted, he closed in on that silvery microphone and read the lines without even glancing at his script.

"My name is Patrolman Arthur Oveson," he said. I bowed my head, containing my embarrassment with a shaky inhale. "I've walked the night beat in Salt Lake City for the past four years. My job: to keep the good men and women of this town safe. I have a beautiful wife and the finest children a father could ever hope for. I can honestly say the last place I ever expected to find myself was on the bad end of that .38 Special wielded by the notorious Running Board Bandit. . . ."

The music flared up again as more cast members poured out from between the curtains and gathered around the microphone.

"Beware of the Running Board Bandit, gentlemen," said the actor portraying Sergeant Noel Gunderson at roll call. "He operates at night, and his method is to crouch low on the passenger side running board of automobiles with his pistol and wait for the unsuspecting driver to get in. When that happens, he pops up like a jack-in-the-box, demanding money. The bandit is armed and dangerous. If you encounter him, exercise utmost caution. That is all."

The actor playing my partner, Roscoe Lund, seemed mousy, with too much pomade in his hair. He bore no resemblance to the genuine Roscoe, whose shaved head, muscular physique, and thick neck frightened off even the most stalwart of lawbreakers. The actor playing him made up for his slight and shifty-eyed appearance by acting the part with a gravelly voice. I had wondered how the scriptwriter, who consulted me months ago by telephone about the particulars of the case, was going to portray Roscoe, a profanity-spewing cop who'd recently given up cigarettes in favor of chewing tobacco and always kept a flask full of some kind of booze in his pocket.

I soon found out.

"Heck, Art, do you really think it's a good idea to put yourself in danger by going out there alone at night with all of them dang robberies happening?" asked the ersatz Roscoe. "You're gonna get yourself hurt or even killed if you insist on being so gol-durn pigheaded!"

Heck. Dang. Gol-durn. A trio of words I'd never heard Roscoe

utter. His tastes were decidedly saltier when it came to exple-
tives.

I chuckled softly as I listened to the performers read one
melodramatic line after another, talking in a way we've never
talked before. I must confess: The part of the show that really
gave me the jitters was the exchange between the radio Art and
the radio Clara. During it, I swiveled on my stool to glimpse
Clara's radiant face and beautiful golden hair, styled in a permanent wave. She must've seen me, because she flashed a pearly
smile in my direction before shifting her gaze back to the actors on stage.

"Oh, Arthur, please do be careful, darling," said the pretty,
petite, and crimson-lipped actress playing Clara. "The thought
of you being robbed by this treacherous criminal is more than
I can bear. Remember, we have children, and I do not wish to
be a widow!"

"I have to do my duty, dear," said Talbot. "You knew when
you married me that you would be the wife of a policeman. Danger, I am afraid, goes hand in hand with the job."

"Oh, Arthur, kiss me!"

The radio Art and radio Clara refrained from kissing as the
orchestra played. I think I spotted Clara winking at me in the
darkness. In that instant, much to my relief, the Bromo-Seltzer
advertisement interrupted the action.

I loosened my collar when it came time for the radio Art to
confront the Running Board Bandit. Memories of that fright-
ening encounter, on a crisp, chill fall night last year, came flood-
ing back to me. The shock of a pistol's cold steel against my
neck, the startling click of its hammer, so much louder when it
is aimed at you—it all made my heart race, then and now.

Until that night, I'd only heard stories from others about

Henry Grenache, the twenty-two-year-old unemployed miner whose purchase of a .38 caliber six-round revolver from a downtown pawnshop last summer set off a chain of late-night robberies around the Salt Lake Valley. The Running Board Bandit quickly became something of a local legend, a spooky story told around dinner tables and campfires. Such tales prompted even the most stout-hearted to check over their shoulders at night and made nervous teenagers rush home before curfew. When my brush with him finally came, it frightened me to the core, bringing me in touch with my own mortality in a way that few events up to that point had. How was I to know that night when I dashed inside the Brigham Street Pharmacy on South Temple and E Street to buy a bottle of milk and a Bit-O-Honey that he'd leap out of the bushes and crouch on the running board of my Oldsmobile with a loaded gun, awaiting my return?

I didn't see his face when I got back in my car, only his silhouette and the glimmer of the weapon aimed at me from the other side of the glass. His voice was muffled. "Raise your hands where I can see 'em!" I did as he demanded and he opened the rear passenger-side door, slithered inside, and pressed the gun to the back of my neck. "One wrong move and I'll blow your brains out. Gimme your wallet. Now. Now!" Shaking, feeling cold steel next to my earlobe, I fumbled for my wallet and passed it to him over the seat. The crack of a heavy gun butt against the back of my head sent my face slamming against the steering wheel. I wasn't sure what hurt worse, the back of my head or the new cut on my lip. I was too frightened to make a fair assessment. But leaning over the steering wheel, I spied the tire iron poking out from under the seat. Grenache's voice told me he was distracted. "See what you've got in here . . . Oh Christ, you're a . . ." I grabbed the long metal tool and swung it at him, connecting with his head. He screamed, toppled backward, and fired his gun. The bullet ripped through the car roof, and a ray of harvest moonlight poured in. A second later, I was aiming my sidearm at him as he rubbed the cut on his head. I switched on the interior globe to get a better look at him. The left side of his face was covered with blood, and greasy strands of hair dangled from the top of his head as he slumped back against the seat, moaning in terrible pain.

The actors at the microphone brought me back to the here and now.

"I can't believe you knocked me in the head with a jack handle, copper!"

"You should know by now, Grenache, that crime does not pay. . . ."

That set off the orchestra. Climactic music filled the radio studio as the two actors stepped away from the microphone. "And now, a final word from the real Arthur Oveson," said the announcer. "Detective Oveson, would you kindly join us?"

The audience clapped as I rose from the stool and crossed the stage. I shook hands with the announcer and all of the actors during the applause.

"You did a splendid job playing me," I told Lyle Talbot.

He smiled with his mouth and his eyes and whispered his thanks.

"Detective Oveson, please step to the microphone," said the announcer. I nodded and moved in close. "I believe I speak for all of our listeners across America when I say that your heroism on that night back in November was truly inspiring."

"Thank you, sir."

"I understand you were given a promotion after this harrowing incident, Detective Oveson."

"Please call me Art," I said. "And yes, I was promoted to the detective bureau. I now command my own squad in the Salt Lake City Police Department."

Scattered applause crackled.

"I see! Congratulations!"

"Thank you."

"Do you have any parting words, especially for the boys and girls listening to our show tonight?"

I nodded. "Yes, I do. Stay in school, study hard, do your homework. And if you ever find yourself in trouble, tell a grown-up, especially if that grown-up happens to be a police officer. We're here to help you in any way we can."

"Thank you, Detective Oveson, for those wise words. And that concludes tonight's episode of *Crime Does Not Pay*, brought to you by Bromo-Seltzer." Dramatic music filled the studio again. "Be sure to tune in next week at this time as we present the intriguing case of Cleveland's Phantom Burglar. For the National Broadcasting Company, this is Red Wilcox bidding you good night from Hollywood, USA."

I white-knuckle-gripped the armrests as the airplane bounced in midair. Between bouts of turbulence, I checked over my shoulder to see Clara and Hyrum in the row behind me, both sound asleep. Now eight months into her pregnancy, Clara's stomach formed a glorious dome under her green frock. Hyrum sucked his finger while he slept, a habit that had persisted since infancy. I caught my breath and faced forward. Our plane, a dual-engine United Airlines with a pair of roaring propellers, descended into a thick brown haze, the result of massive blazes burning up the Wasatch and Dixie National Forests below us. The airplane cabin was designed with one seat on either side of the aisle, for a ten-passenger capacity. When we weren't leapfrogging over clouds, the stewardess would squeeze by, asking if we needed anything. I'd smile, shake my head, and pretend I wasn't in the throes of mortal fear. I kept a United Airlines sick sack by my side at all times, and I closed curtains in a fruitless attempt to ease my terror of heights.

"Ladies and gents," crackled the pilot's voice through a loud-speaker overhead. "We regret the bumpy skies, but we should be past them very soon. . . ."

That's what he said he over Nevada, I thought. Right then, the plane shook violently, to show me who was boss. I gave the sick sack a squeeze.

"It's the safest form of travel, you know."

I looked across the aisle at Sarah Jane, who licked her finger and turned the page of her book. She had inherited her mom's features: hazel eyes, a narrow nose, a light sprinkling of freckles on her cheeks, and chin-length golden-brown hair. She mouthed the words as she read them, and no matter how often the plane shook and rattled, she never once averted her eyes from her book. She showed no hint of fear. How did she do it?

"Come again?" I asked.

"Airlines. Your odds of dying in a car wreck or a train jumping the tracks are a lot higher than in a plane crash."

"Let's change the subject, why don't we. What are you reading?"

She pressed her finger between the pages to hold her place as she closed the book and held it up so I could see the cover. *Little Women*, said the gold engraved lettering, and below: *Louisa May Alcott*. I made a long face and tilted my head. "Isn't this the third time you've read it?"

"Fourth," she said, opening it to where she left off. "I read it again in May, for Mrs. Wells's class. This trip makes four."

I bobbed my head, doing my best to ignore the roller-coaster ride that was this flight. "Four times. That's good. You must really love it, if you've read it four times."

The ceiling speakers hissed and spat and the pilot's voice came on: "We will be landing at Salt Lake Municipal Airport shortly. Those of you sitting on the right-hand side of the plane will marvel at the picturesque view of the city."

Sarah Jane nudged me. "Open the curtains, Dad."

"I'd rather not. . . ."

"C'mon. Have a look. You'll feel better." She tipped her head at the window. "Go on. Do it."

With a trembling hand, I slid open the gray curtain and gazed out. It all appeared so small, that patchwork quilt of earth below, with a surprising number of green squares for a city at the desert's edge. Mountains hemmed in the valley like a fortress, except for the northwest corner, where the Oquirrh Mountains tapered off at the shores of the Great Salt Lake. Even from thousands of feet above the valley's southern end, the downtown and the granite spires of the Salt Lake Temple on the northern side were clearly visible. The sixteen-story Walker Bank Building dominated the skyline, with its towering radio antennae and WALKER BANK spelled out in tall electric-lit words. From this distance, I could even see the giant white *U* built on the side of Mount Van Cott, a symbol of the University of Utah, whose campus of columned, ivy-covered buildings nestled against the Wasatch Range nearby. The airplane dipped lower, its winged shadow swimming over farms and rural roads in the valley's middle. Wide streets intersected in a perfect grid originating from the downtown temple, a deliberate plan by Brigham Young and the early settlers of this place. Thanks to them, it is difficult—if not impossible—to get lost in Salt Lake City.

Parting those curtains worked wonders. The dread I experienced only minutes earlier eased. I uncoiled in my seat and loosened my hold on the armrests. The airplane still jumped about in the skies, but now that we hovered low over the city, it all seemed so much less perilous than before, perhaps because I knew my destination was right under me. Even though I grew up in the next valley to the south, Salt Lake City felt more like home than my actual hometown of American Fork. This is where I lived out my various roles as husband, father, police detective, and member of the Church of Jesus Christ of Latter-day Saints.

Salt Lake City greeted me like an old friend. Salt Lake City, with streets so wide that back in pioneer times a team of four oxen pulling a covered wagon could make a U-turn with room to spare. Salt Lake City, home to ice cream parlors, movie palaces, and the most majestic state capitol building in the country, at the top of a hill overlooking the valley. Salt Lake City, where trolley bells rang like the heartbeat of a vibrant commercial center that a mere hundred years ago was uninhabited scrub. It all seemed so familiar, as if it were part of me, and I part of it.

"See?" said Sarah Jane.

"What?"

"I told you if you opened the curtains you'd feel better."

"You're right."

"I know I'm right." She smiled. "You think the firefighters have got all those blazes licked, Dad?"

I shook my head, craning my neck to get a better look at the swirling smoke clouds swallowing up the tops of the Wasatch Mountains. "Doesn't look like it."

"That's too bad. Mary says half the state is burning up. Her uncle is a volunteer with the Provo Hook and Ladder."

"That's brave of him," I said as we glided low over the airfield.

The airplane touched down on a dusty runway within sight of the Great Salt Lake. With propellers still roaring, it taxied past a cluster of arched steel hangars and some small woodframe buildings that housed aviation schools and aircraft rental joints. It came to a halt near a new municipal terminal—built last year to attract visitors—where dozens of other airplanes were parked. I glanced back at Clara and Hyrum, both awake now and smiling, having slept the entire flight.

"Are we there yet?" said Hyrum, wiping cinders from his eyes. "That was fast."

When the airplane stopped moving, unfastening seat belts clicked away and us passengers rose in unison, yet we all remained hunched thanks to the low ceiling. I pulled our luggage out of overhead compartments and the stewardess opened the door at the rear of the airplane. The kids were out of their seats first, scurrying toward the exit.

"I can't wait to get home and try out that new hammock you got me for my birthday," I told Clara as we inched forward, on our way to the oval-shaped doorway lit by sun. "The way I see it, it won't hurt to miss one day of church."

She shrugged. "Somehow, I get the idea Heavenly Father will forgive you. Last time you missed was back in twenty-seven, when you had whooping cough, and you only missed once, even though when you went the next Sunday you were still sick as a dog. You were hacking away in sacrament meeting. Remember?"

"Oh yeah," I said. "I'll take the rest of the day off, my last few hours of freedom before going back to work tomorrow. Live like a king."

Bowing slightly to pass through the doorway, I maneuvered the two suitcases outside and clanked down the metal staircase. I reached the ground and beheld an unexpected scene: A massive crowd of Ovesons—my mother, three brothers, a trio of corresponding in-laws, and the hordes of children who accompanied them—blocked my way to the airport entrance. Big words in black paint on a homemade banner cried out, WELCOME HOME, RADIO STAR!!! They waved and cheered and erupted into "For He's a Jolly Good Fellow" as I approached. Did I mention that there's nothing Mormons love more than to show up at airports in big crowds to greet arriving family members?

Clara squeezed my elbow and I turned halfway to her as we crossed the sun-drenched tarmac.

"What was that about trying out your hammock and living like a king?" she asked, with a spirited laugh. "Looks like you're going to have to take a detour through your hometown for Mom's pot roast first."

Two

Crowds churned in the Public Safety Building's cavernous lobby. Here, one could encounter a microcosm of the society beyond these walls: purposeful men and women filing complaints or renewing driver's licenses; bleary-eyed hookers in tattered stockings, indifferent to the world around them, and their antsy customers, pleading to be released; sullen truants busted for sluffing school; belligerents who used force instead of words to solve disputes; and, of course, police, multitudes of police, both the plainclothes and uniformed varieties. Some milled about; others moved more deliberately. I fell into the latter category. I darted around men and women on my way to the marble staircase rising to the second floor, the location of my office.

A three-story building at 105 South State, it opened its doors in 1908, first as headquarters of the Young Men's Christian Association. Seven years later, the YMCA relocated to a smaller, less expensive place, and the Salt Lake City Police Department moved in. Public Safety had the look and feel of those stodgy federal buildings you see in the District of Columbia, with its high ceilings, frosted glass windows on the doors, and marble staircases connecting to other floors.

The detective bureau shared the second floor with the court chambers and pressroom, and at any given time of day clacking typewriters echoed through the halls like a troupe of eager tap dancers. The building came with strange charms, such as dimly lit corridors leading to sealed-off doors or bricked-up dead ends. On one floor, a padlocked entrance prevented access to an empty swimming pool that hadn't been used in years. Back in the early twenties, policemen swam laps as part of a calisthenics regimen, but pool maintenance became too expensive and the chief ordered it drained and closed to cut operational expenses.

I arrived at a door with frosted glass that read ROOM 224, and then below that, ANTI-POLYGAMY SQUAD in large black serif letters with gold shadowing. My office.

Once upon a time, not long ago, I used to work a few doors down, in Morals, a thirteen-man unit responsible for busting prostitutes, drug peddlers, bookmakers, pornography merchants, and all other purveyors of vice. We raided illicit gambling joints, holes-in-the-wall that served liquor without a license, and fleabag hotels specializing in noontime whoopee for married fellows and their paid ladies. We confiscated slot machines, bottles of rotgut sans government seals, boxes of stag films and dirty magazines, and nearly every kind of illegal substance you can imagine. For reasons that eluded me, every man in the Morals Squad—including me—was a Latter-day Saint, a fact that irritated the gentiles on the force ("gentile" is a term that Mormons appropriated from Jews to describe non-Mormons), who took to calling us "the Mormon Squad."

My transfer to the Anti-Polygamy Squad happened in March.

On a chilly morning, the mayor of Salt Lake City summoned me to his office without giving a reason why. I arrived with my stomach tied in knots. Mayor Bennett Cummings, a man with a reputation as a crusader, waited in the anteroom to greet me personally, as effusive as I'd ever seen another man. He invited me into his office, where, in the presence of my superiors, Chief William Cowley and Captain Buddy Hawkins, he asked me to head the notorious squad.

The police chief back in 1914, Alonzo Burbidge, had created the unit in response to a series of muckraking articles splashed across page A1 of the *Salt Lake Examiner* revealing that thousands of polygamists resided in the Salt Lake Valley. Their presence greatly embarrassed leaders of the Church of Jesus Christ of Latter-day Saints, whose president, Wilford Woodruff, had issued a manifesto in 1890 banning the practice of plural marriage. Some purists, believing Woodruff had betrayed early church doctrines in exchange for achieving statehood for Utah, insisted on adhering to the controversial practice and continued to wed multiple wives. Police and politicians alike turned a blind eye to the practice until the *Examiner*'s exposés about polygamists not only living, but thriving, in and around Salt Lake City brought national attention to them.

The police cracked down by forming the Anti-Polygamy Squad. Its mission, according to Burbidge, was to "rid our great city of the scourge of plural marriage." Burbidge assigned eight of his top detectives to the squad, to show that his intention to break the "local polygamy racket" (as he called it) was sincere. The squad made some early headway, arresting patriarchs and driving the more conflict-averse practitioners out of the city. However, in time, the police backed away from the effort, opting instead to focus on other crimes that seemed to be more pressing, such as vice and homicides. The squad remained dormant for years, run mostly by one man, Detective John Goetten, until his retirement earlier this year. Goetten had done a halfhearted job of collecting files on suspects and rarely arresting and only briefly detaining the more flagrant zealots.

Three things—Goetten's departure, the election of an overzealous new mayor, and the fame I gained from arresting the Running Board Bandit—resulted in the revival of the moribund Anti-Polygamy Squad with me at its head. "Would you do us the honor of bringing your leadership abilities to this unit?" the mayor asked me. How could I refuse? Still, when he asked, I excused myself from his office, claiming that I had to use the restroom. I nearly killed myself—and one or two other people—sprinting to a row of Mountain States Telephone & Telegraph booths near the building's entrance. I flung open the mahogany-and-glass door, lifted the receiver, dropped a coin in the slot, and called Clara at East High while she was in the middle of choir rehearsal. I told her about the offer and asked her if I should take the job. She advised me to go with my gut instincts. When I voiced concerns that the job would be demanding and may take me away from our baby—due to be born in late July—she told me I was worrying too much. "You made time for the other two," she told me. "You'll make time for this one."

After five minutes on the telephone with Clara, I rushed back to the mayor's office, and—sweating and struggling to catch my breath—said yes to the job, while the perplexed trio of men looked on, perhaps wondering whether I'd lost my mind. The next day, Cummings held a press conference to announce the squad's rebirth. Predictably, the critics made noise right away. The mayor's opposition, mainly city councilors who either coveted Cummings's job or hated him for the toll that his numerous municipal crusades took on them and their allies, lashed out, referring to the squad as a waste of taxpayers' money. Cummings responded defiantly by appointing three men to assist me: Roscoe Lund, a uniformed patrolman; Jared Weeks, a motorcycle cop from the Traffic Division; and Myron Adler, who'd previously toiled away in the basement records room.

Roscoe came at my request. I must admit I encountered some resistance from my superiors when I asked if he could join my squad, due mainly to his long track record of insubordination. Before being reassigned here, Roscoe had been unhappily guiding traffic downtown, the lowest spot on the police totem pole. I promised my commander to keep him on a leash, so the brass reluctantly upgraded him to the detective bureau on a trial basis. If he behaves, Captain Buddy Hawkins, chief of detectives, told me, he'll be allowed to stay on the squad. Roscoe and I had a long history together. We had been partners during our short stint as deputies for the Salt Lake County sheriff's office back in 1930. We were teamed up again in the Salt Lake City Police Department that same year as uniformed patrolmen. Naturally, we developed a strong bond after working together for so long. Roscoe had also grown close to my wife and children over time, visiting our house for dinner once or twice a month and bringing my daughter and son gifts at Christmastime and on their birthdays. Having him on the squad reassured me, knowing such a close ally was in my corner.

The other two men, Jared Weeks and Myron Adler, took time to warm up to. Weeks, a man in his mid-to-late twenties, was particularly hard to read. I always found him upbeat, the kind of fella who said, "Just fine, and you?" whenever you asked him how he was doing. He preferred to call me "boss" and carried a battered leather satchel around with him wherever he went. He never said anything about his personal life or his family—if he even had one. He towered at about six feet eight inches, owing to a case of Marfan syndrome (which Abe Lincoln was thought to have), and his striking features included a golden-haired Caesar cut, blue eyes, and a wide mouth that stood out on such a lean face. He actually had asked for a transfer to the Anti-Polygamy Squad after he saw a posting for it on a departmental job listings bulletin board, so I arranged an interview with him. His responses to my questions were brief yet friendly, and by the time he left, I found myself impressed with his earnestness and dedication. Before arriving here, he had acquired a tan from sitting on a Harley-Davidson day in, day out parked behind a Cream o'Weber Dairy billboard by the side of Highway 91, ticketing speeders. Once on the squad, he immersed himself in researching the unusual world of plural marriage and emerged as something of an expert on all things polygamy, but never in a show-offy way. He was as helpful as he was private. At the end of each day, I always wondered where he went.

By contrast, I found Myron Adler impassive yet talkative, a man who rarely filtered his words before saying them and probably kept no secrets. He'd worked as a clerk down in records since joining the force in early December of 1931. He kept his short, wavy black hair combed neatly to the right, and gazed out at the world through wire-rimmed glasses with thick eyebrows above the lenses. His cleft chin drew attention away from his narrow lips. Alert eyes, enlarged by Coke-bottle lenses, seldom blinked. I could not even venture a guess, from his blank expression, what thoughts may've been racing through his mind at any given moment.

I knew Adler to be the sole Jew on the payroll of the Salt Lake City Police Department. When William Cowley replaced Otis Ballard as chief of police in the fall of 1931, one of the first things he did was hire a Jew and a colored man named Elbridge Davis. It was all a part of Cowley's campaign to prove to the public that the city's police force would no longer tolerate bigotry or discrimination in its ranks. Adler ended up in the records room, the remotest part of Public Safety. I'm not sure where Davis went—I seldom saw him—but it probably wasn't much better. I could not tell, for the life of me, whether Adler was happy to be promoted to plainclothes detective. He was never demonstrative with his feelings. Cowley himself personally promoted Adler to the squad. The chief told me he felt confident that Myron was ready to advance to the detective bureau. However, Cowley exercised caution in appointing Myron to a unit where anti-Semitic prejudice would be minimal, if not nonexistent. The records division's loss was our gain. Myron brought with him an uncanny ability to remember a multitude of tiny details, the likes of which I've never witnessed before. He could tell you how many wives a particular polygamist had, or a suspect's exact street address, date of birth, arrest date, and so on, without even having to look it up. And he'd always be right.

"I'm what the alienists call an eidetic," he informed me the day I met him in March. "Also known as a form-seer. It means I have a photographic memory. It's a rare condition. I was one of eighteen subjects in a study at the University of Marburg, under the supervision of Dr. Erich Rudolf Jaensch. That was about six years ago, before Hitler and his Brownshirt henchmen took over. Too bad. It was a pretty place before that. I'd never set foot there now."

The revitalized Anti-Polygamy Squad had gone to work, in earnest, on the second of April, aggressively tracking down polygamists in our midst. My goal was to carry out mass arrests, to show the mayor that his money and resources were being well spent. I began my mission self-assured. I did not, however, anticipate that my foes would be so cunning. Locating them was the easy part. Unfortunately for me, these men turned out to be astonishingly adept at hiding their transgressions. It only took a few weeks as squad commander for me to realize that I was engaged in a cat-and-mouse game with men who always stayed one or two steps ahead of me. The prospect of catching up to them began to dim. By the middle of June, before I took my family to Los Angeles, Chief Cowley called me into his office. I correctly predicted what he was going to tell me. *Show results, as soon as possible.* I was right. The man wanted to see high-profile busts. Pronto.

The pressure was on.

Our small squad operated out of a spacious room, brimming with natural light thanks to tall windows on the east wall. Four desks easily fit in the office, each with a Royal typewriter, a telephone, a city directory, and a swivel chair. Two guest chairs sat side by side in a corner. Chest-high filing cabinets stood against the walls. The place still had that fresh-paint smell, and an oscillating fan circulated warm air blowing in through the open windows. The view looked out at a half-full parking lot housing a shiny fleet of black-and-white 1934 Ford Model 40 V8 Deluxe patrol cars, along with a scattering of unmarked police sedans.

That Monday morning, Myron and Jared sat at their desks and greeted me with quiet hellos when I walked in the door. On the wall above Roscoe's desk hung a big map of Salt Lake City punctured by colored pushpins that reminded me of Christmas lights. Each pin represented a different polygamist dwelling. Clusters were bunched together in the Avenues, the quaint hillside neighborhood on the northeast bench of the Wasatch Mountains where I lived as well. You could also find plenty of pins around the Marmalade District, an area of nineteenth-century mansions west of Capitol Hill; near Liberty Park in the city's center, where construction crews were still building fresh bungalows; and in the farmlands to the south, down around Riverton, Draper, and Bluffdale, a group of tiny burghs that bid you farewell before you crossed into Utah Valley. The colored pins—there must've been two hundred of them—made our mission seem that much more tangible. I ran my fingers along those primary colors, eager to carry out my first big busts.

Then I spied Roscoe's empty chair. Thoughts of colored pins faded.

"Anyone seen Roscoe?"

"Nope."

"Not yet."

I walked over and perched my hind end on my desk's edge, let out a loud exhale, and ran my hand across my forehead. When I pulled it away, it startled me to see Myron Adler standing before me, holding a pink pastry box.

"Rugelach," said Myron. "They're a traditional favorite. Hannah made them."

I glanced down at the sweet golden-brown crescents. "They look delicious."

"Take two. One won't fill you."

I did as he suggested, biting into one and setting its twin

beside the typewriter. Deliciousness filled my mouth—a flaky shell with cinnamon, walnuts, and raisins inside. I loved every bite and showed it with a long, drawn-out "mmm-mmm." "Dang, that's tasty. Tell Hannah I love it and I want more."

Myron's facial expression stayed strictly deadpan—not so much as a slight grin—and he stood in place holding that box, motionless, like a statue. I used my pants as a napkin for my sugar-and-crumb-coated fingers, then I popped the second half in my mouth and chewed away, repeating the "mmm-mmm," in case Myron had any doubts. "Scrumptious."

"He sounds nothing like you," said Myron.

"Come again?"

"Lyle Talbot."

I finished chewing what was in my mouth and swallowed. "Oh. You heard that on the radio?"

"Yeah."

I waited for him to say something. When he didn't, I prodded: "Well? What did you think?"

"Decent production values done in by a hokey script," he said. "The dialogue was hopelessly contrived and stilted. People don't talk like that in real life. At least nobody I know ever does."

"Thank you for your honesty."

"Don't mention it." He turned to Jared Weeks. "What about you? Did you tune in to *Crime Does Not Pay* on Saturday night?"

Jared didn't look up from whatever he was doing. "I don't own a radio."

Myron faced me. "I jotted down a list of seven mistakes they made in their decidedly fictionalized version of the case, should you be interested. . . ."

"No, that's quite all right," I said. "I'll, uh, take your word for it."

"Suit yourself." Myron returned to his desk, closing the box of rugelach on the way. "If you change your mind, let me know."

"I will."

"How was your trip to Los Angeles, boss?" asked Jared, swiveling toward me in his chair. "Feeling rested and refreshed?"

"Hardly," I said. "We never stopped to relax. The network gave us the royal treatment. We got to stay in a fancy hotel. We went to the beach. We purchased one of those maps of the movie stars' homes and drove through the posh neighborhoods. One of the days we were there, we even got to tour a motion picture studio and saw a movie being made. There's nothing else quite like Los Angeles."

"That's swell, boss," said Jared, with a crooked grin. "We missed you while you were gone, but we held the fort."

"Good to hear," I told him. "Well, let's get back to business. Who's willing to take notes?"

Jared raised his hand.

"Thanks, Jared. So, any breaks while I was away?"

"Still slow going," said Jared, jotting as he spoke. "We were hoping to tie at least three key polygamists to violations of the White-Slave Traffic Act—"

"Also known as the Mann Act," interrupted Myron.

"Which three?" I asked. "Please tell me one of them is Uncle Grand. . . ."

"No, not Uncle Grand," said Jared. "He's too careful. Our pair of witnesses may be able to connect Moss, Barton, and Boggs to those violations. *If* they are willing to testify. That's a *big* if. It's not looking hopeful at this point."

"What about using the mails to send obscene materials?" I asked. "Any progress on that front?"

"We were aiming to pin that charge on Alma Covington,

who's still editing the polygamist newspaper out of his basement," said Myron. "We haven't had much luck so far. I'm combing through back issues as we speak."

"I'm not too hopeful about that option," I said. "It's a tame little thing, hardly what I'd call a smut rag. What about illegal cohabitation?"

"It'll be tough," said Myron. I knew he was right. After the last roundup of polygamists about thirteen years ago on illegal cohabitation charges, the lawbreakers wised up. Nowadays, all of their wives live in separate dwellings, and the patriarchs go from home to home rather than keeping the wives in the same house.

"And the Lindbergh Law?" I pressed.

They shook their heads at the same time. "The witness recanted," said Jared, writing more notes. "She was the mother. Remember? Mrs. Jardine. She was prepared to testify that her twelve-year-old daughter had been kidnapped, forced against her will into the sect, and taken across the border into Arizona, but she backed down. She's afraid of what the polygamists will do to her and her family if she goes on the witness stand."

"Did you tell her—"

"Yeah, of course I did," said Jared testily, lowering his pen. "Told her we could have an armed patrolman placed at her house for protection, at least during the trial. She said no."

"What about Uncle Grand?" I asked.

"No new developments on that front while you were gone," said Myron. "Do you really think it's such a good idea to keep tailing the guy?"

Jared chimed in. "With all due respect, boss, you've been following the man since mid-April and it don't seem to be doing a lick o' good."

"I'll take your comments into consideration," I said, in an attempt to give them the brush-off. "Anything else?"

Myron said, "We know of a former cult member who might be willing to testify that Johnston routinely advocates plural marriage during services at their little church down on Lincoln Street."

"Advocating isn't illegal," I said. "Last I checked there's still a First Amendment. What else?"

"What else do you want?" asked Myron. "We've got a small squad." He glanced at Roscoe's empty chair. "And not everyone pulls his weight."

The comment stung, but how could I quarrel with him? He was right. Maybe carving out a place for Roscoe on this squad hadn't been the best idea after all. I knew what had to be done next: Find Roscoe. Fast. My reasons were purely selfish. Him not showing up to work made me look bad. My ears still worked well enough that I could hear the whispers around the hallway, hushed talk about me, a "yes-man to the bosses downstairs" who got where he was because of his "legendary father," being "suckered in" by my best friend, an "over-the-hill boozer." I tried my hardest to ignore this kind of talk. At the end of the day, however, even though I pretended not to care, I cared very much.

Three

I surged outside into the hazy heat of Salt Lake City, where everything had turned a shade of rust under smoke-shrouded skies. About the only good that could be said of the ugly discoloration that came with being downwind of so many wildfires is that it shielded us, slightly, from the worst of the sun's midday assault. We paid a big price for that shield, though. It reeked of smoke everywhere, and the veil over our heads tinted all things—cars, buildings, the LDS Temple—in sepia tones and left a fine film of ash in many places. These infernos had been months in the making. A combination heat wave and drought that arrived in Utah in the spring had turned forests into tinderboxes, and—just as the experts had predicted—the arrival of summer brought fires to the state. Radio reports told of flames leaping into nearby canyons and making their way closer to the city. Each day, chartered motor buses transported brave men to the front lines of the worst-hit places: Black's Fork, Pine Valley, Crandall Canyon and, closer to home, Big Cottonwood Canyon, where I could see the mountainside glowing orange from my porch late at night. Each day I hesitated to pick up the morning newspaper, fearing more stories of crews unable to contain blazes and young men—boys, really—perishing in ways I didn't even want to imagine.

Behind the wheel of an unmarked police sedan, I drove westbound out of the city on a street called North Temple, over a viaduct that spanned the rail yard, in the direction of the Great Salt Lake. I switched off the police radio. This situation called for my complete attention. Roscoe Lund had to be found and returned to Public Safety before our superiors noticed his absence. The powers that be in the police force had no use for Roscoe, and he responded by playing into their hands. He did this in a variety of ways: not showing up to work; mouthing off to superiors; sparring with other cops, at times with words, at times with fists.

I had been on the receiving end of others' grief for my unswerving loyalty to Roscoe for years now. A few of the more pious Mormons I know had asked me how I—a dedicated churchgoer—could be so close to such a foul-mouthed and hard-drinking rebel. I'd been told by some of my fellow lawmen that my bond with Roscoe has been imprudent on my part and has probably hindered my career in the Salt Lake City Police Department. Myron Adler once expressed his dismay over my attempts to help Roscoe out of jams. "I don't see what you get out of being that dreg's guardian angel," he told me. When I hear those kinds of comments, I usually shrug them off. I'll say something along the lines of "You don't know Roscoe like I know him," or "He's a great guy if you give him half a chance." But the real reason for the closeness between Roscoe and me could not be articulated so easily.

Since our first partnering when we worked in the Salt Lake County sheriff's office, through our time as uniformed patrolmen in the Salt Lake City Police Department, Roscoe had become more like a family member than a friend. He got to be closer to me than any of my brothers. I never had been one to spill my guts to anyone, but I found myself confiding in him on repeated occasions. In turn, he'd tell me about a woman he was seeing, or a place he wished he could go if he had the money (the South Seas came up many times), or he'd recall tales from his colorful youth. So many times we laughed together. Once, when I was talking about my father, I got teary-eyed in front of him. All of those experiences, night after night, week after week, month after month, year after year, cemented our connection to each other. I imagine it was something akin to the relationship that develops between soldiers who share a trench together, though I am fortunate that I was too young to experience the Great War to say that with any certainty.

At the end of the day, put in its simplest terms, Roscoe was my friend, warts and all. As someone who did not have many genuine friends, the few I did have meant a great deal to me. The way I saw it, the occasional headaches and inconveniences that came with that camaraderie were but a small price to pay.

Driving west, with the Wasatch Mountains shrinking in my rearview mirror, I sped into an area of warehouses, cheap luncheonettes, a liquor store, a bowling alley built of adobe, and long stretches of earth between everything. I kept pace with a Union Pacific passenger train, its frenetic locomotive spewing smoke. I neared the sombrero-shaped sign for the Tampico, a Mexican restaurant. I swerved into its parking lot and found a spot between an ice delivery truck and the saddest-looking flivver I'd ever laid eyes on. The building's paint had faded, worn off the brick entirely in some places. The storefront window facing North Temple advertised MEXICAN FOOD SERVED ROUND THE CLOCK.

A call from a downtown telephone booth had brought me out here. It was the second place I called after I didn't get an answer at Roscoe's apartment. The owner of the joint, an old friend, confirmed my suspicions. Roscoe was, indeed, there.

The Tampico had an old-time Mexican feel, with scattered late breakfast customers seated at tables and booths and a mariachi album playing on a behind-the-counter Victrola. Potted cacti were placed everywhere, and the walls showcased framed black-and-white photographs of people I guessed were Mexicans: Mexicans posing by old jalopies, Mexicans working in orchards, Mexicans dancing in courtyards, Mexican revolutionaries riding horses alongside a train.

I knew the owner; sweet old Miguel, one of the nicest fellows I'd ever met. Balding and beefy with an inky black mustache, he always wore a pristine white shirt with sleeves rolled up to his elbows, black trousers, and shiny patent leather shoes. Back in the days when I worked Dawn Patrol, the midnight-to-8 A.M. shift, Roscoe and I would drive out here every night because it was one of the few restaurants open twenty-four hours. Roscoe still dined here frequently.

"Señor Arturo!"

"Miguel! How's every little thing?"

We shook hands and he nodded at the kitchen door. "*Bien!* Our little restaurant, she catch on big!"

"That's swell," I said. "Is Lupe still making those delicious what-do-you-call-'ems . . . ?"

"Empanadas?"

I snapped my fingers. "That's it! Empanadas!"

"Tomorrow and Friday, she make them. Only two bits a box. Best deal in town. You want to order?"

I fished a dollar out of my billfold and handed it to him. "I'll take two. I'll come by and get them tomorrow."

"Good! They ready by, oh . . ." He closed one eye. "Four o'clock. Let me get you your change. . . ."

"No. Keep it."

He stopped in his tracks and smiled. "Thank you, Arturo! Is very generous!"

"Don't mention it." I drew a deep breath. "I believe you have someone . . ."

He flashed a palm, as if to suggest, *No need to say anything else.* "This way."

I followed him into the kitchen, where an army of his relatives fried food, stirred pots, and rattled dishes and silverware. I tailed him over the clay tiles as he entered a darkened back room containing a desk and chair, a davenport, and a corner cot, where somebody slept soundly. The shades were closed. He gave one a gentle tug and it shot up, *flap-flap-flap*-ing several times, letting sunlight flood in. I could tell from the sleeping man's shaven head that he was Roscoe. I crossed the room to get a better look at his face. He'd taken a few punches no doubt, which had left his face marred by bruises and cuts, a fat lip, and a black eye thrown in for good measure. I looked at Miguel, who was watching me intently, waiting for me to say something.

"Who did this to him?"

Miguel shrugged. "He come in last night, about two. First he say he hungry for supper, then he pass out cold. I bring him back here. My sons help."

"Thank you, Miguel. You fellas did good."

"You and Roscoe very good to us, Arturo. You welcome here anytime."

"That's awfully kind. Thanks."

I leaned forward and gave Roscoe's shoulder a shake. He continued sleeping. I repeated the shaking twice, each time longer and more rigorous than before. Not so much as a break in the snoring. I stepped back, straightened, and scanned the room, weighing options.

I turned to Miguel. "Do you mind me getting your bedding wet?"

"Wet?"

"Yeah, is it okay if I get the blanket and sheets wet with water?"

"*Si.* Yes. We got clothesline out back. What you got in mind?"

"You don't happen to have a bucket or a pail . . . ?"

"*Si.*"

"Would you mind bringing it to me full of cold water, please?"

His mouth opened and eyes widened with fear. "Are you sure . . . ?"

"It's all right. He told me he wants me to do it when I can't wake him up."

"If you insist."

"Thanks, Miguel."

Miguel left and I spent the time he was gone hovering over Roscoe, listening to him snore. Labored footsteps approached, water sloshed, and Miguel stood by my side. He handed me a wooden fruit bucket, heavy with water.

"You may want to step away," I gasped, raising it by its handle.

He backed into the shadows, and I lifted the bucket high

with all my might and tipped it upside down. The water retained the shape of the bucket for nearly a second as it plunged through space, pounding Roscoe with a *kersplash*. It worked. Roscoe's eyes shot open when the flood hit him. He tumbled out of the bed, landing on his stomach. He lifted himself onto his hands and knees and grunted while droplets tapped the floor. He then plopped back on his rump and ran his fingers over his sopping head as he squinted up at me.

"Time is it?"

I glanced at my Bulova. "Half past nine. In the morning."

"Day is it?"

"Monday."

"Month?"

"July," I said. "Second. Nineteen and thirty-four."

He held up his hand and I gripped it and helped him to his feet. He swerved and dipped a few times and I worried he was going to fall. He stayed upright, a minor miracle, and made his way over to the chair where his jacket, shirt, and hat rested. I gave him a minute to get dressed and put on his shoes. While he tied his laces, he looked at Miguel, who stood by the door, sheepishly staring back.

"Did I do any damage . . . ?"

"No harm done, Mr. Roscoe."

Shoes on, Roscoe steadied himself on his feet. "Say, Miguel, is your wife still making them, uh . . ."

"Empanadas? *Si!* I tell Arturo here, she make a batch tomorrow."

Roscoe walked over to Miguel and handed him a soggy dollar. "I'll take one. Tell her to throw in some of that hot sauce she makes. That stuff's the bee's knees."

"I get you change. . . ."

"Keep it," said Roscoe. He faced me. "Let's go."

I waited in Roscoe's living room while he showered. He resided on the second floor of a two-story beige brick apartment building at the corner of 200 South and 800 East. Thin walls let me hear someone in the next apartment singing to piano scales. Tall trees outside the open window cooled the place in the dead of summer, and a breeze parachuted the sheer curtains. Roscoe's cats, Barney, a venerable orange tabby, and Millicent, a younger, mischievous tortoiseshell, kept me company while I waited.

The living room was filled with stacks of magazines, a tabletop radio that played crackling music with bluesy horn and a colored lady singing, and an antique table supporting a row of framed photographs. One showed a young Roscoe standing alongside his coworkers from Donovan and Sons, a company that called itself a detective agency, yet really specialized in rental strikebreakers. In another portrait, teenage Roscoe stood by his mother in a photographer's studio, sometime early in the century. The next framed image was a five-by-seven school picture of a young girl that I hadn't seen the last time I was here. I prided myself on being an observant fellow. How did I miss it before? I nudged Barney off my lap and he meowed his protest and leaped to the floor. I walked over to the table and picked up the framed photo to get a better look. I ventured a guess the girl was somewhere in her early teens, with shoulder-length dark hair, a cute squint, and a toothy grin. When hinges squeaked down the hall, I returned the frame to where it sat. Roscoe entered the living room and it surprised me to see what a difference a fresh change of clothes made. Even though the bruises and cuts were still visible, he looked halfway presentable.

"You ready?"

"Yep," I answered.

The sedan's front seat felt piping hot when I slid in and closed the door. A fire engine raced past us with bells clanging as Roscoe got in and muttered something about forest fires. I didn't hear him and I didn't feel like asking him to repeat it. I started the car, steered onto 200 South, and headed downtown. I had no desire to get to the bottom of what happened to Roscoe, but I felt I had no choice.

"You gonna tell me who did it?"

He turned his head to me, swollen-eyed and fat-lipped. "Huh?"

"Your face."

He looked forward. "Remember Pearl?"

"Not the married woman. . . ."

"Don't start in on me."

"Was it her husband?"

He opened a tobacco pouch and stuck a wad between his cheek and gum. When he tilted it my way, I shook my head. "You sure? It's Red Man."

"No thanks."

He tucked it in his pocket. "I know what you're thinking."

I didn't answer him.

"You're thinking: *He oughta settle down. Find himself a wife. Have some kids. Like me.*"

"Actually, I was wondering how that lady's husband bested you."

"What makes you think he bested me?"

"I'm basing it on your appearance. Am I wrong?"

"I tore him apart." He burped and pounded his fist against his chest. "Prick had no idea what hit him."

Roscoe's proclivity for fooling around with married women and his brutish fisticuffs—stories of the latter probably exaggerated for effect—left me cold, and I'm sure he noticed my troubled expression, or heard my sigh of frustration. Once upon a time, I used to harangue him about his reckless ways, but it only made him sore and more reluctant to confide in me. Over time, I grew less judgmental and more inclined to listen the way a good friend ought to. I held out hope that by letting Roscoe find the words to describe his more troubling behaviors, he'd see them more clearly and try to change his ways. He hadn't rounded that corner yet, but the optimist in me refused to give up on him.

I reached the congested intersection of 200 South and State, signaled, and turned right—north—in the direction of Public Safety. We were downtown, which meant I didn't have much time left to be alone with Roscoe. *Change the subject*, I thought. "That girl in the picture, the one in your living room. Who is she?"

"Nona."

"Oh yeah? Nice name. Nona what?"

"Nona your business."

"Oh. It's like that, huh?"

"Yeah, it's like that."

"Sorry. I figured she must be somebody important. If you keep her framed picture in your apartment." I waited a beat. "She must mean something to you."

"Art?"

"Yeah?"

"Her name's still Nona."

"Okay. Fine." On the last block of our drive, I told Roscoe the thing I dreaded saying the most. "I can't cover for you anymore."

"Not now, Art. . . ."

"Yes, now," I said. "You need to realize that you've got a job, and a good one. That's a luxury a lot of men in our day and age don't have. You need to keep that job. Showing up on time in the morning is a good start."

I turned down the shaded alley to the side of Public Safety while Roscoe stewed next to me. Behind the building, I turned into a parking spot and killed the engine.

Roscoe flung open his door and stepped onto the running board, then to pavement. "Listen, thanks for coming out to the Tampico to get me," he said. "But I don't need you looking after me, Art. The way I see it, if the higher-ups can my ass, they'll be doing me a favor."

He slammed his door hard, startling me. As I watched him enter Public Safety, the main thing on my mind right then was that Roscoe had said nothing about the Running Board Bandit episode of *Crime Does Not Pay*. A stabbing pain stuck me above my abdomen, the same sensation I'd felt in the past when someone I loved ignored a milestone in my life.

Four

"Any good news in there?"

Myron lowered today's issue of the *Examiner* and shook his head without taking his eyes off the print. I didn't know why I asked him that question. I guess I'd grown tired of staring at a newspaper for the past half hour and listening to police alerts. He squinted through those thick eyeglasses of his as he read, as if he were still pondering my question in that overactive brain of his.

"It depends," he said.

"On?"

"If you think forest fires burning up half of this state, dust storms burying entire towns on the Plains, Hitler knocking off half of his henchmen, and San Francisco being turned into a ghost town by a general strike are good news." He raised the newspaper, once again hiding behind a curtain of ink. "Looks like they're closing in on the Dillinger gang."

We sat in an unmarked police sedan with the windows open,

down the road from a mansion on Lincoln Street that had been converted into the main branch of the so-called Fundamental-ist Church of Saints. The temperature had climbed into the low nineties, and the few breezes that blew were a welcome relief. We were far enough from our target not to be noticed by visi-tors, who seemed to be coming and going regularly, but still within sight of the grounds.

A wall of hedges prevented passersby from getting a good look at the steep-roofed house with a rounded tower on its west side and a tall chimney so narrow a good gust of wind could have knocked it over. Parallel-parked autos lined the streets, mostly dusty black Fords and Chevrolets from the previous de-cade, taking up curb space in all directions. We'd been parked in the same spot since noon—about an hour now—waiting for LeGrand Johnston to make a move.

Signs of life: Eight women in long prairie dresses that cov-ered everything from neck to feet lined up side by side on the wide gravelly driveway, as if they were accustomed to assuming this formation daily. All of them wore their lengthy hair pinned back into braids and buns, without a loose lock in sight. Before long, the prophet came hobbling down the line with the use of a cane, stopping at each woman, leaning in close for a kiss on the cheek. His beefy driver, in a black suit and cap, walked past Johnston as he kissed the women and opened the door to a lim-ousine. Johnston eventually reached the end of the line and ad-vanced forward to his waiting driver.

When his two-toned black-and-green Packard limousine rolled out of the driveway, I plunged my key into the ignition and the engine turned over right away.

"Look alive," I said.

Myron closed and folded his newspaper, flinging it onto the

backseat. I tailed the Packard up shady Lincoln Street to 2100 South, where it turned left onto the wide, congested road. We had to wait for a break in traffic to make the same turn. On Twenty-First, I leadfooted past assorted restaurants, shops, auto garages, bungalows, and weed-choked lots until we reached State Street, a major north-south artery running up and down the center of the valley. My focus was fixed on the Packard's taillights ahead in the distance.

Northbound on State, I stayed three car lengths behind Johnston's Packard, weaving around a Utah Light & Traction trolley and a few slow cars and trucks. At 400 South, by city hall, I hit a stop signal and I briefly feared we'd lose him, but as soon as the go sign flashed, I stomped on the accelerator and shot forward. In my peripheral vision, I noticed Myron lick his lips nervously and clutch the ceiling strap.

"I don't get it," he said.

"What don't you get?"

"What do you think he's going to do today that he hasn't done since you started shadowing him?"

State Street plugged into downtown at this point. Tall buildings were reflected in the Ford's shiny surface. I considered Myron's question and offered something in the way of a shrug. "We won't know unless we follow him."

"If you asked me, which you didn't, I'd say we're wasting our time."

"Well, we aren't making any progress sitting around that stuffy old squad room."

That shut Myron up temporarily, which was good because I needed to concentrate on finding the Packard. Thankfully it was a unique enough automobile that it was easy to spot circling the block on Broadway (300 South), and braking to turn left on

Main, the next street over from State. I swerved into the left-turn lane, and during a break in the traffic, steered onto Third and caught up to the Packard, letting it turn before I got too close. Johnston's car was heading toward Exchange Place, a cluster of classical architecture that included the federal building and post office. Broadway churned with traffic, packed lanes on both sides, the constant ringing of trolley bells, and car horns blaring.

"I'm sure he's up to no good," said Myron. "Probably trying to send a postcard without a stamp."

I ignored his wisecrack. The Packard eased to a halt, and the driver got out, circled the car, and opened the door for Johnston. I parked at the curb and watched the elderly man hobbling into the post office with the help of a cane, his face shaded by sunglasses and a black fedora. We stayed put while he went inside. Our prowl car was fitted with a police radio, required to remain on at all times, and the alerts hit one after another. *"Calling car twelve! Car one-two! See a domestic disturbance at eight-four-four South, three-zero-zero East,"* droned a woman's voice from the speaker box wired to the dashboard Motorola, the favored brand of patrol cars across America. *"That's eight-four-four South, three-zero-zero east. Neighbors called to report two men quarreling. Liquor may be involved. That is all."*

"Maybe you ought to consider a different approach," said Myron.

"What do you suggest?"

"Find a mole. Pay him well."

I shook my head. "There aren't any finks in this outfit."

He looked at me. "You hate polygamists, don't you?"

"Makes you say that?"

"The way you tense up when you talk about them."

I waited to answer him. "I feel sorry for the women and children. They're victims."

"Maybe the wives want it that way."

I grimaced. "Why do you say that?"

"You know the old saying about the devil you know."

"No woman in her right state of mind would choose that way of life," I said. "Not of her own free will, anyway."

"How do you know?"

"I just know."

"That answer doesn't exactly inspire confidence."

I looked at him. "You really want to know why I hate them?"

"Sure."

"They're deviants. They make a mockery out of all the things I hold sacred. Marriage. Family. Religion. They rule by fear. Nobody in those families dares to step out of line. Do you want me to go on? I could, you know."

Myron began to recite something. " 'If you know the enemy and know yourself, you need not fear the result of a hundred battles. If you know yourself but not the enemy, for every victory gained you will also suffer a defeat. If you know neither the enemy nor yourself, you will succumb in every battle.' "

"What's that from?"

"Sun Tzu. *The Art of War*. Ever read it?"

I felt myself coiling up on the defensive. "What are you saying? That I don't know anything about polygamy? If so, let me tell you—"

"I know, I know. You've got ancestors who were polygamists. You've already said it a hundred times. You think it gives you credibility. It doesn't."

"Okay, smart guy," I said, my voice rising in frustration. "What's your solution?"

"Putting them in jail won't do any good."

"Why do you say that?"

He gestured to the building. "That old man in the post office has nearly two dozen wives, and probably triple that number of children. If you send him to prison, what'll his kin do to make ends meet? Tossing him in jail is only going to make things worse." He drew a breath. "And another thing . . ."

"What?"

"How come it was kosher to have a bunch of wives fifty years ago but not now?"

I eyed the Packard in front of us. "I'm not going to sit here and debate Mormon doctrine with you, Myron."

"I don't blame you," he said. "I wouldn't either if my God kept changing His mind every five minutes."

"If you don't believe in this squad's mission, maybe you should request a transfer."

"What, go back to my dreary job in records and miss all the fun? Not on your life."

Not a second too soon, LeGrand Johnston exited the post office, cane in one hand, burlap mailbag in the other. He moved slowly down the steps to his waiting Packard. With his driver's help, he climbed into the car. I started the engine and followed Johnston's car into the traffic. I was glad to be on the move again. The prospect of continuing this fruitless debate with Myron left me drained. There was, I had to admit, *some* truth in his words, yet his emotionless self-assurance left me cold. Every word he spoke was anchored in his unflappable sense that he was always right. It's pointless to debate a man who thinks he's always right.

For the next few hours, Johnston crisscrossed the city, making rounds that were all too familiar to me. Visiting his wives and offspring, never staying in any one place for too long, had become the old man's daily routine. Most of the women and children on his route resided in modest bungalows dotting the city's residential neighborhoods as far north as the Avenues and as far south as Sugar House. One wife and a trio of youngsters greeted Uncle Grand at the entrance of a two-story Tudor in the Harvard-Yale neighborhood, a ritzy area of tree-lined streets and lavish homes south of the University of Utah. This house, with flower gardens on all sides, was more upscale than the others we'd been to that afternoon.

Five o'clock arrived and we headed back to Public Safety so Roscoe could spell Myron. Roscoe opened the passenger door and Myron, with folded newspaper in hand, tugged the brim of his hat and stepped out. Roscoe got in the car and complained under his breath about the heat as I watched Myron charge—skipping every other step—to the entrance of headquarters, wading into departing policemen ending their shift.

Half past ten at night found us parked near the fundamentalist church on Lincoln Street, where Myron and I had started our long day of surveillance. There were no streetlamps out there, so the moon and the stars were our only light. Roscoe snoozed, breaking out into snoring now and then, his fedora pulled low over his eyes. I watched the house, only able to see glimmers of yellowish light through breaks in the hedge wall.

I blocked out the incessant radio alerts, minding only my own self-pity. These surveillance outings were ripping me away from my family, the most important thing in my life. Earlier in the night, I'd called Clara from a drugstore telephone booth on 2100 South to let her know I'd be home late. She did her best to sound upbeat, but I heard the resignation in her voice. And to think, it was only a few weeks ago that I'd promised her I'd stop working these late nights when summer arrived.

It really bothered me that tonight, Monday, was Family Home Evening, a Mormon custom in which each family got together for a night of fun and games and, in warmer months, evening strolls or auto treks to the ice-cream parlor. *So much for Family Home Evening*, I thought. Was I turning into Buddy Hawkins—my ambitious friend who had swiftly climbed to the position of captain of detectives—willing to push everything aside for my job?

I tried to steer my focus back to the present. *Myron was right*: Johnston—or Uncle Grand, as his followers called him—was careful. He had come back here to his church after a two-hour-long meeting with his apostles at a house belonging to one of them, Alma Covington, on Third Avenue. I had waited in front of Covington's, puzzling over what these codgers could possibly be jabbering about so long. The meeting presumably concluded and the tireless old man left. His driver whisked him to this place, his sanctuary out in the shade trees, the place he stayed on nights when he was busy sorting out church matters until the wee hours. By this time of night, most of the cars at the church were gone. Only Johnston's limousine remained in the driveway.

I thought about calling it a night, dropping Roscoe off at his apartment, and heading home myself. Why was I killing myself for a salary that still required my wife's second income in order to meet our monthly expenses? Had I become one of the police department politicos who I so distrusted, scrambling as fast as I could to get to the top of the ladder? What had the polygamists ever done to me? The keys dangling from the ignition beckoned. The temptation to turn them was great. Yet I held back, for reasons I did not understand.

Time passed. The neighborhood was silent, except for a distant locomotive whistle. I veered in and out of wakefulness, shaking my head and fluttering my eyelids every few minutes to keep awake. I pressed my fingers into my burning eyes and rubbed.

Movement interrupted the stillness. A black Model T truck swerved into the driveway. The light was poor, but I thought I spotted two figures sitting in the vehicle's cab. I switched on the interior light and checked my watch: 11:57. I switched off the light. With the wall of hedges blocking my view, I could not see the new arrivals getting out of the truck, but I heard doors slamming. Now I was more alert than ever, wondering who that was in the truck and why they picked this late hour to drop by. More time ticked away. I stretched my arms and cracked my knuckles. I squirmed in my seat and fidgeted. I drummed my fingers on my knees. Anything I could do to keep from dozing off.

A series of muted cracks startled me. I was pretty sure they were gunshots, coming from inside the church. A dog barked in the distance.

I fumbled for the interior globe. Switched it on. Checked my .38. Full. I snapped closed the cylinder, glanced at the time, 12:12 A.M., and gave Roscoe a shake. He sucked air in through his nostrils, sat up straight, pushed his hat back on his head, and looked around groggily.

"What is it?"

"I heard shots," I said. "Coming from the church."

An engine revved up. Roscoe and I looked at each other, then at the imposing building, partly hidden from view behind the foliage. Rubber tires sprayed gravel and the Model T truck came barreling out of the driveway, screeching around a corner and disappearing into the night.

"Who the hell . . ."

"Let's go," I said.

I got out of the car, not even bothering to pull my keys out of the ignition, and ran across the street toward the house. I balled my hand into a fist and pounded on the front door of the church.

"This is the police," I shouted. "Let me in!"

I rapped on the wood repeatedly with the palm of my hand.

"Stand aside," said Roscoe. He charged shoulder-first, breaking the door open. Wood snapped, splinters flew, and we entered a high-ceilinged foyer. We passed through a chapel with enough rows of folding chairs to accommodate two hundred or so worshipers. A pulpit and an impressive pump organ dominated the front of the room. Hymnbooks filled a bookcase against the wall.

I motioned to Roscoe to follow me upstairs. I advanced through an arched doorway that opened up to a hallway with a set of carpeted stairs. Up the stairs I went to the second floor, where I found a dimly lit corridor with doors on either side. One bore the name LEGRAND JOHNSTON. Entering what appeared to be his office, I got my first whiff of a familiar, sickening odor that always triggered my gag reflex. No mistaking the scent of human blood, with its hint of iron and decay, like beef that had been left out in the summer sun. My cotton hankie went over my nose and mouth.

I found Johnston flat on his back by a coffee table. His driver lay on a davenport.

Uncle Grand was dressed in the same dark suit he had worn earlier in the day. I headed over to him and stooped to get a better look. His dead eyes stared at the ceiling. A dark pool, the color of ripe cherries, formed a perfect circle on the hardwood beneath his head.

The bullet hole in his forehead left nothing to the imagination. Another bullet had struck him at the base of his neck. His upper shirt and necktie were saturated in red, but I suspected most of his blood had drained to the floor. My eyes stopped at another hole in his stomach, a crater that was black in the center surrounded by red. Billowing drapes moved like ghosts, blown by wind from the open window. I skirted the body, taking each step slowly until I reached the curtains and hand-parted them. I leaned my head out the open window. Side yard. Treetops, but nobody down there.

I returned to Johnston's body, and Roscoe began examining the driver. With my handkerchief, I fished a billfold out of his front pocket and checked its contents. The murderer had not stolen his cash—sixty-eight dollars by my count. The wallet contained other items: a motor vehicle operator's license; an Intermountain Indemnity insurance card; a University of Utah football schedule for 1933; a Zion's Bank 1934 card calendar; an IOU dated 2-23-34 from L. Boggs for the sum of $1,278; and a business card from the Delphi Hotel, 233 South State. I stuffed it all back in the billfold and placed it in his pocket in the same position it'd been in when I found it. Next I went over the rest of the body. The assailant had left a fancy watch on Johnston's wrist. Careful not to touch it, I lifted the cuff to get a better look. Black-faced Elgin with art deco gold numbers. I let go of the cuff and spent a while—I don't know how long—gazing at that trio of bullet wounds.

"I got his wallet."

I turned to Roscoe, who handed me the driver's billfold. First thing I saw inside: OPERATOR'S LICENSE—1934—UT DEPT. OF REVENUE. The license said his name was Volney Chester Mason. It listed him as residing at a Garfield Avenue address. I put the license back. The wallet contained a five and several dollar bills. I found a few cards: Seagull Photography Service on West Temple. Deseret Gymnasium membership card. GRANVILLE SONDRUP (and below that) ATTORNEY-AT-LAW. The bottom left-hand corner said: MCCORNICK BLOCK, SALT LAKE CITY. I tucked the cards back in the wallet and slipped it in the man's pocket.

I stooped to get a better look at the driver. Shot in the left eye. Blood all over his head and face. Blood covered his shirt and seeped into the davenport's upholstery. His right hand still held a pistol. It was an M1911 single-action, semiautomatic, black as the night. Tempted though I was to pull it out of his hand and get a better look at it, I left it alone for the homicide detectives to examine. I noted that his pistol was aimed in the general direction of the south wall. I left it untouched.

"There's a hole in the wall over there," said Roscoe. "Who knows if this gun made it."

"We'll find out soon enough," I said, finding the little black entry point in the wallpaper.

"He looks familiar," said Roscoe, gesturing to Mason. "But I don't know his name."

"Maybe he's one of Johnston's followers," I said.

"I'm betting he's hired muscle," said Roscoe. "I've seen him around, back when I was in that line of work."

The men weren't going anywhere, so I sidled to a bathroom off Johnston's office. Toilet, sink, and medicine cabinet, clawfoot tub with the white curtain closed. Towels hung on bars. Medicine cabinet: empty. I shut off the light.

A sound in one of the neighboring rooms startled me.

I aimed my gun and advanced stealthily. I peered into what seemed to be a guest room, complete with a four-poster bed, a bureau topped with a crocheted ruffled doily and washbasin, and a framed photograph of LeGrand Johnston hanging on the wall. I wondered if this was where the prophet's concubines slept after auditioning to join his big family.

I turned to leave, but a muffled movement coming from the closet stopped me. I crept toward it, using my handkerchief to grab the knob. I opened it and pointed my gun inside. I reached up inside and pulled a chain. An electric globe flashed on to nothing but a row of dresses that had been spread apart, as if somebody had already searched inside of it. My heart began to slow, and I turned to leave when I spotted a pair of black shoes with shiny buckles on the closet floor below the dresses. My eyes followed the shoes to a pair of ankles, then ankles to shins. I brushed the hanging clothes aside with my arm so that a girl came into view. She couldn't have been any older than thirteen. Her calico dress must have been unbearably hot. She kept her brown hair woven into braids, her blue eyes reflected the light from above, and a dimple formed a tiny canyon in her chin.

I knelt slightly and showed her my badge.

"I'm Detective Arthur Oveson, Salt Lake City Police Department," I said. "I'm not going to hurt you. I'm a policeman. What's your name?"

She didn't respond. When I touched her arm, she didn't pull away, didn't budge at all. She continued to stare blankly ahead. I wondered what, if anything, she'd seen. What put her in this state?

"Who is she?"

I faced Roscoe, framed by the doorway, gun drawn as he sized up the girl.

"I don't know," I said, blowing a sigh. "I have a feeling it's going to be a long night."

Five

On the sedan's driver's-side running board, I sat hunched with my elbows on my knees, savoring a breeze, even though it brought smoke from forest fires. A line of police cars and the morgue wagon were parked in front of the mansion-turned-church. Sitting out here at two A.M. was preferable to getting in the way of the homicide dicks and lab boys doing their job on the second floor. My mind still had not fully absorbed the shock of finding the bodies of Johnston and his driver. I spent a while remembering those weeks of tailing Johnston around the valley, wondering if there was something I missed that should have led me to expect tonight's awful turn of events. But nothing came to mind. My eyes burned with dryness and I wanted to be in bed at home instead of here. Roscoe had already caught a ride downtown with one of the prowlers that had left earlier. I told him I'd fill him in tomorrow. I stayed put, waiting for an update from Lieutenant Wit Dunaway of the Homicide Squad.

Eventually Wit left the crime scene with his partner, Pace

Newbold, and came to see me. Pasty-skinned and chinless, New-bold was my age, thirty-three, and he harbored a passionate dislike of Mormons, probably because he'd once been one and had had a bad parting of ways with the religion. As for Wit, a man in his mid-fifties, years of hard work had elevated him to senior homicide detective. His receding dark hair capped an oval face with pinholes for eyes and a permanent scowl. Tonight he arrived in a wrinkled black suit and crooked red tie. His grim act concealed real intellect and a splendid sense of humor. He'd learned his streetwise sensibilities in Boston, where he'd been one of the ringleaders of the big police strike in '19. Tonight he seemed subdued, probably owing to the hour, although he grinned at me as he approached.

"It's the radio star," Wit said. "I should've brought my autograph book."

"Hello, Wit," I said. "Pace."

"Why are you still out here at this ungodly hour?" asked Pace. "Didn't anybody tell you the ice-cream joints are all closed?"

Verbal sparring was the last thing I wanted to do. *Leave the witticisms to the witty*, I thought. "I was shadowing Johnston."

"I thought so," said Wit. "I appreciate you asking the night dispatcher to contact me. This is big. In fact, I telephoned Cowley at home. Woke him up, but I figured this is important enough to disrupt his beauty sleep. Look, Art, I'm happy to keep you apprised of our investigation. But I expect the same from you. Cooperation is a two-way street, you know."

"Sure, all right."

"Let's start with *why* you are here so late."

"I told you. I was tailing Johnston."

"At this time of night?"

I nodded. "I've been at it for months now, trying to catch him engaging in some sort of illegal activity. Up till today, it's been pretty dull."

"So you didn't see this coming?" asked Wit.

"Nope."

"Got any idea who Johnston's wheelman was?" asked Pace.

"Volney Mason? I don't know anything about him."

"Ain't seen him before?"

"Just driving Johnston. Roscoe suspects he was hired muscle."

"What about the girl in there?" Wit asked.

"What about her?"

"She hasn't said a word so far," said Pace. "She say anything to you?"

"No."

"You haven't seen her before tonight?" asked Wit.

"No."

"Earlier you said you saw a pickup truck leaving the scene right after you heard shots," said Pace.

"Yeah," I said. "I'm quite sure it was a Model T truck."

"But you're not certain."

"The lighting was poor."

"Didja get plates?'

"No." Before either man could lob another question at me, I gestured to the mansion. "Anybody else in there?"

"Other than the girl and the two stiffs, no signs of life," said Wit.

"I presume there aren't any suspects yet?" I asked.

"Only the girl," said Pace. "We found a pillowcase on her containing what we presume are her belongings. Knitting. Fabrics. Needlepoint. Oh, and a Western Motor Coach bus ticket from St. George to Salt Lake City, dated Friday, the eighth of June. No ID on her, though."

"Do you think there's any chance she had something to do with it?" I asked.

Wit plunged his hands into his trouser pockets and rattled coins. "She's stunned. Unless she's got Garbo's acting chops, I'm guessing she saw something, but she's too shocked to speak. She might be able to help us find who shot Johnston. *If* we can get her to talk."

"What's going to happen to her?" I asked.

"We're taking her for questioning, then they'll stick her in the fun house," said Pace.

The fun house—the Utah State Industrial School, a three-story brick-and-stone building from the last century, built around a castle-like tower, pressed against the Wasatch Mountains in Ogden, a town forty miles north of Salt Lake City. The so-called "school" served as the state reformatory for young lawbreakers. From what I'd heard, survival of the fittest reigned inside of those walls.

"That won't help," I said. "They'll make mincemeat out of her."

As I spoke those words, a pair of patrolmen escorted the girl to a police car. Light from the nearby church lent an ethereal glow to her heart-shaped face and gingham dress, as though she were a ghost from 1847 who had suddenly materialized in the night. She made eye contact with me briefly, then dipped her head as one of the officers helped her up to the running board and into the backseat and closed the door. Wit mentioned something about going home and crawling back into bed. I wasn't listening. I was too busy watching the police car leaving, its taillights disappearing around the corner.

. . .

Salt Lake City's roads were mostly empty at three A.M. I slowed at L Street, where I left-turned north, climbing the steep hill to our bungalow. I steered into the driveway, cut off the engine, and got out of the car. On my way to the front door, a hypnotic scene on the eastern side of the valley grabbed my attention: the Big Cottonwood Canyon fire cast an eerie orange light on the mountains. I worried about the firefighters putting their lives on the line, battling blazes and rescuing homes like mine.

The Ovesons of L Street lived in a handsome brick bungalow with a columned porch and pretty flowerbeds that Clara took care of. Ours was a neighborhood of ancient trees that touched the sky, where children played in the street and people kept their porch light globes burning late. At three in the morning, however, the block was dark and sound asleep.

I was too anxious to sleep. There's no stimulant quite as powerful as finding a pair of dead men. In the dark silence of my house, I felt haunted by the faces of the victims. Their lifeless expressions appeared vividly each time I closed my eyes, like a couple of restless apparitions. No chance of me hitting the sack with that on my mind. A tug on a lamp chain furnished a soft glow in the living room, and I ambled over to the rolltop desk, where I retrieved a brown leather-bound scrapbook.

Entering the kitchen, I turned on the lights, sat down at the table, and leafed through the scrapbook's contents: newspaper clippings, Photostats of police reports, and an official police photograph of a man with piercing eyes, high cheekbones, an aquiline nose, and a bristly mustache. I removed a picture of my father, Willard Oveson, to get a better look at it. Taken in 1908, back when he was the lead inspector in the Salt Lake City Police Department, it showed him in his prime. I smiled at my father's image before I slipped it back into the photo corners glued to the page. I missed him, and thumbing through this scrapbook was one way of getting closer to him. But I knew that if I turned too many pages, I would reach the articles and crime scene reports containing the details of his murder on a wintry night in 1914. Was I ready to go back there again? Was *now* the ideal time?

I closed my eyes and pictured my unconscious father dying in a hospital bed. That was the last time I ever saw him. I chased away the memory. Too many dead men were wandering in my head.

A pair of hands gripped my shoulders, startling me so badly I leaped out of my seat. Standing behind me in her robe and pajamas, Clara took several steps backward, wide-eyed and openmouthed, before bursting into laughter.

"Aren't you the jumpy one?"

"Sorry. You alarmed me. Coming up behind me like that."

She flashed her pearlies, came closer, and hugged me. Her pregnant belly pressed against me as she squeezed tighter. I returned her embrace and kissed the golden finger curls on top of her head. She placed her chin on my chest and stared up at me with her hazel eyes. "I heard you come in the front door a few minutes ago. Why didn't you come to bed?"

"I'm anxious, I guess."

"Any particular reason why?"

"Rough night."

Her smile faded. "What happened?"

"Double homicide."

We let go of each other and her expression turned serious. "Who . . . ?"

"LeGrand Johnston was shot," I said. She knew who he was.

She'd heard me ranting and raving about him plenty of times. "So was his driver, Volney Mason, who also worked as Johnston's bodyguard. You'll read about it in the papers soon enough."

"That's terrible," she said. "I have no love for polygamists, but nobody deserves—"

"No," I interrupted. "Nobody."

"You poor thing," said Clara, pouty. Her smile returned. "Hey! How about some ice cream to soothe your jangled nerves?"

"Sure," I said. "Why not?"

"Good! I'll dish us up some and you can tell me all about what happened tonight."

"If it's all the same to you, I'd prefer to talk about something else."

"Oh. Of course. Sure. I get it."

Clara's slippers slapped tiles on her way to the icebox, where she removed two cartons, one of Keeley's nougat ice cream, the other Keeley's peach—both hand-packed at our favorite ice-cream parlor—along with a couple of bowls, a pair of dessert spoons, and an ice-cream scoop.

"Pick your poison."

"Both."

"Wow. It must've been a hard night."

She let out a juvenile giggle as she scooped up ice cream, clinking metal on porcelain. While she was at it, I closed the scrapbook and nudged it aside, so it was no longer sitting right in front of me. She brought two bowls of ice cream and placed one in front of me, pulled out a chair, and sat down across the table from me. We both ate ice cream in silence for a few minutes. I finished mine sooner and scraped the bowl with my spoon—*tink, tink, tink*—so as not to miss any.

"Good news. They've hired a substitute to teach my classes this fall," said Clara. "And Cliff told me I might be able to get my maternity leave extended into the winter. That is, if we can afford it."

Cliff was Clifford Reynolds, the principal at East High School.

"Music to my ears," I said. "The more time you can spend with the baby, the better."

"I'm aiming for at least six months off," said Clara. "I feel better, knowing the baby will be with Ruby after I go back to work."

Ruby was Clara's older sister. She boarded children, providing day care out of her home, to make extra money.

"I will too," I said. "You getting kicked all the time still?"

Clara laughed. "Kicked. Punched. Elbowed. Somersaults. You name it."

I stood and took my bowl over to the ice-cream cartons for seconds. "I know it's not exactly comfortable for you," I said. "But I'm glad to know we have such a robust little one."

"I hope you'll be saying the same thing when you get up in the middle of the night to change diapers," she said. "Remember your promise?"

"Yeah, I remember," I said. "I stuck to it with the last two. I won't renege on this one."

"You'd better not."

I returned to the kitchen table with my dollops of ice cream and resumed eating. Clara licked her spoon clean, dropped it in the bowl, and pushed it aside. That's when she spied the scrapbook and knew right away what I had been doing when she touched my shoulders and gave me such a powerful start. Her eyes narrowed at the sight of it and she gave me a stern look.

"Why do you have that out?" she asked.

I shrugged. "No reason. I'm just looking through it."

She reached over and squeezed my hand in hers. "You're tormenting yourself again."

I tugged my hand free of hers.

"I'm not. I just . . . I miss him. That's all."

"Is that *really* all?"

"What other reason would I have?"

"Last time I found you looking through that scrapbook, you said something along the lines of you'll never be able to measure up to him. Ring any bells?"

"What's your point?" I asked.

"I don't think it's healthy, you turning him into a legend," she said. "It's like you're competing with a phantom who will always outrun you."

"Because I'm weak," I said. "Is that what you're saying?"

"That isn't what I meant and you know it," she said angrily. "Stop putting words in my mouth. You're the last person I think of when I hear the word *weak*. I mean, my goodness, Art, how many police detectives do you know who've had their stories broadcast on an episode of *Crime Does Not Pay*?"

"That was the Hollywood version of me," I said. "Dad would've been able to see right through it."

"Oh, Art, why do you do this to yourself?"

"Because there was nothing brave about what I did that night to Henry Grenache," I said. "The entire time he had that gun aimed at me, I was terrified that he was going to actually shoot me, and I wasn't ever going to see you or the children again. The only reason I came out of that ordeal in one piece was because there happened to be a tire iron within reach. That radio show made everybody think I was some kind of hero. . . ."

"But you are a hero!"

"No, I'm not," I said. "It was just dumb luck and fast reflexes. Heroism never entered the picture at any point."

"There you go again! Why do you always have to tear yourself down?" she asked. "It's a rigged contest, Art, because you're never going to let yourself win."

"It's different for you, Clara," I said. "Your father is still alive."

"Don't hand me that 'you'll never know, because it didn't happen to you' business," she said. "That's just your way of trying to shut me up. After all, how could I possibly know how you're feeling when my dad is alive and well, and all I have to do is pick up the telephone and ring his house?"

"I hope to God you never lose him the same way I lost mine, because nobody should ever have to experience what it's like to not be able to say good-bye to someone who's that important to you, to someone you love that much," I said. "It's twice as upsetting to know that he died so . . . in such a . . . well, that he died the way he did. Knowing the last thing he ever saw was his killer, and the last thing he ever felt was getting shot."

"Sometimes I think you wish it'd been you instead of him," said Clara. "But you're here, and you're alive, and you punish yourself with this foolish notion that you'll never be half the man he was."

"I guess that's my own particular demon," I whispered.

Clara's arms, folded over her chest, rose and fell gently with each breath. I sensed she felt defeated by this conversation and couldn't take any more arguing. So she changed the subject. "Why don't you tell me about the two men you found tonight?"

"Aw, shoot, Clara, I told you I'd rather not. . . ."

"I won't go to bed until you do, and I won't let you, either. Keep it short. But don't leave out any of the important details. Go."

I recounted the crime scene to Clara, describing it vividly. Talking through it distracted me, made me forget about the scrapbook and my father. My vocal cords grew raw from all the talking, and I reached a point at which I was too exhausted to speak. I leaned back against the hard wood of my chair, threw my arms up into a stretch, and yawned.

"Thanks for telling me about it," said Clara. "Want to go to bed? You have to get up for work in a few hours."

"I appreciate you reminding me," I said, coming out of my yawn. Rising from my chair, I lifted my ice-cream bowl to put it in the sink.

"Leave it," she said. "I'll wash it in the morning."

I set it down and reached for the scrapbook.

"Leave that, too. Sometimes I wish you'd burn it."

How to respond to that comment? I didn't. Instead, I said, "We need more ice cream."

"I'll pick some up tomorrow," she said. "Good news. Keeley's has brought back that South Seas Island coconut kind you loved so much last year."

Hand in hand, we headed to the bedroom, and she closed the door, letting darkness swallow us. Without even bothering to remove a stitch of my clothing, I belly-flopped onto the bed, my head barely touching the bottom of the pillow. Somewhere in the haze of fading into unconsciousness, Clara spoke, but I was too exhausted to acknowledge her words. "Don't you want to change into your pajamas?" Slumber seized me at that point, carrying me into a land of dreams.

Six

Police Chief William Cowley kept me waiting in the anteroom of his office, on a velvet armchair, one of several facing a long desk. There, a Betty Boop–ish secretary in a floral dress typed slavishly whenever some three-piece big shot passed through the room, only to switch back to filing her nails when the coast was clear. Her desk nameplate identified her as INEZ SPOONER, and from time to time, she'd stop her emery board to blow on her nails and glance at me. Somewhere behind her desk, a radio played a forlorn tune performed by the unmistakable birdlike voice of Annette Hanshaw. I sat there, right ankle propped on left knee, reading—but not really reading—an issue of *Popular Mechanics* from last fall that I had pulled off a stack of magazines on an end table. The cover showed a futuristic art deco speed train racing across the countryside. On the chair next to me sat a stack of cream-colored file folders and a small box containing photographic slides that I had brought over for this morning's meeting.

"I recognize you," said Inez Spooner. "You're that Overtson fella, the one that busted the Running Board Bandit."

I looked up from the magazine. "Oveson."

"Begging your pardon?"

I said it slowly. "O-vuh-son. No *R*, no *T*."

"Oh yeah, Oveson," she said. "I remember your face from the papers. Real crackerjack, the way you nabbed him. Serves him right, stickin' up decent people."

"That's nice of you to say. Thank you."

"You sounded keen on the radio," she said. "It makes your voice lower."

"Oh, that? That was an actor playing me."

Her face brightened for the first time. "Which actor?"

"Lyle Talbot."

Her eyes went saucer wide. "*The* Lyle Talbot? From *Fog Over Frisco?*"

"The same."

"Gee, that's swell! Did you get his autograph, by any chance?"

I hesitated, as if about to make a grave confession. "I forgot."

"Now how on earth could you forget something like that?"

Chief Cowley's office doors opened at the right time. I dreaded the prospect of being interrogated over my failure to obtain Lyle Talbot's autograph. An older woman with platinum curls, wire-rimmed spectacles, and a maroon collared crepe dress poked her head out and her eyes scanned the room, stopping at me. "Mr. Oveson? We're ready for you."

On my way to Cowley's office, lugging my stack of file folders, I noticed Inez Spooner typing once more, and I had no doubt she'd stop as soon as that matron was no longer standing in the doorway. "Famous movie star and you don't get his autograph," she said under her breath, fingers dancing on the Underwood keys. "What a disgrace."

The chief's assistant closed the doors behind me. Inside, paneled walls matched a mahogany conference table in the center of the room, surrounded by tall chairs, several presently occupied. Chief Cowley rose from his spot at the head of the table and came over to me to shake my hand. He stood at only five feet, seven inches tall, yet his formidable presence fooled you into thinking he towered over seven. He kept his hair slicked back, his eyeglasses low on his nose, and his dapper mustache neatly trimmed. He had the most prominent chin I've ever seen on a man, even more than President Roosevelt's. He seized my hand with a grip that almost fractured bones, so I knew he meant business.

"Welcome, Detective Oveson," he said. "Please, come in and be seated. Anywhere you wish."

"Thank you, sir," I said. I faced his assistant and handed her the box of slides. "Were you able to arrange use of the projector?"

"Yes, it's right over there," she said, gesturing to a wheeled cart. "Top slide first?"

"Yes, please," I said. "Thank you."

While Cowley's assistant went over and loaded the slides into the projector, I gravitated to the unoccupied end of the table, nearest the door, and Cowley returned to his spot. I never quite knew what to make of Cowley. He seemed competent enough, but his rise to the top spot in the force grew out of a checkered history. Sometime around the close of 1931 or opening of '32, Mayor Bennett Cummings replaced the outgoing police chief, Otis Ballard, with his good friend Bill Cowley. Ballard retired so he could—in his own words—"take up the rod and reel full-time." But there was more to Ballard's departure than a desire to spend more time fishing, and everyone from the lowliest traffic cop to the highest deputy chiefs knew it. Ballard's early retirement was tied to a scandal in the winter of '31 that rocked the Anti-Vice Squad. It was a complicated story involving cops who accepted bribes in the form of money, liquor, and prostitutes; mass firings of a squad commander and detectives for allegedly participating in said racket; and an overzealous new mayor, Cummings, who wanted to wipe out every last vestige of corruption, even if it meant destroying the careers of a few innocent men in the process. At least three Anti-Vice detectives had been driven out of the force without any evidence linking them to illegal activities. For Cummings, their presence in the squad was sufficient reason to discharge them. Moreover, Ballard had never played any part in the scandalous behavior that had been going on for years. Yet he had been the chief of police at the time when the worst instances of corruption were occurring, and that was good enough for Cummings to accuse him behind the scenes of being "inept" and "asleep at the wheel." Since Ballard was so popular among his men and the public at large, Cummings would never utter such statements in public. He chose instead to apply quiet pressure. It worked. Ballard was out and Cowley was in.

Needless to say, Cowley wasn't terribly popular in his own force. That had to do, in part, with him being an outsider. Cummings brought Cowley in from Boise, Idaho, to introduce a fresh face, someone capable of rising above the internecine conflicts that had been plaguing the force for so long, and restore the department's tarnished image.

My thoughts returned to the present. To Chief Cowley's left

sat Wit Dunaway, looking as grim as ever with freshly slicked-back hair to go along with his perpetually angry expression and folded arms. To Cowley's right was my longtime friend Buddy Hawkins, captain of detectives. That made him my boss, the figure in the police bureaucracy whom I answered to directly. He was several years older than me, about thirty-nine or forty. Over time, his reddish hair had gone blond, and for a man with five kids and a police detective's salary, he was dapper, probably the ritziest dresser I knew. I always thought he married into money, but knowing little about his wife's background, I could never be certain. He had an angular jaw and blue eyes, and for some reason he reminded me of the motion picture actor Spencer Tracy, even though the two didn't look much alike. He and I used to attend the same ward, which is the Mormon name for a local congregation, but when my family moved to the upper Avenues two years ago, we switched wards. Despite this, Buddy and I had stayed good friends and frequently updated each other with the latest news about our families and our church activities. Buddy also harbored ambitions I lacked. He had political savvy to spare. He played golf on Saturday afternoons with all the right men. He befriended Utahns in high places. Judges. Politicians. Newspapermen. He was going somewhere, but he was patient and methodical about it, willing to take it slowly and follow whatever opportunities opened up for him.

The woman with curls—whom Cowley quietly introduced as Mabel—pulled out a chair and sat at the table's midsection, opened a stenographer's notebook, and readied her pen. I lifted a nearby pitcher of water and filled the empty glass at my side. I trembled with nervousness. Butterflies darted around in my stomach.

Cowley broke the silence. "I was impressed with the

dramatization of your capture of Henry Grenache on *Crime Does Not Pay.* It was a spectacular publicity coup for the department. And you were in top form."

"Thank you, sir," I said. "I was quite happy with it myself."

"I'm sure your family is proud, too." Cowley gestured to the other men at the table. "As you can see, I've invited Captain Hawkins and Lieutenant Dunaway here so that we might discuss, in greater detail, the tragic homicide that occurred at the headquarters of the Fundamentalist Church of Saints last night, and what is to be done about it."

"Yes, sir," I said.

"As of now, the murder of LeGrand Johnston has been categorized as a joint investigation," said Cowley. "It will require close coordination between Homicide and your squad, Arthur. I've spoken to Mayor Cummings this morning. He has taken a strong personal interest in this case. There is pressure being brought to bear on him from the city council for your squad to show results. A rapid solution to this case would be precisely the sort of breakthrough the mayor wishes to see."

Cowley swiveled his chair toward Buddy. "Do you mind continuing, Charles?"

Buddy once told me that the only people he let call him Charles were his mother and Chief Cowley. I smirked when I heard the name spoken. Buddy cleared his throat and scanned the listeners around the table. "This is a high-profile homicide. The national press has taken a strong interest in this case already. Our operators have logged telephone calls from newspaper reporters as far away as London, Berlin, and New Delhi. Rumor has it the *New York Times* is putting this story on page one of tomorrow's edition. That stands to reason. LeGrand Johnston was the head of the largest polygamist sect in the world. I'm sure you can begin to understand why a prompt resolution to this case is of the utmost importance."

Buddy stopped and glanced at Chief Cowley. Cowley nodded and mouthed the words "thank you." "Arthur, you'll be working closely with Wit here," said Cowley. "I was hoping that you would apprise him, as well as us, of the progress your squad has made in its ongoing investigation of Johnston's notorious cult."

"Yes, sir. Most certainly." I pulled the dossier folders closer. "We—that is, the other three squad members and myself—have spent the last three months monitoring local polygamists, with the goal of building cases against them. These files are the tip of an iceberg that represents months of hard work—surveillance, research, direct cooperation with other units—and I have every reason to believe our efforts are going to pay off soon. If someone can dim the lights . . ."

Mabel went over to the twin doors and turned a wall dial. That, combined with Buddy closing the drapes, blocked much of the light out of the room. I whispered thanks and Buddy sat down next to the slide projector and switched it on, beaming an apparition on the screen that came into focus with the turn of a knob. The blob shape-shifted into an elderly white-haired man with a turkey neck and wearing a wide-brimmed black hat. His eyes and mouth open, he seemed surprised his photo was being taken. The slide showed him crossing a tree-lined road with a row of jalopies parked curbside behind him.

"Gentlemen, this is one of the victims of last night's brutal homicide, LeGrand Johnston, the seventy-nine-year-old leader of the Fundamentalist Church of Saints," I said. "It's a breakaway offshoot of the Church of Jesus Christ of Latter-day Saints. His followers called him Uncle Grand and they believed he was in direct contact with God. We estimate that he had somewhere in the neighborhood of twenty-two wives, but we can't be sure. There are thousands of polygamists who make their home in the Salt Lake Valley. Some are independents, with no connection to any specific sects or offshoots. But thousands maintain ties to Uncle Grand's cult. We've been operating under the assumption that if we target the heads of this sect with arrests and prison time, we'll behead the monster—so to speak—and send the other cultists fleeing." I paused. "Next slide, please."

Buddy pressed a button. *Click-click.* Next came an image, taken through shrub branches, showing a distant black-clad figure in a wheelchair, being pushed by a tall, lean man, and surrounded by a trio of bodyguards. The camera was far enough away from the man in the wheelchair that his face was not visible, but his dark hat and overcoat stood out. Two of the brawny men escorting him looked directly toward the camera lens, with one pointing a finger as if he had just realized someone was snapping pictures from the bushes.

"We believe the man in the center of photo with the hat is Rulon Black, second-in-command of the cultists," I said. "This photo was snapped by an ex-cultist. Unfortunately, you can't really see him in this picture. We have no other known photographs of him from the past thirty years, so we can't be sure of what he looks like today. Naturally, his reclusive tendencies have made him seem more sinister and given rise to plenty of rumors."

"Give us a for instance," said Cowley.

"I've spoken to a handful of men and women who've managed to escape the sect," I said. "They've all indicated there's a power struggle of sorts going on inside of the Fundamentalist Church of Saints. It apparently pits Rulon Black here, who supports moving the church and all of its members to a more remote location to escape the interference of authorities, against LeGrand Johnston, who prefers to remain in Salt Lake City and practice polygamy more out in the open, not in the shadows. So far, the rank-and-file members are divided, with some staying here and others moving to Dixie City, the fundamentalist settlement on the Utah-Arizona border."

Click-click. An outdoor portrait at a one-room schoolhouse, with four rows of ten kids each, all high school students, dressed in the attire of the 1870s.

Click-click. Same as before, yet zoomed in on the back row. Grainy, out of focus, but one can make out an acne-scarred kid with bristly hair, wearing a button-up sweater over a light shirt. Alert eyes, mouth almost nonexistent, protruding ears.

I narrated: "Here's the only known photograph we've been able to obtain of Rulon Black's face. It's his tenth-grade school photo from 1875. Next, please."

Click-click. A gangly man, late forties, head like a bobbing oil rig, eyes wide, major overbite, seated in a chair at a rolltop desk.

"This is his son, Eldon Black," I said. "This photograph is from about two years ago. There is some speculation that he's the real driving force behind Rulon's affairs. He's cunning and nakedly ambitious. Next slide."

Click-click. Two men in suits, standing near a wall. On the left: a tall man, thinning hair, handsome in a sleepy-eyed way, wearing bifocals perched on his bulbous nose, with deep lines etched in his face, and a crooked polka-dot bow tie below a jutting Adam's apple. Age: early sixties. On the right: a short man, circa mid-fifties, with a receding widow's peak, prominent cheekbones, a slight scar above his lips, and sporting tailor-made pinstripes.

"These are two very important figures in the Fundamentalist

Church of Saints," I said. "The man on the left is Alma Coving-ton, and on the right is Carl Jeppson. Covington edits a little pro-polygamy newspaper called *Truth* out of his house on Third Avenue. Jeppson runs a floral shop on Second South. Both men are considered to be part of Johnston's inner circle, although nobody can say for sure if they have any contact with Rulon Black." I paused. "Next slide."

Click-click. LeGrand Johnston leading five men—ages rang-ing from forties to sixties, all attired in dark suits—across des-ert flats. Behind them are dusty autos, scattered junipers, and a mesa.

"This," I said, "is a picture of Johnston with five of his apostles, Heber Moss, Guy Hammond, Lyman Boggs, Nordell Christensen, and Amos Barton."

"What exactly does it mean to be an apostle in this bizarre cult?" asked Cowley.

"An apostle would be an important patriarch in the church," I said. "It means he's got money and influence, he's close to the prophet, he's married to several wives, and he probably owns a decent chunk of real estate. The sheriff of Kane County took this picture in Kanab, the day the men went into town to pick up supplies. The polygamists are buying up land on the border, which they'll use for their United Brethren scheme—"

"United what?" asked Wit Dunaway.

"United Brethren," said Buddy. "It's a project to build a cult-ist utopia down on the border of Utah and Arizona. As Art mentioned, they already run a town down there, Dixie City, on the Arizona side. It's crawling with polygamists. They control everything—the city council, the school board, all the busi-nesses. Even the mayor has eight wives."

"I don't understand why they all don't just move down there," said Cowley. "It'd make life a whole lot more pleasant for us. We'd be rid of them, and we could finally lick this notion of Salt Lake City being a hotbed of plural marriage."

"With all due respect, sir, we oughtn't to underestimate the connection that many members feel to Salt Lake City," I said. "I'm not just talking about Johnston. A goodly number of the cultists were born and raised here. This town is the devil they know, so to speak. They don't necessarily want to relocate to some tiny burgh out in the middle of nowhere. But if Rulon had it his way, they'd all be living in Dixie City."

Sitting in darkness, looking at slides, it took all of my will to hold back from making derisive comments about these men. Their faces, pasty and sagging and full of malevolence, bothered me, pricking something deep inside. They stoked the flames of my animosity, in a way that no other group of people ever has. Part of me silently rejoiced that LeGrand Johnston was dead. Most modern Mormons—and by modern, I mean dedicated churchgoers of the twentieth century—viewed the polygamists with the strongest scorn imaginable. "Polygs," we called them.

Reasons for this powerful dislike were numerous. The simplest explanation, the pat one, was that polygs made a mockery out of marriage and family. Yet in my more reflective moments, I was willing to concede that my hatred for the men in my slide show was rooted in my inability to come to terms with the lives of my ancestors. Not so long ago, my great-grandparents on both sides engaged in plural marriage, practicing the same custom as the men I now detested.

"Lights, please," I said. Mabel switched on the lights and my eyes transitioned back to clarity in time to see everybody in the

room staring at me, waiting for me to utter something insight-
ful. "I wish I could advise you on suspects, but the truth is, I
don't have the foggiest idea who could have murdered Johnston,
or why."

"We need to strike while the iron's hot," interjected Cowley.
"This homicide changes everything."

"Our first move will be to arrest the leaders," said Wit. "Two-
man interrogations will run all day and into the night if need
be. If we squeeze these sonsabitches hard enough, they'll rat out
who plugged their prophet and cough up a lot of other dirt about
their operations. I'm telling you, aggressiveness is our ally."

"I'm not so sure about that," I said. "You'll be playing right
into their hands. They'll give us the silent treatment and squawk
about religious persecution to the press. And they've got one of
the best lawyers in the state defending them to boot. No, it seems
to me you've got to go at it a different way."

Wit shook his head. "What has your squad been doing since
the start of April, anyhow? Playing checkers?"

"We've been trying to build cases," I said, ignoring Wit's jab.
"Our goal is to see these men serve jail time."

"What sort of cases?" pressed Cowley.

I opened the top folder and summarized the file before me.
"We've turned up evidence that apostles have probably violated
the Mann Act, the Comstock Laws, and the Lindbergh Law. All
of these are federal offenses, and it's my hope that we might be
able to try these men before a federal grand jury. . . ."

"What about illegal cohabitation?" asked Cowley. "Surely
that's still against the law in this land?"

"The men marry one woman legally," I said. "The rest of the
wives are sealed to the husband in secret ceremonies. Each wife
lives in a separate place, to avoid arrests."

"I agree with Dunaway," said Cowley. "Round up key figures, put 'em under the hot lights, and sweat it out of them. I bet by the end of the day you'll squeeze out some confessions. If we play our cards right, we can use this thing to finally wipe out the fundamentalist cult in this city once and for all."

I opened my mouth to speak, but Buddy beat me to it. "This is a closed and tight-knit community we're talking about," he warned. "None of these people will testify in court against each other. It's exceedingly difficult to prosecute them. They cover their tracks, and they aren't keen to cooperate with the police."

"I'm sure their resolve will crumble when they see the inside of our jail cells," said Cowley confidently. He looked at Wit. "What do you need to conduct these arrests?"

"As many men as Becker can spare on short notice," said Wit. "We can begin as soon as ten o'clock this morning. Art here can provide the names and addresses of the apostles. I'll ask Bringhurst for quick warrants. I promise you we'll break these men by day's end."

"Good. I do *not* want this case to drag on," said Cowley, eyeing me, then Wit. "You two work together. Coordinate. Do whatever you have to do to find the murderer. We have two squads working on this. If there isn't a breakthrough soon, I'm going to feel the heat from Cummings. I *really* don't want that. Understand me?"

"Yes, sir," I said.

"Yep," said Wit.

Cowley stood, all smiles and good cheer. "If you'll excuse me, I have a meeting in city hall in five minutes and I don't wish to be late."

I scooped up my file folders, collected my slides from Mabel, and silently dreaded what lay ahead. As we filed out the office door, Wit glowered at me in his usual *it's-too-early-for-this* deadpan style.

"Looks like we're going to be collaborating," he said.

"Yes," I said, mustering as warm a grin as I could. "It certainly does."

Seven

I passed through the open sliding door of a large gray warehouse that stood behind Public Safety. Inside, forty uniformed men— eight wide, five deep—stood at attention, with Detective Lieutenant Wit Dunaway and Captain Earl Becker standing at the head. Off to Wit's side, a dozen or so of Wit's plainclothes homicide dicks, including Pace Newbold, waited for orders. Outside, it was hot, but in here, the air managed to stay cool under the cover of a thirty-foot-high ceiling. Behind the men, a fleet of twenty police paddy wagons waited, each with black paint so pristine it reflected the glare from overhead spotlights, and all of those vulcanized tires still gave off a factory-fresh rubber scent. Myron Adler and Jared Weeks, in fedoras and suits, stood in sunlight beaming through a tall window. I made eye contact with Myron and mouthed the word "Roscoe." He closed his eyes and shook his head. I tried not to show disappointment, but it was hard. I walked up to the front of the uniformed patrolmen and looked at their faces. Visors hid eyes, but their noses and mouths came in all shapes and sizes. Each man wore regulation black, with a thick belt, a diagonal shoulder strap, a crisp white shirt and black necktie, gleaming chest badge, cream-colored jodhpurs, and boots that went almost to the knees. Wit approached me and whispered, "Ready to go?" I nodded. He walked up to the front of the phalanx.

"Gentlemen," he said. "Thank you for taking part in this operation at such short notice. We are about to conduct raids on the homes and businesses of the heads of the largest polygamist sect in the United States. I can promise you the press will be watching us. Our purpose in carrying out today's arrests is to interrogate these men until one or more of them breaks and coughs up information that will enable us to solve last night's double homicide. As such, we need to carry out this operation with the highest level of professionalism. There is much at stake today. Whatever your views on polygamy happen to be, that's of no concern to me. What matters is that a series of murders has taken place inside of their tight little circle, and the perpetrator of this heinous act must be brought to justice, with no delay." He paused and scanned their faces. "I have obtained warrants from Judge Bringhurst to conduct searches of the polygamist-owned residences and businesses. If you happen to find anything tying a particular individual to last night's homicides, you are to report directly to me. Do I make myself clear?"

In almost perfect unison, they responded, "Yes, sir!"

"Good." Wit walked over to Captain Becker, who handed him a clipboard. Wit skimmed the assignment roster and nodded, then returned to his place in front of the men. "Squad A will be led by myself, Squad B by Detective Newbold, Squad C by Detective Oveson, and Squad D by Detective J. Weeks." Wit lowered the clipboard and looked out at the men. "Any questions?"

There weren't any, a good sign. Wit handed the clipboard to Becker. "Fellas," said Wit. "I don't believe in luck, but I'm wishing it to you anyhow. Now, what are you standing around for? Get moving!"

The formation broke. Patrolmen scattered in all directions. Paddy wagon engines roared, and men filed out the doors to get in black-and-whites. Roscoe chose that moment to show up. His cut and bruised face was still recovering from the beating he'd taken. About the best that could be said is that it looked better than it did yesterday. Wit gave him the evil eye as he walked past. I handed Jared his warrant and patted him on the shoulder, then I reluctantly approached Roscoe to have a word with him about his lack of punctuality. He saw me coming and gave me his best *what now?* face.

"You're late."

"Can we do this some other time?" he pleaded.

"I need you here at work each day on time."

"What can I say? It was one of those mornings." Up closer, he appeared even more disheveled, and not merely due to his roughed-up face. Unshaven, shirt untucked. I caught a whiff of booze. He noticed me studying him. "What?"

"Like I said the other day, I can't keep covering for you."

"Then don't. Cowley and Hawkins can go to hell. They can't stand me 'cause I ain't Mormon and I don't play their games."

"For crying out loud, Roscoe, all you have to do is show up on time and do your bit—"

Shaking his head in frustration, Roscoe left while I was in mid-sentence, heading off in the direction of the open entrance, only to be swallowed up by the brightness of the morning sun.

"What's his problem?"

Myron stood by my side, watching Roscoe head out into the light.

"Wrong side of the bed," I said.

"Too bad you have to put up with that guy. To call him a big, dumb ape would be an insult to big, dumb apes the world over."

Jared came over with a grim expression. "Wit's making a big mistake, boss," said Jared. "If you ask me, this is overkill, using all of these lawmen for just eleven arrests. This is only gonna make things worse."

"It's what Wit wants," I said. "It's his investigation now."

Wit strolled over and gave us the *something wrong?* glare, the one you get when your superiors do not actually want to know if something is wrong. I smiled and shook my head and we all went our separate ways. I nabbed Roscoe outside and he rode along with me, while Myron joined Jared in Squad D, prepared to assist in the arrests. Roscoe and I ended up riding along with a pockmarked, bristly-headed young officer named Kimball. Roscoe sat in back and I took the passenger-side front seat. None of us said a word as Kimball turned out of the parking lot, part of a long police convoy dispersing to all parts of the valley.

Under smoky skies, a line of police cars and a paddy wagon slowed in front of a redbrick building near the intersection of 200 South and 200 East. SUNSHINE FLORAL said a long sign spanning the entrance and display windows. A smaller sign read GREENHOUSE IN REAR. In a corner of the front window, owner Carl Jeppson had hung a poster of the ubiquitous National Recovery Administration (NRA) blue eagle, showing the mighty New Deal thunderbird with a gear in its right talon and lightning bolts in its left. WE DO OUR PART, it said. A star-spangled

sandwich board sign out front announced, ASK ABOUT OUR PATRI-
OTIC FOURTH OF JULY SPECIALS! Kimball killed the engine and the
three of us got out of the car. On my way to the entrance, I
stopped and whirled around toward the men behind me.

"Follow me. I'll do the talking."

I turned the knob and pushed the door open. A brass bell
rang. Inside, my eyes adjusted as I moved forward between
shelves of flowers on either side in all shapes and colors. The
temperature plunged thirty degrees, thanks to a walk-in refrig-
erator with its door wide open. I could see that it housed a huge
supply of roses. Roscoe came in after me and assumed a tough-
guy pose near the entrance. At least he'd tucked in his shirt and
appeared more presentable. In the rear of the store, four women
sat at a long wooden table, wrapping bouquets in paper, taping
them closed, and cutting ribbons with scissors. They ranged in
age—I guessed—from twenties to fifties, with their braided hair
pinned back in buns, wearing pale blue home-sewn dresses that
reached their ankles. Behind them, a door opened and I recognized Carl Jeppson, an apostle in the fundamentalist sect. You
couldn't mistake him for anybody else, thanks to a receding
widow's peak, high cheekbones, and a scar that formed a fault
from his nostril to his mouth where he once had a cleft lip. He
was sweating profusely, as if he'd emerged from a steam bath,
and the whites of his eyes had gone pink.

"Hello," I greeted him.

"May I help you?"

"Are you Carl Jeppson?"

"Yes. Is something the matter?"

I took out a black leather wallet and showed the badge inside. "Lieutenant Arthur Oveson, Salt Lake City Police Department. You're under arrest."

His face lost all color. "What on earth for?"

I opened my mouth to respond, but Roscoe, who now stood by my side, beat me to it.

"Polygamy, which is a violation of state laws," he said. "We have a warrant from Judge Nestor Bringhurst to search—"

"How dare you come inside my shop and disrupt my business!"

I motioned to Kimball, who moved past me, maneuvered behind Jeppson, and began to cuff his wrists. Jeppson started flailing before Kimball could finish. "See here, you can't do this!"

"Give me your hand." Kimball lunged for Jeppson's arm and twisted it downward, causing Jeppson to groan in dismay. Metal rattled and snapped and then the handcuffs were on securely. Jeppson looked like he was about to start sobbing.

"This is an outrage!" he shouted, his voice cracking. "My attorney is Granville Sondrup! He's in the McCornick Block on First and Main. Fifth floor. Telephone Wasatch one-zero-seven-nine. What are your names again?"

"Lieutenant Arthur Oveson."

"Detective Roscoe Lund."

He growled between clenched teeth. "This time tomorrow, you two will be picking up litter, if you're still employed at all!"

I blinked at him and said nothing, yet I felt the hatred—toward him and his entire way of life—welling up in me. Roscoe stayed quiet, too—a rare show of restraint for someone usually so quick with a snide comeback.

Kimball motioned for two officers to escort Jeppson to the paddy wagon. Jeppson bucked and writhed as the men led him past me. "This is a calamity!" he cried. "I have a reputation in this community! This place has been in business since 1910!

How dare you! My attorney is Sondrup! S-O-N-D-R-U-P. First name, Granville. G-R-A-N-V-I-double L-E."

It took two patrolmen to load the twisting, hollering Jeppson into the back of the idling wagon. I followed them out to the curb and watched them carry out the grim task with quiet determination. Even after they closed the rear doors, I could still hear muffled shouts. "You'll hear from my attorney! You'll rue this day! So help me . . ." The wagon roared off on the short drive to Public Safety.

Reluctantly, I went back inside to the four women seated at the table at the back of the room. Roscoe was already leaning against the counter, scrutinizing their every move. They had stopped wrapping bouquets and were frozen like statues, doing their best to avoid eye contact with me. They shared the same forlorn expression, and they seemed to stare blankly down at the work awaiting them. I'm sure I was the last person they wanted to see at that moment. Still, some part of me yearned to make nice with them, to assure them that I did not mean any harm. When I reached up to tip my hat, I startled the youngest of the four, who was probably in her twenties and already trembling.

"Ladies," I said. "I'll let you get back to your work."

One of the older women, round-faced with sunken eyes and dark gray hair, raised her head, frowning, resisting tears.

"It's not enough that he was excommunicated," she said. "Now you come in here and drag him out of his place of business, like he's a . . . a . . . a common criminal."

"Quit your bellyaching. He's a suspect in a homicide investigation," said Roscoe.

I glared at Roscoe and gave a little headshake to show my disapproval of his "bellyaching" comment.

"He has children!" she yelled, rising to her feet. "He didn't harm anybody!"

The woman beside her, young and frail in appearance, rose and squeezed the gray-haired woman's arm and pulled her back. "Please, Hilda. It won't do any good."

Hilda's shoulders drooped and she began convulsing with sobs. She sat back down, followed by her petite coworker.

"Are you his wives?" I asked the women.

"Don't answer him," cautioned Hilda through a veil of tears.

The women stayed silent. I had no desire to remain in that shop a second longer. My conflicted feelings of guilt and hostility—the former for disrupting their lives, the latter from my dislike of polygamy—jousted in my mind and my heart as I watched those women resuming work, cutting strips of brown paper with scissors, taping the wrapping around bouquets, tying shiny colored ribbon around the packages, and not a single one acknowledging my presence.

Nothing left for me to say or do here. I faced Kimball. "His office is in back," I said. "I presume your men have been briefed about what to look for?"

"Yes, sir," said Kimball. "The captain informed us."

"Good. Put a couple of men on it and let's get out of here."

"Yes, sir."

I gave the women at the long table a backward glance on my way out, with Roscoe tailing close behind. I sensed they were pleased to see us leaving, although they couldn't have been half as relieved as I was when I walked out of that shop. From a young age, I'd been taught that polygamists were deviants and not true to the current church. At that moment, I felt overwhelming feelings of hostility toward these people churning inside of me. Roscoe grinned at me as he stuffed a wad of chewing tobacco in his mouth. He didn't care. Cynicism with two cubes of apathy was more his cup of tea. Unlike me, he was not saddled with the burden of being a true believer.

"This is it. Slow down."

Officer Kimball swerved to the curb and into the shadow of an enormous old tree near the corner of Third Avenue and T Street. Behind us, the police cars and the paddy wagon that had barely deposited Jeppson at the jail imitated our move. The vehicles halted in front of a two-story bungalow, brick on the first floor and shingles on the second, with a long columned porch surrounded by low-trimmed shrubs. I picked up the newspaper on the seat between Kimball and me and unfolded it. The banner at the top said TRUTH in old English calligraphy, and below it were the words THE ORGAN OF THE FUNDAMENTALIST CHURCH OF SAINTS.

"That's their birdcage liner," said Roscoe from the backseat. "Puts even the most alert parakeet to sleep."

"Let's go, fellas," I said.

The three of us got out of the car and formed a semicircle with officers from the other vehicles. I advised them to enter the house if we weren't out in five minutes. Roscoe and I trotted up concrete porch steps. The screen door was closed but the front door open. I pressed the doorbell button and a buzzer went off inside. I waited half a minute. Nothing. A wind chime rang softly in the breeze. I pressed the button and waited once more. Nothing again. I opened the screen door and, holding the warrant in my left hand and taking out my .38 with my right, moved into the front entrance hall. Roscoe eased the door closed quietly and followed me. A forlorn symphony played somewhere in the distance. We went from room to room. All the blinds were

drawn. It was dark in each place we checked. The furnishings
came with that fresh smell of something recently carted out of
a Sears and Roebuck freight. I opened a hallway door and the
music suddenly got louder. Roscoe looked at me with a nod, as
if acknowledging this was the place to go.

The door opened up to a set of stairs descending to the basement. I started down, taking each step slowly, and the wood
moaned under my heels. Roscoe kept pace behind. Halfway
down I caught my first glimpse of a small army of women, all
dressed in the same type of heavy homespun, working away at
newspaper production. The long basement room housed what
appeared to be a professional linotype machine used for making newspapers and other printed items. Beyond it, like the great
Sphinx of Egypt, sat a printing press, dark and metallic and full
of intricate parts, with rolls of newsprint nearby. The symphony
had grown louder, now rising to a string instrument crescendo,
and I realized it was being played on a phonograph. Seven, no,
eight women I counted, probably ranging in age from twenty to
sixty. They stole looks at the two of us, never stopping what they
were doing.

A man sat on a swivel chair at the linotype machine's key-
board with his back to the basement stairs so that I couldn't see
his face. His fingers danced on the keys until my final footstep
sounded a loud creak on the aging wood below my feet. He froze,
raised his head slightly, and turned just enough to give me a
fleeting peek at his profile before shifting back again. He reached
to his right, to the phonograph sitting on a small table near his
workstation, lifted the needle off the record, and closed the machine's cover.

"He was only thirty-one when he died."

I still couldn't see his face.

"Who?" I asked.

"Schubert. That's his Symphony number eight in B minor. The Unfinished Symphony."

"Are you Alma Covington?"

"Yes."

I held my badge shoulder level, but he kept his back to me. Roscoe fished out his badge, too, and displayed it. "Detective Arthur Oveson, Salt Lake City Police Department. This is Detective Lund, my partner. You're under arrest."

"May I finish putting the finishing touches on the next issue? It won't be long."

"He said you're under arrest," echoed Roscoe.

He spun toward us in his swivel chair. His bifocals rested on the end of his nose, too large for his narrow face. "What is the origin of that name?"

The question took me aback. "Which one? Oveson?"

"Yes. I'm curious to know."

"How come?"

"Please humor me." He leaned far forward in his chair, smiled slyly, and whispered, "I'm a genealogy fiend."

Roscoe and I stole glances at each other. I put away my wallet and shrugged. "I suppose if you traced it far enough back, you'd end up in Denmark."

"Ah, a sturdy people, the Danes," he said. "That's where I went on my mission as a lad. Copenhagen. It's an extraordinary city, full of breathtaking architecture and gardens. Have you been?"

"No."

"You must go! The Rosenborg Castle Gardens is one place you are required to visit before you die! Lush. Full of exotic plants. Rich in history."

"I hate to cut off the geography lesson," said Roscoe. "But you're still under arrest."

"So I am! Well then, let's not delay this process another second."

He rose to his feet and came over to us with a confident stride, holding his hands out as if offering them to be cuffed. Roscoe maneuvered around me, brought Covington's arms behind him, and snapped the handcuffs on. The women gathered to bid a silent farewell to Covington, whose oddball grin never went away. He didn't seem the least shaken up by what was happening, which ran contrary to every other arrest I'd made since joining the SLCPD. I started to wonder about his sanity, whether he possessed any.

"Aren't you curious about why you're being arrested?" Roscoe asked, stepping to Covington's side.

Covington eyed me intently, ignoring Roscoe's question. "You're not related to Gustav Oveson, are you?"

I instantly recognized the name: my paternal great-grand-father. He crossed the Atlantic in the nineteenth century with other Danish converts to Mormonism. I nodded. "I am, as a matter of fact. Why do you ask?"

"I see. You know something? I think we're related."

I looked at Roscoe and tilted my head toward the basement steps. He escorted Alma Covington to the main floor and out the front door. I had no desire to find out whether I was really related to him.

"Lead the way, boss," said Roscoe, unable to wipe that smirk off his face. "You do the talking."

We surveyed the scene at our third and final stop of the day, a two-story redbrick house in an isolated part of town northwest of the state capitol. By now, the men in our police convoy knew the routine, and they milled about on the hot sidewalk while I conducted my business. Up here were squat, sullen little dwellings with closed blinds, tucked away under canopies of catalpa, ash, and maple trees. About half the driveways contained a jalopy. Most of these houses dated back to the last century, constructed at the bottom of a hill, baked daily by the hot sun. The area attracted plural marriage zealots who stubbornly maintained the practice long after the Church of Jesus Christ of Latter-day Saints forbade it in 1890. Except for a handful of elderly men who had married multiple wives in their youth and then stopped after the 1890 ban, the Church aggressively excommunicated practicing polygamists. Outcasts preferred neighborhoods like this—cut off enough that the police rarely visited, yet sufficiently close to still have access to the city.

Roscoe shadowed me up front steps and I knocked on the screen door. Ten seconds passed. I turned around and looked over Roscoe's shoulder at an ancient black delivery truck with the words ROCKY MOUNTAIN COAL COMPANY on its sideboards as it rattled south on 200 East. I turned to knock again when the inner door opened and a lanky man around fifty years old appeared on the other side of the screen.

Eldon Black.

He had me beat in the height department by a few inches. A layer of thinning brown hair topped an oblong head, a paleskinned noggin barely wide enough to showcase his bug eyes, turned-up nose, and protruding mouth. I don't know as I'd call him homely—that's a crummy thing to call someone—but Clark Gable had nothing to fear. Maybe he'd get handsomer with age.

"May I help you?"

I held my badge face level. "Detective Art Oveson, Salt Lake—"

"You were in the papers. You captured the Running Board Bandit."

"Yes, I did."

"That was fine work," he said. He craned his neck to see over my shoulder, and he swallowed hard when he saw Roscoe and, beyond him, the uniformed officers down by the street. "What are you doing here?"

"Eldon Black?" I asked.

No reply. No nod or any other movement. He hovered ghost-like on the other side of that thick screen, not even blinking.

"Do you know why I'm here?"

"The prophet is dead."

"How did you find out about his death?"

"Word travels fast. I suspect you wish to question my father? He's not here, I'm afraid."

"Where is he?"

"At his compound in northern Arizona."

"Is he planning on coming here?" I asked.

"He's frail. He's in no condition to travel."

"I see," I said with a nod. "Is it safe to say that you function as his representative, then?"

"Yes."

"You're under arrest," I said, fishing out my warrant.

He didn't bother examining the warrant. Instead, he pressed the screen door outward, a spring moaned, and he pulled the thick, arched wooden door shut behind him. He locked the door and pocketed the key, then faced me with his hands extended outward, side by side, dangling at the wrists. "Cuff me."

Eight

The roundup of polygamist apostles from the Fundamentalist Church of Saints the day after the murder of their prophet, Le-Grand Johnston, went textbook smoothly. The eleven men we arrested, all older—most in their forties, fifties, sixties—and dressed in dark suits, each requested to see their attorney, Granville Sondrup, but otherwise said nothing. Meanwhile, polygamist wives—about thirty strong—lined up at the front desk clerk, asking when their husbands would be released. Impossible to ignore in their prairie attire, these women seemed to be frozen in time at around 1851. This bizarre gathering, naturally, attracted the press hounds, who came out in full force with photographers and began snapping pictures. One duo, reporter Abner Clayton and his youthful shutterbug sidekick, Tommy Phelps, found their way to the basement jail cells and managed to line up a photograph of all the polygamist apostles we'd just arrested, right before they were taken to their jail cells.

After the flash went off, a uniformed officer broke it up. "All right, c'mon, the show's over. Right this way to your temporary accommodations, gentlemen!"

The subdued men filed into their cells and heavy steel doors squealed and clanged shut, with the loud striking of metal against metal as they locked. Behind bars, the men stayed eerily silent, staring out at me with rage in their eyes. I took in the scene, shook my head in disgust, and headed to the marble stairs leading up to the detective bureau. Clayton, the reporter, a lean, pockmarked fellow in a brown hat and greenish jacket, went up the steps with me to the first floor, and up the next flight.

"Detective Oveson, I loved you on the radio!"

"Thank you, Ab," I said. "That's awfully kind."

"Don't mention it. By the way, how do you respond to the accusation that the Salt Lake City police are stifling these people's religious freedom with these arrests?" asked Abner.

"Who's making that accusation?" I asked.

"Shoot, I don't know," said Abner. "Me, I guess."

"The men in those cells are suspects in a murder investigation." I stopped halfway up the stairs, turned, and looked down at Abner to drive my point across. "They're apostles in the Fundamentalist Church of Saints, which means they're part of Johnston's inner circle. As I'm sure you've figured out by now, they're uncooperative in the extreme, and we have reason to believe, based on our past interactions with them, that not a single one of them would have submitted willingly to questioning unless we arrested them. They left us with no choice."

"Aren't you violating their rights by arresting them in this manner?" pressed Abner. "Aren't you targeting them merely because they disagree with the Church of Jesus Christ of Latter-day Saints and have the gumption to—"

"This has nothing to do with the LDS Church," I shot back firmly. "We are conducting a homicide investigation and we cannot rule any of those men out as suspects unless we've had a chance to question each one separately. Is that clear?"

"Why arrest all of them?" he asked. "I mean, we've had other homicides in this town before and you don't round up dozens of people. . . ."

"C'mon, Ab, do the math! We didn't arrest dozens! There are eleven men downstairs, ten of 'em apostles in the Fundamentalist Church of Saints, and the other one's the son of Johnston's successor, who's nowhere to be found. That's not even a full dozen, much less 'dozens' plural."

"All right, you got me on that one," said Abner, grinning sheepishly. "What about you, Detective Oveson? Aren't you a Mormon?"

"Yeah, I am," I said. "What of it? Mormons rejected polygamy long ago."

"You must have ancestors who were polygamists," he said. "How do you feel about them?"

"This isn't about my ancestors, or yours, or anybody else's," I said. "It's about finding out who murdered LeGrand Johnston and Volney Mason. And believe me when I say we will find out. Now, if you'll excuse me, Ab, I've got a meeting I'm late for."

I continued up the stairs, and Abner called out from behind me. "Crack this one and you might be on the radio again!"

Half jogging, I passed my office and went instead to the Homicide Squad's meeting room at the end of the corridor. Wit Dunaway sat on top of a long desk in the front of the room, thumbing through a report in a folder. All of the other men from the

Homicide and Anti-Polygamy squads sat in wooden chairs. I peeked up at the clock as I planted my bottom on a hard seat near Roscoe. A few minutes past three o'clock.

"Art, how nice of you to join us," Wit said. "Now we can get started."

Light laughter around the room, and maybe a scowl from Pace Newbold, who could always be counted on for a dirty look.

Wit eased off the desk and began pacing, scanning the room as he briefed. "Interrogations will occur under my supervision. A stenographer will be posted in each room, so please speak up and make sure your suspect does likewise. I understand their attorney, Mr. Sondrup, will be sitting in on as many of these as he can, so show him some courtesy. If you get any bites, no matter how small, come see me."

The door flew open and in strode a Homicide dick, J. D. Lythgoe, gaunt and gray haired, the old man of the bunch in his early sixties. He walked up to Wit and said something that I could not make out in a hushed tone, but Wit was concentrating on his every word, nodding slowly the entire time. Lythgoe took his seat behind me and a soft "Thank you, John" came from Wit.

"I've just been told by Detective Lythgoe that Mr. Sondrup, the attorney for the suspects, is downstairs as we speak advising his clients not to cooperate."

Angry whispers and furrowed brows spread around the room.

"You know what to do," said Wit. "Get busy."

Desk legs scraped linoleum. Men stood. A line formed at the door. Amid the muted conversations, Wit walked over to me.

"Why don't you start in on Covington, since you brought him in," he said. "We've still got the girl in a separate holding cell.

She's stubborn as all get-out, I'll give her that much. Maybe this mute routine of hers isn't an act after all. Anyhow, I'm going to go to work on her one more time before the fellas from the State Industrial School drop by to haul her off. When you're done, maybe you can check in and see how things are shaping up." His face brightened. "Oh yeah . . ."

He opened his file folder and took out an eight-by-ten picture and handed it to me. I looked at it. It was a mug shot of the girl from the Lincoln Street church.

"Do me a favor, will you?" he asked.

"Sure."

"Ask around, see if any of the men know her. Maybe we can ID her that way, if she's intent on keeping her trap shut."

"Will do."

After talking to Wit, I went to the long hallway of interrogation rooms in the basement, conveniently located near the jail cells. The corridor was packed with plainclothes detectives and a sprinkling of patrolmen, and I could hardly hear myself think in the din. I carried the picture of the girl in my hand as I squeezed past them. Officer Gus Nibley, uniformed and without a speck of dust on his cap's visor, wormed through a wall of men to hand me an incomplete police report attached to a clipboard with Alma Covington's name at the top and a freshly sharpened pencil, the tools I needed to start my interrogation. Normally soft-spoken, Nibley had to raise his voice considerably for me to hear him.

"He's in room five, sir!"

"Thank you, Officer!"

"Things are getting off to a rough start," he said above all the other voices. "These men are all mum, closed up tight as drums. Sondrup is going from room to room, giving orders not to cooperate. The no-good son of a—"

"How are the wife and kids, Gus?" I asked.

He seemed surprised at my question. "Never better. Yours, sir?"

"Things are looking sunny on our end," I said. I tucked the pencil in the spring clip.

"Pleased to hear it, Lieutenant. Do you need a partner, sir?"

"Something tells me I'm better off alone with this particular fellow. Thank you, though."

I slipped into room five and, closing the door, silenced the hallway din. I spied my reflection in the two-way mirror: still as gangly and awkward as ever, and my messy hair could use a good combing. In the corner of the room, a brunette stenographer in a green dress readied herself over her stenotype as I pulled out a chair, sat down, and turned my attention to Alma Covington. My interaction with him had been limited, yet I could sense this was a man whose intelligence outshined that of his polygamist brethren. Unlike the others, he struck me as erudite and cultured, a man who knew there was more to life than how many women he married.

"I have a few questions I'd like to ask you, Mr. Covington," I said.

The machine snapped away as the stenographer's fingers struck keys.

"I assume you're here to discuss LeGrand Johnston."

"Yes."

"My attorney has advised me not to say anything."

"That is certainly your right."

"I respectfully disagree with him," Covington said. "We

polygamists have been hiding from the world for too long. It's high time we be more outspoken and prouder of who we are. We need to show the world we're not freaks. We need to move into the twentieth century, so to speak."

I nodded. "Those are encouraging words."

"So ask away, Detective."

"Thank you," I said. "I wish more polygamists shared your openness."

"They're a misunderstood people." He spoke as though he were an anthropologist studying them from a distance. "It stands to reason why they distrust the outside world. They're like the Mormon pioneers of yore, hounded, judged, driven from place to place."

I could have launched into one of my anti-polygamy tirades, but I held back. *Let the baby have his bottle*, I reasoned. Besides, until now, not a single polygamist had shown the slightest willingness to speak to me. Who knows if this opportunity would ever present itself again?

"You're right, I want to ask you about Johnston," I said. "Do you have any theories about who might've murdered him?"

"The question is *who'd want to*," he said. "He was a gentleman. A thinker. A visionary. A finer man could not be found."

"I've heard rumors about a power struggle in your church," I said. "Is there any truth to these claims?"

His eyes moved searchingly, as if he needed to inspect the room to reply. "No."

"You hesitated," I told him. "You had to think it over."

"Every religion has its divisions. We're no exception. But I know of no one in our church who'd want to end Grand's earthly existence. We've lost our prophet, seer, and revelator. We've lost an extraordinary man who gave us, in his talks and his writings, an enchanting vision of the future. Yes, I'm afraid we've lost a great deal more than most people realize."

His self-assured posture loosened. His shoulders slumped. Eyes closed. His sadness now showed in a way that it hadn't before, and it seemed genuine.

I allowed him some time. I looked at the stenographer. She smiled at me.

"Are you getting all this?" I asked her. "Do you need us to slow down?"

"You're doing just fine," she said.

I turned back to Covington. "Sorry for your loss."

He stiffened upright, eyes wide, still serious but no longer in the grip of despair. "I know of nobody in our church capable of murdering Grand, especially in the terrible way it was done."

"How about outside of your church?"

"There are rival groups, but most pose no threat."

"Is there one that could've been behind this?"

He lowered his head, as if silently deliberating how much to reveal.

"Please," I said softly. "I need you to level with me."

He inhaled deeply through his nose. "It's small. It's called the Assembly. Short for the Assembly of Apostolic Saints of Final Days."

"What a mouthful," I said. "Have they got a leader?"

"Yes. Orville Babcock. He owns a used car lot on State Street called Babcock Motors."

"Do you think this Babcock character had it in him to kill Johnston?"

"I'm not saying he did. I'm not saying he didn't. I know the two men were once close, but they had a parting of ways.

Orville went off and started his own church. Since then, he's been denouncing Grand with alarming frequency."

I snickered a little, instantly fearing I might've offended Covington.

"Did I say something amusing?" he asked.

"A breakaway sect of a breakaway sect? Is there a word for that?"

His grin was subtle, but there. "Who knows?"

"So you think this Babcock might have had something to do with Johnston's murder?"

"I really don't know. Some of his attacks on Uncle Grand have been harsh. Be that as it may, it's a big leap from saying bad things to doing bad things. I guess you'll have to look into that yourself."

I nodded. "What happens now? Does Rulon Black take the helm?"

"Pending the approval of the apostles," he said. "I'm sure they'll vote to confirm him."

"He's a rather mysterious fellow."

"How so?"

"Well, for starters, nobody's ever seen him."

"He's an elusive man, no question."

"So he's real?"

"Of course. What sort of question is that?"

"You can't blame a fellow for asking."

"I can count on just two hands the number of times I've been in his presence, and only from a distance or in dark surroundings. He's self-conscious about his appearance. I imagine it must have something to do with the attempt on his life."

"You mean somebody tried to kill him?"

"Oh good heavens, yes."

"Who?"

"The assailant is still unknown. The attack left him disfigured and confined to a wheelchair, I'm sad to say."

"When was this?"

"Years ago. You'd have to ask him the exact date. Dear Uncle Grand always had a real soft spot for Rulon. After the attempt on Rulon's life, the prophet declared that Rulon could stay an apostle and keep living in seclusion in his compound on the Arizona border."

"I don't recall seeing anything in the police files about him being attacked."

"He didn't report it to the police."

"Why?"

"The police aren't exactly sympathetic."

"Well, you people *are* lawbreakers."

"There are unjust laws, Detective Oveson." Covington smiled, and when he squinted, crows' feet formed at the corners of his eyes. "Although I suspect a man of your zeal does not stop to consider that."

Another comment best ignored. "When you say Rulon was disfigured and wheelchair-bound, what happened to him?"

"There's no point in describing it. It's all gossip."

"Do you think whoever his attacker was might've had a hand in murdering LeGrand Johnston?" I asked.

"It's been so long," he said. "I don't see how there could be a connection."

"One last question?"

"Sure."

"The night Uncle Grand was murdered, there was a young woman there, at the fundamentalist church. Do you know who she is?"

He shook his head and made a slight pout. "The prophet knows a good many people, male and female. Did you bring a picture of her?"

I showed him my eight-by-ten of her.

"Where is she now?" he asked.

"Do you know her?"

He looked up from the photograph as he pushed it back to me. "I'm afraid not."

"To answer your question, she's in protective custody."

"Oh. Why don't you ask her her name yourself?"

"She won't speak. Something frightened her and she isn't saying anything."

"Do you suppose she saw . . ." His words trailed off, as if he could not finish his sentence.

"Who knows?"

It wasn't my imagination: He seemed genuinely stunned by the news of the girl. He knew something he wasn't saying, I could tell that much. I asked again, "Do you know her?"

He grinned. "Does anybody really know anybody?"

"Do *you* know *her*?" I repeated.

"She looks familiar," he said. "Beyond that, I can't say."

"Who were all those women?" I asked.

"Which ones? You mean back at my house?"

I nodded.

"That's my production staff on the newspaper," he explained. "A real dedicated bunch."

"How many of them are your wives?" I asked.

"I have but one lawfully wedded wife to speak of," he said, now sporting an ear-to-ear *you-can't-fool-me* grin.

"Uh-huh. Got any children?" I asked.

"Only daughters." There was a tinge of disappointment in

his voice, but that smile spread across his face once more. "Perhaps the Lord will one day bless me with a son."

"Thank you for your time," I said. "This has been helpful."

I leaned forward, extending my arm across the table, offering the hand of friendship. He shook it, without hesitation.

Carl Jeppson squirmed in his chair and turned his glass of water around and around in circles. He blinked rapidly. He cleared his throat repeatedly. When he felt like I was not saying enough or staring at him too much, he'd get irritated and ask, "What?" No question, the man was agitated. The room's bright lights added to his discomfort, and he kept pressing his fingers into his eyes and rubbing.

"I don't appreciate being dragged out of my place of business, in full view of passersby," he said. "I've a reputation to uphold." He paused a few seconds and looked me up and down. "I think the police are using this crime as a pretext to come down hard on our community."

"That's not so," I said. "All we're trying to do is figure out who murdered your prophet and his driver. You people ought to be helping us. Instead you're treating us like we're your enemies. I don't get it."

He puffed his cheeks and blew air. "I've been advised by my attorney not to—"

"Let me show you something."

I handed him the photograph. His eyes widened and his mouth opened slightly when he saw the girl, but then he tried to conceal his surprise. He flicked his fingertips at the picture and it slid across the tabletop.

"Who is she?"

"I don't know."

"Yes, you do."

"Are you calling me a liar?"

"If you say you don't know her, then yeah."

"She's not somebody I recognize."

"Maybe she's one of Johnston's wives?" I guessed aloud.

"Grand only had one wife in his time on earth, his dear Lucinda, who he met and married back when he—"

"Cut it out," I said. "Look, I know the man's a polygamist, no matter what you and the others say. He's the head of the Fundamentalist Church of Saints, a church that openly advocates plural marriage. And he is—or was—the kind of fellow who lived by example. I know he had many wives. I've been following him around for nearly three months and I've seen him stop at their various houses. I've counted at least fifteen here in Salt Lake, and I know for a fact he's got more in Dixie City. So you might as well come clean and let me know how many wives the old bird had, because I'm tired of playing these guessing games."

"I object to your line of questioning," protested Jeppson. "Grand was a respected businessman and a brilliant theologian. He was a self-made man, raised in dire poverty. Any other man born into those circumstances would've come out of it with a hardened heart, but he didn't. He stayed generous until the end. I find it offensive in the extreme that you'd reduce this man's life to how many wives he was sealed to during his earthly existence. Of what concern is that to the police, and how does it relate to the murder of our prophet?"

I smiled at him.

"What?" he asked, his pupils doing a nervous dance.

"Prophet, my foot," I said. "He wasn't a prophet."

"How can you say that? What makes you so cocksure?"

"Because I can tell a confidence man when I see one," I said.

"Joseph Smith was a prophet. Brigham Young was a prophet. Heber J. Grant is a prophet. Not Johnston. No, he was as crooked as the day is long. That's what he was."

His posture sagged with defeat. "I remember reading about you in the newspaper, back when you were promoted. Even though I hated that your squad was back in business, your remarks to the reporter encouraged me. You said people shouldn't judge others that are different, or jump to conclusions. You said you'd arrest polygamists only if you found evidence of them committing crimes. Remember?"

I leaned in close to him, for effect. "Tell me something. If we hadn't arrested you, would you have come in voluntarily if we'd asked you to?"

That shut him up. I snatched the picture of the girl and left. No point in quizzing a man as uncooperative as Carl Jeppson.

Nine

The other interrogations were fruitless. I went from room to room, observing detectives questioning suspects. Granville Son-drup, a lantern-jawed, middle-aged man in a chalk-stripe three-piece suit and bright red tie, with a head of thick, prematurely gray hair, sat in on as many of the exchanges as he could. But because they were happening concurrently, it was impossible for him to attend each one. When present, he'd frequently lean over and whisper into the ear of his client. Then the nodding apostle would straighten and say either "I refuse to answer that question" or "I don't know." Most of the polygamists were uncooperative, some even combative. Their expressions—a mix of twitches and glares—spoke volumes, even as their voices stayed silent. When they answered questions, after the rare granting of approval by Sondrup, their replies came out terse, often snarled. During each session, I would interrupt and show the photograph of the girl to the suspect. No one recognized her. Or so they claimed.

Wit paced the halls, stopping now and again to watch through the two-way windows. His coworkers knew to stay out of his way. He dropped his cigarette on the linoleum, crushed it under his heel, and blew smoke out his nose. "Eldon Black is in there," he told me when I'd finished with another polygamist, jerking his head in the direction of room three. "Peery gave up on him a while ago. Why don't you see what you can do?"

"Yes, sir."

I entered room three, shut the door, and took a seat across from Rulon Black's shifty-eyed, bucktoothed son. The elder Black's police dossier sat on the table. I placed the photograph of the girl down next to it, opened the folder, and thumbed through its contents.

"Hello, Mr. Black."

"I have nothing to say to you, Detective."

I slid the eight-by-ten photograph at him. He glanced at it. His eyes returned to me. "All questions may be directed to Mr. Sondrup."

"What's her name?"

"Did you hear what I said?"

I knitted my fingers together and cracked my knuckles. That got a wince out of him. "What's her name?"

"My, my, but you are persistent, Detective Oveson."

"I want a straight answer," I said. "All I'm asking is who is she?"

"Am I a suspect in last night's murders?"

"Not necessarily," I said. "Not at this point, anyhow."

"Then I'm free to go? I've been here for two hours. Two and a half hours, actually."

I ignored his remark. "You're not going to tell me her name?"

"I'll repeat what I said, because evidently you didn't hear me. Please address any questions to Mr. Sondrup, attorney at law."

"How about I address a question to you and you answer it. I'll start with: Why is LeGrand Johnston lying in the morgue?"

He inhaled sharply through his nostrils. "I don't have the foggiest idea."

"What about his driver, Volney Mason?"

"I don't know that, either."

"No guesses?"

"You're wasting *your* time and *mine*," he said. "I do not know who killed them. All I know is that a great man lost his life, and I wish to leave now so I can spend time properly mourning the loss of my prophet with the other members of my faith."

"I've heard there was something of a rift between Johnston and your father," I said. "Care to comment on it?"

"No."

Tough nut to crack, I thought. He kept his cool. Not even a bead of sweat.

I pressed him: "Which is it? No, you don't care to comment on it? Or no, there was no rivalry?"

"They were close," he said. "This *rivalry* you speak of, I've never heard of it before now."

"Suit yourself," I said. "We'll revisit that one later. Johnston had, *what*, twenty-two wives? Maybe one of them got jealous and decided to kill him."

"Your desperation is starting to show, Detective."

"Why do you say that?"

"I don't know where you get your foolish ideas," said Eldon. "LeGrand only had one wife, Lucinda. *One wife*, singular, not twenty-two."

"On paper, that's true," I said. "But in your church's secret ceremonies, he was sealed to lots of wives, not just one."

"Tell me, Detective, are we here to talk about the murders that happened last night at our church, or the custom of plural marriage?"

"Talking about one doesn't rule out the other," I said. "LeGrand Johnston was, after all, the head of the largest polygamist sect in the United States. . . ."

"No, Detective, he's a prophet in a legitimate church whose members are being persecuted by the authorities. Is it any wonder so many of us are pulling up our stakes and leaving this place? We're merely carrying on the traditions of the early Mormon pioneers, searching for a haven where we can—"

I slammed my palm on the table, startling him only slightly. "Hey!" I shouted, pointing my finger. "Don't you dare compare yourselves to my church's founders! You hear me? Because there is no comparison!"

His grin returned. "I believe I've found your raw spot."

I calmed down, lowered my voice. "How come I've never seen a photograph of your father?"

He narrowed his eyes in surprise. "A photograph?"

"Yeah, a photo, a snapshot. Doesn't like having his picture taken?"

"That's a peculiar question, Detective," said Eldon. "I don't see what it has to do with why I'm here."

"I find it strange I've never seen him," I said. "No picture, no . . . nothing."

He studied me for a moment. "Like most families, we keep all of our pictures in a family photo album."

"Does each wife get one?" I asked. "A photo album, I mean."

"Again, I'm not really comprehending why you're asking this

line of questions," he said. "It hardly strikes me as germane to the matter at hand."

"Let me rephrase the question: Do *you* have a picture of your father I can borrow? It'll help our investigation greatly."

"You want to borrow a picture of my father?"

"If I promise to return it safely," I said, "may I?"

He shook his head. "No."

"Why not?"

"Detective Oveson, *with all due respect*, I have more important things to do than sit here and explain why I'm not going to give you a picture of my father."

"I see no reason to drag this out any longer," I said. Easing my chair back to leave, I paused before I stood. "So far, you people aren't acting like you want to see us nab the killer in this case. It makes us think you're holding out. Maybe hiding something."

He shifted his attention to the two-way mirror, as if he were trying to see beyond his reflection. I took that as an indication that he no longer intended to cooperate with me. I reached across the table and picked up the picture of the girl sitting in front of him and rose to my feet.

"Detective Oveson." I stopped halfway to the door and turned to Eldon Black. "When you've been hounded and harassed by the authorities as much as we have, it has a way of eroding your faith in the fairness of the justice system."

I left because I am sure had I stayed in that room, I would have said—or done—something I'd later regret.

"This is outrageous!"

Granville Sondrup, attorney at law, had a loud voice, and was legendary for shouting his courtroom summations. On this day, it hurt my ears, and I could tell from the unpleasant grimace on Wit's face that I wasn't alone. Worsening matters, we had to sit in Chief Bill Cowley's office and listen to this man carrying on about how horribly he thought his clients had been treated by the Salt Lake City Police Department. Buddy Hawkins sat in on the meeting, keeping his arms folded in uneasy silence.

From behind his stately desk, Cowley listened intently and smiled at all times, a gesture of courtesy. Other than a candlestick telephone, the only other items atop that massive chunk of art deco rosewood were the components of an onyx desk set: a dual fountain pen holder, a letter rack, a perpetual calendar, and galloping horse bookends with no books in between. The walls in the office were so white they stung my eyes when I looked at them. I'll give the police chief this much: The windows opened up to a fine view of the Wasatch Mountains. Whether he actually took time to savor it was a different story.

"You've arrested eleven of the most respected citizens of this community," Sondrup said. "You did it in a way that was so public, so conspicuous, that I can't help but conclude that you were deliberately trying to humiliate my clients!"

"Jesus Christ!" hissed Wit. "I can't believe I have to sit here and listen—"

"Wit, please," said Cowley, shaking his head disapprovingly. He rotated his chair toward Sondrup. "Mr. Sondrup, this is standard procedure in a high-profile homicide. It's not unusual to arrest and temporarily detain multiple suspects in a case of this nature. Our resources, alas, are limited, and bringing these men down here together allows us to complete the initial phase of our investigation."

"I want my clients released immediately," he said. "Moreover, the men I represent wish to know when you're going to open up the second floor of their church."

"Come again?" asked Buddy.

"Inside of the building on Lincoln, the stairs are blocked off by ropes and there are policemen standing guard, intimidating my clients."

"Oh, for hell's sake," said Wit. "Intimidating . . ."

Sondrup ignored Wit: "They must be ordered to leave the premises at once and open up the second floor so that my clients have access to what's up there."

"It's a crime scene," protested Wit.

"It's a place of worship, and the entire second floor is cordoned off. It's a clear violation of the religious freedom of my clients."

"We'll endeavor to open that up as soon as possible," said Buddy, his gaze shifting back and forth between Sondrup and Cowley. "Wit has assigned two of his most capable detectives to that location, and they should be wrapping up shortly."

Sondrup knitted his brow. "And another thing . . ."

"Yes?" asked Cowley.

"What *exactly* is Detective Oveson doing working on this case? Last I heard, he's not in Homicide."

"Oveson is assisting with relevant information from his ongoing investigation into the local polygamist community," said Buddy. "He has been bringing Detective Dunaway up to speed about the current situation."

"You know the old expression," said Sondrup. "If it waddles like a duck and quacks like a duck. You know what this looks to me like?"

"What?" asked Cowley.

"A crackdown."

Cowley shook his head and turned his palms up. "Mr. Sondrup . . ."

"I'm merely commenting on the optics of this thing."

"Granville . . ."

"What?"

"Don't let their paranoia rub off on you," reasoned Cowley. "I know you're smarter than that. This is not a crackdown. It's anything but."

"We're in the middle of the worst hard times in the history of this country," said Sondrup. "Crime rates are on the rise, and you're dedicating valuable men and resources to a campaign of harassment and intim—"

"That's a load of shit!" snapped Wit. "You can't seem to get it into that thick skull of yours that the leader of this cult was found shot to death *in his own goddamn church!* Given that, I'd say we've been proceeding with kid gloves."

"I object to your use of foul language, Detective Dunaway," said Sondrup. "And the fact that you used the word 'cult' to describe their church shows a real lack of respect on your part."

"Fuck you, Sondrup, and the horse you rode in on!"

"Wit, this isn't helping," said Buddy. He looked at Sondrup. "Mr. Sondrup, what can we say to talk you out of this lawsuit you plan to file against us?"

Wit's outburst had gotten to Sondrup. I could see his hands trembling slightly. "At this point, *nothing*, Captain Hawkins. I'm going to sue the SLCPD for violating the civil liberties of my clients. Nothing you say or do can stop me at this point."

Sondrup got up and left, slamming the door. Cowley tilted back in his chair, staring up at the ceiling, lost in his thoughts. Buddy studied him for cues. The veins on Wit's neck bulged and his forehead had turned red. I sat still, saying nothing, waiting for someone to speak.

Wit broke the uneasy silence. "The nerve of that bastard!"

"The mayor called me," said Cowley. "He isn't happy with how this thing is going."

Wit spoke through clenched teeth. "He isn't, is he?"

"For a crusader, he hates controversy," said Buddy.

Cowley said, "Mayor Cummings got wind of the fact that the *Examiner* is running a story about today's arrests at the top of A1 alongside coverage of the murder, and he's worried it's going to cast him in a poor light. He presented me with a list of demands."

"Oh?" I asked, hoping to head Wit off at the pass. "What are they?"

"He wants the Anti-Polygamy Squad to stay out of the case," Cowley told me.

Wit jerked upright in his chair. "What the hell . . ."

Cowley went on: "Cummings agrees with Sondrup. He says it's not the mandate of Art's squad to get involved with homicide cases."

"You mean we're supposed to stay out of it completely?" I asked in disbelief.

"Publicly, yes," explained Buddy. "Naturally, you two may share information, as long as it's done on the quiet."

"What else does this sonofabitch want?" asked Wit.

Cowley resumed: "He's demanding that we release all of the polygamists promptly and refrain from further arrests until we have airtight evidence linking one or more of them to the homicides. He also wants a written report justifying today's arrests."

"Why, that no-account prick!" Wit shot up to his feet so

abruptly, he tipped over his chair. "How dare he second-guess us!"

Cowley shrugged and shook his head. "I don't like it any more than you do, but we need to do what he says. Bear in mind, the mayor's opponents are already talking about a public inquiry into the conduct of this department."

"Public inquiry?" said Wit, turning his palms up in frustration. "Where do they come off . . ."

"The point is, if we release these men now, there's a chance Sondrup will drop his lawsuit," said Cowley. "We need to play ball on this one."

Those veins in Wit's neck were getting more prominent, and his facial color now resembled that of a beet. "What about Johnston? What about his driver? Are we supposed to just forget about those two small details?"

"Do as the chief says. Go downstairs and let the polygamists go," ordered Buddy. "Keep your investigation out of the papers from here on out, and Art . . ." Buddy looked at me. "Don't touch it."

"Yes, sir," I said.

When Wit left, he slammed the door even harder than Sondrup, a feat I thought impossible. Cowley continued to recline far back in his chair, seemingly unfazed, although his slow, solemn blinks revealed a man pushed to the edge by stress. Buddy motioned to me with a subtle head jerk that I should go, too. I rose from my chair, tugged my hat brim, plunged my hands in my pockets, and smiled at the two men on my way out the door. I figured they both needed to see at least one friendly face that day.

Ten

At the end of the workday, I caught Tom Livsey in the corridor, closing his office door on his way home.

" 'Lo there, Art," he said, locking up. "Got any plans for the holiday?"

"A big barbecue at the Oveson homestead in American Fork," I said. "You?"

"Who knows with this darn drought? I hear they might cancel the fireworks at Liberty Park, what with everything so dried out. That won't sit well with my kids."

"That's a shame." I pointed to a door with MORGUE on the frosted glass. "Mind if I take a peek at your new tenants?"

"Make it snappy."

"Shouldn't take more than a few minutes."

Tom unlocked the door and I followed him into a high-ceilinged room with tall windows, operating tables, and lab sinks. He threw a switch, electrifying rows of globes overhead. Bleach fumes assaulted my eyes as we crossed octagonal tiles to a wall of morgue refrigerators, four high, six across. He pulled rubber gloves on his hands and picked the top towel off a stack. He tossed it to me and I caught it with a puzzled expression.

"Just in case."

I held the towel near my face as Tom unfastened a lever on a morgue drawer and slid it open, like a massive filing cabinet. He peeled back the sheet, revealing lifeless LeGrand Johnston with that puckering hole in his forehead, thoroughly scrubbed and drained of blood. His flesh had turned paler and sagged more than it had last night. The wisps of white hair on his head came into focus more clearly, as did the wrinkles on his neck and torso and his prune lips. I glimpsed the other two bullet holes, at the base of his neck and in his flabby stomach. Surveying the damage, I wondered if his soul had reached a better place. I supposed I'd never know.

"Shot three times with a .32. Same caliber used on the driver."

"Any sign of the firearm?" I asked.

"I'm afraid not. We have Volney Mason's .45 caliber sidearm, which was used to fire a shot into the wall of the church, but not the one used to shoot the victims."

"Did the police contact the next of kin?"

"Yes, they did this morning," said Tom. "That'd be his wife Lucinda. Her son drove her here earlier this afternoon and they identified the body."

"What was her demeanor?"

"Weeping, but not distraught."

"When she was here, did you happen to mention the girl at the crime scene?"

"I did."

"And?"

Tom shook his head. "She insisted that her husband was

alone, taking care of business at the church, that there wasn't a girl with him. She has arranged with a mortuary to pick up her husband's body."

"When are you releasing it?"

"Thursday. The family is planning a Saturday funeral in Dixie City."

"Polygville."

"Yep. Let me ask you, Art: Has Wit had any luck figuring out who the girl is?"

"Not yet. She either can't talk or won't talk, and the polygamists refuse to identify her. It's all a part of their crazy code of silence, I guess."

I watched Tom pull the sheet over Johnston. "Two homicides," I told him. "You're a busy man."

"Care to see the other fella?"

"Sure, if you don't mind."

"Not at all."

Once more, he pulled a lever, gripped a handle, and used his weight to pull the drawer out of the wall. This time I did the honors, folding down the white linen covering the dead man. The first thing I noticed was the dark, scrubbed-out canyon where his left eye used to be. My eyes dropped to a toothbrush mustache that I had failed to notice on Monday night when I first saw him, the kind worn by Oliver Hardy, Charlie Chaplin, and Adolf Hitler. Death had transformed his face into a waxy, insubstantial mass of flesh, with his lips forming an ugly leer.

"What about his next of kin?"

"Mason's estranged wife dropped by during the noon hour and ID'd him," said Tom. "Apparently, he's got a mother and a sibling or two. Pace Newbold told me they live in the Minneapolis–St. Paul area and they lost contact with him years ago. The wife has no money, so it looks like the city's going to foot the bill for burial." Tom pointed at the sheet. "Finished?"

"Yeah. Thanks."

Tom pulled the sheet back up, walked the drawer closed, and fastened the lever shut.

"Did Johnston have anything else on him, other than his wallet?"

"No." Tom's brow wrinkled while he peeled off his gloves. "Come to think of it . . ."

He disposed of his gloves, led me out into the corridor, and shut off the lights and locked the morgue door him. He then went into his office—he was in there about half a minute—and came out with a file folder in hand. Out of it he pulled a tattered yellow handbill with creases and a bloodstain in the corner.

"This was in his jacket pocket," he said.

Big letters spanned the top, like an Old West "Wanted" poster. A NEW DAWN IN HOMESTEADING! Next line, smaller font: 170,000,000 ACRES OF PRIME LAND STILL AVAILABLE FOR SETTLERS! My eyes dropped to a longer message in a smaller type:

Have you ever wondered what it's like to own your own homestead? *WONDER NO LONGER!* Prime home-stead land is still plentiful in the western states. In these hard times, having a piece of land to call your own is the dream of millions. There is prime land for the tak-ing. Alas, most men are unaware of how to claim that land under federal Homestead Act laws. Do *YOU* know the rules? Well, friend, keep reading, for this is your chance to *BEAT THE DEPRESSION!* The goal of the Golden Valley Improvement Association is to help you obtain the homestead of your dreams. We will work with you through every stage of your application, and our ultimate reward is to see you farming on a piece of land that you can call your own. Don't wait another day! Send us your name, contact information, and return postage. We will arrange a meeting with you to discuss making your dream of being a homesteader come true. Mail to: Golden Valley Improvement Association, Box 130, Salt Lake City.

The bottom proclaimed, TODAY'S PIONEERS ARE THE SUCCESS STORIES OF TOMORROW. I flipped it over. On the back, someone had scrawled in smudged ink: *DELPHI, RM 308.* The only Delphi I knew of was the Delphi Hotel, a flophouse on State Street that I'd visited many times as a Morals Squad detective. With eight-bucks-a-month rooms, the place was a magnet for alcoholics, dope fiends, narco dealers, prostitutes, drifters, the unemployed, and frugal gents who led their mistresses in through the back door and rented rooms by the hour. Livsey watched me, expecting me to give back the handbill. I steadied myself to ask a question I dreaded asking.

"May I take this?"

He closed the folder. "You know the rules, Art."

"I'll be careful."

He thought it over and nodded his approval. A subtle nod, though, which told me he had misgivings, and I'd better take it while I could.

"Thanks."

I was halfway to the stairs when he called out, "Happy Fourth of July, Art."

I tipped my hat. "You too, Tom."

"Remember. Don't come to work tomorrow!"

We both got a good laugh out of that one.

Had I been another minute later, I'd have missed the two orderlies escorting the girl from last night's crime scene to a Chev-
rolet with a state seal on its door idling out front. In an act of
overkill, they'd chained her in shackles, and pulled her by the
elbows on a forced march to the exit. I gave chase from the stairs,
dodging people, till I breathlessly caught up with the men in
white and the girl between them. "Hey!" They turned, spinning
the girl with them, rattling chains, eyeing me as if I were a luna-
tic asylum escapee. One of the men toted what appeared to be
a tattered white linen bag of some sort, made bulky by all of the
things stuffed into it. I guessed those were her belongings.

"Where're you fellas taking her?"

"To the State Industrial School."

"Feller upstairs signed off."

The timid girl in homespun stood no chance in that pit of
juvenile despair, where the guards thought a good beating was
exactly what every inmate needed. I'd do whatever it took to
stop these men from putting the girl in the reformatory, even if
it meant fighting them with my fists. I hoped it wouldn't come
to that.

Right then, Buddy Hawkins crossed through the lobby, on
his way somewhere, perhaps home. A spectacular coincidence.

"Art," he said. "What's going on?"

"Buddy! Just the man I wanted to . . . They're taking the girl
away. The girl from the crime scene."

Buddy gave me his best *Are you nuts?* squint. "Yeah. Of

course they are. What other choice do we have? She won't tell us her name or address, so we can't contact her family. Besides, she might be a witness to a homicide. In fact, for all we know, she might've . . . Well, you know."

"A girl like that, dressed like an old-time schoolmarm, doesn't stand a chance in the reformatory. That place is the worst possible mix of little league psychopaths-in-training and guards who can't be bothered. Do you really want to put her in that kind of jeopardy?"

"It's either that or jail," he said. "It doesn't matter to me."

My next words I spoke impulsively. "She can stay at my house."

Buddy gazed at me as if I'd lost my mind. "Have you run this by Clara?"

"Well, no. But the girl's a minor, and I happen to know that according to the law, I can take custody of her if I . . ."

Buddy yanked me aside, nearly giving me whiplash. "Have you taken leave of your senses, Art?"

"Look at her! She's terrified. . . ."

"Yeah, and she might be a murderer. Did you ever stop and think of that?"

"Surely you don't think . . ."

"I don't know what to think, Art. She won't even say her name!"

"Maybe she's mute."

"Who knows? All I know is we're doing her a favor by putting her in the Industrial School."

"Oh, you mean the same way we did Ellis Frandsen a favor?"

Buddy knew instantly who I was talking about. Ellis Frandsen was a fourteen-year-old boy who came from a troubled home and repeatedly ran away, thanks to frequent beatings inflicted on him by his father. Last year, after an especially harrowing night of his dad's savagery, Frandsen was admitted to the hospital to recover. The investigating detectives from the Youth Bureau, Oscar Saunders and Sam Alcorn, made a big public stink in the local papers about Frandsen's woeful tale in order to drum up support for a long overdue child protection bill being drafted in the state legislature. Coincidentally, a judge ordered that Frandsen be released from the hospital to the State Industrial School for an indeterminate length, until the matter of his living arrangements could be resolved. When Frandsen was well enough to be discharged, a hospital administrator drove him to the reformatory, as per the judge's orders. Poor Frandsen. Three days into his stay, he was taken out of his bunk in the dead of night to a secluded spot in the building by an unknown perpetrator—or perpetrators—tied up, gagged, tortured, and murdered. That made him the eighth person to die in the custody of the youth reformatory since it first opened. Half of those had been suicides, the rest homicides. The dead all shared the common trait of being vulnerable boys and girls—in other words, the Ellis Frandsens—too weak and terrified to defend themselves against their assailants or withstand the rigors of confinement in the institution. Days after Frandsen was found dead in the boiler room, his father climbed up on a stool, pulled a homemade noose around his neck, and stepped off. Frandsen's killer still hadn't been caught.

I was determined that this young woman standing before me in the lobby of the Public Safety Building would not become victim number nine.

Buddy glared at me. "All right, you want her? She's all yours. But you're responsible for her, Art. And if we find out she had anything to do with Johnston's murder, she goes straight into an isolated unit in Ogden. You got that?"

"Yeah. I got it."

Buddy looked me up and down. "I hope you know what you're doing."

He turned to the orderlies, both wondering what was going on. "Let her go," said Buddy. "She's going with *him*."

I took the girl to the office of the Anti-Polygamy Squad. I found it a friendlier setting than the interrogation rooms, which always seemed so intimidating and cold to me.

Her eyes caught my attention first. Wide-open, irises splashed with blue, pupils reflecting light. Someone unfamiliar with her might assume those eyes were full of innocence, yet I wondered what they'd seen on the night of Johnston's murder. She made no noise. Even her breathing was silent. She sat in a chair next to my desk, and her eyes stayed fixed on her shoes. Her thick lips contrasted with her leanness. Hair cascaded to her shoulders in damp waves. She carried a battered, soiled pillowcase weighted down with assorted odds and ends.

The clipboard on the table held a report by Dr. Eugene Calderwood, resident alienist at the state hospital, who happened to be making his routine jailhouse rounds at Public Safety earlier in the afternoon. I lifted it to get a better look at his mostly illegible penmanship. I could make out "Jane Doe" standing in for her name, and on the line designated "Condition," partially decipherable cursive said, "Unknown if muteness is temp or perm." I set the clipboard down and studied her. She avoided eye contact with me.

"I don't know if you can understand me."

No reply.

"We met last night. Remember?"

When I reached for my badge wallet, she cowered. "I'm not going to hurt you. I want to show you something."

I placed the open wallet on the table, badge up. The shiny surface flashed gold light on her cheek.

"I'm a policeman. I want to help you."

Her head plunged, chin to chest, hair shrouding her face. I flipped the page on the clipboard. "Physician's Recommendation: Confinement at State Industrial School." My eyes darted to the girl.

"You almost got put in the State Industrial School. You know what that is?"

She became as still as a statue.

"It's a youth reformatory. It's about the worst place on earth."

She lifted her head. A little.

"I can help keep you out of there. But I need you to help me."

I closed the wallet and pushed it into my pocket.

"What's your name?"

Silence.

"Do you have a name?"

She ran her tongue over her lips. I thought she might speak for the first time. She did not.

"Did you know LeGrand Johnston?"

No reply.

"Was he a relative?"

It wasn't my imagination: Her shakes got worse.

"A friend?"

Her eyes wandered right, left. No sign of speaking, or even attempting to.

"Can you tell me how you knew him?"

I waited a beat.

"If you tell me, maybe I can help you."

She said nothing. I opened my top-center desk drawer, took out a pad of paper, and rummaged around until I found a sharpened wooden pencil. I placed the pad on the desk next to her, which made her inch back slightly in her seat, and I smacked the pencil atop the paper.

"Do you know how to write?"

She appeared mystified, as though I were from Mars.

I spoke louder, my voice sharp with urgency: "Are you able to write things down? Like your name? Or any words? Or can you draw a picture or something? Even a . . . a . . . a stick figure or shapes or anything? Anything at all?"

She seemed paralyzed, unable to move. I slumped back, folded my arms, and sighed in frustration. This was going nowhere.

"Didn't anybody ever teach you how to write?"

Tears fell from her eyes, tapping the table. One . . . two . . . followed by a steady drip. I watched the top of her head. Her lips tightened and her body convulsed. I wanted to reach out and touch her hand, but I dared not. It would scare her. I used words instead. I reached for a box of disposable paper handkerchiefs, yanked out three, and handed them to her. She hesitated at first, but then she accepted my offering and used them to dab the tears and snot off her face.

"I know you're in a dark spot right now," I said. "I've been in dark spots, too. Sometimes things seem so bad, you feel like there's no hope of any light getting in. You know what? It won't always be this dark. The light will come back. And instead of spending all of your time thinking about everything you've lost, you'll start to see all of the wondrous things around you, the things nobody can ever take away."

I gave her time to take it all in. She stopped trembling. The tears ceased. She watched me reach for a candlestick telephone, lift the receiver, rattle the hook a few times with my thumb, and wait for the operator.

"Number, please."

"Wasatch one-four-eight-four."

"Please hold." Pause. "Now connecting." Another pause. "Sorry, that number is busy."

I waited a few minutes and repeated the action, with the same results. I lowered the earpiece onto its cradle, pushed the telephone aside, and looked over at the girl, who kept her head dipped slightly to avoid eye contact with me.

"You're going to come home with me," I said. "To my house. I have a wife and two children, and we would like it very much if you could stay with us for a while. I think you'll like it, if you give it a chance."

Her eyes finally met mine.

Eleven

Outside, standing on the porch in front of Clara, I'd never seen her so furious.

"I'm saying you should have asked me first, Art!"

"I tried to call you."

"Oh, don't hand me that balderdash about the line being busy." Clara folded her arms above her pregnant tummy. Her toe started tapping, too. The combination folded arms/toe tap robbed me of any hope that this would end well. It meant she was genuinely sore. "I was on the telephone with my sister for all of twenty minutes, Arthur J. Oveson!"

"Look, they were going to stick her in the reformatory up in Ogden," I said. "What was I supposed to do?"

She swatted my forearm with her hand. "You don't know what she's done or what she's capable of! We've got children, Art! Have you forgotten?"

"If I thought she was dangerous, I wouldn't have—"

"Listen to yourself! You act like you know anything about

her! Tell me something, Sherlock Holmes, did you even notice the wedding ring on her finger? What's the story behind that? You're the expert. Enlighten me!"

Her comment blindsided me. I hadn't seen the wedding ring on the girl. Nor had any of my fellow detectives. Or if they had seen it, they'd neglected to tell me. How on earth did I miss something so significant? I had not even bothered looking for one. My first impression of the girl was that she seemed so young, hardly marriage material. Why would I keep an eye out for a wedding ring? Clara could plainly see I was bewildered, based on my open mouth, searching eyes, and loss for words.

"Oh, you missed that little detail, did you?" she said.

Hinges creaked. Clara and I jerked our heads in the direction of the screen door. Hyrum stepped out onto the doormat, wearing his felt crown hat, chewing on a licorice stick while he watched us.

"Hi, sweetheart," said Clara, turning toward him. "Is there something I can do for you?"

"I want to watch you fight," he said.

"Oh, honey, we're not fighting," said Clara, with a warm smile. "We're just having a conversation."

"Is it about the girl in the house?" asked Hyrum.

"Yeah," I said. "We were fight—"

Clara glared at me.

I rephrased: "We were discussing her, yes."

Hyrum shot me a curious look. "Who is she?"

"Sweetie, why don't you go inside?" suggested Clara. "We'll be in in a minute or two."

"That means longer," he said, feeding the licorice into his mouth. "More like ten minutes."

Clara looked at me and whispered, "He's so brainy for a five-year-old."

"Like his sister," I whispered.

"I can hear what you're saying, Dad."

I leaned in close to Clara. "His hearing's good, too."

"I heard that, too."

Clara managed a smile. "Please, wait inside, dear. I promise we won't be more than about another minute out here."

He nodded, his jaws working away on that licorice. Reluctantly, he opened the screen door and stepped inside. He was only in there for a second or two before he poked his head out.

"Inside," said Clara. "Please."

The screen door banged shut. Clara faced me.

"And who's going to watch her during the days, while you're at work?" Clara held up her palm, as if to stop my reply. "Wait a second, the answer is coming to Clara the Clairvoyant. It's getting clearer and clearer. Well, what do you know? I'm going to watch her! After all, I'm not teaching in the summer, and except for a couple of hours here and there when I'll be training the substitute who'll take my place while I'm on leave, I'm at home with the children until the baby arrives. So you just assumed I would watch her! Right?"

"Yeah, more or less."

She hit me again in the forearm. I rubbed the soreness away.

"How long is she going to be here, Art? Days? Weeks? Months?"

"Okay, you've got me," I said bitterly. "I'll take her back. Sorry I put you through this."

I started for the door, but Clara stepped in my path. She hesitated, but found the words.

"I know you did what you thought was right," she said. "And I love you for it. I can never stay mad at you for long."

She ran her fingers through my hair. "You're aided by your adorability. But I stand by my initial complaint. It was wrong for you to bring her here without asking me. We're not just husband and wife, Art. We're partners. Everything we've done up until now in our relationship has been based on love *and* mutual respect. But it doesn't work if you pull a stunt like this. Understand?"

"Yes," I said, in a real tone of remorse. "I am sorry."

She gestured to the door. "We'd better go back inside. Don't think for an instant this conversation is over, though. There are lots of details we have to iron out, when the kids aren't around. Obviously, she can't stay here forever. She's probably got family somewhere who're worried sick are about her."

"I know. I agree."

Hyrum poked his head out again. "It's been more than a minute!"

Clara laughed. "We're coming."

"Would you mind saying grace, S.J.?" I asked.

"Sure," said Sarah Jane. "May we all bow our heads?"

Heads dipped around the dinner table. I peeked to see if our guest was bowing her head. She was. I closed my eyes.

"Our beloved Father in Heaven, we're thankful to be sitting down to dinner as a family with our new friend," said Sarah Jane. "Bless Mom for preparing this meal tonight. Please bless this food that it may nourish and strengthen our bodies, to help us to do the good we need. Bless those who are not here to share this meal that they, too, may find the nourishment they need.

And bless our new friend here, that she may have the things in life she wants and needs. We say these things in the name of Jesus Christ. Amen."

"Amen."

"Amen."

"Amen."

The girl didn't say "Amen." She kept her head bowed.

"Thank you, honey," said Clara. "Would you start passing the roast beef?"

"Yes, ma'am," said Sarah Jane.

The food went around the table. I plunged the carving fork into the roast beef and lifted a hefty piece onto my plate. Next came the creamed baby peas and pearl onions, then steaming mashed potatoes, followed by cooked carrots. A basket reached me and I pulled a hot roll out from under the forest-green linen napkin. The girl, seated directly across the table from me, was not filling her plate. She stared at her empty plate, the same way she had cast her eyes downward in my office, without budging. For the first time, I noticed the wedding ring on her finger that Clara had mentioned earlier, a shiny silver band. Hard to believe I had missed it before. But so had other detectives, including Wit Dunaway, not to mention the police alienist, which made me feel slightly better about my own ineptitude. Clara looked at me, as if to say, *Well?* I closed the green napkin over the rolls and sent them to Hyrum, seated beside me.

I spoke across the table to the girl. "You must be hungry."

As expected, she said nothing. She didn't even raise her head.

"How about I fix you a plate?" I said. "S.J., could you hand me her plate?"

Sarah Jane picked up the plate in front of the girl and gave it to Hyrum, who passed it to me. I began scooping food, identifying it as I went. "Some peas and pearl onions—nobody makes 'em better than Clara. Let's see, some carrots. Mashed potatoes. Gotta get you a good mountain going here." I picked up my fork, which I hadn't used yet, and began pressing a gravy crater. "See, the idea here is you gotta make a space for the gravy." I exchanged my table fork for the carving fork to lift roast beef onto her plate. "You may wanna stay away from the horseradish. It'll put a hem in your stocking."

I tipped the gravy boat over the girl's plate and filled the mashed potato crater and covered the roast beef. "Voilà! Hyrum, I appoint you on a knight's errand. Would you kindly deliver this to the fair maiden across the table?"

"Dad, you're being corny."

"Sorry. Do you mind?"

He lifted the plate with both hands, circled the table, and placed it in front of the girl, who'd raised her head enough to watch me serving her.

"As the Frenchmen say, bon appétit!" I said, raising my glass of milk in a toast.

Before I could drink it, the girl began eating, and with a vengeance. She spooned peas into her mouth, stuffed half of a roll in there, and lifted the roast beef with her fingers and bit into it. We Ovesons sat in stunned silence, watching this hungry girl cleaning her plate in record time, before any of us even touched our food. She stopped chewing, despite a full mouth, painfully aware of us staring at her.

I smiled. "Like I said, bon appétit!"

The rest of us started eating, and the hungry girl resumed filling herself. The dour expression on Clara's face as she chewed softly seemed to say, *What have you gotten us into?*

. . .

"Jack Benny, with Frank Black and his orchestra!"

Lavish band music crackled out of the speaker of our four-legged radio console, with Sarah Jane and Hyrum hovering around the coveted ebony knobs. The girl sat on the davenport's middle cushion, cautiously observing through an outsider's eyes. Clara, seated on a floral armchair, was knitting something for the baby. Having just finished washing the dishes, I wiped my wet hands with a striped dishcloth and draped it on the back of a living room chair to dry.

"Is it on the Red Network?" asked Hyrum.

"Yes, it's the Red Network!" snapped Sarah Jane. "It's K-D-Y-L."

"The dial has to be precise."

"You don't know what that means," said Sarah Jane scornfully. "You heard a grown-up say it."

"I do so know what it means!"

"You two cut it out," said Clara.

"And now for that man of mirth, humor, jokes," said the radio announcer, *"Rochester, Buffalo, Cleveland, and all points west, Mr. Jack Benny on track five!"*

"Hey, let's listen to the *A and P Gypsies*," suggested Hyrum as Benny launched into his monologue.

"It's not on tonight," said Sarah Jane. "It's on Monday nights."

"Are you sure about that?"

"Yes, I'm sure. I've got the schedule memorized."

"Betcha don't know when *Amos 'n' Andy* comes on."

"Mondays. Before *A and P Gypsies*. Give me a hard one."

"Little Orphan Annie?"

"Thursdays at seven."

I studied the girl visitor. I could plainly see that she was relaxed around Sarah Jane and Hyrum. She seemed to find them safe, knowing they would not harm her in any way. My attention shifted to the soiled beige pillowcase near her feet, where I assumed she kept her possessions. The girl noticed me looking at her. She reached down and pulled her lumpy pillow-case closer, so it rested against her leg. She watched me uneasily, her eyes warning me not to touch her pillowcase. I nodded. I hoped she would interpret it as a sign of respect.

Sarah Jane and Hyrum erupted in laughter.

"Did you hear that, Dad?" asked Hyrum.

I looked over at my children. "Sorry. I must've missed it."

"Nobody's funnier than Jack Benny," Hyrum told me. "Not even you."

Sarah Jane laughed with the radio audience. Hyrum went wide-eyed. "What? What? What did I miss?"

"I'm not going to repeat it," said Sarah Jane. "Just shut your trap and listen."

Late at night, a blizzard moves in over Salt Lake City. Snow falls sideways, creating a whiteout. Churning clouds above swirl into a foreboding dark gray.

The twelve-year-old boy runs through the streets on that freezing night in 1914. Even with his coat on, his skin is numbed by harsh winds. He sprints through snowdrifts, past storefronts where electric lights burn. He knows his dad is out here, and knows his father's life is in danger. That's why his legs move as fast as they do, spraying snow, driven by a faint hope that he can turn this tale's ending into a happy one.

The boy is out of breath, overcome with fatigue, thighs burning, heart thumping so hard it feels as if it's going to leap out of his chest. He knows if he does not find his dad soon, the worst will

*come to pass. A streetcar rattles past, bell clanging, disappearing
into a swarm of snowflakes.*

*He hurries across the street. A horseless carriage slams on its
brakes and skids across powder, with lantern spotlights trembling
and horn blaring. The boy ignores the driver, pressing on, reaching the sidewalk in one piece. He makes his way to the next street,
West Temple. Shops are scattered in this part of town, separated
by vacant lots, wooden fences, and utility poles. Snow is everywhere: in the air, on the ground, coating the boy, who breathes in
frozen crystals through his mouth as he tries to catch his breath.
He comes to the corner of West Temple and 800 South, now in
front of Morrison Grocery. The owner of this place—an ex–police
officer—was gunned down a few weeks ago in cold blood, along
with one of his sons. Tonight the boy has a feeling that he might
find his father here. Morrison and Dad were friends, and Dad insisted on investigating his murder.*

*But on this night of squalls, the lad cannot find his beloved
father. He trudges through whiteness to a lit display window with*
MORRISON GROCERY *painted on the glass and a* CLOSED *sign hanging
in the door. Footsteps approach from behind. The boy spins for a
look. A shadow-figure in a bowler hat and long coat steps out of
the snow like a ghost.*

*The figure grips his bleeding abdomen and topples to a bed of
snow. His eyelids flutter like butterfly wings. His mouth opens and
he struggles for air. Blood gurgles between his lips and forms droplets on his mustache. Blood seeps between his fingers. The shirt he
is wearing—pristine when he left home this morning—is crimson-
soaked.*

"Dad!"

*The boy falls to his knees by his father's side. The wetness of
damp snow seeps into the boy's clothes, yet he hardly notices. He*

reaches out to touch his father and finds the man's bloodstain is warm to the touch.

My eyes opened. Darkness enshrouded me. I ran my palm over my wet face and gave my eyes a chance to adjust to the darkness. With the dream over, I needed to adjust to the here and now. Clara slept on her side, back to me, partially covered with a sheet and blanket, humming with each exhale. My arm snaked under the covers around her waist, and only the slightest pressure from my fingertips against her pregnant belly triggered a kick from the baby. A warm wave shot through my body, slowing my heart, and my breathing grew more measured.

Lying on my back, I watched leafy shadows bounce in the moonlight, and the night sounds—crickets, wind blowing branches, a train—blended in my ears. I tossed and turned, in pursuit of a comfortable position. Minutes passed. No point in denying it: Mr. Insomnia had come to pay a visit. I threw my legs over the edge of the bed, sat upright, stood, and slipped on my cloth robe. I closed the door on my way out.

I switched on the hallway light and crept to Sarah Jane's room to peek in on our young guest. The door was ajar. *That's funny, I thought it was closed before I went to bed last night.* I nudged it farther. Imagine my surprise when I looked in and saw that the girl was nowhere to be seen. Sarah Jane, meantime, slept soundly on the cot. *Where did she go?* I wondered. I heard a floorboard creak right outside the bedroom. I rushed out to find the girl stepping out of the door to the basement stairs, located midway down the hallway. My heart performed a crazed horse gallop right then.

"What were you doing in there?" I whispered.

Why am I asking her? She can't talk, I thought. She swallowed hard and the color drained out of her face. She developed a case of the shakes.

"C'mon," I whispered. "Go back to bed, okay?"

She nodded. I watched her get into bed, and this time I left all of the doors open—Sarah Jane's and the one to Clara's and my room. I lay awake for hours, wishing I could go back to sleep, and wondering what the girl had been doing in the basement.

Twelve

The Olds rattled southward, past farms and fields and mountains, soon crossing the divide at Point of the Mountain between
Salt Lake Valley and its neighbor to the south, Utah Valley. On
the radio, Dick "Hotcha" Gardner's smooth voice sang "Say,
Young Lady" to a bouncy orchestral accompaniment by George
Olsen & His Music. The windows were down and the warm air
blew in, but it felt nice and cool against our perspiration-covered
skin. We crested a hill and looked down into Utah Valley, a vast
bowl that—like its sibling to the north—is bordered by the
Wasatch Mountains to the east and a freshwater lake—Utah
Lake—on the west side. From this high up, we could see the
patchwork landscape below, and the remainder of our drive was
steadily downhill.

I felt the weight of Clara's stare. I looked over at her, and she
adjusted her flowery velvet hat as she watched me. "Are you sure
this is a good idea? We could cancel, you know."

"That's not such a good idea," I said. "We spent last Fourth of July with your family. My mom's expecting us this year."

"I don't know how comfortable our daughter feels about lying," Clara said, wincing as she said the word "lying."

Sarah Jane leaned forward so her head rested on the upholstered seat between her mother and me. "I don't mind, not when it's for the greater good. Dad's right. They're never going to understand why we took her in. It's easier for everyone involved if we stretch the truth a little."

"Stretch the truth?" asked Clara, her painted red lips spreading into a smile. "Is that the new euphemism for lying?"

"It's not new at all," said S.J. "Mark Twain said it all the time."

"You don't have to do this, sweetheart," Clara told Sarah Jane. "Nobody's asking you to."

"I know. I volunteered. Remember? I even invented a name for her. *Priscilla.* I call her by her nickname, Prissy. I've known her since second grade, and she's mute, so don't count on her to be much of a conversationalist at the dinner table." Sarah Jane slumped back into her seat, between her little brother and the girl. Sarah Jane had loaned the girl a sky-blue dress with white lace and short sleeves, and it fit perfectly. Sarah Jane looked at the girl and smiled. "Isn't that right, Prissy?"

I saw in my interior rearview mirror that the girl smiled back and lowered her head, fixing her gaze on her lap, but she flashed S.J. a quick, coy look.

"Priscilla," I said with a nod and another glance to the rearview mirror. "I like it."

"So do I," said Clara. "That's a grand name."

I steered off the highway at American Fork, turning right on a road that took me to my childhood home, sending a high column of dust in our wake.

The Fourth of July barbecue at the Oveson homestead in American Fork was only slightly less epic than a Cecil B. DeMille movie, and I mean *slightly*. The line of autos in front of the porch could easily be mistaken for a used-car lot. In the vast backyard behind the farmhouse, a pair of long picnic tables accommodated feasting adults at one, children at the other, all of us dining under hazy skies, with a breathtaking view of the mountains to the east. My mother—called Mom Oveson by everyone—sat at the head of the table, a spot once reserved for our now deceased father. Soft-skinned, she had a gentle face with some age spots and a head of curly salt-and-pepper hair, more salt than pepper these days. The children—a baker's dozen when you counted my daughter's friend, "Priscilla"—ate at the table nearest the barn. At first, nobody paid much attention to Priscilla, which I took to calling her because it seemed as good a name as any. In keeping with her behavior the previous day, she didn't say a word. She sat still among the boisterous and excited cousins, occasionally smiling, rocking back and forth gently as she got used to a crowd of unfamiliar people. I kept an eye on her at all times, occasionally missing what other people were saying in the process.

"Art, dear."

I turned around and faced the picnic table. My heart raced, as if I'd just gotten caught doing something terrible. "Yeah?"

"Bess here asked you a question," said Clara.

"Oh, sorry," I said. "What was the question?"

I looked at Bess, a roly-poly brunette with a permanent wave like the rest of the women at the table, but a little more makeup than the others. She smiled. She had lipstick on her teeth. "What did you think of the crib?"

I needed a moment to absorb the question. "Oh yes, the crib. It was lovely. It was in perfect condition."

Bess's husband, Grant, smirked. Two years my senior, my elder brother Grant didn't much care for me. The feeling was mutual. He never missed an opportunity to say something negative and try to put me in my place. Sometime in our shared past, an adversarial relationship had taken hold. I did my best to ignore his comments, but it wasn't always easy. Even our jobs seemed competitive. Over the years, Grant had climbed through the ranks of the Provo Police Department and now served as its chief of police.

"Do you have the baby's room all decorated, Clara?" asked Eliza, John's wife.

John, second oldest of the Oveson brothers, was sheriff of Carbon County, a part of the state renowned for its rich coal deposits and its militant miners' unions. He somehow always stayed jovial, slapping backs and laughing at dumb jokes, and was by far the most strapping of all of us. He had married Eliza, big-hearted and sincere, and someone who never hesitated to say what was on her mind.

"We still have to pick out wallpaper," Clara told Eliza. "Otherwise, I think we're all set. Don't you, honey?"

I looked up from my chicken leg and potatoes. "We're ready for the new Oveson to arrive."

"You want my advice?" asked Margaret, Frank's wife, as she dabbed her lips with her linen napkin. "Give the baby cod-liver oil."

My eldest brother, Frank, worked as an agent with the Federal Bureau of Investigation, in the federal building in downtown

Salt Lake City. The job required traveling, and Frank often took his family to Washington, D.C., where they once dined with J. Edgar Hoover. His wife, Margaret, a confident redhead, could be something of a cold fish and a know-it-all, but essentially harmless.

Clara reared her head back in curiosity. "Cod-liver oil?"

Margaret nodded, working food out of her molars. "It promotes healthy evacuations."

"Oh, for heaven's sake," said Bess. "Surely there must be a better dinner-table topic than passing stools. Pass me the rolls, will you, dear?"

Grant handed her a basket of hot rolls wrapped in linen.

Margaret ignored Bess and went on: "Regularity is so important in the lives of babies. One bowel movement a day is critical to the good health—"

Frank cut her off: "I'm afraid I'm going to have to side with Bess on this one, honey. It just doesn't go with the cornbread."

"I heard a doctor on the radio the other day saying a baby oughtn't to be swaddled," said Eliza. "Babies prefer to move around, you know. They love to throw their arms and kick and whatnot. We learned that by the time we had Wayne. Why, we had him in loose-fitting clothes all the time and he was just as content as could be. Wasn't he, dear?"

"Darn tootin'," said John, his mouth stuffed with food. "Whatcha gonna name the critter?"

"Dear, please," said Eliza. "Swallow what's in your mouth before you speak."

John wiped his mouth with his napkin and swallowed his food in a loud gulp. "Shoot, sorry. Got a name picked out for the new kid?"

Clara and I said "Emily" at the same time.

"Emily if she's a girl," Clara said.

"And Clarence if he's a boy," I said.

"Why Clarence?" asked Grant.

"We like the name," I said. "I used to love Clarence Mulford's books when I was growing up."

Grant laughed. "Oh, you mean the hack who wrote the Hopalong Cassidy tales?"

"Now, dear, don't call him a hack," said Mom. "They're fine books."

"You got something against that name?" I asked Grant.

"Don't mind me, Arthur," said Grant, chuckling. "Go ahead and name your baby after a spinner of cowboy yarns. If that's what toots your horn."

"Doggone it, Grant, leave the kid alone, ya turkey," said John. "Ignore him, kid. That's a fine name."

"Sarah Jane's friend is awfully quiet," said Eliza. "What's her name again?"

For a second, I forgot Sarah Jane's made-up name for the girl. My confusion showed, I'm sure.

"It's Priscilla," said Clara.

Priscilla! I smiled and nodded in agreement.

"Remind me how they know each other?" asked Margaret.

"It's an old friendship," I said. "It dates back a ways."

"Sarah Jane told me they know each other from school," said Bess.

Margaret leaned over her plate of food, lowering her voice. "I'm pretty sure she's mute. She hasn't uttered a single word. That's unusual for a girl her age."

"It could be she's just shy," said Eliza.

Bess tilted sideways, peering over John's shoulder to get a better view of the youngsters at the next picnic table. She resumed eating her spareribs. "Which is it, Art?"

"Which is what?" I asked.

"Is she mute or is she shy?"

"She's mute," I said, my voice full of hesitation. I hated lying. I was terrible at it, too. For all I knew, I might've been telling the truth. "It just adds to her shyness."

"How long has she been that way?" asked Eliza.

"As long as I've known her," I said.

"I've never actually known a mute," said Bess. "I mean a *real, actual* mute, someone not capable of saying a single word. Not until now, anyway."

"I wish I knew a few more mutes than I do," said Margaret.

Bess stopped chewing and glared at Margaret. "What's that supposed to mean?"

"I wasn't meaning you, of course," said Margaret. "I meant *in general.*"

Bess gave her a surly look. "Yeah. Uh-huh. In general."

"Got any big trips lined up, Frank?" asked Clara.

Frank raised a napkin and dabbed the corners of his mouth. "Hoover is sending me to the City by the Bay," he said. "Frisco."

"He returned from Chicago last week," said Margaret. "They had him working on that big crime wave out in the Midwest. Dillinger and Pretty Boy Floyd and what have you."

"Why San Francisco?" I asked.

"Haven't you been reading the papers?" sneered Grant.

"Reds have turned the place into a ghost town," said Frank, scooping beans on top of his ham. "Not even the trolleys are runnin'. The strikers have got one of them Workers', Soldiers', and Sailors' Councils set up and running the show. Bunch of

Moscow-trained agitators, calling it the Supreme Soviet of the Golden State. We can't let 'em get away with it. Next thing you know, the reds will be taking over Seattle and Los Angeles, control the whole Pacific seaboard." He lowered his voice and gestured to a blue bowl. "Hand me the corn, will ya, dear?"

Margaret passed him a bowl loaded with boiled cobs.

"Seems like everything is falling apart," said Eliza. "I don't dare pick up the newspaper, or watch a newsreel, for fear of more bad news. I don't think this country can take much more of these hard times."

Frank waved his free hand while he used the other to scoop food into his mouth. "Baloney! Greatest country on earth, and she ain't goin' nowhere, I'll tell you that much."

I twisted my upper body and turned my head to see the girl. With her chin pressed to her chest, only the top of her head was visible. *Who is she? What is she thinking? What did she see the night . . .*

A pointy-toed shoe nailed me in the shin. Whoa! It hurt like mad. I swung around. It got my attention. Clara jerked her head in the direction of Grant. I looked at him. His arrogant grin returned. "He was daydreaming again."

"I was just checking on the girl."

"I'm sure she's fine," chuckled Grant. "It's not as though the little cannibals are eating her alive or anything."

"Something you wanted?" I asked him.

"Are you on the trail of any suspects in this polygamist murder?" Grant asked, probably knowing the answer already.

"Yes."

He arched his eyebrows. "Oh? Care to reveal any details?"

"It's early yet," I said. "Wasn't even forty-eight hours ago."

Grant laughed as he lifted his corn on the cob.

"Did I say something funny?" I asked.

He gnawed on his corn for a moment, and then he set it down and wiped his hands with his napkin. "Why don't you come right out and admit it?"

"Admit what?"

"Someone I trust told me the Salt Lake police are in over their heads," he said. "To hear this man tell it, you fellows blundered the case yesterday by jumping the gun with mass arrests. I don't know who planned that move, but I'm guessing it was someone who had no idea what he was doing, or who he was dealing with."

Grant waited for me to take the bait. He lifted his corn on the cob and went back to gnawing. With a full mouth, he asked, "Well?"

In my younger years, back when Grant and I used to verbally spar all the time, I would've opened fire on him. Hurled insults. Taken potshots. Called him a name. Or two. In fact, I sensed the others at the table watching us, fearful of some sort of showdown.

I decided not to give him what he wanted.

But I did lean over my plate of food, to build up a little tension. "I'm not at liberty to comment on the investigation at this stage. If I could, I would. But, well, rules are rules."

I looked over at my mother. "Mom?"

"Yes, Art?"

"This is the best fried chicken I've ever tasted," I said. "You've really outdone yourself this time."

"Why, thank you, dear."

I went back to eating lunch, and I winked across the table at my elder brother Grant. His response? A sneer.

• • •

On that stretch of highway between the valleys, multitudes of stars and planets glowed in the sky. We reached the pass a few minutes before midnight. Ahead of us, the distant lights of Salt Lake City twinkled, and a shooting star disappeared behind the black wall of the Wasatch Range. The reflection in the rearview mirror revealed the children in the backseat—S.J., Hyrum, and the girl—all had fallen asleep. With both hands on the steering wheel, I checked on Clara, who watched me with sleepy eyes, doing her best to resist the onslaught of slumber. She scooted closer to me and rested her head on my shoulder while I drove. I kissed her honey-colored hair and promptly went back to staring out at the headlights' beams. She squeezed my knee.

"Too bad about the fireworks."

"Maybe next year."

Clara waited a while to speak. I thought she had fallen asleep, but then she glanced fleetingly behind her. "She did well, all things considered."

"The girl?"

"Priscilla."

We both chuckled at S.J.'s pseudonym for the girl.

"Good thing I talked her into letting me take that ring off her finger," said Clara. "Your sisters-in-law would've noticed, and imagine the grilling we would've been subjected to."

"Especially Bess," I said. "She's the gossip queen of Utah."

That got a laugh out of Clara. Then we were quiet for the next mile or so.

Clara said, "She spent a lot of time by herself. After the picnic, I noticed her sitting under the tree, by the canal." Clara paused. Something was on her mind. "Who do you think she is?"

"I don't know."

"She must've had a reason for being there. At the crime scene, I mean."

"I suspect she knew one or both of the deceased," I said.

"You don't think she could have . . . . that she's the one who . . ."

Clara couldn't bring herself to say it. I knew what she meant.

"I doubt it. But when push comes to shove, there's no way of knowing."

The car reached a steady clip at fifty miles per hour in the night, and distant lights came closer, until we zoomed past an off-ramp to a filling station, market, and motor lodge, each open all night. I was going to say something to Clara about the girl being a gentle soul, and that I couldn't imagine her taking someone else's life. But by that time, Clara had fallen asleep, and her breathing grew louder, turning into borderline snoring.

Now I was the only one awake in the car, or so I thought, until—about five miles away from the city limits, I checked the rearview mirror and noticed the girl's eyes were open, staring blankly, with a slow blink. I spent the rest of the drive puzzling over who she was, and why I had found her in that closet on the night of the murders.

Thirteen

The briefing in the Anti-Polygamy Squad office commenced at eight thirty A.M. sharp. My eyes burned from a lack of sleep, another gift on my doorstep from Mr. Insomnia.

Jared Weeks: *present.*

Myron Adler: *present.*

Roscoe Lund: *absent.*

"Anybody seen Roscoe?" I asked.

"Nope," said Myron. "Shock of the century, and we're only a third of the way through it."

I leaned back in my chair with rolled-up shirtsleeves and a loosened tie.

"Word came from Cowley on Tuesday," I said. "We're off Wit's homicide investigation."

Their faces lit up for the first time that morning.

"What?" Jared shook his head in disbelief.

"Why?" asked Myron.

"Politics," I said. "Wit has already pulled his men off the crime scene."

"Looks like Granville Sondrup plays golf with all the right people," said Jared.

"What're we supposed to do now?" asked Myron.

"What we've been doing all along," I said. "Minus my surveillance of Uncle Grand, of course. We need to keep building cases against these men. We're not in the homicide investigating business."

"Big mistake, arresting all of those fat cats at once," said Myron. "The *Titanic*'s maiden voyage went smoother than yesterday's interrogations."

I shrugged. "I'm sure Wit believed the polygamists would all crack under the pressure. Clearly, he underestimated them."

"They're a devout bunch," said Myron. "To satisfy my morbid curiosity, I drove past the Lincoln Street church this morning. It was packed. I'm assuming they were all mourners."

"Now they've got their very own martyr," I said, glancing down at my notes, zeroing in on the words "Model T truck?" in my familiar block letters. I looked at Myron. "What about running a check on the truck I saw at the church on the night of the murders? I didn't see the plates, but I did notice it was a Model T."

"That's directly related to the homicide case," said Myron wearily. "We're not supposed to go near it. Remember?"

"I'll look into it, boss," said Jared.

"Myron is right, this is a delicate matter, so let's keep it strictly on the down low," I told Jared. "Check with Pace Newbold, see what Homicide knows. No point in reinventing the wheel if he's already on it. I suspect the Homicide dicks just haven't gotten that far, otherwise they'd be coming to us asking for a list of local polygamists. I suggest you compare that list against the motor vehicle records of registered Model T trucks at the state department of revenue."

"Will do, boss, and mum's the word," acknowledged Jared, reaching for his spiral notebook. He licked his finger and turned pages until he found what he was looking for. "I've got one promising lead here. Harold O'Rourke is an investigator with the Federal Emergency Relief Administration, based out of Flagstaff. He went on a fact-finding trip to Dixie City that took him door to door, questioning townsfolk who happen to be on federal relief rolls. He found plenty of instances of multiple women listing the same man as their husband on applications."

I straightened in my chair with interest. "So you're saying . . ."

"Written evidence of unlawful cohabitation," he said, closing his notebook and tossing it on his desk. "And from a New Deal relief agency, no less."

"Are all the applicants on the Arizona side?" I asked.

He shook his head. "Some, but a handful list residences in both states."

"How on earth did you find out about that?" I asked.

He lifted a folded newspaper off his desk. "There was a story in this morning's *Examiner*. Says O'Rourke is planning to testify before Congress later this month."

"Any hope of him sharing those records with us?"

Jared shrugged. "I got ahold of his secretary this morning. He's currently on the road. He'll be back in Flagstaff on the ninth, I'm told."

"Good work," I said.

I opened a folder on my desk, took out a familiar yellow handbill, and walked it over to Myron. It astonished me how quickly he read it. He finished it in seconds, flipping it over and noting the Delphi Hotel reference scrawled on the back. That at least got raised eyebrows from him. He offered it to me, but I shook my head.

"You keep it," I said.

"Golden Valley Improvement Association." Hard to tell whether he was looking at me through those glasses. "Same outfit as Golden Valley Enterprises, I'm assuming."

"It's a front," I said. "I suspect they've got their hands in a lot of cookie jars. I was hoping you'd look into it."

"It may entail some joyriding to the counties in question," Myron said.

"Use an unmarked," I advised. "Less conspicuous."

Myron gestured to Roscoe's empty chair. "The invisible man can come along for the ride."

"Don't worry, I'm going to have a word with him."

"It doesn't do any good," said Myron, putting on his hat. "If you ask me, he's about as useful as a ham sandwich at a bar mitzvah."

"How long you gonna be gone for?" I asked.

"Who knows?" he said. "I'll call from the road."

Myron left with the tattered yellow paper in his hand.

It was quiet again. Roscoe's empty chair bothered me. My wristwatch said 8:55. *I'll give him till nine*, I thought. *Then what? Lay another ineffective lecture on him? What good'll that do?* On the bright side, Jared was at his desk, jotting in his notebook. My curiosity about him suddenly got the best of me, a welcome distraction from Roscoe. I realized he had said something a few minutes ago that wasn't quite right, and it began to needle away at me. I propped my right ankle on my left knee and kept a close eye on him. Without looking back at me, he stopped writing and lowered his fountain pen. He turned his head slightly, enough to reveal an edge of right ear and a sliver of profile.

"Something up, boss?"

"How did you know about that O'Rourke fella?"

"I told you, there's an item in this morning's . . ."

"That's bunk. I get the *Examiner* delivered to my doorstep each morning, and I never saw that article."

"Oh, it's there, all right. You must've missed it."

"That so? Why don't you show it to me?"

He swiveled around and sized me up. "I mighta found it some other way."

"What other way?"

"I'd rather not say, if it's all the same to you."

"Cough it up. Now. And while you're at it, maybe you can explain why you're the only man on the force who requested to join this squad?"

The question surprised him. "I reckon I thought this would be a good opportunity for me to be promoted to the detective bureau so I could get experience . . ."

"Cut it out, Jared, and level with me. How is it that you know so much about these people?"

He knew I had him cornered, figuratively speaking. "You really want to know?"

"That's what I'm asking."

He gazed at me and stood, like the beanstalk spiraling into the clouds, and put his little fedora on his large head.

"I've got a better plan," he said. "I'll show you."

"Right here, boss. Slow down."

I braked, halting the black Ford in front of a mansion.

The Queen Anne, inside of a picket fence, took up a major chunk of the block of B Street where it stood. A typical leviathan from the last century, it was the type of formidable abode that might've once housed a powerful Mormon Church official, a mining magnate, or a senior partner in a successful law firm. Up close, however, it appeared more run-down, more battered by age, than it did from afar. Still, it was a fine-looking specimen, with its fancy white spandrels, rounded tower, bay windows, and wraparound porch, all of it capped by a steep roof with a pair of dormers that had shades pulled down indoors, forming sleepy eyes.

"This it?"

"Yep. There's parking right over there."

I steered curbside, put the car in park, and shut off the engine. "Are you going to tell me in advance what this place is? Or is it going to be a surprise?"

"Wait here."

Before I could even get out and open the driver's-side door, Jared was crossing the street, lifting the gate latch, and jogging up to the porch. He tugged the string to an old-fashioned doorbell. Half a minute later, the door opened wide enough for him to squeeze inside. *Presto*, he was gone. I stepped off the running board, closed the car door, and strolled to the shady sidewalk, where I found relief under a canopy of leafy tree branches. I leaned against a gnarled trunk for what seemed like a while.

I got tired of waiting out in the heat. I retraced Jared's route across the street, past the picket fence, up the walkway to the front door. I almost knocked. Voices from inside stopped me. The door was made of sturdy wood, with a trio of leaded windows level with my head, obscured by interior curtains. I pressed my ear to the surface. Jared's muted words mixed with those of a woman, coming and going out of my range of hearing. Ten minutes came and went, but I didn't hear much. From Jared, I picked up the words "boss," "trust," and "fair." The woman's words were slightly more distinct, but not much. "Police, "Grand," and "children" were three words I could clearly make out. It all got me wondering: Why had Jared brought me here? Why couldn't he simply tell me back in the squad room where he came by that information about Harold O'Rourke?

The doorknob began to turn. I gave myself whiplash standing straight.

"Boss," said Jared from the doorway. "I thought I asked you to wait."

"You did," I said. "But it was taking a while and I thought I'd . . ."

In the darkened vestibule behind him, I detected the faint presence of a woman, her eyes and mouth wide with concern.

"You said he was waiting across the street!" Her voice cracked with urgency.

"You mind?" Jared asked me, jerking his head in the direction of the Ford parked across the street.

"Not at all."

I headed back to the car, startled slightly by the intensity of the door slamming behind me as I passed beyond the picket fence. I got in the police sedan, shut the door, rolled down the window, and waited another seven or eight minutes. Jared soon emerged from that enormous house, and within a minute, he was once again sharing the front seat with me.

He stared forward at the road ahead, his face glistening with sweat. "It was too soon. Gimme a little more time, boss."

"Who is she?"

"Can we go?"

"Not until you give me some answers. Why'd you bring me out here?"

He squirmed in the heat of the car, licking his lips. "I need more time."

"You're not going to tell me who she is?"

He shook his head. "I can't. Not right now."

"Fine," I said. "I'll go question her myself. . . ."

He grabbed ahold of my arm, which stopped me from opening the car door. "I'll make you a deal, boss. Give me a couple of days to soften her up. That's all I ask for. Then you'll have all the answers to all your questions." When I didn't respond, he said, "I didn't have to bring you here in the first place. Please trust me on this one."

"Okay, you've got till Monday," I said. "If I don't have some answers by then, I'll come back and question her myself. Understand?"

He nodded. "Thanks, boss."

I started the car and drove away. I dropped Jared off at Public Safety so he could make inquiries about the mysterious Model T truck I had seen the night of the murders. I spent the rest of that hot July morning driving to the places that LeGrand Johnston visited on his daily outings. I went to bungalows and apartment buildings. I stopped off at a Sears and Roebuck kit house on a sparsely inhabited rural road by the foothills of the Oquirrh Mountains and then journeyed to the opposite side of the valley, to a Tudor mansion south of the University of Utah. I knocked on doors, lots of doors. They all began to blend together in my mind. The intrepid few who actually bothered opening the doors were women. All of them looked the same, with their gravity-defying hairdos done up in buns or braids, and stark black puff-sleeved dress extending to the wrists and ankles, which I assumed was reserved for mourning (although when I asked one if that's what it was for, she would neither confirm nor deny it). I found the women to be either morose or angry. I asked a lot of questions. They furnished terse replies, shedding no new light on anything, and each one referred me to her attorney, Granville Sondrup.

Fourteen

Roscoe entered the Anti-Polygamy Squad office in a rumpled suit and a tie resembling a noose waiting to be tightened. He crossed the room to his desk, carrying some sort of flat, square object wrapped in brown paper, about the size of a real estate sign. His face still suffered from discoloration and scabs, the result of that beating he'd taken a few days ago, but he was on the mend and looking better than when I last saw him. He seemed extraordinarily cheerful for showing up at work so late. He took a pouch of Red Man out of his pocket and stuffed a wad in his mouth. Seated at my desk, reviewing my squad's file on LeGrand Johnston, I felt my resentment toward Roscoe welling up when I saw him. *He can't keep neglecting his job like this*, I thought.

"Where were you all morning?" I said, my voice tight with frustration.

"I got something neat I want to show you, Art," he said, battered face beaming.

"Buddy asked me about you again today," I said. "I lied and told him you were out following up on some leads. I hate lying."

"Ah, to hell with him," he said with a dismissive wave.

"Are you going to answer my question?" I asked.

Still grinning, he asked, "What was it?"

I closed the file in front of me and then swiveled my chair toward him.

"Where were you this morning?" I asked.

He tore the brown paper off a sturdy square piece of cardstock with a logo on it that looked like it was professionally designed. He handed it to me and I held it up to get a better look. Inside of a hive surrounded by a few buzzing bees it said, BEEHIVE DISCREET INVESTIGATIONS. Below that: EST. 1934.

"Ta-dah!" he said with a Cheshire Cat grin. "What do you think?"

I looked at him. "Private investigator?"

"No more answering to those fools downstairs. What do you say?"

I handed it back. "Looks nice."

"It ought to," he said. "That thing cost me half my paycheck. The designer told me if I liked it, he'd paint it on the door and window of my new office."

"New office?"

"I'm starting my own agency," he said. "Come with me. We can be partners."

I chuckled. "Gumshoes, huh?"

"Just like in *Black Mask*," he said.

"Funny thing, I don't seem to remember any of the detectives in those mystery magazines worrying about where the next paycheck is gonna come from."

"Before you say no, just hear me out," he said. "My old boss at the Denver and Rio Grande Western told me he'd set me up in an office at the Rio Grande Depot. He'll also give me some part-time work running security at the yards, till I get on my feet."

"Those are some ritzy digs."

"What do you say?" he asked. "You in?"

"This place isn't perfect," I said. "Far from it. I've got grievances of my own. But the pay is steady. Things aren't getting any better out there, either. The soup lines still go around the block. If you want to take your chances out there, go ahead. I'm staying right here."

He grinned at me. "The invitation is always open."

"Thanks. So when are you leaving?"

He shrugged. "I'd like to save a little money on this job first, build up a nest egg. . . ."

"Fair enough," I said. "Until then, I need you to promise me that you're not going to take any more paid daytime leaves from your job to take care of personal business."

"All right, that's reasonable."

"While you're here, you need to show up on time and pay careful attention to your job," I said. "Speaking of which, I could use help right now, at a used-car lot."

He sneered in disbelief. "You need advice buying a car?"

"I'll explain on the way there," I said.

A square building, mostly windows, stood in the middle of a sea of autos, in the shadow of a sign for BABCOCK MOTORS. Multicolored pennants flapped and rainbow pinwheels pitched in the dry grass buzzed like airplane propellers, thanks to a breeze sweeping through the area. Out here, on 800 South and State, the car dealerships reigned supreme, though they shared the street

with motor inns, greasy spoons, cigar stores, taverns, tattoo parlors (for after you're done at the tavern), and pawnshops that did
a brisk business in hard times. None too prosperous, this part
of Salt Lake City, but I imagine every city has an area like it.
Roscoe and I parked along 800 South and crossed the street,
assaulted by a bunch of small advertising signs: SIXTY-DAY WRIT-
TEN GUARANTEE, ASK US ABOUT OUR CREDIT PLAN, DRIVE AWAY IN A
CAR THAT'S LIKE NEW. I'd briefed Roscoe about Babcock on the
way down. Once at the lot, I spied a portly little man, dressed old
fashioned–like, with a straw hat, vest, bow tie, and shirt garters,
reminiscent of a Dixieland band member. He gesticulated
wildly as he spoke to a young couple.

Roscoe tugged his hat low over a pair of tinted glasses to keep
the sun out of his eyes and chewed a wooden match, switching
on his gruff cop routine, which no longer fooled me after all
these years. It was all an act, a part of his shtick, as they say on
the vaudeville circuit. I, on the other hand, went from car to
car, skimming windshield stickers. Some decent deals could be
had here, especially if you were willing to go back into the last
decade. Shielding my eyes with cupped hands, I peered into
the window of a handsome little '27 Oakland sedan, light blue,
listed at only seventy-five dollars.

"You're not actually thinking of buying a car from this asshole, are you?" asked Roscoe.

I moved in close to him. "Do me a favor. Keep the gutter
language to a minimum. These people are quite religious."

"Help you gentlemen?" a voice called out behind us.

We turned at the same time to face Mr. Dixieland, who I assumed was Orville Babcock. His straw hat shaded bulging
eyes, and one of his front teeth was made of gold. Not a tall man,
maybe five foot five, he had a flabby chin darkened by a

five-o'clock shadow, and I could smell his sweet-scented hair tonic even under that hat of his. "Slippery" seemed a good word to describe him.

"Are you in the market for a newer model, or a little number from the good old days?" he asked.

"Are you Orville Babcock?"

"Yes, sir."

I showed him my badge. "Detective Art Oveson, Salt Lake police. This is my partner, Detective Lund. We'd like to ask questions about LeGrand Johnston."

The smile on his face flew south. No more gold tooth for us. "I haven't seen him in years," he said. "He and I haven't been in touch since nineteen and twenty-nine."

"Can you tell me more about your parting of ways?"

"We're fundamentalist Mormons, he and I. That was what we had in common in the first place."

"I suppose that makes you a polygamist, like him?" asked Roscoe.

He seemed to consider Roscoe's question as he whipped out a cotton hankie and dabbed his glistening neck. Ultimately, he opted not to respond to it. "If this is about his murder, I can assure you I played no part in it."

"You left LeGrand's cult and founded your own," said Roscoe.

"I prefer 'church,'" said Babcock. "Otherwise, that's accurate."

I pressed: "Did anything in particular trigger your falling-out with Johnston?"

"God told me to abandon LeGrand's corrupt church," Babcock said, with a straight face.

"God told you?" asked Roscoe, lowering his sunglasses to reveal skeptical eyes.

"Yes."

"Does God talk to you all the time?" asked Roscoe.

"Yes."

Roscoe pressed: "What does God tell you?"

"He gives me advice."

"What kind of advice?" asked Roscoe. "Wash behind your ears and wipe with toilet paper?"

Babcock ground his teeth and I thought I spotted a vein bulging out of his throat. "I take great umbrage at your remarks, Detective Lund!"

Roscoe leaned near me, perplexed. "Umbrage?"

"Let me," I whispered. I stepped closer to Babcock. "I apologize if Detective Lund's comments offended you. I just have a few more questions."

"I told everything to the police," he said.

"You did?" I asked.

"Yes, five years ago, after my break with LeGrand, I went to the police to report his vile practices. Isn't there some record of my testimony?"

"I haven't seen anything about it in our files," I said. "If you'd cooperate with us again, it'd be mighty helpful."

"LeGrand is an instrument of the devil. My church is the one true church, the one that Heavenly Father has established on earth as—"

"Shit almighty, Babcock, cut the preaching and make with the specifics," said Roscoe.

I whispered to Roscoe, "Gutter talk." His posture slackened slightly with compliance. To Babcock, I said, "What issues did you two disagree over?"

Babcock glowered at Roscoe, although he calmed down after shifting his attention back to me. "I hated LeGrand for supporting the banishments. I thought it was a cowardly and immoral thing to do."

"Banishments?" I asked. "What do you mean?"

"It happens down in Dixie City, around the time the boys turn twelve or thirteen. Certain ones get drummed outta town, sent away to fend for themselves."

"Not all of them?" asked Roscoe.

He shook his head. "Only those judged impure by the prophet's council."

"What's the prophet's council?" I asked.

"It's a tribunal that operates in secrecy. They run their own star chamber and mete out harsh punishments. Most of the boys have no choice but to run away, find somewhere else to live. A lot of them end up here in Salt Lake City. Some woman runs a sort of halfway house for runaway polygamist kids."

"What's her name?" I asked. "She might be helpful."

" 'Fraid I can't help you there," he said. "I don't know her name. I've only heard of her. The point is, LeGrand and his apostles are making a mockery out of plural marriage. It's a way of life sanctioned by the Lord, but they've turned it into something dark and terrible. I keep trying to persuade Carl to get out of it."

"Jeppson?" I asked. He nodded. I said, "Do you think he'd be willing to cooperate with us, if we promised him protection?"

"He's scared," said Babcock. "These men . . . you don't know what they're capable of. I saw firsthand with Len Orton."

"Who's Len Orton?" asked Roscoe.

"He's one of the reasons I left Grand's church," said Babcock. "Orton was an apostle in the church who began questioning some of the church's crooked practices. One day, he failed to show up at his place of business. He repaired cars. Wasn't like him to miss work. Ever. His wife filed a missing persons report, but Orton was never found. I have a pretty good idea what happened to him."

"What?" asked Roscoe.

"He's deep in some crevice somewhere nobody's ever gonna find him."

"What year did this happen?" I asked.

He closed his eyes and thought it over. "Mmm, nineteen and twenty-six."

"Maybe he had some sort of accident," I suggested.

He opened his eyes and laughed. "Sure. Right. Uh-huh. An accident. Just like Caldwell Black, Rulon's younger brother. He started getting funny ideas, too. He went around telling anybody who'd listen that the fundamentalists were up to no good, sinning with young girls and making dirty money hand over fist. He went missing, too."

"When?" I asked.

"Four years ago," said Babcock. "His house burned to the ground, killing his wife and three of his children. Caldwell's body was never found. That happened in Dixie City, too. Town marshal chalked it up to a faulty furnace. That's a laugh."

"What do you think happened to him?" I asked.

"I don't think *anything*, Mr. Detective. I *know* darn well what happened to him. He's in the same slot canyon as Len Orton. They've tried to kill me, too, a couple of times. Fired shots into my lot here a few years back. I'm pretty sure they're trying to poison me now. They regard me as a threat."

Roscoe chuckled. "You're starting to sound paranoid, Babcock. Maybe we oughta be making rubber room reservations for you."

Babcock sneered. "Mock me all you want. God knows I

speak the truth. Just wait until we find out what happened to those boys who went missing in May."

"What boys?" I asked.

Babcock swallowed hard and got nervous. "You mean . . . you don't know?"

"Know what?" asked Roscoe.

Babcock shook his head. "I need to get back to work. I'm a busy man."

"Bullshit!" snapped Roscoe. "You can't go jackassing like that and then just drop it. What do you mean *missing boys?*"

"I see what you're trying to do," he said, taking a few steps backward. "Sniffing around here, asking all of these questions. Well, it won't work. You've got to get up pretty early in the morning to fool this old catfish."

"These boys you mentioned," I said. "Who are they and when did they go missing?"

He waved a hand in the direction of State Street. "I'm going to have to ask you both to leave. I won't answer any more questions unless I have my lawyer present."

Nodding, I took one of my business cards from a holder I kept in my pocket, placed it on the hood of a car, and looked at Roscoe. "Got a pencil on you?"

He plucked one out of his pocket, all the while glowering at Babcock, and handed it to me. I jotted my telephone number on the back of my card and returned to the pencil to Roscoe. I handed Babcock the card and he arched his eyebrows at it.

"If you happen to think of something you think I should know, call me," I said. "Day or night, it doesn't matter. I've written my home telephone number on the back of the card just in case."

He pocketed the card and we set off, back toward our car.

We were halfway across the lot, passing rattletraps with new sets of tires, rusted areas painted over, and dents pounded out, before Roscoe spoke. "You let him off easy, Art. I was prepared to beat the shit out of him until he coughed up more information."

"You don't understand," I whispered out the side of my mouth. "This is the most information anybody's given us since the murders. If we push him too hard, he's gonna go cold on us. If we bend a little, give him some elbow room, we can come back for more. We don't want him thinking we're the enemy, Roscoe."

We'd almost reached 800 South when I heard Babcock call my name. "Oveson!" I turned around to see him standing in the middle of all those autos.

"I noticed you were ogling at the Oakland!"

"She's a beaut!" I shouted back.

"You can't beat that price! Want to take her for a spin?"

"Let me talk to the missus and I'll get back to you!"

"Tell the little lady that for twenty extra bucks, I'll throw in a car radio!"

"I will! Thanks!"

Roscoe and I started again in the direction to the car.

"All right, we'll back off for now," conceded Roscoe. "But please tell me you're not going to buy a car from that weasel."

"Just humoring him," I said, winking as we crossed the piping-hot pavement.

Fifteen

The bitty bell jingled when I closed the flower shop door. The strong scent of roses greeted my nose. A familiar-looking group of four women on the other side of the counter in the rear of the store briefly stopped assembling and wrapping bouquets to watch me. One leaned to another and whispered, and both—like all of the others—stared at me as I walked in with Roscoe following me. Something about the combination of the chilled air, dim light, and bright, fragrant blooms comforted me, enough to make me consider how pleasant it would be to take a nap in here. I reached the counter, a little higher than my waist, and rested my palms on the surface near the brass cash register.

"Mr. Jeppson?" I asked.

"He's not here," said a black-haired, olive-complected woman in a pale blue dress. She was probably around my age.

"Where is he?" asked Roscoe, scanning the place.

"We don't know," answered a similarly dressed redhead. "He didn't tell us where he was going."

"We have no idea when he's going to be back," said another.

Roscoe bowed to admire orchids in a vase. "We'll wait."

"We aren't sure when he'll return," the redhead reiterated. "He'll probably be gone a long time."

Roscoe shrugged. "We haven't got any pressing engagements."

"Don't let us interrupt you," I said.

"He's right," said Roscoe. "Go on doing what you were doing."

We waited. And waited. Five minutes ticked by, then ten. I leaned against the counter for support. Roscoe strolled up and down the center of the store, examining prearranged bouquets in vases behind sliding glass doors. The women went about their business, trimming flowers, arranging them with baby's breath or assorted greens, trying their hardest not to look at us. I was starting to fear that we might be there all day long. After a half hour of this, one of the women, young and big boned, with ruddy cheeks and auburn hair, stood so abruptly that she sent her chair skidding backward. She opened the door to the back room, slipped inside, and slammed it behind her, startling a couple of her coworkers. Roscoe and I looked at each other for a second, then returned our attention to the women still slaving away behind the counter.

"Got any Dr Pepper?" Roscoe asked.

The women ignored him, but one—the redhead in blue—gave him a forlorn eye and shook her head.

"I didn't think so," he said, with a sly grin.

The big-boned woman emerged from the back room with Carl Jeppson in tow, fancied up in his three-piece Sunday finest and bringing with him a palpable sense of dread. He approached the counter and puffed his cheeks and shook his head disdainfully.

"It's bad enough that you fellows tore me away from my shop on one of the busiest days of the year and kept me languishing in a jail cell for hours, even though I committed no crime." One could not miss the bitterness in his voice. "Now you're back for more, I see. You can't leave me well enough alone, can you?"

"What can we say?" asked Roscoe. "We've taken a shine to you."

"Please be brief," he said. "I've had it up to here with these disruptions."

"We don't intend to stay long," I said. "The reason we're here is you weren't entirely forthcoming with us the other day, Jeppson."

"Oh?"

"You left something out," I said.

"What?"

"You never mentioned those boys who went missing in May."

His face lost all color. His mouth moved for a few seconds, but at first no words came out. "What are you talking about?"

"You know what I mean," I said. "Same way you knew who that girl was in the picture I showed you the other day, even though you said you didn't. You know more than you let on."

He glanced over his shoulder, then he sized me up. "Outside?"

I nodded. He took a second or so to jot something on a slip of paper, then dropped the pencil on the counter and placed the paper in his pocket. He rounded the counter and led the way to the exit. A moment later, Jeppson, Roscoe, and I stood in triangle formation in the late-afternoon heat, where the traffic made my eardrums throb. At first when Jeppson spoke, I couldn't hear him above the steady roar of automobile engines. I lifted my finger to my earlobe and pleaded with him to talk a little louder.

He cleared his throat and raised his voice so it was barely loud enough for me to hear him.

"Please mind your own business," he said.

"We can provide police protection," I said. "Whoever it is you're afraid of . . ."

"You know my attorney's name, Detective," he said. "If you'll excuse me, I have to prepare for a trip out of town."

"Where to?" asked Roscoe.

He furrowed his brow. "Not that it's any of your business, but I'll be attending LeGrand Johnston's funeral in Dixie City. I don't wish to be delayed any further."

I said, "We have a few questions. . . ."

He moved right up to me and began shouting at the top of his lungs. "I have nothing to say to either of you! My attorney is listed in the city directory! Leave! Now!" Then he leaned in close and whispered, "Don't look at the sedan parked across the street. Check your shirt pocket after you go."

He walked away. *Ding ding.* The sign in the flower shop door flipped from OPEN to CLOSED. Out of the corner of my eye, I spied the sedan he'd mentioned, a late-model brown Hudson, with a driver and a front-seat passenger. The sun's glare on the windshield and the brevity of my glance prevented me from getting a good look at the men inside. Carl Jeppson's yelling had all been for show. I didn't want to look at the slip of paper he'd given me, for fear that whoever was in that car might notice.

Roscoe and I crossed the street to our unmarked police car, opened the doors, and climbed inside. Pulling the door shut, I reached in my pocket and tugged out a piece of paper slightly larger than a fortune cookie fortune. I opened the folded slip in my hand to see what he gave me.

Neat uppercase print said simply *HELP US.*

I handed it to Roscoe. He read it, said "Hmm," and gave it back. I looked at my rearview mirror in time to see the Hudson parked behind us leave the curb, make a U-turn, and speed west on 200 South. Who those two men were and where they were going, I had no idea. I wish I'd seen their faces.

"Did you get a look at the plates?" asked Roscoe.

"No," I said. "You?"

"Afraid not."

"Jared's running a check on Model T trucks," I said. "I'll add brown Hudsons to his list."

Perched on the swivel chair's edge, gazing out the window at the smoky skies, I lifted the telephone receiver and tapped the cradle a couple of times. I listened into the ebony earpiece and waited. The line crackled with distant party-line voices coming and going like ghosts waltzing in a ballroom.

"Operator. May I help you?"

"Long distance," I said. "To the sheriff's office, Kingman, Arizona."

"Hold the line, please."

"Yes. Thank you."

The other end of the line purred with a trio of rings before somebody answered.

"Sheriff's office. May I help you?" asked a woman's throaty voice.

"Is this Kingman?"

"It most certainly is. How may I help you?"

I introduced myself and said, "I'd like to speak to the sheriff, if he's in."

"Hold the line."

I did as she asked. A couple of clicks later, a man came on, sounding even more gravelly than the woman who answered the line. "Sheriff Colborne here."

Once more, I introduced myself. When I addressed him as Sheriff Colborne, he asked me to call him by his first name, Burke. "Much obliged, Burke," I said. "I've got a few questions. It shouldn't take long. Is now an okay time?"

"No better time than now," he said. "Slow day here in Kingman."

"Dixie City is in your county, isn't it?"

"Polygamistville. Certainly is. What about it?"

"How often does your job take you out there?"

"I steer clear of the place. They don't want me there. I don't want to be there."

"But you *have* been there, correct?"

"Couple of times, yeah."

"Do you know anything about some apostles in the Fundamentalist Church of Saints who went missing a while back? Their names were . . ." I closed my eyes to recollect. "Len Orton and Caldwell Black." I opened my eyes again. "Ring any bells?"

"No, sir. They coulda been before my time. You say they disappeared?"

"Some time back. I don't know any of the details. On a related subject, you didn't happen to hear anything about some boys from Dixie City who went missing in May, did you?"

He paused again to consider the question. "No. Can't say I have."

"We have a girl in custody who's mute. She's probably thirteen, I'm guessing. We have reason to believe she's from a polygamist family, but she hasn't said a word. She can't—or won't—say who she is, and we're stumped as to her identity. Nobody has claimed her. We've more or less reached a dead end with her."

"If she won't say who she is, how do you know she's got po-lygamist kin?"

I took several minutes to explain to him that I had found her at a murder scene, Le Grand Johnston's, in fact, and that she was being held somewhere safely. I didn't tell him she was staying at my house. I figured he didn't need to know that.

"Sounds like she's been down a troubled road," he said. "Too bad. Sorry I can't help you. I don't know anything about her."

"You haven't heard about a missing girl from Dixie City?" I asked.

"No, sir. No missing boys, no missing girl, nothing like that. Even if there were, I'd have no way of knowing."

"I don't understand."

"Dixie City's got its own law," he said. "Marshal Ferron Steed. He's more an enforcer than an officer of the law. Takes orders from his fundamentalist bosses. He can't stomach me. The feeling is mutual. There are a couple of goons in his em-ploy called the Kunz brothers, Dorland and Devlin, two of the worst bottom-feeders to ever set foot in Arizona. I'm certain they've left a trail of bodies out in the desert. I have no way of proving it, mind you, 'cause ain't no way anybody's gonna find where them bodies are buried."

"How'd you come by this information?"

"Let's just say the rumor mill operates at full capacity around here," he said. "From what I've heard, Steed and the Kunz bro-thers answer to Rulon Black. He runs the show down here."

"Why all the secrecy?" I asked.

"They're racketeers, the polygamists," said Colborne. "They use their religion as a cover to hide their crimes."

"When you say crimes . . ."

"It's all grapevine."

"It'd help me if you'd elaborate," I said.

"I don't know all the specifics. Put it this way. They've got their own empire up there. And, like most empires, parts of it are none too savory. Beyond that, I don't care to speculate over the telephone with someone I don't know."

I felt queasy from this conversation. "These boys who disappeared in May, surely somebody must miss them?"

"Yeah, sure, maybe their loved ones. But Detective, there are a million places in the desert where you can dump a body and nobody's ever gonna find it. That goes doubly so for children. It doesn't help any that the polygamists quit applying for birth certificates for their newborns years ago, so we have no way of knowing how many children live in Dixie City."

"No birth certificates," I said. "That doesn't make sense."

"These folks aren't like you or me. They live in the shadows. They hide everything. They leave no telltale signs." There was a long pause. "I feel bad."

"Why?"

"I'm sure there's more I could've done, and could be doing now. Problem is, these people are always one step ahead of me. They guard their secrets carefully."

"Thank you for your help, Sheriff," I said.

"I wasn't any help, I'm sure. I'm afraid in this instance, nobody can help you. So long, Detective."

Sixteen

"Permission denied!"

I had only been in Buddy Hawkins's office for a few minutes before he blew up, and I was already starting to regret my decision to run my idea by him.

"I'm surprised you'd make this request! What's gotten into you?"

"I'm getting nowhere here," I said. "My men and I are running around in circles."

"And what do you think you're going to find down there that you can't find here?"

I shrugged. "I won't know until I go there."

"This wouldn't have anything to do with the murders? If so, let me remind you that you have no business—"

"I know, I know," I said. "That's Wit's turf."

"Once you leave the city limits, you're out of your jurisdiction."

"The law allows me to question people outside of Salt Lake City, even out of the state, if need be."

"Let's not split hairs. You and I know the polygamists own Dixie City. They run everything, from top to bottom. Law enforcement, the courts, municipal politics, the schools, you name it. It's their town. The last thing we need right now is for you to go down there and raise a ruckus. . . ."

"Who said anything about a ruckus? All I want to do is talk to a few locals, find out what I can."

"Is this Roscoe's idea? It sounds like the kind of crazy thing he'd cook up."

"No. I have a feeling there are things happening down there. . . ."

"Things? What kind of things? What are you talking about?"

I closed my eyes in an effort to piece my thoughts together. "I'm trying to figure how it all fits."

"How what all fits?"

I blinked open my eyes. "The girl who's not saying a word, who we found at the murder scene, I think she's somehow tied in with the polygamists who've taken over an entire town down on the Arizona strip. I can't help but believe that this business with the homestead land and the boys who went missing in May—"

"Whoa! Back up a second. Homestead land? Missing boys? What on earth are you talking about?"

"I don't know exactly," I said. "I'm still trying to make sense of it all myself, and not having a whole lot of luck. Look, all I know is that by pushing these polygamists out of Salt Lake City, we're sending them to a place where they can do the things they do away from public view. You know, out of sight, out of mind."

Buddy smirked. "Oh, so now you're having second thoughts? You want us to roll out the red carpet and hand them the key to the city?"

"C'mon, Buddy, you're oversimplifying things."

"The polygamists are giving our church a bad name," said Buddy in a voice tense with exasperation. "People who aren't Mormons look at these crazy nuts and all of their wives and get the wrong idea. They start thinking all Mormons are a bunch of crackpot polygamists. That's why Mayor Cummings gave the go-ahead to get the Anti-Polygamy Squad back off the ground. He thought—as do I, as does Chief Cowley—that pushing the plural-marriage zealots out of the city limits could only be a positive thing, not just for Salt Lake, but for the future well-being of our faith. Now, after three months of heading said squad, you march into my office and tell me you don't think this is a good idea? It's a little late in the day for that, Art. Don't you think?"

"I know there is something bad going on in that community, and if we don't do something about it—"

"Where's your proof?"

It took me a few seconds to consider his question. "Proof?"

"Yeah. Show it to me and I'll consider your request."

"All I have are bits and pieces, little fragments that are troubling, but taken together . . ."

"That won't cut it."

"What *would* cut it? A couple more homicides?"

Buddy squinted with contempt. "Don't do this."

"Don't do what?"

"You come in my office, you tell me something *bad* is going on, but you can't even say what it is. What am I supposed to do?"

"I want to go to Dixie City, and I'd appreciate your support."

"As what?"

"What do you mean, as what?"

"How many times do I have to tell you? You have no authority down there. What're you gonna do, start arresting people? You can't even issue traffic tickets in Dixie City!"

"Some boys, I found out, went missing there in May. Give me permission to go to Dixie City to look into it. That's all I ask."

"We're going around in circles." Buddy paused to sigh. "I'm not going to give you my blessing on this one."

It occurred to me, then and there, that Buddy's number one priority was his own future. I'd always known Buddy was a political animal with his sights set on elected office, yet I'd forgiven him for this in the past because I believed that deep down inside, he shared my abiding commitment to doing right.

He said, "Now that I have addressed your foolish request to go to Dixie City with an emphatic no, will there be anything else?"

"No." I shook my head. "No, nothing else."

We said our good-byes and I put on my hat as I left. I followed the corridor lined with oil paintings of past police chiefs out to the bustling lobby, where Roscoe leaned against a marble column, chewing on a matchstick. His fedora was tilted on his head, and Lord in Heaven could he use a shave.

"The answer's no," I said glumly.

"So when do we leave?"

I cracked a crooked smile. "I'm not going."

"You mean you're actually going to listen to that prick?"

"I'm not going to disrespect my superior, and that's all there is to it."

"All right," he said slowly, as if he thought I was making the biggest mistake of my life. "But don't say I didn't offer."

"I appreciate it, old friend. I think I'm gonna call it a day. Want a ride home?"

He smiled and shook his head. "That's all right. I'll catch the interurban. See you tomorrow, Art."

"G'night," I said.

He turned to leave, but I called out his name and he stopped and faced me. "Yeah?"

"Remember: Get here on time tomorrow," I said. "I know you can do it."

He chuckled and gave his fedora brim a tug before he turned to go.

It turned out that Clara, Sarah Jane, and Hyrum all had a prior engagement: a cousin's birthday party on Clara's side of the family. This left me alone for the night with the mute girl, who needed a break from family get-togethers, we decided. Come dinnertime, I warmed up homemade chicken noodle soup and the two of us sat across the table from each other. She ate slowly and seemed more comfortable, less tense than she had been the other day. When we were done, I put the dishes in the sink and planned to wash them after she went to sleep. The two of us went into the living room and listened to the radio for a while. The news on KSL, "brought to you by Pep 88 Gasoline," was full of grim talk of Nazis and forest fires and labor strikes. A music variety show aired afterward, and that's when the girl got up and left for the kitchen. I could hear silverware and dishes shifting. I stood and walked over to the kitchen door. I spied her tilting a box of Super Suds over the basin of water and begin scrubbing away with a Brillo Pad. Before long, the bowls and silverware and glasses were pristine and placed out to dry on the wooden dish drainer.

"Thank you."

She swung around suddenly, as if startled.

"I was going to do those. Thanks for doing them."

She swallowed hard, and her eyes darted nervously from me to the dishes and back again.

"Can you understand me?" I asked. "Nod for yes."

She backed up a couple of steps, bumping into the sink.

I said, "I don't wish to hurt you. You know what I'm saying, don't you? If you know how to do dishes and use Brillo Pads and Super Suds, you must be able to communicate with others."

I sensed her tensing up. Her breathing quickened. She placed her hands over her solar plexus, as if guarding herself.

"You were there, at the fundamentalist church, the night of the murders. What did you see? Can you write?" I pantomimed with an invisible pen, my flat hand doubling as paper. "You know, write. If I were to get you a pencil and a piece of paper, could you write down what you saw?"

She blinked at me, still coiled up.

"Are you able to write? Or read?" I asked. "Are you literate? Do you know English? Look, you need to help me, if I'm going to . . ."

The sight of the frightened girl made me stop. I knew I'd pressed her too hard when I saw her body—her hands, arms, head—trembling under my shadow. She sank her teeth into her lower lip, and her wide eyes became watery. I backed away from her a few steps, instantly feeling remorse over my actions, even though I hadn't said anything spiteful. I'd scared her, and I imagined a girl who wore a wedding band this young in life had probably been frightened by one too many men.

"Sorry," I said. "Thank you for doing the dishes."

She left. I lost track of how long I stood there, regretting what

I'd done. It must have been a while, because when I went to check on the girl in Sarah Jane's room, I found her sound asleep. I went into the living room and listened to the rest of the variety show on the radio. Around half past nine, I checked on her again. She was still asleep. A photograph of an adolescent boy had found a new home on the nightstand. I picked up the snapshot and looked at it by the light of the hallway. The boy, likely twelve or thirteen, with a mop of dark hair, a tentative smile, and a plaid shirt, leaned against a split-rail fence. I set it down where I had found it and glimpsed the thick beige pillowcase that held her belongings, sitting on the floor, tucked partially underneath the bed. *Should I? Shouldn't I?* I leaned over the bed where she slept. Her eyes were closed and heavy breaths swished through her nostrils.

I ignored any doubts, squatted low, reached inside of the pillowcase, and began pulling out its contents. Strips of plain and floral and calico fabric; a battered tin that once held Sweet Clover brand pure lard, now home to a wad of seven or eight soggy dollar bills and close to three dollars in change; a porcelain doll in a dark Victorian dress and a matching ruffled derby; a bottle of Sloan's Liniment with the cap screwed on tight; a small stack of movie magazines, all with pretty actresses on the covers; a cloth pouch filled with spools of thread, a thimble, and sewing needles; a road map printed by Sinclair Oil; a bus ticket from St. George, Utah, to Salt Lake City; a bag of hard candy; and at the very bottom, a pillow with words in needlepoint: *GOD BLESS OUR HOME*. Nothing else. I sighed a sigh of resignation and began putting everything back where I found it. I closed the door and returned to the radio, where some sort of police drama flooded out of the upholstered speaker.

Car lights swept into the driveway around eleven. I went out and waited on the porch in warm night air that smelled of burning wood. Clara shut off the engine, she and Sarah Jane got out of the front of the car, and I opened the rear door to find my sleeping son. Without saying a word, I carried Hi off to bed and tucked him in. I returned to the living room to find my daughter waiting for me.

"Good night, Dad," said Sarah Jane, rising from the armchair, throwing her arms around me. I hugged her back.

"Nighty night, angel," I said.

She pulled back and smiled warmly. "Don't let the bedbugs bite."

"I love you," I said.

"I love you too."

She went off in the direction of her room.

Clara switched off the radio, came over to me, put her arms around my neck, and leaned in for a peck on the lips. We gave each other a loving smile. She smelled of something flowery, maybe a new perfume she'd bought at one of the downtown department stores.

"How did it go tonight?" I asked.

"How do you think it went? Leroy got inundated with presents. The kids all raised merry Cain. S.J. sat in a corner, as usual, and Hyrum made everybody laugh with his Jack Benny impersonations."

I let out a soft laugh as we released each other. "Sounds like I missed another rollicking night of fun and frivolity."

"You got off easy, mister," said Clara. She turned serious. "How is she?"

I decided not to say anything about my brief yet aggressive grilling of the girl. "She did the dishes and went to bed early."

Clara's eyes widened. "Washed the dishes, huh? How sweet of her."

"Mom. Dad. She's gone."

Sarah Jane stood in the doorway with a spooked expression. I bolted past her, down the hallway, flinging her bedroom door open with such force that it knocked a picture frame off S.J.'s bureau.

It sent shock waves through me to see the empty bed where our guest had been sleeping earlier in the night, its sheet and blanket pulled all the way down like a peeled banana. The bedroom window was wide open, kept in place by a piece of lumber. Sarah Jane appeared by my side, forlorn and scared, staring at me expectantly for answers.

"You found it like this?" I asked.

"Yes."

"Did you hear anything before you came in?"

"No."

Clara came into the room while we were talking. She went over to the window, leaned forward, and poked her head out to get a better look. The window looked out onto the backyard, lit only by the moon. She straightened and turned to me, and I looked at her to see if—by any remote chance—she noticed anything. She shook her head.

I stepped closer to the bed, got down on all fours, and tilted my head low to the floor. I found nothing under the bed. I went to the closet, opened the door, and was greeted by a rack of hanging dresses. I stooped to get a better look down below, where S.J. kept her shoes, but I didn't see any sign of the girl. I closed the door.

My insides ached with guilt about my decision to search the girl's pillowcase. No doubt about it, I had let my zeal take over, and my actions left me ashamed. It could very well be that she was feigning sleeping when I went into her room, and saw me take that old pillowcase stuffed with her things, and she knew I went through her belongings. With my wife and daughter watching me, waiting for some sort of cues, I put my hands on my waist and sighed.

"Time to make a couple of telephone calls," I said.

Seventeen

"I've really fouled it up this time," I said. "She was supposed to be in my protective custody." I slapped my hand on my chest for emphasis. "In *my* care. I couldn't even do that right. What was I thinking? I should've let her be sent to the reformatory up in Ogden, like Buddy told me to do in the first place."

We were conducting an emergency powwow in my living room, with lemonade and cookies provided by Clara. I wasn't thirsty and I certainly wasn't hungry, although the others were digging in freely.

"Go easy, Art," Roscoe told me. "You did the right thing by helping that girl. Don't always be second-guessing yourself."

"You said you looked in on her around nine thirty?" Jared asked.

"Yeah, nine thirty, somewhere thereabouts."

"What time did your daughter discover she wasn't there?" Jared asked.

"My wife and children got home from the party around

eleven. Maybe eleven-oh-five. Sarah Jane went into the bathroom and brushed her teeth, changed into her PJs, and then noticed the girl was missing." I drew a deep breath. "It's like the Lindbergh kidnapping. The window open, the girl missing, the—"

"For crying out loud, now you're getting dramatic," said Roscoe. "It's nothing like the Lindbergh kidnapping."

"It's exactly like it," I said. "I go in there, the bed is empty, the window's open . . ."

Roscoe turned his palms up. "You were where—in the living room—when it happened?"

"Yeah. Yeah, listening to the radio."

"If there were some kind of commotion, you'da heard it," said Roscoe. "No, this ain't anything like the Lindbergh kidnapping."

"What are you saying?" I asked. "You think the girl left on her own?"

Roscoe nodded. "It's possible. What do we really know about her? What's going through that head of hers?"

Jared reached for a cookie. He snacked while Roscoe pulled out a silvery flask, uncapped it, and tilted it against his lips. He took two hard swallows and gasped, capping it again and slipping it into his pocket.

"I don't even know where to start," I said. "Maybe I should just fess up to Buddy and let the chips—"

"Steer clear of Buddy," interjected Roscoe. "He'll bust your balls and pile on the *I told you so*'s thick as cordwood, then the prick will go straight to Cowley. That's how he operates. Nothing against him, I know he's your friend and all. But he's a grade-A politico, a chain-of-command pencil pusher who doesn't understand that there's a time and a place to bend the rules, if not break 'em."

Jared chewed his cookie in a hangdog silence that was un-characteristic for him. I said to him, "Well?"

"Well what, boss?"

"You're as familiar with these people as anybody I know," I said. "What does your gut tell you?"

"She went back."

"Went back where?"

"Didn't you tell me she had a bus ticket on her?"

"Yeah. From St. George."

"St. George is only forty miles away from Dixie City. I'm guessing the girl probably scraped together enough money to buy a bus ticket to get here. There's a good chance she lit out tonight to go back home to be with her kin."

"What makes you think her family is from Dixie City?" I asked.

"She's one of *them*," said Jared. "I can see it, plain as day, by the way she styles her hair, the design of her dress, even by how she carries herself. She's from one of the clans. I'm ninety-nine percent sure of it."

"I think a trip to Dixie City is in order," said Roscoe. "If we stay here, we're just gonna get in the way of the Homicide dicks."

"Buddy gave me explicit orders not to go," I said.

"Art," said Roscoe, arching his eyebrows.

"Yeah?"

"Fuck him."

"Oh, that helps! *Eff* Buddy! That helps a lot."

"No, not *eff* Buddy," said Roscoe. "*Fuck* Buddy. There's a dif-ference."

"Easy for you to say. If Buddy finds out I went to Dixie City, it'll land me in serious hot water," I said.

"Either way, your goose is cooked," said Roscoe. "The girl

disappeared while in your protective custody. Now, I know it's not your fault, and I hope you know it's not your fault. But when the mayor gets wind of this, it's curtains for our little squad."

He was right and I knew it. I just didn't want to admit it. But I also wasn't eager to make this trek down to Dixie City that Roscoe was suggesting. "Maybe we should wait until after Johnston's funeral on Saturday," I suggested. "Give the people a chance to mourn without us getting in their way."

"That may be why she's going down there," said Jared, his mouth still full of cookie. "Just keep your distance from the funeral. They don't want you there, and your presence is gonna get them all riled up. Observe it from afar. You best take your field glasses with you."

After a prolonged silence, I looked at Roscoe. "Will you go with me?"

"Of course," he said. "You don't even need to ask."

I turned to Jared. "What about you?"

He stopped chewing and ran his tongue over his teeth. "Can't do it, boss."

"Why not?" I asked.

He swallowed what was in his mouth. "I've got a meeting at one o'clock in the afternoon with that clerk over at the state department of revenue's vehicle division. He's the same fellow I spoke to yesterday when I went out there to request registration records on Model T trucks and brown Hudsons. They need twenty-four hours' notice to rustle up those documents, and I don't want to stand him up after he went to all that work. Besides, with Myron out of town, it makes sense to have someone in the office for at least part of the day, in case someone calls."

"Good point," I said.

"Art," said Clara, from the arched entrance to the room. "A word, please?"

In the hallway, Clara and I stood face-to-face, and I found her visibly shaken.

"I don't want you going to Dixie City."

I didn't know she'd been eavesdropping. Maybe I should've arranged to have the meeting at Public Safety. Oh well. Too late now. Besides, I knew I'd have to tell her if I was going to leave town. It just caught me off guard, knowing she was listening in on us.

"I have to," I said. "I have no choice."

"Yes, you have a choice," she said. "Talk to Buddy . . ."

"Clara . . ."

"I'm being serious. Tell him the truth. Tell him all about the girl and what happened here tonight. He knows you meant well, that you didn't want to see the girl suffer in the reformatory."

"Clara, I have to try to find her," I said. "Even if I return empty-handed, I need to be able to tell Buddy I gave it my best shot."

"You know nothing about Dixie City," she said, choked up. "You've no idea what to expect. You're going down there blind."

I leaned in close to her. "Nothing bad is going to happen to me. Trust me. I'll be fine."

She looked down, fighting the tears. I curled my index finger under her chin and gently nudged her head upward. Our eyes met. She bit her lower lip.

"I'll be fine."

The drive on U.S. 91 south snakes through desert valleys dotted with sage and juniper and mesquite trees and surrounded by stubby mountains that from a distance appeared slate gray with a hint of purple. I drove while Roscoe slept on the passenger side, his hat pulled low over his face. My only company was a two-knob radio that came installed in the Olds for an extra ten bucks when I ordered her from factory Detroit. From time to time, I'd fiddle with dial and pick up chatter or music. For five whole minutes, WGN clear-channeled its way out here from Chicago, broadcasting a dance orchestra from the White City Ballroom. The station soon crackled its way into oblivion, leaving me alone with all of those pops and hisses. The drive went on like this for hours, with nothing to do but turn the radio dial and hope for something, anything.

Nearing St. George, at the bottom of the state, the terrain turns to red sandstone, rising high into sheer faces that instantly make you feel small. *Real small.* With one hand on the wheel, I picked up a folded sheet of paper on the front seat and glanced at directions from St. George to Dixie City, written in the familiar handwriting of Jared Weeks. Before we left, Jared furnished a name, Oscar Larsen, Dixie City's justice of the peace, a non-polygamist and owner of the only boardinghouse in town. The polygamists in Dixie City all held Larsen in high regard, according to Jared, primarily because he was fair-minded, although it helped that he had founded the town back in 1911.

Roscoe's head dipped low, and the man snored louder than the car's engine. I envied him. My eyes burned and grew heavy from a sleepless night. My plan: find this Larsen fellow, see if he'd rent rooms by the night, eat an early dinner, and get a good night's sleep. Tomorrow was the funeral. I was dreading it. Jared's advice to watch it from a distance made sense. Maybe we'd spot the girl among the mourners. Maybe we wouldn't. At this point, I was feeling desperate and willing to do anything to find her. Planning these things out in my head helped ease doubts that dogged me as I turned off 91. Unfortunately, those doubts persisted—intensified, even—as I sped east on a narrow, barely paved road, forty or so miles away from Dixie City. Was I doing the right thing by defying Buddy's orders and coming down here? Was I on a fool's errand? How on earth would I ever find a single, solitary girl—who may have been a polygamist wife—in a town teeming with such women?

Oscar Larsen, a wiry man with white hair, crinkly eyes, and a Roman nose, watched us from a rocking chair on the porch of his boardinghouse. At first glance, he came across as intense and distrusting. His leathery exterior, heavily tanned, with faded work clothes torn and dirty in spots, conveyed a toughness that must be a prerequisite for surviving out here among the mesas and the junipers. I parked my car on the dirt road, in front of his two-story Victorian house, prompting Larsen to stand and amble to the porch stairs.

"Help you fellers?" he asked, watching me lift the fence latch.

"I'm Art Oveson," I said, pushing open the gate. "This is Roscoe Lund. We heard you take in lodgers here."

"Who gave you that idea?" He folded his arms and remained stone-faced.

"A friend of ours," I said. "I hope he was right."

"Your friend got a name?"

"Jared Weeks."

"Weeks, huh?" His eyes wandered searchingly. "Weeks, Weeks. Hmm. I used to know a family by that name. Most of 'em up and moved a while ago. But I am acquainted with one, a daughter, who stayed put." His fixed his gaze back on me. "I think her name was Lillian. Yeah, that's it. Lillian. I don't suppose she's any relation to that friend of yours. She dropped her maiden name when she got married. Unfortunately, she died some years ago." He paused to ponder something. "I don't know how this Jared feller come to know about our boardinghouse here."

"Christ, does it really matter?" asked Roscoe, matchstick on his lip. "We ain't freeloaders. We come bearing greenback."

He scowled at Roscoe. "I don't rent to just anybody."

I showed him my badge. "I'm a detective with the Salt Lake City Police Department."

He looked at Roscoe, who fished out his badge as well.

Larsen nodded in acknowledgment. "Are you here to attend LeGrand Johnston's funeral?" he asked. "It's tomorrow, you know. But don't expect to get in if you weren't invited."

"We're not here for that reason," I said. I squatted, opened my leather grip bag, took out a police mug shot of the girl, stood, and showed it to him. "We're looking for this girl. Do you know her?"

He looked at it two seconds and returned it. "No."

"Have you heard about some boys who went missing in May?" I asked, returning the photo to my bag.

"If boys went missing, I'd know about it. The town marshal, Ferron Steed, would've mentioned it to me."

"Got any ideas about who'd want to put a few slugs in Le-Grand Johnston?" asked Roscoe.

"I'm afraid I was never closely acquainted with the man." He twisted right and spat tobacco into a porch spittoon next to the rocking chair. "Anyhow, these people aren't keen on outsiders. They've got their own form of justice. It's called blood atonement. They don't have any reason to believe that big-city police like you fellas are going to carry it out properly, either. If someone from inside their little world did kill Johnston—and I'm not saying that's so—then the killer has signed his own death warrant."

"Or *her*," said Roscoe, dipping into his own pouch of Red Man.

Larsen grinned, showing his tobacco-stained teeth. "Yep."

"Maybe you'd be so kind as to show us a room," I said. "Is there a restaurant in town where we can eat?"

"Only one. The Covered Wagon. It's in the middle of town. You can't miss it."

"Much obliged," I said, with a tug of my hat brim.

"Don't expect to find a reception committee waiting to give you the key to the city," said Larsen. "These folks aren't partial to outsiders. I'm one of the few non-polygamists they let live around here. That's because I founded this town."

"You founded Dixie City?" I asked.

"I'm called the town founder, but that's something of a stretch," he said. "There were plenty of polygamists living in these parts long before I arrived. All I did was sign the papers of incorporation in 1911, to make it officially a town."

Roscoe turned in the direction of a craggy butte beyond the picket fence. A tumbleweed rolled by. "Some town," he said.

Our host glared at Roscoe. "I'll show you to your room."

Eighteen

To get to the Covered Wagon Café, we walked along Central Avenue through Dixie City. In my hand I held a picture of the unknown mystery girl, whose disappearance from my house last night still had me baffled and shaken. I couldn't get her off my mind, and I hoped I'd locate her in this strange place that seemed to have been frozen in time eighty years ago. A high mesa at the town's edge, splashed with red and orange, overlooked the place like a petrified tidal wave. The walk along the wide road took us past block after block of modest wood-frame houses.

This was where the rank-and-file fundamentalists—the "common folk," or "the salt of the earth," as Johnston used to like to call them—resided. By contrast, the wealthy patriarchs lived outside of town, in secluded fortresslike compounds behind high walls. This arrangement was no accident. It meant that visitors to this place were given the impression that all polygamists were simple folk.

The streets appeared mostly deserted at first, yet soon we saw signs of life. Curtains parted in windows and dark figures gazed out. Men, women, and children watched from front yards. Teenage girls who looked as though they'd just leaped out the back of prairie schooners circa 1854, clad in ankle-length dresses with long hair pinned in buns, whispered to each another, pointed fingers, and stayed out of our way. I didn't see any adolescent boys, but it was impossible to miss the women peeking over fences, children climbing trees to get a better view, and the elderly watching us from porches.

We focused on the road ahead. I knew a little about the history of this place, mainly from bits I'd picked up over the past few months in our investigation. Long before Oscar Larsen signed the articles of incorporation that officially turned Dixie City into a town in 1911, the early Mormon pioneers built an outpost here in the 1850s, to facilitate Brigham Young's plan to send families to these parts to try their hand at growing cotton. Young hoped profits from the crop would enrich the cash-strapped Church, and he cited the lucrative cotton trade in the South as an example. Alas, southern Utah's desert terrain could not compete with the rich soil of Alabama or Georgia. The Mormons abandoned the community and it deteriorated into a ghost town. When the Church disavowed polygamy in 1890, paving the way for Utah to achieve statehood, there was talk that authorities were poised to crack down on plural marriage zealots. Rising fears of mass arrests triggered a southward exodus. Thousands of fundamentalists moved to these parts, looking to avoid jail time. Despite this trend, the more stubborn polygamists stayed put in Salt Lake City. The wealthy ones quietly began buying up land along the Utah-Arizona border, while holding on to their property in the city.

Roscoe elbowed me, snapping me back to the present. We

had crossed into the business quarter. Not much to it: a one-pump filling station, a bank (with a scowling guard standing out front), a local mercantile with a CLOSED sign in the window, Zion Auto Repair, and the Covered Wagon Café. As we passed Zion Auto Repair, a burly auto mechanic in oil-stained blue coveralls wiped his hands on a rag and watched us.

The Covered Wagon was your typical small-town eatery. I surveyed the long, narrow room, with a lunch counter on one side, checkered-cloth-covered tables in the center, and booths against the other wall. The joint was half full, with a primarily older male clientele and a handful of female diners. Three officers of the law, with dark pants, khaki shirts, and town marshal insignias, swiveled around on their barstools to get a better look at us. The awkward weight of a dozen or so pairs of eyes fell upon us as I closed the door.

Roscoe broke the thick silence. "There's a booth at nine o'clock. Let's nab it."

We walked over to a wall booth and slid into the maroon seats. A nervous young brunette in a blue dress with a white apron approached with eyes begging us to go away.

"We're closed," she said softly.

"Doesn't look that way to me, sister," said Roscoe.

"The others were here when we closed. They'll leave as soon as they're done."

Roscoe gestured at a couple at the next table who hadn't gotten their order. "Them too?"

"They got here as we were closing. They're waiting on their dinners."

"What time do you close?" I asked.

"Now," she said. "We close now."

I checked my wristwatch. "At quarter to six?"

"We close at five thirty," she said. "Sorry, I'll have to ask you to leave."

Quick on her feet, I thought.

"Is there another restaurant in town?" I asked.

"There are a bunch in St. George," she said.

"That's a long way to go for eats," I said.

"We're closed," she repeated.

The town marshal, a short, stocky man with hair pomaded tightly to his head and a deep dimple on his chin, stepped up alongside her. Grinning, he lifted his trousers with curled thumbs and gave us both a going-over. A nameplate under his chest badge said FERRON W. STEED.

"Help you boys?"

"We're hungry," said Roscoe. "We want menus."

"I don't know if you heard Talena," said Steed, pointing at the waitress. "Place is closed."

"We don't plan on being here long," I said. "We're staying at Mr. Larsen's boardinghouse, only they, uh, weren't expecting us for supper. We're good for it. We've got money."

"There's a place in St. George called the Metropolitan," said Talena. "I hear they've got the best southern fried chicken in the state of Utah."

"We've been on the road all day," I said. "If you could see your way clear to . . ."

"You fellas like meat loaf?" asked Marshal Steed.

I smiled up at him. "Who doesn't?"

He faced the waitress. "I'm sure Roy has some meat loaf left in the kitchen. Have him fix it up with a couple of sides. While you're at it, bring a bottle of Heinz."

"And a cup of coffee," said Roscoe. "Better yet, bring the whole pot."

"We don't serve coffee," said Talena.

"Bottle of cold beer, then," said Roscoe.

"We don't serve beer either," she added.

"Root beer?"

"No. Sorry."

"What about water?" asked Roscoe. "Or is that not available either?"

"Two glasses of water coming right up."

"With ice, if you've got it, toots," said Roscoe.

"Yes, sir," she said, heading fast to a swinging kitchen door.

"Nothing beats Roy's meat loaf," said the marshal. "Mind if I pull up a chair?"

Roscoe mumbled, "To be honest, I'd prefer you—"

I cut him off: "Please, join us."

Steed lifted an unused chair from the next table, saying something out of earshot to the couple seated there. He returned to our booth, slid the chair close, and sat down, letting out a loud exhale and grunt as he made himself comfortable. "Much better. Now, where were we?"

"Waiting for our grub," said Roscoe.

"I didn't get your names," said Steed.

"I'm Art Oveson. This here is Roscoe Lund."

He shook hands with me. "Good to know you."

We released our grips and he offered his hand to Roscoe, who waited a few seconds before capitulating.

"What brings you two fellas to this neck of the woods?"

"We're vagabonds," said Roscoe. "Bitten by the wanderlust bug, making our way across this enchanting land of ours by auto."

"We're detectives," I said, giving Roscoe the *cut-it-out* eye. "With the Salt Lake City Police Department."

"Oh? You're a little outside your domain."

I set the picture of the girl on the table in front of him and he leaned forward to get a good look at her.

"Do you know this girl?" I asked.

"She looks familiar."

"What's her name?" asked Roscoe.

"I said she looks familiar," Steed told Roscoe. "I didn't say I *know* her."

"So you don't know who she is?" I asked.

"Why don't you let me hold on to this picture," he said. "I'll ask around."

"I'm afraid I can't let you do that," I said. "I need it."

He picked up the photo, smiled tauntingly, and showed no signs of giving it up. "Does this pretty young thing have something to do with you men being here?"

"She's one reason," I said. "There are others."

"What might those be?" asked Steed.

"Can I get my picture back, please?" I asked, pointing to it.

"I'd like to hold on to it," said Steed. "In case."

"Give it back," said Roscoe.

I gave Roscoe my best *let-me-do-the-talking* glare, but he ignored me.

"The young lady in that picture has gone missing," I told Steed. "She's a witness in a double homicide. We need to find her. And I need to have the picture to show people what she looks like, I'm afraid."

"Are you referring to Uncle Grand's murder?" Steed asked, finally handing me the picture.

"Yes."

"He was shot in Salt Lake City, not here," said Steed.

"But the girl is from around here," said Roscoe. "We have reason to believe . . ."

"Well, I can save you time," said Steed. "We're a town of law-abiding folk. You won't find any murderers around here. They're all running around up in Salt Lake City."

"Just the same," I told him, "we'd like to follow up on all of our leads."

Our meat loaf arrived on a tray, along with a pitcher of ice water speckled with condensation droplets and a couple of glasses. The girl set our plates in front of us, filled our glasses, and placed cutlery inside of folded napkins on the table.

"Enjoy," she said. She rushed back to the counter, perhaps fearful of a confrontation at our table.

Fork in one hand, knife in the other, I inspected the steaming contents of my plate. I raised the fork above the meat loaf when Steed slid the bottle of Heinz closer and uncapped it.

"You've got to have ketchup on it," he said. "It brings out the flavor."

I thanked him under my breath, doused the delicacy in ketchup, and spread it around with my fork. I dug in. It was the best meat loaf I'd ever had, probably because I was so famished. Roscoe was already a third of the way through his, washing it all down with water for a change.

"News of Uncle Grand's death hit folks 'round here hard," said Steed. "Only thing you all are gonna accomplish is opening up the wounds."

"Thank you for your advice, Marshal," I said. "My partner and I would like to spend a day or so here to rule out certain things."

"What exactly are you ruling out?" Steed asked, itching his cheek.

"Shit," said Roscoe. "We're ruling out shit."

Steed scowled at Roscoe. I butted in: "We're following up on leads."

Steed's features softened when he looked at me. "What kind of leads?"

"Information that may help us capture Johnston's killer," I said.

"I can't imagine what leads would bring you to Dixie City."

"We prefer to play our cards close to our chest," I said. "I'm sure you get it."

"No. I don't, I'm afraid."

"Why you doing this?" Roscoe asked Steed.

"Doing what?"

"Crowding us out."

Steed grinned, showing teeth. "I thought I was being cordial."

"Look, Steed," said Roscoe, "if your little city upon the hill can withstand the scrutiny, then get the hell out of the way and let us do our work."

The grin stayed on Steed's face as he leaned back. "You got quite a mouth."

Steed's deputies, two of the heftiest men I've ever laid eyes on—twins with brown eyes, walrus mustaches, and round, shaven chins—strode up behind him. Both had on black Stetsons and their hands hovered near their guns. Steed sensed their presence on either side of him and gestured with a backward jerk of his head. "These here are the Kunz brothers. Dorland and Devlin. They assist me when troublesome elements rear their ugly head in town."

I laid down my fork, having made a significant dent in my dinner. "I've had enough," I said. "What do you say, Roscoe?"

Roscoe had initiated a staring match with the Kunz brothers, and his right hand dipped below the table, presumably to
reach for his firearm. I knew Roscoe had the spine to challenge
these men to a fight. Whether he'd come out on top was a
different matter, one I didn't care to find out. When I squeezed
Roscoe's arm, it brought him back from the brink.

I fished out my coin pouch, opened it, and stirred its contents: quarters, dimes, nickels, pennies.

"It's on me," said Steed. "Your money's no good here."

"You sure?" I asked.

"Yep."

"Thank you," I said, snapping the pouch shut. "We'll be leaving now."

"A fine idea," said Steed. "You all get a good night's sleep.
Leave bright and early in the morning, before the funeral. You
can go out the way you came in."

Nineteen

Water dripped at irregular intervals on my forehead. Lying flat on my back atop the cold escarpment, I puzzled over it, because there were no clouds in the night sky. Only stars. Yet these big dollops of water would plunge out of the heavens and nail me. Each drop made a sharp sound when it hit.

The dream ended when I opened my eyes. My vision adjusted to darkness. Moonlight filtered into the window through the leaves, and when the wind blew, shadows of branches danced on the floor.

I sat up in bed.

CRACK!

The sound at the window startled me. I threw my legs over the edge of the bed, got up, and walked across the room to the window. Roscoe snored without stirring, making me wonder what it would take to awaken him.

CRACK!

This time, I saw the rock hit the window. My wristwatch said 2:18 A.M.

CRACK!

Open the window, I thought, *before a rock hits too hard*. I lifted the window as high as it'd go and the next stone pelted me in the chest. *Ow!* It hurt. I backed away and rubbed the sore spot. I knelt and picked the rock up off the floor. That would've been the window breaker.

I peered out the window. Between cottonwood leaves I saw a silhouette of a girl or woman standing in the side yard.

"Stay there!" I called out, loud enough for the thrower to hear. "I'm coming down!"

I stumbled in the night, pulled on my shirt and trousers over my temple garments, and sat on the edge of my bed to put on my shoes.

"What's going on?" asked a groggy Roscoe. Lurching upright, he rubbed cinders out of his eyes.

"We've got a visitor."

"At this hour?" Roscoe grunted as he rolled out of bed. "Time is it?"

"Not quite two thirty."

"Where you going?"

"Outside."

"Wait! How do you know it ain't some crazy polygamist come to kill you?"

"A crazy polygamist wouldn't throw rocks at the window," I said. "Besides, I can see it's a woman."

"You think it's her?" he said, clearly referring to the missing girl.

"I'm not sure. It's hard to see. I didn't get a good enough look."

Roscoe's belt buckle clinked as he pushed a leg into his pants, then the other. He pulled his trousers waist high, zipped, and tightened the belt.

"Go back to sleep," I said. "I'll take care of it."

"Somebody's gotta watch out for your scrawny behind," he said, buttoning his shirt.

"All right. C'mon."

Roscoe followed me on the trek through the hall, down the staircase, across the foyer, and out the front door. Out in the warm air, a symphony of crickets performed as we rushed down the porch steps. I spotted the figure, a woman in a long dress, standing beside a tree in the side yard.

"This way," I whispered back to Roscoe. "Watch your step."

Closing in on our late-night caller, I got a better look at her face. It was Talena, the waitress from the Covered Wagon. A strap on her shoulder held a leather bag buckled shut.

"I'm sorry to wake you," she said. "I overheard you earlier tell Steed that you were staying at Mr. Larsen's."

"What can we do for you?" I asked.

"I'm as good as dead if anyone finds out I'm here." Her voice trembled. She glanced in both directions. "That's why I came so late."

"Sounds like you've taken a big risk," I said. "Tell us why."

She crouched, unbuckled her bag, and fished something out. She handed me a snapshot. I struggled to get a better look at it under the faint light of the moon.

"Here."

She pulled a flashlight out of her bag and passed it to me, one of those long and heavy numbers. I switched it on and shined light on the picture. I instantly recognized the boy in the picture as the same boy in the cherished photograph belonging to the mysterious girl staying at my house. I am pretty sure that Talena saw my eyes widen with recognition, or maybe my Adam's apple jump.

"You know him," she said, more a declaration than a question.

"I've never met him."

"But you've seen him."

Roscoe sidled toward me and saw the photo before I shut off her flashlight and returned it, along with the picture, to her.

"Is he alive?" she asked.

"I don't know," I said.

Her eyes widened and her voice grew panicky. "What do you mean you don't know?"

I shushed her. "Try to keep it down. I've only ever seen a picture of him."

"Who else has a picture of him? Nelpha? Is she alive?"

"Hold on, hold on," said Roscoe. "We're getting ahead of ourselves. Why don't you start by telling us the boy's name?"

"I thought you already knew," she said. "His name is Boyd Johnston. He's my brother."

"You two any relation to LeGrand Johnston?" I asked.

"He is—*was*—our father."

"I'm sorry for your loss," I said. I gave her a moment to collect herself. She shook when she inhaled and I feared she'd start crying. I headed her off with a question: "You mentioned somebody named Nelpha?"

"Yes. Nelpha Black, Rulon's youngest wife. That was her picture you showed to Steed at the Covered Wagon."

"I see," I said. "We're looking for Boyd and Nelpha and anyone else who might've gone missing around here. We'd appreciate you telling us what you know."

Talena said, "I was hoping you'd tell me. I haven't seen my brother in a while. I'm scared something bad happened to him. You said you saw a picture of him?"

"Yeah, as a matter of fact—"

"We got a few more questions to ask you first," interrupted Roscoe. "Can you be a little more precise about when it was you last saw your brother?"

"This would have been, oh, late May," she said. "I knew something wasn't right. He quit coming to church. I no longer saw him around town. It wasn't like him, never to come around like that."

"Where do you suppose he went?" I asked.

"They banished him," she said.

"Banished?" Roscoe asked. "What do you mean?"

Her eyes lit up in the darkness, and at first I couldn't tell if she was afraid to answer or relieved someone had the nerve to ask. "It happens around the time the boys reach their teens. They get sent away, forced to go off and fend for themselves."

"All the boys get banished?" asked Roscoe.

"No, only the ones judged impure by the apostles. It's all secret-like. One day a boy is gone, just like that." She snapped her fingers for effect. "That's what happened to my brother. Truth is, all of the boys in town live in fear of being sent away, out into the desert."

"Don't the families of these boys miss them?" I asked.

"Oh goodness, yes," she said. "Whenever a boy disappears, you can hear his mother wailing. It's a terrible noise. Some mothers get real scared and upset and they search all over town for their missing sons. The apostles tell the townspeople to accept it. They say banishments are a part of life and the will of God.

That doesn't make them any easier, especially when it's your son who gets pushed out."

"These boys wouldn't survive a week out in this desert," I said.

"The way I hear it, most make their way up to Salt Lake City. A goodly number of the boys stay with Claudia."

"Who's Claudia?" Roscoe asked.

"She used to be a child bride, till she ran away. I heard she got herself a big house up in Salt Lake City. She takes in the banished boys and child brides who run away."

"I noticed your wedding ring," I said. "Were you a child bride?"

"I got married at age twelve. My last name isn't Johnston anymore. It's Steed. Talena Steed. I'm the wife of Ferron Steed."

"Damn. I don't know what's worse: being married to that goon, or getting married when you're only twelve," said Roscoe. "Both are about equally tragic in my book."

Talena didn't quite know how to respond to Roscoe's comment, but she did her best. "The apostles say the girls are at their purest when they're young. They say a young girl makes old men feel young again. That's how the apostles look at it."

Roscoe noticed my teeth grinding, and maybe the glint of rage in my eyes, even in the darkness. He said, "We've heard some other boys went missing, too."

"Yes. There were three others who disappeared around the same time as Boyd. There was the Christensen boy. Garth Christensen. Frankie—um, Franklin—Boggs. Chester Hammond. Ches, they called him. They were all around the same age—thirteen, fourteen, fifteen. All of 'em went missing in late May and they haven't been seen or heard from again."

"You mean they didn't make it up to Salt Lake City?" asked Roscoe.

"No."

"How do you know?" I asked.

"Couple of the sister wives are still in touch with Claudia," said Talena. "She tells 'em what's what."

"Why those four?" asked Roscoe. "Any idea?"

Talena shook her head. "I don't know. Don't make no sense, exceptin' for Boyd. Rulon found out about Boyd and Nelpha. After that, Boyd up and vanished."

"What exactly was it that Rulon found out?" I asked.

"Nelpha and Boyd were close. Real close. Even after Nelpha married Rulon."

"So Nelpha was a child bride, too?" I asked.

"Yup. She's probably thirteen now. Maybe fourteen. I'm not sure."

I could no longer conceal my sighs of disgust. No point in trying, I figured.

Talena went on: "Nelpha and Rulon were wedded, but that didn't stop Nelpha from sneaking away with Boyd. I recollect seeing the lovebirds out by the creek one day, holding hands. They took risks, spending all this time together. I've heard Rulon is a jealous man. I heard whispers going around that Rulon found out about Boyd and Nelpha. Some say Rulon thought Satan got into my brother, but I can tell you right now that wasn't so. My brother is as good a boy as you'll ever find."

"Do you have any idea why Nelpha made the trip up to Salt Lake City?" I asked.

Talena said, "I don't know Nelpha all that well, but she's first cousins with Eliza. Eliza's my best friend. Eliza says Nelpha took off one night and went all the way up to Salt Lake City to find

Uncle Grand to tell him what happened to Boyd. Boyd being Uncle Grand's son and all."

"Can we talk to this Eliza?" asked Roscoe.

"I don't think it's a good idea," said Talena. "She's in the same boat I am. Child bride. I got a feeling her husband won't take too kindly to you fellas questioning her."

"We'll leave her be," I said. "This Nelpha. What did she look like?"

Talena spent the next couple of minutes describing— to a T—the girl who had stayed at my house. It gave me the chills, hearing her detailed outline of the girl's appearance, and she confirmed that Nelpha was mute. *They have to be the same person*, I thought. *There is no way she could be describing someone else.* I politely excused myself. I hurried inside the house and up to the room where we were staying. I found the picture of the girl and brought it downstairs with me. I closed the screen door gently, crept down the porch steps, and handed the photograph to the girl. She shined her flashlight on it and began to weep. I gently tugged the photo free of her grip.

"She's alive, isn't she?" asked Talena, wiping tears. "Please say it's so."

"Yes, she's alive," I said. "She was staying with my family. But she ran away. I need to find her. She's a witness in a murder investigation, and she needs to be protected."

"What about my brother?" she asked. "Can you find him?"

"We'll try," said Roscoe. "We can't make any promises."

She lifted the bag's strap over her shoulder. "I got to be going. I'll cut out the back. They're watchin' this place."

"Who?" I asked.

"Dorland and Devlin," she said. "They drive a brown car. That's why I jumped the fence in the backyard, so's they wouldn't see me." She paused and the light of the moon illuminated her gentle smile. "You know, Mama always said that if I prayed hard enough, God would send angels down to help us."

She bolted in the direction of the backyard. Her footsteps picked up to a run. Somewhere out there, a rickety wooden fence squealed under her weight. The night took her away as quickly as it had delivered her.

Where we stood, we could not be seen from the street in front of Larsen's house. I walked to a set of neatly trimmed chest-high hedges nearby. The sedan came into view, parked by the curb across the street. I was hunched down far enough and it was sufficiently dark that the two figures in the front seat could not see me. I wondered: *How long have they been there? Why are they watching us?*

"That must be their car," I said. "I wonder if they saw Talena . . ."

I checked over my shoulder but saw no sign of Roscoe. *Where did he . . .* I took off toward the backyard, jogging across the grass, dodging trees, stumbling a couple of times in the darkness. I hiked out to the arroyo behind the Larsen place and put up a thorough search with only the moonlight to guide my way. No sign of Roscoe. I returned to the boardinghouse and spent the next few hours lying awake, tossing and turning, worried sick about my friend.

Twenty

The morning sun blazed in the sky, baking everything around us. I parked the car up the road from the cemetery, under the shade of an Arizona Ash. We were at the top of a hill overlooking the grounds, distant enough to remain unnoticed by all of the mourners streaming in through the gates, yet sufficiently close to command a good view through the black iron railings surrounding the sea of dry grass and tombstones. A thick layer of perspiration covered both of us, and I was starting to imagine the sun brushing up against the earth at any moment.

My eyes burned from lack of sleep. It had been a long night. Talena Steed dropping by out of the blue coupled with Roscoe wandering off into the night and not telling me where he was going fueled my insomnia. When he finally crept back into the room, around quarter past seven, I was splashing water on my face over the basin. I asked him where he'd been. He muttered something containing the word "pussy," and I had no intention of asking him to repeat it.

His decision to light out in the middle of the night created a quiet tension between us. I picked up my canteen off the floor of the car, unscrewed the top, and gulped water out of it. Even though the warm water tasted metallic, I didn't care. It still came as a relief in that heat. I tilted the canteen toward Roscoe.

"No, thank you," he said, patting the flask-shaped bulge in his unbuttoned jacket. "Got my own."

I capped the canteen and placed it on the floor beside my feet. Then I raised my binoculars, which brought me closer to the action. A maroon hearse led the way through the main entrance, followed by a line of chugging automobiles, dusty and slow moving. Men, women, and children, most attired in black, filed into the cemetery on a sidewalk through an opening that passed under an arched doorway built of stone, surrounded by iron bars on either side. I heard the passenger-side car door open and close, and I lowered my binoculars see Roscoe walking toward the cemetery. Slightly panicky, I flung my door open, nearly falling out onto the pavement in my rush to get out.

"Where are you going?" I asked, closing the door, hurrying to catch up.

"To pay my last respects," said Roscoe, tugging his fedora low to shadow his face.

"Are you crazy?" I asked. "They'll see you."

"I don't care. They know we're in town. I'm sick of this hiding-out horseshit."

Roscoe was walking at such a fast pace that I had to jog a little to keep up with him. "Come back to the car," I said. "That's an order!"

He stopped and faced me. "With these people, you gotta make noise. Rattle the cages. Let them know you mean business, that you're not giving up until you find out who put their prophet in the cemetery. You coming? Or you wanna go back to the car and fiddle around with your spyglasses some more?"

He resumed his walk, and so did I.

I said, "Something tells me I'm going to regret this."

"Only one way to find out."

We continued down the dirt road until we reached the cemetery gates at the bottom of the hill. We entered under that arched stone opening. My stomach was in a state of free fall, but it calmed down after we found a shaded spot near a big oak tree, a comfortable distance from the ceremony. We were eventually spotted, and I spied a few pointing fingers and leaning whispers. It was there that we stood and listened to endless speeches about what a great human being LeGrand Johnston was, along with solemn hymns sung by the entire crowd during the in-between breaks. I recognized all of the apostles who we'd arrested days ago. They sat side by side on a line of folding wooden chairs under a white tent on steel poles at the front of the crowd. I did not see Rulon Black among them, but he might have been somewhere else in the crowd. Only two of them refrained from giving us the evil eye: Alma Covington, who had the makings of a coy grin the entire time, and Carl Jeppson, who kept fidgeting and avoiding glances in our direction. Eldon Black could not take his eyes off us throughout the entire ceremony.

Back at Larsen's boardinghouse after the funeral, we had visitors waiting on the porch.

Two bodyguards in suits and hats, one swarthy and clean-shaven, the other with thick eyebrows and a long brown beard plunging to the middle of his chest, flanked Eldon Black, who wore a three-piece outfit the color of his last name and a somber black tie to match. When he walked toward me, his bony knees poked out the fabric of his pants and his arms swayed like those of a loose scarecrow flailing on a windy day. His enormous jaw formed a smile of recognition and his eyes glowed with the intensity of a man convinced he sat at the right side of Heavenly Father.

"We meet again, Detective Oveson," he said. "How good of you to come to the funeral."

We shook hands.

"Mr. Black," I said. "What can I do for you?"

He eyed Roscoe. "You must be Detective Lund."

"No, I'm Dick Powell, traveling incognito," said Roscoe. "Want me to serenade you with 'Shadow Waltz'?"

The lean man's wince conveyed disgust.

"My father is indisposed right now," he said. "He has appointed me his messenger, and he has a business proposition for you."

"And what might that be?" I asked.

"I would prefer to talk at our family compound," said Eldon. "In private."

"Where is your compound?"

"A short airplane ride from here."

I swallowed hard and suddenly developed a severe case of cottonmouth. "Airplane?"

"It's a Waco cabin biplane," said the bearded bodyguard. "It's safe. I've flown her a hundred times."

"She has four seats," said the swarthy one. "The big guy will have to stay."

"Fuck you," said Roscoe. "You stay."

The swarthy tough advanced toward Roscoe, but Eldon raised a toll-bridge arm to stop him and offered a diplomatic smile. "We'd prefer Mr. Lund stay here."

"He's my partner," I said. "Where I go, he goes."

The placid expression on Eldon's face did not change. "Very well. Duke will stay. In exchange, I ask that you two consent to be blindfolded."

"Blindfolded?" asked Roscoe in disbelief.

"It's a deal," I said.

Roscoe leaned in close. "You crazy? You gonna let this asshole blindfold you?"

I gripped his elbow and pulled him under a cottonwood tree, out of earshot of Eldon. "It's a small price to pay."

"You'll have to remind me of that while we're falling to earth after these crazy fuckers have shoved us out of the plane," Roscoe hissed.

"I don't like it any more than you," I said. "Don't even get me started on how much I hate flying. But Eldon Black isn't going to try knocking off a couple of Salt Lake police detectives. It's too risky, and he knows it."

"All right. I'll do this for you. I wouldn't do it for anyone else, though."

I was hoping to encounter more resistance from Roscoe, because once he stopped, I knew what came next, and I dreaded it.

This airplane bounced more than the last one I'd flown on, which was turbulent as all get-out. Unlike the last plane, this had no armrests—too cramped a cabin—so I spent the entire time squeezing my knees. The flight's only redeeming quality was its brevity. We were up in the sky for a half hour. Odd how much slower thirty minutes passes in a flying tin can than it does when you want a little extra shut-eye on a Monday morning.

Our hosts tied a mean blindfold. Not a ray of light got in, adding to my sense of vulnerability. Our landing caught me off guard. I felt the airplane slowing to a halt, followed by the sound of a door opening and a warm wall of air rushing in. Hands pulled me out of the craft, and once on terra firma, I felt a sense of relief. I also found that my inability to see anything heightened my other senses. I could, for example, feel dirt under my shoes as we crossed the runway. I heard the soft whispers of women and children, but I couldn't tell what they were saying.

We entered darkness. The sun no longer throbbed down on us. A heavy door closed. The air turned chilly and our footsteps echoed. Hands stopped me, like a brake. Men spoke to one another in hushed tones, a little above a whisper, yet in words indecipherable. We resumed walking, turning several times before reaching our destination. The blindfolds got peeled off. We stood inside of a gated elevator. We shared the narrow car with Eldon and the bearded bodyguard. Behind us, the gate rattled shut, humming started, and mild nausea hit me when the elevator began going down. It halted and the bodyguard maneuvered to let us out.

We entered a long, mausoleum-like room, all marble except for the carpeting on the floor. Art deco light fixtures on the ceiling bathed the room in a golden light. Eldon Black led us to a wide desk unlike any I'd seen, consisting of marble columns holding up a glass surface, lit by a mysterious source. He gestured to a pair of marble benches in front of the desk. Roscoe and I sat on one while Eldon circled the table and sat down on a high-backed chair on wheels. His bodyguard loomed behind him. My eyes moved up to a puzzling sight. For reasons I did not understand, directly above the desk were four big, black theatrical spotlights mounted to the ceiling. They were shut off. They made me wonder if this place had once been a theater where plays were performed. When the talking started, I quickly forgot about them.

"Thank you for coming all the way out here, Detective Oveson," Eldon said. He glanced over his shoulder at the bearded bodyguard behind him. "The bag, please."

"Yes, sir." The man moved aside his Rip van Winkle beard to pull a set of keys out of his pocket. He unlocked and opened a sliding steel door in the corner of the room and went inside. He was gone a minute or so. He returned with a leather bag, which he placed on the table near Eldon. Eldon unzipped the bag and lifted out a stack of bills, one of many in there, bound by a currency strap. He flung it across the table and it skidded to the edge, teetering briefly before dropping. I leaned forward and scooped it off the floor. When I straightened, I bent the stack and ran my thumb over the edge. There must've been a thousand dollars in my hands. I placed it on the edge of the table and slid it back. It smacked into the case that'd been its home.

"There are ninety-nine more of those in the bag," said Eldon. "It's all yours if you bring the girl back here alive."

"What girl?" I asked.

"I believe you know who I'm talking about," said Eldon.

I propped my right ankle on my left knee, making myself as comfortable as possible on that hard, cold surface. "I'd like to make sure we have the same girl in mind."

"What girl do *you* think I'm referring to?"

"You tell me," I said. "Then I'll let you know if we're talking about the same girl."

"Don't you know her name?" he asked.

"You're the one who brought her up," I said. "We can do this all day if you want."

"Nelpha Black," he said. "What do you say to my proposal?"

"You're offering money in exchange for her?"

"A hundred thousand dollars," he said, leaning back in his chair, knitting his fingers together, as if in prayer.

Roscoe chimed in: "A hundred grand buys a lotta clean skivvies where I come from. This Nelpha must mean something to you people."

"She's Father's youngest wife," said Eldon. "Father is protective of her."

"Your old man's got what? Twenty, thirty wives?" asked Roscoe. "What difference is one wife more or less gonna make? The prick already has a harem the size of Cleveland, while a handsome gent like me is doing well to get a date with Rosy Palm."

Eldon glared at Roscoe, then looked at me. "Is he always like this?"

"Only when he's in a good mood," I said. "What he's trying to say, in his own crude way, is that we don't think you're leveling with us about why you want to see Nelpha Black returned."

"Hours before he was slain, the prophet told his apostles he was planning to meet with her that night. Maybe she witnessed something that would shed light on why this tragedy occurred. We believe in blood atonement, Detective Oveson, and we intend to carry it out against the fiend responsible for murdering Uncle Grand. Since the police aren't able to do their job . . ."

"Ouch," said Roscoe. "Now you've gone and hurt my feelings."

"Some cooperation would help," I said. "So far we've come up against a wall of silence from your camp. I wonder who's spooking your people into clamming up."

"Members of our church exercise free will, Detective," said Eldon. "We've nothing to hide from the police."

"In that case, you won't mind me asking a few questions," I said.

"Go ahead."

"Let's start with Nelpha Black," I said. "Why'd she leave here and go to Salt Lake City?"

"I don't know. I'll ask her that very question when she returns."

"Do you want to know my theory?" I asked.

"If you have one percolating in that policeman's brain of yours, yes, by all means."

"I think she went there looking for someone. Boyd Johnston, maybe?"

Again, I detected no change of expression. He was icy, this one. "What do you know about him, Detective Oveson?"

"What I need to know."

"Which is?"

"Enough."

He dropped his hands in his lap. "So that's your theory? She went to Salt Lake City to find Boyd Johnston?"

"It's one theory."

"What's another?"

"She went to Salt Lake City to relay a message to Uncle Grand about Boyd's disappearance. And maybe—*just maybe*—she mentioned something about the other boys who went missing. It's possible the news upset the prophet, but my guess is he already knew it, along with all of the other shady things that happen down here."

"Oh? What sorts of things?"

"You know, the usual," said Roscoe. "Girls being forced to marry at age twelve. Adolescent boys banished from the community. Throw in some unscrupulous business dealings, and it stinks like a fish market in Death Valley."

"I won't dignify these absurd charges with a response." Eldon patted the leather bag. "My offer still stands."

"Do you honestly think," I said, "that we'd trade her for money?"

Eldon stared coldly at me. "Everybody has a price."

"I don't," I said. I gestured to Roscoe. "Neither does he."

"Oh yes, you do," said Eldon. "You just don't know it. A price comes in many forms. It can be a bribe. But it can also mean something unpleasant happening to you, or someone you love, if you decide not to cooperate."

"Sounds like a threat," I told him.

"It's not," he said. "I'm merely trying to define 'price.' As a Mormon, you ought to know what the word means."

"Sure I do," I said. "Trading Nelpha for a hundred thousand dollars is a price I'm not willing to pay."

"So be it. You'll be flown back to Dixie City. Blindfolded, of course."

Ten minutes later, I was back aboard that little airplane with Roscoe, lifting off into the sky, unable to see anything and silently praying for a safe flight.

Twenty-one

Leaving Dixie City after settling up our bill with Oscar Larsen, I experienced a wave of relief, eager to get home to my family. We drove north on an uphill grade, and I was glad to see Dixie City and the mesa that overlooked it getting smaller in my rear-view mirror. The sun made me squint while I drove, and I did not even bother turning on the radio, because it wouldn't pick up anything. The highway hugged a rising slope, and to our right the ground dropped precipitously into a ravine. Roscoe and I didn't say a word while I drove, both too exhausted to speak. We rounded a corner so that Dixie City was out of sight, and that's when we came upon a pair of dark blue Model A's with gold stars painted on the doors. I knew them to be law enforce-ment autos. They were parked on a gravel shoulder at the edge of the cliff near an area where the guardrail had been torn apart. Roscoe and I exchanged a quick look, and he motioned for me to pull over. As I steered onto the gravel, three familiar-looking men came into view, standing near the spot where the green-painted wooden barrier had been reduced to smashed splinters.

I shut off the car, and the two of us got out and walked toward the men, our shoe soles crunching gravel. The Kunz brothers watched us with their fiercest glares, and Ferron Steed remained motionless, blank eyed and openmouthed, as if drugged or in a trance. I peered over the edge. Two hundred feet or so below us, the remains of a crumpled car were smoldering in the shadows of the cliff. Roscoe and I set off in search of a way down. About ten yards to the south, we found a sloping embankment that led to a trail snaking to the bottom of the steep face. Roscoe and I hiked down a narrow path to the base of the cliff, sliding on the pebble-covered ground, and at one point, I nearly went over the edge. Roscoe grabbed my arm and helped me avoid that unfortunate fate. We ventured on, watching every step, until we reached level earth and walked another thirty yards or so to the wreckage of what had once been a green Plymouth, I guessed a '28 or '29 model. It was on its side, the engine hissing steam and dark smoke, and every inch of it was broken and smashed and twisted. Through the shattered windshield glass I saw the lacerated face of Talena Steed, as lifeless as could be.

"Stay back," Roscoe said. He gestured to a puddle of gas on the ground near one of the tires, widening as it drained out of the tank.

I overheard the Kunz brothers giving Steed directions to the bottom of the hill and telling him to watch his step. I turned toward them and watched as they reached the bottom of the path and approached the car. Steed, who'd been strangely catatonic when we got here, deliberately slammed his shoulder into me as he walked by, and I could finally see a hint of bitterness in his previously blank expression.

"Can't you see that's my wife in there?" he mumbled.

One of the Kunz brothers—I couldn't tell them apart, so I wasn't sure which one—came right up to me so his face was a few inches from mine, and his features quivered with rage. "You don't belong here," he said menacingly. "This is the scene of an accident. We'll attend to it. Go back to Salt Lake City. Leave us be."

"This isn't an accident," I said.

He moved closer to me, nose to nose, so I could see the pores on his face and a crumb in his moustache bristles. "Maybe *you* killed her by coming down here, sticking your nose where it don't belong, stirring up trouble. Poor gal might still be alive if it weren't for you."

My heart thumped hard in my chest, and a rage like I'd never experienced before bubbled up in me. I eased away from him and took a breath, fooling him into thinking I was surrendering. He never saw that punch coming. A flash of pain shot down my knuckles when they connected with his chin, sending him tumbling backward into the dirt.

"Come on, you bastard!" I shouted. "You want to take on somebody, you take on me!"

He moved in a flash, and his haymaker to my chin made me see stars. Now I was the one on the ground, my face numb with shock. He took out his revolver and aimed at me and I swear I saw his trigger finger wiggle, but the sound of a clicking gun hammer stopped him. Roscoe came over with his .38 pressed at Kunz's head, and he was as cool as a mountain stream in November. One more revolver hammer got pulled back, and the other Kunz now had his gun pointed at Roscoe in a grim deadlock.

"Looks like we're all fucked," said Roscoe. "Unless, of course, cool heads prevail. I say we all lower our pieces, and my friend and I will clear on outta here."

All three men lowered their guns at the same time. I managed to stand up on my feet and I dusted myself off. I shook my sore hand, and the weight of the Kunz brothers' fury-filled stares proved almost more than I could bear. Steed was still strangely emotionless, as if not entirely present, like his wife's death meant nothing to him. We hiked back up to the road, with Roscoe coming up behind me, keeping a vigilant eye on the marshal and his deputies below. Back in the car, Roscoe reached over and gently patted my knee.

"Let's go home," he said.

After stopping to fill my tank in St. George I motored across a succession of dry valleys, with the late afternoon turning to evening, and the shadows of hills growing taller by the minute. For part of the drive, Roscoe slept with his hat pulled down over his face and his head dipping so his chin touched his chest. Sometimes his snoring was louder than the car's engine. Twilight brought a welcome drop in the temperature, and a cool breeze blew through the open window, ruffling my hair. I regarded it as a gift after enduring the heat of Dixie City. Somewhere in central Utah, Roscoe sat up straight, tilted his hat back, and looked out at the scenery—what there was of it—shaded by a darkening sky still splashed with hues of orange, purple, and indigo. He wiped drool off his mouth with his sleeve and he let out a sigh.

"You've got a hell of a right hook," said Roscoe. "Remind me not to ever get on your bad side."

That made me laugh. "I'm tougher than I thought."

"That you are," he said. He was quiet in a reflective way. "What you did back there was crazy as hell. But it took guts. You did what you had to do. I'm proud of you."

"Thanks." Driving at a decent clip, hands gripping the wheel, I still felt sick to my stomach at the thought of what we'd been through. "If it weren't for me, she'd still be alive. I should've listened to Buddy."

"That's horseshit," he said, packing a wad of Red Man into his mouth. "Where'd you come up with that damn fool idea?"

"That wasn't an accident," I said. "The Kunz brothers saw her talking to us last night. I'm sure of it."

"It ain't your fault that they're a couple of cold-blooded killers," said Roscoe. "Them two got ice water running through their veins. Their old man was a crackpot polygamist, living way out in the middle of nowhere. He used to beat the hell out of his boys while reading scripture to 'em. No wonder they murdered a Navajo kid named Jimmy Nakai when they were only fourteen. Of course, the sheriff of San Juan County was too lily-livered to bust 'em for—"

"Hold on a second, is all that true?" I asked, struggling to keep my eyes on the road and not on Roscoe.

"Yeah. Sure it is."

"How do you know so much about the Kunz brothers?"

"That walk I went for in the night," he said. "I went and jimmied the lock at the marshal's office and looked through his files."

The news astonished me. "You didn't."

"I did."

"How could you?"

"It was easy. That's a flimsy lock Steed's got on the back door. . . ."

"No, I mean that's a huge risk you took," I said.

"After throttling Kunz at that crash scene earlier, I'd say you don't have a leg to stand on lecturing me about risk taking."

"All right, you got me," I said. "So what happened?"

"I was in there about an hour and a half. I've got a feeling I only saw the tip of the iceberg. That prick Steed is either running a blackmail racket out of his office or somebody's using him to dig up information on others. He's got files on nearly every single one of the big-shot patriarchs, and a whole lot of other folks in that town."

"What's in these files?"

"Dirt," said Roscoe. "Surveillance photos, reports on the apostles' movements, private letters that I'm guessing were stolen. A lot of what's in those dossiers confirms our worst suspicions—you know, all of the accusations about underage marriages, crooked land deals, and those poor boys who got kicked out, left to fend for themselves. Hell, half of these sorry old prunes are diddling each other's wives, as if they're not getting laid enough by their own small armies of señoritas at home. The only man Steed didn't have a file on was Rulon Black. It makes me wonder if Steed is Rulon's goon."

"When were you going to tell me all of this?" I asked.

He sideways-glanced at me. "I'm telling you now."

"Did he keep a file on LeGrand Johnston?"

"Yeah, but nothing on who might've killed him," he said. "Steed is thorough. I'll give him that much. From what I saw, he keeps copies of everything, including carbons of his own letters."

I nodded. "Did you happen to run into any information on the four missing boys?"

"Can't say I did," said Roscoe. "I did find one gem. Steed kept a file on Nelpha."

"You're kidding!"

"Nope. I figured you'd wanna see it, since she's staying with you. So I took the liberty of lifting it."

"Are you serious? You stole the file?"

He looked over at me. "You'll thank me."

I pulled up to Roscoe's apartment around ten o'clock at night. We said our good-byes, and he got out of the car, closed the door, and started to walk away. "Hey, Roscoe," I called out. He stopped about halfway to the door, turned around, and came back to my idling Oldsmobile, lifting his foot onto the running board and resting his elbow on the car door, where the window was rolled all the way down.

"Listen," I said. "I don't know how to thank you for all your help. Sometimes I think if it weren't for you . . ."

"Art?"

"Yeah?"

"Don't mention it." He winked and patted the car door twice. "See you Monday."

Minutes later, I steered into the driveway of my house in the high Avenues, killed the engine, and collected my suitcase and the file on Nelpha Black. The lights were on in the house, so I checked my appearance in the car's exterior rearview mirror and concluded that I looked terrible and it would take too much work to make me halfway presentable. I drew a deep breath and headed up the walkway. Opening the front door triggered a stir in the house, with Sarah Jane, Hyrum, and Clara coming to welcome me. The kids were in their pajamas, and everybody greeted me with hugs and overlapping greetings.

"She's back, Dad!" said Sarah Jane. "She's here!"

"Who?"

"The girl! She came back!"

I reared my head in surprise. "Nelpha's back?"

Now Clara looked confused. "Nelpha? Is that her name?"

"Yeah, Nelpha Black," I said. "It's a long story. Where is she?"

"C'mere, Dad!" said Hyrum. "We'll show you."

My children each took an arm and towed me down the hallway, toward Sarah Jane's room. Sarah Jane reached for the knob and opened the door as quietly as possible, and a soft light from the hallway bathed Nelpha as she slept soundly on Sarah Jane's bed. A blanket and sheet covered most of her, although her hair spilled out on the pillow. On the floor, near the foot of the bed, sat her soiled pillowcase.

Where did she go? I wondered.

I wanted to examine the contents of Steed's file on Nelpha, but my children reminded me it was Saturday night—and in the middle of summer, no less—so it wasn't too late for some family time. It didn't take much coaxing for me to join them in the living room. The more time we spent together, laughing, playing games, listening to the radio, the less I thought about that file and the troubling death of Talena Steed.

As Clara and I lay in bed, she told me about arriving home from the grocery store with the kids that morning to find Nelpha inside the house, coming up the basement stairs. Clara wondered how long Nelpha had been down there, but she was so happy to have her back, she chose not to dwell on it. I told Clara about the episode several days ago when I had found our mystery girl emerging from the basement. I wondered aloud if there was any connection. Clara shrugged it off, chalked it up to curiosity on the girl's part. But I thought about it. A lot.

Hours later, lying in the darkness of our bedroom, listening to Clara breathing in her sleep, I wondered: Where had Nelpha gone? It seemed unlikely she could have hidden in the basement that entire time. Did she actually leave the house? If so, was she with somebody? Why did she come back? I recalled something

Roscoe had said before we left for Dixie City, a comment to the effect that I knew nothing about Nelpha. He was right. At that point, I hadn't even known her name. I had no reason to trust her. She could have been capable of murder, for all I knew.

I got up in the night and crept into the living room. I switched on a lamp and sat down at my desk with my new acquisition, the file on Nelpha Black from Steed's office. DIXIE CITY POLICE REPORT, said a top sheet, with a snapshot of Nelpha Black stapled to it. I went straight to her stats:

LAST NAME: BLACK
FIRST NAME: NELPHA
MIDDLE NAME: MARY
DATE OF BIRTH: FEBRUARY 6, 1921
PLACE OF BIRTH: RUBY CREEK, UTAH
PARENTS: MR. AND MRS. ALMA COVINGTON

It surprised me to read that Alma Covington, the quirky apostle in the Fundamentalist Church of Saints who edited the newspaper called *Truth* out of his basement on Third Avenue, was her father. He was one of the few arrestees earlier in the week who had made half an effort to be friendly to me. I remembered showing him the photograph of Nelpha during the interrogation at Public Safety and asking him if he knew her. "I'm afraid not," he said. *Was he the one she visited while she was gone?* I wondered. I quickly ruled out that possibility when I remembered that he was in Dixie City for LeGrand Johnston's funeral.

I read on.

STATUS: MARRIED, JUNE 15, 1933
SPOUSE: BLACK, RULON T.

CURRENT PLACE OF RESIDENCE: R. BLACK COMPOUND, NEAR DIXIE CITY

The line about her marital status literally made me nauseous. *Only thirteen years old*, I thought. *How could they?* This was why I found these men so repulsive. In my eyes, marrying multiple women was a troubling offense; wedding little girls, however, was beyond the pale. That seemed to me to be completely unacceptable, with no room for compromise, and no shades of gray. I had to put my fury aside in order to concentrate on reading. My eyes dropped to the summary of her disappearance, right below her stats.

COMPLAINANT: BLACK, RULON T.
DETAIL OF EVENT: Rulon Black visited the station at 14:45 on Thursday, May 10, 1934, to report that his youngest wife, Nelpha, went missing two days previous, on May 8. The subject was last seen at Mr. Black's compound by two of his wives and one of his daughters sometime around half past seven on the morning of May 8. Eyewitnesses reported that the subject was running in haste. Rulon Black's daughter Braylea, the last person to see Nelpha Black, watched her enter a barn where there is a tunnel that lets out near Big Water Creek. Deputies D & D Kunz investigated the opening of the tunnel at the creek and found footprints in the sand, but no sign of the subject. Subject remains at large and is believed to be traveling in the direction of Salt Lake City, where she has kin. Rulon Black stresses that it is urgent that we find her, as he is protective of the girl and wishes to see her returned

alive. Signed, *FERRON W. STEED, Marshal, Dixie City, Arizona.*

I thumbed through the rest of the police file to see if I could get any sense of this girl or why she was here in Salt Lake City. I worked my way through pages of typed reports and anonymous tips, each contributing a new layer to an increasingly complicated portrait of Nelpha as a troubled girl. If you believed the folder's contents, Nelpha at age seven beat up three bullies who tormented her for being a mute, at age nine stole a revolver belonging to her father and shot a bullet into somebody's window, and at age eleven set a barn on fire that belonged to a polygamist patriarch and watched it burn to the ground. As I worked my way through the pages, I kept running into certain words repeatedly: "willful," "spiteful," "rebellious," "defiant," "disobedient."

I came across a photograph taken from a distance of Nelpha with Boyd Johnston. They were standing side by side on the banks of a creek, holding hands, smiling at each other. I puzzled over who might've taken the photograph and why. Was it one of Rulon's goons? Marshal Steed or the Kunz brothers? I guessed it to be a surveillance photograph, though I didn't know for certain. I checked the back for a date or some other handwritten hint that might help me understand it. Nothing.

Flipping pages, I found a police incident document toward the bottom of the folder that caught my attention. It bore the date Monday, May 14, 1934. My eyes dropped to the body of the report: "Sheriff Steed has ruled out Missus Black's involvement in the rash of thefts that commenced last month and have spread at an alarming rate to the compounds of virtually all of our beloved apostles. The incidents began in late April and have continued as recently as the date of suspect's disappearance. Sheriff Steed interviewed Rulon Black at length this morning and Black stated in the strongest of terms that Nelpha played no part in the bold acts of larceny that have shaken our town."

I picked up my pencil and jotted the word "larceny" on my pad of paper. I drew an arrow, and on the other side of the point I wrote "Nelpha," followed by a question mark. I wondered: What was stolen? Money? Precious heirlooms? Maybe the perpetrators took items that could easily be resold at a pawnshop, like phonographs or firearms or musical instruments. Or it could've been all of the above. If Nelpha was involved in the thefts, how could she single-handedly move the stolen goods to Salt Lake City? How was I going to get any answers to these questions when Nelpha couldn't say a word?

Twenty-two

"It may surprise you to know that I have no intention of raising my voice today," announced Buddy Hawkins, almost joyfully.

Those words ended nearly five minutes of silence, the longest five minutes of my life. It was Monday morning, a little past nine. I'd spent the previous day—Sunday—in church and afterward, at dinner with my family, fearful that this moment might come. Sure enough, Roscoe and I occupied a pair of side-by-side chairs in Buddy's office, the same place I had sat last Thursday when he told me not to go to Dixie City. Outside, a dry thunderstorm unleashed flashing lightning and coughed up thunder that shook the glass panes. Unfortunately, there was no rain to go with it, a common occurrence in Utah, but one that only exacerbated the dangerous forest fire epidemic across the state. Even without the precipitation, it seemed appropriate weather for the tongue thrashing we were about to receive.

"You see, shouting doesn't do any good," he said, rolling his chair closer to his desk, where he propped up his elbows. "Remember our meeting on Thursday, Art?"

"Yes."

"Would you say that I raised my voice at that meeting?"

I made a long face and nodded slowly. "A few times."

"Do you recall what we discussed that day?"

"I wanted to go to Dixie City."

"What did I tell you at that meeting?"

"You told me I oughtn't to—"

"No, I never used the word 'oughtn't,' " he interrupted calmly. "I *ordered you* not to go Dixie City. Would you say that's a fair characterization of my position last Thursday?"

I nodded. "Yeah."

"After our meeting, what did you do?" asked Buddy.

"I went home and I . . ."

"Jump ahead," said Buddy. "To the next day. Friday. What did you do on Friday?"

"I drove down to Dixie City."

"With or without Roscoe?" asked Buddy.

"With," I said.

"Despite what?" asked Buddy.

"Despite you advising me . . ."

"Despite me *ordering* you . . ."

"Despite you *ordering* me not to go."

Roscoe said, "Buddy, there's something you should know—"

Buddy gaped at Roscoe and cut him off: "Roscoe?"

"Yeah?"

"There was a movie in the theaters about six or seven years ago called *The Jazz Singer.* Remember? Al Jolson. Blackface. 'Mammy.' Ring any bells?"

"Sure," said Roscoe. "Who didn't see it? It was the first talkie ever made."

"Precisely. Before that, what were all other movies?"

"Silent," said Roscoe.

"Right!" said Buddy. "Now, unless you want to be selling apples on a street corner to make ends meet after you leave here, you'd better be exactly like all of those movies made before *The Jazz Singer.*" He leaned over his desk and hissed, "Silent."

Buddy resumed his soft-spoken interrogation of me. "I don't suppose you were planning to inform me of this excursion of yours?"

I shook my head. "No."

"I didn't think so. You must be wondering how I found out about it."

"The thought did cross my mind."

"This morning, Chief Cowley received a telephone call from Granville Sondrup, representing his client, Deputy Dorland Kunz of Dixie City. Sondrup informed the chief that you two gentlemen arrived in Dixie City on the weekend of LeGrand Johnston's funeral, and you committed a number of grievous offenses, including disrupting his funeral—"

I protested: "We didn't disrupt—"

"Uh, uh, uh. Let me finish, Art."

"Yes, sir."

"He said the two of you disrupted Johnston's funeral, broke into his office in the middle of the night, and that you, Art, assaulted one of his deputies at the scene of a tragic auto accident involving the marshal's wife." He studied me for a long second. "Sondrup is vowing to go to the press with these disturbing allegations. Is there any truth to them?"

"Not the first two," I said, lying to cover for Roscoe.

"And the third?" asked Buddy.

I hesitated. "You really should hear my side of the story, Buddy."

"You assaulted a deputy?" asked Buddy, betraying no emotion.

"Roscoe and I were leaving Dixie City to come home . . ."

"Answer the question," said Buddy. "Did you assault a deputy?"

"Yes."

"What *exactly* did you do to him?"

"I punched him in the face."

"What on earth ever possessed you to . . ." Before finishing his sentence, Buddy held up his index finger. "No, wait. I don't want to know. You're both suspended, for an entire week, without pay. During that time, you are not to conduct police business of any sort. If you violate the terms of your suspension, you will be fired. Once your suspension is up, you will be allowed to return to work on Monday, July sixteenth. There will likely be a disciplinary inquiry into this matter at a future date. Furthermore, a follow-up suspension, demotion, or job dismissal may occur if your superiors decide to pursue one of those courses of action in light of the outcome of the inquiry."

He gave us a brief pause to let this news sink in.

"And I never had to raise my voice once," he finally said. "Dismissed."

Roscoe and I left Buddy's office without saying a word. It was the first time I've ever seen Roscoe too dismayed to speak. His bravado must have flown south. We put on our hats in the corridor on our way to the exit. I asked Roscoe if he needed a ride home. He shook his head. On the way down the steps in the rear of the Public Safety Building, I heard a familiar voice calling my name. I stopped my downward trot and turned to see Jared Weeks at the top of the stairs, waving at me. I headed up until I reached him.

"Thought I saw you," he said cheerfully. "You comin' up?"

"I can't. I'm suspended."

The smile slipped away from his face. "Suspended?"

"Until next Monday."

"I'm sorry."

"Don't worry. It's not the end of the world."

I moved aside to let a crowd of uniformed officers, fresh out of morning roll call, pass us on their way to the parking lot. I waited until the last man was out of the building and then I smiled reassuringly at Jared. "You're in charge of the squad while I'm gone."

"Sure thing. Does this have anything to do with your trip?"

"Yeah, but I'd rather not go into it," I said. "Any word from Myron?"

"Not yet," Jared said. "On Friday afternoon, I ran that check on brown Hudsons and black Model T trucks over at the state revenue office."

"And?"

"Until two years ago, a brown Hudson, nineteen and thirty model, was registered to Dorland Kunz," said Jared. "Registration lapsed after he moved to Arizona. As for the Model T truck, there are three hundred and twenty-seven of them registered in Salt Lake County, but none of the owners' names matched up with any polygamists. I even ran a cross-check on the maiden names of wives. Came up empty-handed."

I nodded. "Good work. What about that other matter? You know. The woman whose house we paid a visit to last week?"

He averted his eyes and tightened his mouth. "Yeah. I almost forgot."

"Well, you've got a slight reprieve," I said. "If you don't come clean by Monday, things are going to get unpleasant. And that's not the way I prefer to conduct my affairs."

"Yes, sir."

"I'll be at home," I said. "You've got my telephone number."

"Enjoy your time off, boss," said Jared. "Maybe you'll get some long overdue rest and relaxation."

I winked at him. "Maybe."

Jared and I parted ways. I hurried down the stairs, but found no sign of Roscoe when I reached the bottom. Knowing Roscoe, he'd probably gone off to some hole-in-the-wall where he could get drunk.

It was still overcast outside, but the rain never came, and wildfires still spewed dark columns into the slate-gray sky. I got in my Oldsmobile, still dusty from my trip to northern Arizona, and started her up. I drove over to Main Street to visit Keeley's Ice Cream Company, a bright establishment and a favorite destination of kids who were somehow able to scrape together enough coins in these hard times for a scoop of their favorite flavor. This time of morning, most of the tables and booths were vacant, but they'd soon be packed with rambunctious youngsters and a few intrepid adults. Inside, I picked up a couple of quarts of ice cream.

I carried the frigid containers out into the heat and climbed into my car. I started it back up and let her idle a moment while I waited for the traffic on Main to subside. As soon as the flow in both directions thinned out and a streetcar clanged past, I accelerated into a U-turn and then abruptly turned east at 200 South, the route that would get me home the fastest. The drive took me past Carl Jeppson's floral store, and I glanced in that direction as I drove by. Those solemn wives of his in their pioneer dresses were busily unloading crates of potted flowers out of a delivery truck with the name of Jeppson's business, SUNSHINE FLORAL, arched over the painting of a sun shining down on a bouquet of flowers. I drove on toward my house. About two blocks later, it suddenly hit me: Jeppson's delivery truck was a Model T. I couldn't be sure it was the same Model T truck I had seen in the driveway of the fundamentalist church on the night that LeGrand Johnston and Volney Mason were murdered, but I was more concerned about what Jared had just barely told me back at Public Safety: *"As for the Model T truck, there are three hundred and twenty-seven of them registered in Salt Lake County, but none of the owners' names matched up with any polygamists."* How had he missed this one?

I drove back to Sunshine Floral and confirmed that the truck out front was, indeed, a Model T. I puzzled over it and came up with three possibilities: one, Jared had been careless with the records; two, the truck was not registered under Carl Jeppson's name; or three, the most troubling scenario, Jared had lied to me. But why would Jared cover for Jeppson? What was to be gained from it? Was that truck in front of the flower shop the same one I saw the night of the murders? One way or the other, Jared had suddenly aroused my suspicions in a big way. There was a chance he'd lied to me outright. I aimed to find out if this was so.

I raced home to an empty house, not stopping to wonder where Clara and Nelpha and the kids had gone, and deposited the two quarts of ice cream in the icebox. Then I hurried back out to my car—idling the entire time—and sped down L Street, a road that could match any in San Francisco for steepness, to South Temple. I made record timing getting to Public Safety, steering into the parking lot and making my way over to the farthest possible corner, where I backed into a spot, shut off my car, and waited, hoping for a breeze.

Jared usually took a lunch hour, right at noon sharp. At 11:59, men came spilling out the back doors of Public Safety. One of them was Jared Weeks. I started my car and continued to watch him. He got inside of an unmarked Model A prowler, started it up, and drove toward the lot's exit. I stayed behind him a safe distance. His first stop was Sunshine Floral, where he parked at the curb and ducked inside. By this time, the Model T delivery truck was nowhere to be seen. He emerged from the shop with a bouquet wrapped in green paper, heavily accented with purples and pinks. He carried it to the prowler and was soon back on the road again.

His drive took him to the Salt Lake City Cemetery. The hillside burial ground on the north end of town dated back to 1847, when the first Mormons arrived in the valley. It expanded rapidly in the district known as the Avenues, eventually swallowing up more than two hundred acres of land, and one by one, a sea of headstones and monuments proliferated across the emerald slopes, shaded by high trees and divided by a series of winding roads.

What is he doing here? I wondered.

He parked his car on Fourth Avenue, crossed the quiet street, and began walking up one of the winding paths into the cemetery grounds. I shut off my car and followed. He'd picked a quiet day to come up here. There weren't any funerals happening. He moved beyond a cluster of trees and shrubs, out of my line of vision. If I lost him, it didn't matter, because I knew I'd find his distinctive bouquet sooner or later.

Before long, I spotted him in a remote corner of the cemetery, placing his bouquet at a grave. I hid behind the trunk of an ancient tree and watched. He sat down near a monument and stayed there fifteen minutes. I was a ways away, but from this distance, I could see him wiping tears and rocking gently back and forth. After straightening the bouquet, he rose to his feet and left. I waited for a couple of minutes and then I set off down the grassy hill until I reached the gravestone. I crouched before it and pulled the fresh bouquet back so I could see the name. I felt as though my heart was going to burst out of my chest when I read it.

JARED MORONI WEEKS
Beloved brother, son & friend.
July 9, 1909–November 16, 1923

Twenty-three

Half past four in the afternoon found me back in the lot at Public Safety, doing what I seemed to do best these days: waiting. Jared came lumbering out of the rear doors of the building, presumably calling it a day. Once again, I followed his movements from afar. He walked across the parking lot, waving at coworkers. He climbed on a green-and-brown Harley-Davidson by the chain-link fence and started it. He sped to the exit, and I started my car. I followed him down the alley and out to State Street, where he turned north, heading to South Temple. I remained four car lengths behind him, sitting low in the front seat with my hat brim pulled low over my eyes. He turned east at South Temple and promptly swerved into the next lane to make a left-hand turn onto A Street. I turned east after him and waited for a trolley to pass in the center of the road before I veered into the left lane to turn.

At that point, I lost him. He was nowhere to be seen. I drove up A Street and checked a couple of side roads. I eventually ended up cruising slowly past the house on B Street that I'd visited last week with Jared, but saw no sign of his motorcycle in front of it. I pulled up to the curb on the next block north and shut off the engine, silently contemplating my next move. I did not want to ponder it too long, because it was getting hotter by the minute. I suspected Jared had gone to the house on B Street, because he'd been heading in this direction, though I had no way of knowing for sure. I felt the need to ask him about the Model T truck I saw parked in front of Jeppson's flower shop and that gravestone where he placed flowers at the Salt Lake City Cemetery. The way I saw it, Jared owed me an explanation on both counts. Knowing my goose would be cooked if I confronted him in Public Safety during my suspension, I decided to see if he was here and demand that he level with me.

I got out of the car, crossed the street—clear on both sides—and walked over to the house. It hit me as I sized up the layout of the property and noticed there was no driveway that this was one of those houses with a detached garage located behind it, probably backing out to a gravel or paved road shared with other neighboring garages. I walked around the block to verify my hunch. I was right. I came to a narrow garage alleyway and kept going until I reached the one behind the B Street house. It was a brick number with a big overhead door made of wood. A battered Nash Ajax from the last decade was parked in front of it. I reached for the garage door handle and gave it a good pull and the big door sprang upward and moved along a track into the garage.

I can't say I was shocked to see a black Model T truck parked inside. Still, my heart skipped a beat with a rush of excitement as I squeezed inside. There was not much room between the truck and the wall, and if I weighed thirty pounds more, I wouldn't have been able to sidle to the front driver's-side door. Block letters appeared on the side of the truck spelling out COLUMBIA TRANSPORT, and below that, in a smaller size, FLAG-STAFF, ARIZONA. I stepped onto the running board and opened the door. I scooted inside, leaned over, and opened the glove box. At first, I found nothing out of the ordinary. Registration, maps, an owner's manual, a parts book, an oil-changing log. *Wait a minute*, I thought, as I came across an item of interest. It was a speeding ticket from the Utah Highway Patrol. The word "VOID" had been written across it. It was issued to the driver of a Model T truck, Arizona 1934 license plate number 3GF5. What caught my attention was the date and time: Tuesday, July 3, 1934, 12:30 A.M. The Model T was stopped on State Route 68, heading north, near the U.S. 40 (North Temple) exit. I pocketed the ticket, loaded everything else back in the glove box, climbed out of the truck, and closed the garage door.

I returned to the front of the house on B Street. I reached down and unlatched the picket fence gate. I went up the porch stairs, made a fist, and gave a light knock. Thanks to an interior curtain, the windows on the door were blocked, preventing me from seeing inside. When no one answered, I delivered a second, louder pounding, but it failed to get a response.

I gave the doorknob a turn. It was unlocked. I slowly eased the door forward a few inches, poking my head into the dimness. I saw no sign of life, but I heard music from a radio located somewhere inside.

"Hello," I called out. "Anybody here?"

Going from the blinding sun into this cave-like dwelling, my eyes took time to adjust. Every curtain in the house appeared to be closed and every electric light globe was turned off. I closed the door and advanced down the hall, passing through an arched opening into a room with no lights on. With the Venetian blinds shut, I could make out faint shapes of a sofa, chairs, and a table. The only source of light in the room came from a fancy new console radio playing in the corner. I walked softly over to it. *"Oxydol's Own Ma Perkins,"* said an announcer as an organ went into high gear. *"Starring Virginia Payne as America's Mother of the Air . . ."*

I reached down and switched it off. When I turned, a boy's face appeared before me for a split second—wavy brown hair, wide eyes, teeth clenched—and that's when the heavy object struck my head. It all went black.

"He's coming to. Stand back."

I've been through a lot of pain in my life. At various points, I've been afflicted with polio, influenza, diphtheria, pneumonia, and smallpox—luckily not all at once. There have been times when I thought I would not live to see another day. I have to say, however, that getting hit in the head so hard it knocked me out turned out to be one of the worst forms of pain I've ever experienced. An excruciatingly sore spot on the top of my head, throbbing and sensitive to the lightest touch, sent waves of agony through my body. My vision had gone double. Like Noah readying his ark for the flood, I saw two of everything. My injury-induced optical illusion presented me with doubles of Jared, the woman by his side, and the three boys and the girl peeking into the room from the hallway.

I figured out I was lying on a bed. I attempted to sit up straight, got dizzy, bent, and vomited over the edge. It splattered on the floor and I fell back on my pillow, in no shape to move. Seeing a dark bloodstain on the pillowcase by my head didn't comfort me. My double vision eased up and I got a good look at

the woman for the first time. An oval-faced brunette with hair
that reached her chest, her straight eyebrows topped a pair of
lovely, sunken green eyes that seldom blinked and watched me
with an intensity I could not ignore. Her mouth hung open, and
I wondered if she was waiting for me to do or say something.
Behind her, three boys and a girl—all teenagers—stood shoulder to shoulder, observing my every move.

"Who hit me?"

"Sorry, boss," said Jared. "One of the boys got antsy."

I looked around for the boy, thinking I'd catch him among
those few kids in the hallway. I didn't.

"He could've killed me," I said wearily.

"You shouldn't have sneaked in like that," said the woman.
"You scared him."

"Be sure to apologize to him." Such sarcasm was not typical
for me. Then again, neither was having a lump on my head half
as big as a boiled egg. "How long was I out for?"

"Half hour," she said. She winced when she looked at my
head. "You should have it looked at."

"I will, as soon as I get to the bottom of what I came here
for." I kicked my legs over the edge of the bed and stood up,
careful to avoid my own vomit. One of the teenage boys arrived
with a dripping-wet strip of cloth and a dustpan to scrub up the
mess, and I circled around him. Eyeing Jared, I considered confronting him about the cemetery. But with all of those kids
around, I opted for a delay.

I looked at the woman and held out my hand. "I don't believe we've been introduced. I'm Detective Art Oveson, Salt
Lake City Police Department."

She hesitated, then shook my hand. "Claudia Jeppson."

"Any relation to Carl Jeppson, the florist?" I asked.

"I'm his daughter."

"I see," I said, releasing her hand. "Is there somewhere we can talk?"

"Why don't we all go sit in the kitchen," suggested Claudia.

"Can I use your telephone first?" I asked, thinking I should let Clara know where I was.

"We don't have one," said Claudia.

We found spots at a table in the center of a spacious kitchen. Sunlight beamed in through a window above the sink, shining brightly on a black-and-brown checkerboard linoleum floor. At Claudia's insistence, a boy of about fourteen or fifteen presented me with a package of frozen peas. I followed Claudia's advice and placed it on my head. It felt comforting against the throbbing wound. She made tea and let it steep inside of a ceramic pot in the middle of the table. She went over to a glass cupboard and fetched cups and saucers and returned to fill them. The youths watched us through two doorways leading into the kitchen, one from the hall and the other from the living room. I counted eight in total—three girls, five boys. I still didn't see the one who hit me.

"Would you care for some tea, Detective Oveson?"

"I don't drink tea," I said. "But I'll take a glass of water, please."

Jared filled a glass with water from the tap and gave it to me, and I gulped it down fast. He refilled it. I polished off the second one faster than the first.

"Want more, boss?"

"Maybe later. Thanks."

Claudia sat across the table from me, poured a cup of tea, and stirred in a pair of sugar cubes. "Before we begin, I must ask," she said. "How is Nelpha?"

Her question surprised me. I adjusted the bag of peas, in search of a colder side. "Fine."

"I understand from Jared that she's staying with you? Is that so?"

"She's doing well." That was the most Claudia was going to get out of me.

"Why did you come here, Detective Oveson?"

"Why don't you start by telling me what on earth would drive one of those boys to hit me like that?" I asked.

"There've been some prowlers in the neighborhood," said Claudia.

"Wouldn't you say he overreacted a bit?"

Claudia dodged the question. "What else would you like to know?"

She still appeared slightly blurry in one eye, making me worry about the effect of this blow to my head. "Start by telling me about yourself."

"Jeppson's my maiden name," she said. "I was married for a time."

"What was your husband's name?"

"Alma Covington," she said. "I take it you know him?"

"I've met him." I gave her time to sip tea. "You must not be all that partial to him if you gave up his last name."

She shrugged. "He forced me to marry him when I was thirteen."

"Must've been awful," I said.

"It was years ago," she reflected. "I was only a girl. The night before I was to be sealed to him, I told him I didn't want to be his wife. He didn't care. My father pleaded on my behalf to halt the ceremony, but Uncle Grand refused to stop it. Before that, I always used to think Uncle Grand was a kind man with a good heart. I was naive. I know better now. I don't have any illusions anymore about him."

"How'd you end up here?" I asked.

"I ran away from Covington's place," she said.

"The one here in town, over on Third Avenue?" I asked.

"No. He also owns a homestead down around Dixie City. That's where I lived. I couldn't take it anymore. I made my way to St. George, where I jumped a freight heading north. All I had was a bottle of water, and I somehow, miraculously made it here alive. I stayed with Papa the first few months I was here, in one of the back rooms of his flower shop. I knew it was risky. Papa would've gotten in a heap of trouble if he was caught sheltering me. Alma owned the house nearby—still does—on Third Avenue. That's too close for my comfort. Papa found out about this place, on sale for a song. It was run-down back then. Papa knew the fella selling it, and he bought it and let me live here. At some point, I started taking in runaways from the other polygamist families. Kids just like I was. Scared. Confused. Needing a place to stay. Child brides. Banished boys. They help me around the house, in exchange for room and board. By and by, we got it looking pretty nice, I'd say. Don't you think?" She paused to let me nod. "The older ones eventually get on their feet and fly out of the nest, make room for the younger kids."

"I imagine a place like this costs a lot of money to run," I said, looking around the spotless kitchen.

"My father helps me."

"He sounds generous," I said.

"He's the kindest man I've ever known."

I nearly said, *I'm sure that ain't saying much.* But I knew to refrain. "What about Nelpha Black?"

"What about her?"

"How do you know her?"

"Runaway. Got here in early June. Can't speak. Writes notes to communicate."

"So she *can* write?" I said, half asking, half declaring.

"Yeah. Why?"

"I tried a few times to get her to write something. She wouldn't. I figured she didn't know how."

"Maybe she had her reasons."

"It's possible," I said. "These notes you mentioned—what did she say in them?"

"She told me she was planning to meet up with Uncle Grand to tell him something. She asked me if I'd help her find him."

"Did she tell you what she wanted to talk to him about?" I asked.

"No," said Claudia.

"You didn't happen to save these notes?"

"I don't know where they are."

"That's a long way to come to talk to Johnston," I said. "It must've been important, whatever it was she wanted to tell him."

"I guess."

"You didn't ask her what it was about?"

"No."

"Got any guesses?"

"No."

"Do you have any reason to believe that Nelpha had a hand in killing him?"

"Not at all."

I nodded slowly and ran my fingers along the table's pock-marked surface. "Have you ever heard of Boyd Johnston?"

"No," she said. She said it quickly, almost before I was finished saying his name, which made me wonder if she was telling the truth. "Who is he?"

"He's one of Uncle Grand's sons," I said. "In the Dixie City branch of his family. Boyd went missing in May. He was only twelve or so. He vanished, along with a few other boys. Nelpha got to be quite close to him. I suspect that's why she wanted to meet with Uncle Grand, to discuss his disappearance. I can't be sure of that, though."

I turned the bag of peas around and pushed the frozen coldness into the raw area on my skull. It hurt something fierce. I considered Claudia's words, although I had a difficult time collecting my thoughts due to the pain.

"Who set up Nelpha's meeting with Uncle Grand?"

"I asked my father to," she said.

"Was he at the meeting?"

"No."

"Were you?"

"No."

"Then how do you know he wasn't there?"

"I dropped Nelpha off at the Lincoln Street church that night. It's usually quiet there during the week. Uncle Grand told my father it would be an ideal place to meet."

"Why didn't you stay for the meeting?"

"Uncle Grand wanted time to talk alone with her. He promised to telephone me when Nelpha was ready to be picked up. I didn't have any reason to doubt him. So I went home. I waited a few hours. The telephone call never came. I got nervous. I drove back to Lincoln Street, thinking I'd pick her up."

"What kind of car do you drive?" I asked.

"A Nash Ajax," she said. "Nineteen and twenty-six model."

I recalled the Model T truck I saw the night of the murders, and I thought of the one that I'd just seen inside of her garage. I kept those bits of information to myself. I didn't want to put her on the defensive. For now, I had to keep the focus on the timeline of the murders. "What time did you go back?"

"I can't remember. I didn't look. I got down there and I saw all of those police cars out front. I got nervous. I turned around and came back home. To be honest, I didn't want the police meddling around here and bothering the children."

A wristwatch check told me it was quarter after six. I had at least a dozen more questions I wanted to ask Claudia, but all of those teenagers watching me from the hallway made me antsy. I rubbed the sore spot again and groaned. That was the closest thing to a transition that I could offer to bid Claudia Jeppson farewell.

"I'd best be getting home. It's coming up on suppertime." I looked at Jared. "Jared?"

"Yeah, boss?"

"I'd like to have a word with you alone."

"Sure thing."

"Can I see her?" Claudia asked.

"Nelpha?"

"Yes. I want to talk to her, Detective. Make sure she's okay."

"She's okay."

"I need to see for myself."

I looked at her forlorn eyes and her open mouth, so pleading. "I'll consider your request," I said.

Her nod came slowly. "Thank you."

I stood and walked over to Jared. "You," I whispered. *"Outside."*

Twenty-four

"Start by telling me who you are."

"What do you mean, boss?"

"You know precisely what I mean," I said, looking over at him.

We sat in the front seat of my car. The windows were rolled down. Some kids rode past us on bicycles, jingling their handlebar bells. The overcast skies provided sweet relief from our long, dreary heat wave, although we had received next to no rain, just ample amounts of lightning and thunder. I could tell from the way Jared looked away, and the way he rubbed his left forearm incessantly with his right hand, that he was in no mood to talk to me.

"Imagine my surprise when I found Jared Weeks's gravestone at the cemetery," I said. "Who does that make you?"

He became momentarily indignant. "Were you following me?"

"I'm asking the questions," I said. "If that's Jared Weeks in the cemetery, who are you?"

"I'm Jared's little brother."

"What's your real name?"

"Aaron Malachi Weeks."

He fiddled nervously with the buckle on his bag. He needed prodding.

"Was your family polygamist?" I asked.

"Yep."

"You come from Dixie City?"

"I was born near it, grew up in the area, yeah."

"Were you banished?"

"Yep."

"Tell me about it," I said.

"Not much to tell."

"Try me," I said. "Or I'll go have a word with Buddy. Tell him what I know."

He stared at me in silence, perhaps wondering if I'd really go through with it. I guess he decided not to take that chance, because he began talking.

"Jared and I were close. Real close. We grew up on a ranch my father owned outside of town. We had the same mother. We were born only a year apart. And let me tell you, we did everything together. Ate dinner together. Explored the outdoors together. We drank out of the same tin cup whenever we were thirsty or brushed our teeth. We loved to go swimming in the creek during the summers. We had a favorite spot where the water was deep, but there wasn't much of a current, so it was safe. We shared a bedroom, and at night, when the lights went out, that's when the fun started. We'd tell each other stories. He could always tell 'em way better'n I ever could. He had a real way with words. He'd describe what a big, wide world it was out there, beyond this dry old desert full of Gila monsters and coyotes. And I'd shut my eyes and just listen. You know, take it all in." He fell silent for a moment. I sensed him getting choked up. He drew a deep breath and continued. "Yeah, we were as close as any brothers you'd ever find."

"So what happened?" I asked.

He looked at me. "You mean why did we get sent off?"

"Yeah."

"Our mother passed away in the fall of twenty-three. We all saw it coming. She'd been sick for several years. I was twelve at the time. Jared was thirteen. A week after her funeral, we got driven out into the desert. Dropped us off in the middle of nowhere. We were told we were men now, and we had to make it on our own. I had no idea where we were. I got scared and I cried, like I never cried before. But Jared told me that God was looking out for us, and that everything would be okay. He promised me that if I kept up with him, he'd take me to a place that he'd heard about up in Salt Lake City—somewhere we could call home, where we'd be safe."

"That's a long ways," I said. "How'd you make it all the way up here?"

"We walked a long distance, but we made it to the highway, and Jared said we could get a ride by sticking our thumbs up. He said they called it hitchhiking, and he read about it once in a magazine at a general store in Kanab, when our mother was stocking up on supplies. We gave it a try, thumbing for a ride, and sure enough, a big delivery truck stopped for us. The driver said he was going all the way up to Cache Valley to pick up some chickens from a farm up there, and he told us he'd drop us off in Salt Lake City. We were so excited we jumped up and down for joy. I remember Jared telling me, 'See, I told you so. Didn't I? God is looking out for us.'"

Jared dipped his head, and he struggled to maintain his composure.

"It turns out that God must've been sleeping on the job," he said bitterly.

"Why do you say that?" I asked.

"He let my brother die."

"How?"

Still looking down, Jared said, "We rode all the way up to Salt Lake City in the back of that delivery truck. Wasn't any covering. No tarps. Nothing. Only the elements. It was cold, rainy—the kind of weather you get in November. We even got some snow part of the way. When the truck driver dropped us off at the railroad depot, he gave us some coins to use a telephone booth to call Mr. Jeppson. He was the man who Jared heard was helping the boys who got kicked out. He was about the nicest man I ever knew. He came down to the station in the middle of the night to pick us up. But by then, my brother had a fever and he developed a bad case of the shivers. His condition was so bad that Mr. Jeppson took him to the hospital right away. Jared came down with pneumonia. The doctors did everything they could. He didn't make it. After that Claudia took me in. I was pretty broken up over things. Everyone I grew up around was gone—my mother, my father, my brother, my home. But Claudia told me one thing that always stayed with me."

"What's that?" I asked.

"She said to me—and these are pretty close to her exact words—'If you give up, your brother died for nothing.'" He bit his lower lip and looked over at me. "I started going by his name because it was my way of keeping part of him alive."

"I'm sorry," I said. "You got a lot of rotten breaks in life, Jared."

"It's all about the math," he whispered.

I reared my head in puzzlement. "The math?"

"Half of the babies being born to polygamist wives are girls and the other half are boys. If you're looking to build a plural marriage utopia in the desert where one man gets to marry as many wives as he wants, then there are two ways around this problem. Either you recruit lots of new women to come and live at the settlement. And I can tell you right now there ain't a long line of 'em waiting to get in. Or—"

I interrupted: "Or you can get rid of boys."

"Polygamists called them surplus," he said.

"So that's why you wanted to join this squad," I said.

"I wanted to do my small part to bring those men down."

"I see. Not to change the subject too much, but when Nelpha lit out last week, you knew she didn't go back to Dixie City. Didn't you?"

"I don't know what you mean."

"You sat in my house, in my living room, and looked me in the eye and told me you thought she was going back to Dixie City," I said. "All that time you knew she didn't."

He was quiet for a while. Finally, he said, "I thought it would help for you to go down there. So you'd finally begin to understand what you were up against."

"She came here, didn't she?"

This time he didn't answer.

"Is Claudia Nelpha's mother?"

Jared shook his head. "Claudia ran away from Dixie City twenty years ago. Nelpha's only thirteen."

"So that must mean Claudia is her aunt?" I asked.

He chuckled. "We're all kin, all related to one another somehow."

"What about the Model T delivery truck I saw in front of Jeppson's store this morning?" I asked. "Surely if you'd gone over the motor vehicle records and matched them against the names of polygamists, you would've caught that one. Are you covering up for Carl Jeppson, because he helped you?"

He stared at the car floor, not saying a word.

I briefly considered confronting Jared about the Model T truck I found parked in Claudia's detached garage, but it seemed like the wrong time. Naturally, I wondered how it got there and if it was the truck I had seen speeding away from the Fundamentalist Church of Saints the night of the murders. But I knew Jared was covering up for Claudia, and I felt like I could not trust him.

"Listen, Jared. I know you're still holding out on me."

"Why do you say that?"

"You lied to me about the check you ran on Model T trucks," I said. "So far I don't hear you denying it."

"There's a lot of history you don't know, boss," he said. "I'm trying to prevent innocent people from getting harmed."

He went silent on me again, and I was beginning to feel woozy from the blow I had taken inside of Claudia Jeppson's house.

"Level with me a little more," I said. "You've already helped me with everything you've told me. Go the rest of the way."

He shook his head. "I've got to go, boss. I'm all talked out. Sorry."

I watched him get out of the car, close the door, and cross the street. He headed up the walkway and porch steps, and went inside Claudia's house. I pitied him. The poor man had endured more suffering in his youth than many people experience in a lifetime. But what could I tell him to give him peace of mind?

The last person to assure Jared that everything would be okay had left this world grimly and unceremoniously not long after making that promise.

"How on earth did you get this?" asked Dr. Henry May.

"It's a long story," I said, watching him disinfect the needle with rubbing alcohol.

The gash in my skull required five stitches. To bind up the wound, Dr. May made a house call and brought along his electric clippers, which he used to shave a portion of my head while I sat on a chair in the kitchen. He numbed my flesh with a topical anesthetic and stitched above my right ear. When he was done he passed me a handheld mirror so I could survey the repair job. The bald spot with the fault line running down the center gave me a freakish appearance. Knowing this bizarre new look would draw stares and possibly even ridicule, I asked him to shave the rest of my head, so I was bald everywhere.

"Are you sure?"

"Yes, sir," I said. "I'm sure."

He turned on his clippers and they buzzed ominously as he ran them over my noggin until all that remained was faint fuzz. Clumps of auburn hair rained down on the floor, some of it on my shoes. He turned off the clippers and handed me a mirror, and I inspected. Shocked by the Roscoe Lund cue ball look, I thanked him, and we shook hands and he went on his way.

In the living room, Clara, Hyrum, Sarah Jane, and Nelpha waited for me. Clara burst into hysterical giggles when we came out of the kitchen and she saw my new look, muttering something about "Roscoe's twin brother." This was a welcome change from her mix of tears and outrage when she first saw the cut on my head.

Sarah Jane giggled too, and Nelpha even got in on it by smiling gently.

"You look like Frankenstein, Pop," said Hyrum.

"Oh, a wise guy," I said. I rolled my eyes up into my head, bared my bottom teeth, and did my best impersonation of the Boris Karloff monster.

"Dad, it's still Family Home Evening," said Sarah. "It's two-for-one night at the Rialto."

"Yeah? What's playing?"

"*Footlight Parade!*"

"Hey, I took you to that last time it was in town," I said.

Sarah Jane gestured to smiling Nelpha. "She hasn't seen it."

"What are we waiting for?" I asked. "To the Rialto!"

The Rialto promised "iced air." And it delivered.

I could practically see the steam with each exhale. We crossed the lobby and entered the movie palace through swinging doors. A flashlight-toting usher led us down a flight of steps to an unoccupied row of seats. I tipped the lad in the maroon monkey suit for guiding us away from the cigarette smokers so we didn't have to breathe in their foul-smelling fumes. The Rialto, formerly the Kinema Theater, boasted 820 seats under a ceiling as high as heaven. The theater filled up each Monday night because families could get in half price (hence, TWO-FOR-ONE NIGHT spelled out in tiny blinking lightbulbs in the lobby). The only catch was the Rialto showed re-releases on Mondays, films originally out in theaters a while back. Tonight's feature, *Footlight Parade*, had played in the movie houses in the fall of '33, but it returned for a revival on *el cheapo* night. Despite having seen *Footlight Parade* before, I was happy to watch it again.

After the newsreel ended, a musical fanfare sounded with the arched words WARNER BROS. PICTURES, INC. floating above the wavy VITAPHONE pennant. The sound track filled the theater as credits to *Footlight Parade* rolled as if listed in a turning drum. I clapped when my favorite actor, with his tough-guy grin, appeared on the screen above the words JAMES CAGNEY AS "CHESTER KENT."

Footlight Parade moved fast. Lavish musical numbers climaxed with bathing beauties on a giant waterfall swimming and dancing to Busby Berkeley choreography. Cameras filmed the action from above, capturing elaborate, shape-shifting geometric patterns, all to the effervescent sounds of voice and orchestra. For an hour and a half, I almost forgot my life was careening like an out-of-control auto, just as I almost forgot about that stitched canyon on my freshly shaven head.

Almost.

Twenty-five

I knew I'd likely end up in serious trouble for what I was doing, but I didn't care. Desperate times sometimes call for desperate measures. Holding a newspaper in my right hand bearing that morning's date, I barged in through the door with the name CAPTAIN C. W. HAWKINS on its pebbled glass. In the anteroom, I strode past his secretary, Beryl Paisley, a spinster in her fifties with curly salt-and-pepper hair. She stopped typing, watched me with horrified eyes, and leaped out of her seat to put herself between Buddy's office door and me. She revealed her nervousness with her quivering turkey neck and jittery hands, which she lifted to my chest to push me back.

"You can't go in there!" she said. "He's in a meeting right now!"

I gently brushed her aside with my arm, which got a bewildered whine and huff out of her. "Begging your pardon, Miss Paisley," I said, "but I really need to get in there. Now."

"He's talking to the district attorney. . . ."

I ignored her and pushed Buddy's door hard. His furious expression when I entered told me I might end up unemployed for what I was doing. The DA, Walter Rasmussen, a slick politico with brown hair pomaded flat against his head and a special fondness for double-breasted navy blue Brooks Brothers suits, sprang out of his chair, aghast at my abrupt entrance. He straightened his wire-rim glasses and stayed silent as I crossed the plush carpeting. I slammed the newspaper on his desk, flattening it out with the palms of my hands. There was no missing the headline: POLICE CHIEF ABOLISHES CONTROVERSIAL POLYG SQUAD. Below that appeared a subhead: COWLEY DENIES CONNECTION TO RECENT MURDERS.

"Do you want to tell me what this is all about?" I half asked, half demanded.

Buddy rose and circled around his desk, hooked me by the arm, and pulled me toward his door. "Excuse me a minute, will you, Walt? This won't take long."

He took me to the anteroom and pulled his door closed, and when he turned to me, I noticed the red splotches on his neck. He only got those when he was flying into a rage. "Just what in the hell do you think you're doing?" he asked through clenched teeth. "I'm in the middle of a very important meeting with the district attorney. Have you any idea how wildly inappropriate you're being, Art?"

"Put yourself in my shoes," I said, plucking off my hat. "Can you imagine how awful it is to find this out in the newspaper?"

Buddy looked horrified when he saw my bald head with the stitches on the side. "What happened . . ."

"Long story," I said. "Best saved for another time."

"I tried telephoning you at your home last night, but nobody answered," said Buddy. "It's over, Art. As of this Friday at five P.M., your squad is no more. Next Monday, you're returning to Morals, demoted to junior grade. Roscoe is back to guiding traffic, Myron—"

"You don't have to tell me. We're going back to our old jobs. It's all spelled out in great detail in the article."

"It was either that or Sondrup was going to go straight to the press and reveal all of the gruesome details about your Dixie City excursion," said Buddy. "He cut a deal with Cowley and Mayor Cummings. If they pull the plug on the squad and cease all harassment of his clients, Sondrup will drop his lawsuit against the city and the department. One way or the other, your squad is shutting down. The mayor has gotten nothing but grief ever since he revived it, and your recent escapades have only given ammunition to his opposition in the city council."

"All right, then I'll talk to the mayor," I said. "Tell him what's what, help him see the error of his ways."

"Oh, I wouldn't do that if I were you. Believe me, I had to stick my neck out to keep you on the force, because if Cowley and Cummings had it their way, you'd be unemployed. The last thing you ought to be doing is storming into people's offices and giving them a piece of your mind, especially mine! I'm the best friend you've got right now. I'm the reason you're still working here. Oh, and must I remind you that you're still suspended? If you don't leave Public Safety this instant, you're going to become yet another statistic. Am I making myself clear?"

"We can't stop now, Buddy," I said. "These polygamists are more dangerous than ever, and if we don't make some effort to stop them . . ."

"You had that chance, Art," he said grimly. "You not only

dropped the ball. You threw it away. You were doing an admirable job of building cases against these men, but you were done in by your pigheaded impulsiveness."

How to respond to such a comment? Whatever wind was in my sails when I first entered Public Safety, Buddy took it away right then. His glower softened, and he let out a sigh.

"Go home and rest for the next few days," he said. "There's a wisdom to knowing when it's over, Art, and to accepting that." He waited a beat before turning to leave. "Don't let the polygamists become your white whale."

I nodded. He returned to his office and closed the door. I suddenly became aware of Beryl Paisley watching me, and I straightened my hat on my head and walked out of that anteroom trying to preserve as much of my dignity as I could.

"Just the man we're looking for!"

Wit Dunaway and Pace Newbold approached me outside the rear entrance to Public Safety on my way to the parking lot. I kept my hat pulled low, hoping they wouldn't notice my newly hairless head. Their fierce expressions told me they weren't happy. In fact, Pace—sweating profusely in this oppressive July heat— glared at me like he wanted to break my jaw. We met up at the chain-link fence enclosing the lot.

"What can I do for you fellas?" I asked.

"There's been a break in the case," said Pace. "We'd like to have little Miss Pioneer back."

"Oh yeah?" I asked. "What's cooking?"

"That's on a need-to-know basis," said Pace. "And you don't need to know."

"We're playing our cards close to our chests on this one," said Wit. "I'm sure you understand, Art."

"I thought we were sharing information," I said.

"Last I heard, you're suspended," said Pace. "I'd say that renders our little arrangement null and void, wouldn't you?"

I was angry, and he could see it in my face. "I'm concerned for the girl. That's all."

"Of course you are," said Wit. "If you really want to know, we found a .32 caliber Harrington and Richardson in the hedges outside of the fundamentalist church. Somebody in a hurry must have tossed it out there, without thinking it through clearly. We're tracing the registration right now, but fingerprints on it match the ones we took off the girl we found at the murder scene. So you can either bring her here or we'll gladly drop by your place and pick her up. It's six of one and half dozen of the other."

I felt my heart beating hard. Could that gentle soul staying under my roof really be a killer? Then again, how much did I know about her? She'd already lied to me by pretending not to know how to write. And where had she gone last week when she left my house? One thing was certain: These questions weren't going to answer themselves while Wit and Pace waited for my response.

"She's camping," I blurted out. "With Clara's family, up in the Uintas."

They shot suspicious glances at each other. Wit looked me up and down. "I thought most of the campsites were closed, on account of the forest fires."

"They found one that's open," I said. "Not too far from Kamas."

"That's what? An hour's drive from here?" asked Pace. "That gives you time to get in your car and go pick her up. If you don't bring her to Public Safety this afternoon, we'll pay a visit to your house after work today. Remember, we can arrest you if you choose not to cooperate."

"On what grounds?" I asked.

"Obstructing a homicide investigation," said Pace. "After reading the headlines about your squad in this morning's edition, I don't think that's a desirable option for you. And Oveson? There ain't no ice cream in jail, if you get my drift."

Pace and I entered into an angry staring match, and the slightest provocation could have set either one of us off. It's a good thing Wit was there. He sensed the tension and—ever the diplomat—knew precisely what to say.

"At the end of the day, we want the same thing as you," he said. "We just want to know who pulled the trigger on the gun that killed Johnston and Mason that night at the church. Like it or not, the girl is the prime suspect."

"What about the Model T truck I saw driving away?" I asked.

"There are plenty of Model T trucks on the roads," said Pace. "In the absence of any license plate numbers, or a description of the driver, there's not much we can do."

"That's not so," I said, trying my best to stall them. "You can match registration records available at the office of revenue against the names of polygamists."

I left out the part about ordering Jared to do that. My goal was not to give them information. It was to steer them in another direction, to buy me some time. I could not bring myself to believe that Nelpha had had a hand in the killings. My reasons were not necessarily rational or backed up by evidence. It all came from a pang originating in my gut. I had visions of Nelpha cowering in fear in a ratty old bunk at the State Industrial School, the target of bullies and guards alike. The justice system was not always kind to the vulnerable, especially someone unable to speak, to find the words to defend herself.

"It wouldn't hurt to give it a shot, but we'd need those names from you," said Wit, snapping me back to reality. "Have you got them handy?"

"I can give them to you on Monday, when my suspension ends," I said. "I'm not allowed in Public Safety until then."

Pace grinned. "Say, what did you get suspended for, anyhow?"

I hesitated. "I went to Dixie City against Buddy's orders."

"What else?" asked Pace.

"What do you mean?"

"There's gotta be more to it than that," he said. "C'mon. Cough it up."

"When I was down there, I punched someone."

Pace dipped his head and broke out into laughter. Wit's smirk escalated into a big smile and he began convulsing with laughter, too.

"You're having us on," laughed Pace. "*You?* Assaulted *someone?* What are you, Max Schmeling?"

"I've got to go," I said, tugging my hat brim. "See you around, boys."

I excused my way between them.

"Art," Wit called out. "Don't make us pay you a visit. You follow?"

I glanced back at Wit. "Yeah. Thanks."

Back on the road in my Oldsmobile, I noticed the brown Hudson sedan in my rearview mirror, and someone inside watching me through binoculars. It tailed me as I drove home. I engaged in evasive maneuvering. Instead of driving east on South Temple, the route I usually took to get home from Public Safety, I drove south on State and turned right on 200 South. Now going west, I checked the mirror once more. The Hudson still shadowed me. Based on the shape of its headlights, vaguely resembling upside-down teardrops, I pegged it as a '32. I kept driving west, past assorted shops and auto mechanics, three-story office buildings and the Sweet's Candy Company, past the Khan Brothers Grocery building and a cluster of eyesores called the Keyser Warehouses.

I wove around traffic. I glanced at the mirror's reflection. Still there. The car never got close enough that I could read the license plate, but even from this far away I could make out the Kunz brothers inside. When I reached 300 West and the stately Denver and Rio Grande Western Depot came into view, I swerved north with screaming tires. I approached the equally grandiose Union Pacific Depot and the Bamberger Depot, the terminus for the interurban railway. I knew of an alley shortcut north of the Bamberger where I could ditch my pursuer. I accelerated and picked up speed. The Hudson grew smaller in my mirror. I cranked the steering wheel as much as possible. Hard right into the alley. I braked and put the car in park. I sat there for ten minutes. No sign of the Hudson.

I drove home, gripping the steering wheel tightly all the way, determined to get something—*anything*—out of Nelpha.

Twenty-six

Plumes of smoke, miles high, obscured the tops of the Wasatch Mountains on the east side of the valley as I steered into the driveway of my home and killed the car's engine. Vexing as the fires were, I had other matters on my mind to contend with. I walked through the front door of my house, yelled out "hello" but got no response. On the table by the front door, Clara had left a note saying that she'd borrowed her father's Model A to take the family out shopping, and they'd be back in a while. I sat down on the couch and perused the other headlines in that morning's *Examiner*. All bad news. Fires. Heat waves. Dust storms. Unemployment. Nazis. Sometimes newspapers only make everything seem worse. I folded it in half and tossed it onto the table as the front door opened and a cacophony of joyful voices filled the house.

Clara, Sarah Jane, and a girl I almost didn't recognize as Nelpha strolled into the living room, aglow with happiness. Nelpha could have stepped right out of an MGM movie, with her chin-length permanent wave and short-sleeved floral dress with splashes of bright reds, blues, teals, and yellows on white. I thought back to the night I found her, hidden in a closet, trembling in her homespun, terrified of the sight of me. I never would've guessed this beautiful butterfly had been waiting to break free of her cocoon. She looked so happy, so radiant.

I hated to do what I knew I had to do.

Clara's face brightened when she saw me. "Hi, honey! There's something you should see!"

I cracked a grin. "Okay."

"Ta-da!" said Clara, gesturing to Nelpha. "What do you think of this marvelous young lady?"

Slightly embarrassed, Nelpha stared down at her new black shoes as she smiled.

"We took her to ZCMI to buy some new dresses," said Sarah Jane. "Then to the Crystal for a permanent wave. What do you think, Dad? Doesn't she remind you of Loretta Young?"

"She looks beautiful," I said with a warm smile. "You look beautiful, Nelpha."

"She's got lilac spray, too!" Sarah imitated an Englishwoman. "I believe the proper name is 'eau de toilette.' "

Sarah Jane giggled and Nelpha raised her head with that humble, sweet smile still there.

"I took the money out of our rainy day fund," said Clara. "I'll pay it all back over the next few months."

"No need," I said. "You did good. I'm glad. By the way, is Hi here?"

"He's with George. What's wrong, Art?"

I looked at Nelpha. "I need to talk to you. I was wondering if we could go in the kitchen?"

"What's this about, Art?" asked Clara.

"I just need to talk to her," I said. "It won't be long."

"Is everything okay, Dad?" asked Sarah Jane.

"I need a few minutes of Nelpha's time. That's all."

I put my arm around Nelpha's shoulders and led her into the kitchen, with Clara and Sarah Jane standing by and watching nervously. Wooden chair legs groaned on the floor as I pulled out a seat for her and she sat down. From my rolltop desk in the living room I fetched a pencil and a few pieces of paper. I returned to the kitchen, sat down across from Nelpha, and pushed the pencil and paper toward her.

"They're coming for you," I said.

"Who is?" asked Clara, standing in the doorway.

I turned to Clara. "The police are paying a visit to this house, tonight, to arrest Nelpha. She's going to be in a lot of trouble if she doesn't help me out."

Clara entered the kitchen, arms folded above her protruding belly. "When were you going to tell me this?"

"I only just found out myself," I said over my shoulder to Clara. I looked at Nelpha. "I need you to write down what happened the night of Uncle Grand's murder."

She bit her lower lip and tensed up.

"I think you saw what happened to Uncle Grand the night he was killed," I said. "Listen, if you had anything to do with it . . ."

She shook her head vigorously, as if protesting. Her features twitched with dismay.

"If I'm going to protect you, I need to know what you know," I said.

I picked up the pencil and went to place it in her open palm, but she jerked her hand away. She placed her hands on her lap under the table and lowered her head, her way of withdrawing into that turtle shell of hers. I couldn't let her do that. There was too much at stake.

"It's not a matter of locking you up in reformatory anymore. They want to try you for murder. Double murder. I can't help you if you don't help me."

She stared at the pencil I placed in front of her. Her fearful eyes met mine. Her jittery movements reminded me of a bird in a cage being attacked by a cat.

"I know why you're afraid," I said. "I know about Boyd Johnston disappearing, and the other boys, too."

She shook her head when I mentioned Boyd Johnston.

"No?" I asked. "No what? They didn't disappear?"

She didn't respond. I began reciting the names of the lost boys.

"Garth Christensen. Franklin Boggs. Chester Hammond. Any of those names sound familiar? Are they the reason you left home and came all the way up here to talk to Uncle Grand? I know for a fact that Boyd was your friend. You wanted to help him, and that's why you went to Uncle Grand. Isn't that true?"

Her nod was slight, but I saw it.

"His disappearance has something to do with the two murders," I said. "Tell me this much: Am I right?"

No more nods or headshakes came my way. If it weren't for her trembling, I'd think she'd turned to stone.

"Please," I whispered, with a hint of desperation in my voice. "Write down what happened that night."

She did not budge. Not an inch. Her newly permanent-waved hair shook, along with the rest of her.

"It's too hard for her."

Sarah Jane stood next to me, looking at her frightened friend on the other side of the table.

"She's scared, Dad."

Clara approached Sarah Jane. "Why don't you and Nelpha go to your room? I want to talk to your father, sweetheart."

"Okay," said S.J. "Come on, Nelpha."

As Nelpha rose to her feet, I knew I was not imagining things when I saw her mouth the word "sorry." She followed Sarah Jane to her room. The door at the end of the hallway closed. Clara and I were alone now.

Clara pulled up a chair and sat down beside me. Her pregnant belly, now larger than ever, made her squirm in search of a comfortable sitting position.

"Why do the police want her?"

"They think she murdered LeGrand Johnston," I said.

Clara turned pale. "What—why?"

"They found a gun that someone threw out at the fundamentalist church the night of the murders," I said. "It has her fingerprints on it. It doesn't look good."

"Oh my God."

The phone rang. I went to the hallway, lifted the receiver, and brought it to my ear. "Hello."

"It's me."

I instantly recognized Myron Adler's voice.

"Myron! Boy, am I glad to hear from you. How was your outing?"

"I've never been to Branning's," he said, instead of answering. "Their chili is legendary."

"That it is," I confirmed.

"Are you hungry for a late lunch? I'd like to share the findings of my expedition, and I'd rather not discuss it on the telephone. You know, party lines and what have you."

"When?" I asked.

"I'm calling from a telephone booth in the lobby of the Sem-loh. So I'm pretty much there. When can *you* be here?"

"Can you give me some time?" I asked.

"Sure," he said. "How about an hour?"

I spied my wristwatch. 12:56. "Two o'clock it is. See you then."

I lowered the earpiece onto the cradle. Clara now stood in the hall, a few feet away from me, expecting me to share what I knew.

"Who was that?"

"Myron," I said. "He was out of town for a few days. I'm going to meet him a little later to discuss his trip. But there are other, more pressing matters to attend to right now."

"What should we do about Nelpha?" she asked.

"They're going to charge her with murder," I said. I looked at her. "If she's here, they'll arrest her. You think you can stay at your sister's for a few days?"

"Of course."

"Has she got room for the kids and Nelpha?"

"Yeah. I could also stay at my parents'."

"Better make it your sister's," I said. "I love your mom and dad, but they ask too many questions. Maybe you could use your parents' Ford for a few more hours. Give George's mom a call. Tell her where you're staying. Ask if she'll drop Hi off there."

"We could get in trouble for this," said Clara. "What if she's . . ."

Clara couldn't bring herself to ask it.

"Then I'll do everything in my power to see to it that she'll get a fair trial and decent legal representation," I said. "But Clara, just as sure as I'm standing here, I'm certain she's inno-cent. Even if she pulled the trigger that night, something terrible pushed her to that point, and we owe it to her to figure out what it was. We've come this far. Please, let's just do this one thing. . . ."

We embraced. I kissed her on the cheek and then our lips touched. We released each other and went to work packing. It is striking how quickly you can pack when you stay focused. Forty-five minutes later, I loaded suitcases into the backseat of her mother and father's Ford Model A, mindful to carve out a space for one of the girls to sit. Clara waddled out to the car in a floral crepe dress, along with a hat to keep the hot afternoon sun out of her eyes. Behind her, Sarah Jane led Nelpha by the arm out the front door, down the porch steps, to the idling auto. I exchanged hugs with my wife and daughter, while Nelpha observed with uncertainty in her eyes. I walked up to her and gently put my arms around her and pulled her close. I briefly considered telling her that everything was going to be okay, but how could I say something that I knew might not be true? Instead I let go, stepped back, and smiled down at her. She returned the smile. I felt a wave of sudden happiness—a real relief from the stress I'd been under all day—to see her smile like that. I watched the car back out onto the road and speed downhill, eventually disappearing out of sight.

Twenty-seven

If one were to compile a list of the seven culinary wonders of the world, surely Branning's chili would have to be included on it. People drove from as far away as Evanston, Wyoming; Fort Collins, Colorado; and Elko, Nevada, to partake of the steaming, aromatic delicacy. After the first bite, your mouth caught on fire and you began to wonder whether you'd live to see another day. By the time you reached the bottom of the bowl, you'd sacrifice nearly anything to figure out how to make it. The owner, Ralph Branning, kept the recipe a closely guarded secret. Rumor had it he wouldn't even let his loved ones see it. Whatever ingredients he used, however he made it, his little tile-floored joint on the ground floor of the Semloh Hotel, with a big sign out front that spelled CHILI in lightbulbs, consistently drew a sizable noontime crowd. The menu contained a few other staples: hamburgers, steaks, tamales, and even a bizarre concoction called a Ham Waffle, which I avoided like the dickens, but it's safe to say that two-thirds of the lunch clientele came for the chili.

Myron Adler, as stone-faced as Buster Keaton and dressed in a suit that must've been much too hot for this weather, selected a table near the storefront window, which gave us a prime view of congested traffic on Second South. He set his hat on the table and began crushing saltines in his hand, sprinkling them over his chili. Next came the ketchup. Three whacks of the bottle's bottom sent a red flood pouring onto his lunch.

He capped the bottle and leaned it my way.

"No thanks."

I kept my hat on, to cover the unpleasant wound on my freshly shaven head. We dined briefly in silence. At some point, Myron fished the familiar folded piece of paper out of his jacket pocket and passed it to me. I unfolded the tattered yellow sheet and read the words again. A NEW DAWN IN HOMESTEADING!

"Have you figured out what this thing is about?" I asked.

"I believe so," he said, chewing his food and napkin-dabbing his mouth.

"And?"

He drank half of his glass of water and let out a little "ah" when he set it down. "I spent all day Friday going through the records at the land offices in St. George and Kingman. Get this. At least thirty thousand acres in Washington County, Utah, and sixty-five thousand in Mohave County, Arizona, all of it designated as Homestead Act land, has been given to applicants who listed room 308 at the Delphi Hotel, Salt Lake City, Utah, as their address on the application forms."

"How'd they find these dummy claimants?" I asked.

"They printed thousands of those handbills. Blanketed the

soup kitchens, hobo camps, and transient shelters with them. When the polygamists would get a response at their P.O. boxes, they'd tell the sap to meet them in their room at the Delphi on State Street. That's how they persuaded the poorest of poor men to apply for homestead land."

"Aren't these men expecting to get land out of the deal?" I asked.

"I imagine not many of them read the fine print on the forms," said Myron. "I'm sure some could barely even read the handbill."

"I don't get how all of these men could be swindled out of their land without reporting it to the police."

"You raise an important point," said Myron. "I was just getting to that. It didn't take long for the polygamists to realize their original scheme was full of holes. It left too many loose ends, too many witnesses, and it could've easily backfired on them. That's why they came up with a different approach."

"What would that be?"

"Based on my research down there, that little handbill racket accounts for only a small portion of the illegally obtained land. The polygamists wised up and figured out a way to get their minions placed in these land offices. It's not like they're highly coveted jobs, even in these hard times. The polygamists switched from hoboes to dead people."

"You mean . . ."

"I matched the names on the applications with lists from cemeteries in the region, including the one in Dixie City, and since the start of 1933, most of the land claimants had been dead long before they actually filed their papers. So either we're dealing with ghosts that understand the complexities of government bureaucracy . . ."

I finished his sentence: "Or the polygamists are taking names off of cemetery records and their lackeys in the land offices are signing off on all of these claims and filing them away, assuming nobody will ever notice."

I folded the handbill and gave it back to Myron. "If that's all true," I said, "then it's the biggest land swindle I've ever heard of."

"And it's not confined to Washington and Mohave counties, either," he said. "These men have used similar loopholes to amass land in Garfield County, Colorado, not to mention northern Nevada and the border of Idaho and British Columbia. That's in addition to the tens of thousands of acres they already own in Texas and Mexico. All told, we could be looking at upward of a quarter of a million acres of land in as many as eight different states and three countries."

I reared my head in surprise. "Don't tell me you went to the land offices in all of those places?"

"No. That information came from Harold O'Rourke, that field agent with the Federal Emergency Relief Administration who Jared mentioned. He's been investigating these and a lot of other legally questionable polygamist activities."

"So you met this guy?"

"Yeah, he got back into Kingman yesterday after being on the road for a while. We sat down in his office and he talked for close to three hours. I learned a lot."

"Such as?"

"The polygamists are sitting on top of a multimillion-dollar empire," said Myron, eating a bite of chili. He chewed for a moment. "They've got investments in oil, real estate, construction, radio stations, aviation, and even motion pictures. O'Rourke says these men are racketeers who go about their business under the cover of religious convictions. And on top of all that, they're getting federal relief money coming into Dixie City. All of it is lining the pockets of rich apostles. They're living high on the hog in big fortress homes, with all the luxuries. Meantime, most of the followers live in hovels with dirt floors and no electricity."

"What's O'Rourke waiting for?" I asked. "Why isn't he nailing the polygamists?"

"He still needs more evidence," said Myron. "It's like we've said a hundred times: These men are nothing if not careful."

"If we could somehow get our hands on the financial records of the polygamists . . ."

Myron shook his head while he ate. "It won't be easy."

"How did O'Rourke come by all of this information?"

"He has a connection on the inside," said Myron. "He knows the accountant, who also happens to be one of the apostles. The fellow is feeding O'Rourke all kinds of information."

"Who's the accountant?" I asked. "Maybe we can talk to him."

"O'Rourke won't say. My guess is the fellow is disillusioned, probably found out about the investigation and secretly went to O'Rourke."

I snapped my fingers, and Myron noticed me glowing with excitement. "I bet I know who it is."

"Who?"

"Carl Jeppson."

"Do you think so?"

"With his business acumen, it wouldn't surprise me," I said. "Let me ask you something. How is O'Rourke planning to use this information?"

"He's building a case at the federal level to charge them with fraud. While he's at it, he's going to move to cut off the relief aid going into Dixie City and Vermillion Creek. That's the incorporated community on the Utah side, across the border from Dixie. The rich polygamists keep property on both sides. That way, if there's a raid by state authorities, they can sneak over the state line and lie low until it all blows over."

"Did you get any sense of where Uncle Grand fits into all this? I mean, he is the head of this church. I expect his hands are dirty."

Myron shook his head. "I get the impression he was a figure-head, a grandfather type who mostly stayed out of the shady dealings of his church. That's why he preferred Salt Lake to Dixie City. He figured he'd let the young Turks do their own thing with the United Brethren experiment out in the desert while he stayed comfy around here, wooing new converts and visiting his local wives."

"So maybe—*just maybe*—when Nelpha came all the way up here to tell him about his missing son, it jolted Johnston into the realization that not all was well down Dixie City way."

"That's one scenario," said Myron.

"How could Johnston not know, though?" I asked. "I guess the bigger question is: How is it that these men have gotten away with committing so many crimes for so long?"

"It's not hard to understand," said Myron. "The polygamists use the same tactics as the mob. They operate in secrecy, intim-idate their followers, and murder those who get in their way. They bribe judges, law enforcement, elected officials. They keep a low profile and try hard to stay out of the press. I can see why they get away with it."

I spent the next half hour filling Myron in on everything that had happened while he was gone. I went into detail about the trip to Dixie City, the meeting with Talena Steed, the funeral, Talena's death, and my assault on Dorland Kunz. It made me feel better to talk about it, although I'm not altogether sure that

Myron heard a single word I said. He appeared to be in a trance the entire time he was listening. No nodding. No "Uh-huh, uh-huh." No questions or comments. He simply sat there, taking it all in. After I finished talking, he remained quiet for another minute or so, and I began to wonder if he had gone catatonic on me.

Finally, Myron asked, "So are the newspaper reports true? Is the squad really going to be shut down?"

"Yep."

"So, am I back in records?"

"It looks that way."

"What about you?" he asked. "What's next for Arthur Oveson, master sleuth?"

"The Morals Squad," I said. "This time Monday, I'll be netting hookers and raiding secret slot machine joints."

"Sounds delightful."

"We've still got three and a half days," I said. "A lot can happen in that time."

"I thought you said you're suspended until Monday," said Myron. "Doesn't that mean you're off the job?"

I shrugged. "Technically. Yeah. But I've never read the fine print on suspensions."

"We could ask Buddy," said Myron. "I'm sure he'd be tickled to clarify the rules."

"I'd prefer to leave him out of it." I fished out my wallet, took out a familiar slip of paper, and handed it to Myron.

He unfolded it and read the words *HELP US*.

"I'd rather talk to the man who wrote *that*," I said.

He returned it to me. "Where did that come from?"

"Carl Jeppson," I said, putting it back in my wallet.

I suddenly recalled the police file on Nelpha that Roscoe had given me. "You didn't happen to find out anything about a rash of thefts down in Dixie City, did you?"

"Thefts?"

"Yeah. These would've been in the spring. April. May."

"No. Nothing about any thefts."

"Listen, I could use your help these next few days."

"*My* help?" Myron shook his head. "With all due respect, I'm lying low. You should, too. We're lame ducks. We might as well start acting the part."

We finished our lunch, and when we got up to leave, I plunked a few coins on the table as a tip for the waitress. I could tell Myron wanted no part of this investigation any longer. In fairness to him, he'd already put countless hours of work into this squad. His willingness to drive hundreds of miles to southern Utah and northern Arizona, a long and arduous journey that he made without a single complaint, exhibited a level of commitment that was exceedingly rare in this profession, even among seasoned detectives. To call Myron dedicated would've been an understatement. This quiet and unassuming man had been nothing less than heroic. The news of the squad closing down seemed to hit him hard after all of the work he'd done.

All that is simply to say that I was not about to argue with Myron's "lame ducks" comment. He was probably right, after all. On the way out of Branning's, I thanked him and held out my hand. He stared at it for several seconds and then shook it, and while he did, I felt a touch of sadness. I'd miss Myron Adler, the same way I would be unhappy to part ways with Jared and Roscoe. I wished my little squad had more time. That's all I really wanted, just a little more time.

. . .

Half past five in the evening found me sitting on my porch swing, watching the smoke from distant fires. I knew Wit would be on time, and I no longer felt apprehensive as I watched the unmarked police sedan pulling into my driveway. Make no mistake: I had been nervous earlier. The prospect of being arrested for refusing to cooperate with Wit and Pace in their homicide investigation caused me no end of consternation. But at a certain point, I became convinced of the rightness of not cooperating. As Myron pointed out earlier over lunch at Branning's, the polygamists ran a multimillion-dollar empire, and the only way for a David like me to go up against a Goliath like that was to stare my fears down until all that was left standing was a resolve to do the right thing.

A pair of car doors slammed, and the homicide detectives approached me with their toughest tough-guy swaggers.

"I think you know why we're here, Art," said Wit.

"Where's the girl?" asked Pace, looking around the front yard, as if she'd been out here a second ago planting a sapling.

"She's gone," I said.

Pace walked up the steps and sat down on the porch swing next to me. My bald head elicited a chuckle from him. "What happened, Oveson? Lose a wrestling match with a lawn mower?"

"Something like that," I said. "Like I was saying, the girl isn't here."

"Still camping, huh?" Pace asked.

"What can I say? She likes the outdoors."

"Jesus Christ, Art, are you really gonna make us do this?" asked Wit.

"Don't even bother," I said, looking up at his pained face. "You're wasting your time and mine. If you couldn't keep all of those hardened polygamists behind bars last week, what makes you think it's going to go any better with me?"

Pace said, "When Buddy gets wind of this . . ."

"Tell him," I said. "Shoot, call him right now and I'll tell him. The only thing he hasn't done yet is fire me. If I lose this job, I'll find another one."

"When did you suddenly grow some cojones?" asked Pace.

I extended my hands outward, and Wit and Pace looked at each other with exasperation.

"Jesus Christ, I'm not actually going to cuff you," said Wit. "Let's go."

They loaded me into the backseat and slammed the door hard, slipped into the front, and started the auto, backing out of the driveway and coasting down our steep road. They were sore at me for calling their bluff. But I maintained my defiance. A few weeks ago, if somebody had predicted the police would be swooping down on my house to arrest me for sheltering an accused murderer who also happened to be the wife of a polygamist, I would've laughed off such a comment as crazy beyond all words. Yet here I was, prepared to accept whatever punishment should befall me for refusing to give up Nelpha Black.

Twenty-eight

Pace and Wit kept me waiting over an hour in an interrogation room in the basement of Public Safety. At one point, I asked the uniformed rookie in the hallway to escort me to the restroom for some much-needed relief. Back in the brightly lit box of a room, my behind began to ache on the hard chair, and the hands on the wall clock pointed to six forty-five when the door finally opened and Wit and Pace entered. Pace closed the door behind him and the two men sat across the table from me, neither bothering to apologize for detaining me for so long. Pace was holding a stack of eight-by-ten black-and-white photographs, which he placed on the table and pushed across to me. They must have been freshly developed, because they still smelled of darkroom chemicals. He gestured for me to pick them up.

I lifted the pictures—three in total—and started with the top one, the distinct silhouette of an airplane high in the sky, its wings and tail visible against the haze in the background. The tops of pine trees appeared in the foreground. I placed the top photo on the table and examined the second, a similar shot of the airplane, but this time with a black speck under it. A third photograph zoomed in closer to the airplane—still faraway, but slightly nearer—and the speck from the previous image turned out to be a human figure, arms and legs flailing, plummeting to the earth from hundreds, possibly thousands, of feet in the air. Not a pleasant image to behold.

I pushed the photos back to Pace and awaited an explanation.

"They were taken Sunday by a Civilian Conservation Corps shutterbug named Clifton Frost," said Pace. "He was photographing a wildfire near Swains Creek in Kane County, down in southern Utah."

"It's this guy's job to go all over the place snapping pictures of all the good things the CCC is doing," said Wit. "That way, when President Roosevelt asks Congress to give the agency more money, he can show slides of these fellas planting trees, building dams, and fighting forest fires."

Pace cut in: "Anyhow, Frost looks up and notices this plane flying about a thousand feet high, directly above the fire. At first he didn't think anything of it, but then he notices it circling and bobbing and flying erratically. So he starts taking pictures of it. He happened to capture this scene of a man getting pushed out of the airplane, right over the blaze."

"After that, the airplane flew away, according to Frost," said Wit.

"Who's the victim?" I asked.

"The sheriff's office down in Kanab retrieved the body and they've identified it as Carl Jeppson," said Pace. "They contacted us this morning to say the body will be shipped up here for a formal autopsy. Tom Livsey will do the honors with the help of Jeppson's dental records."

My mouth fell open. I could not conceal my shock. I pictured that little note Jeppson had slipped to me on the day Roscoe and I visited his flower shop: *HELP US*. I suspected Jeppson had been the mastermind behind the polygamists' incredible financial success, and I also had reason to believe that he had turned informant to assist with Harold O'Rourke's federal investigation. I knew that he provided crucial financial help to his daughter, who had been sheltering the banished boys and runaway child brides from Dixie City. It made me forlorn, knowing the one apostle with a kind heart, and haunted by remorse, died in such a horrific fashion. This was homicide writ large, carried out by men of power, unlike the seemingly spontaneous shooting that claimed the lives of LeGrand Johnston and Volney Mason. My stunned silence, I'm sure, spoke volumes.

"The dead man was a hell of a mess, scorched by the flames," said Wit. "He still had his billfold on him, with his ID. The sheriff of Kane County was kind enough to courier us copies of Frost's photographs. It goes without saying, but I'll say it anyway, that this is being treated as foul play."

"You look as though you've seen a ghost," said Pace.

"Why would the polygamists chance it like that?" I asked. "With all of those CCC firefighters in the area?"

"This is the first summer the feds have trucked the CCC men out to combat the wildfires," said Wit. "In past years, if some remote part of southern Utah went up in flames, they just let it burn."

"They probably didn't know there were CCCers in the area," said Pace. "With all of that smoke in the sky, I'm sure visibility was limited."

"We think this is all tied to the double homicide we're investigating," said Wit. "That's why we need to see the girl. She was there the night of the shootings and her fingerprints are all over the murder weapon."

"She's a key suspect," said Pace. "We'd like to have her back, if that's not too much to ask, Oveson."

"Like I told you earlier, she's camping," I said.

Pace smacked the table with his palm, startling me. "I'm tired of your stalling, Oveson! I want some answers!"

"Or what? You're going to lock me up?" I snapped back. "Is it curtains for me, Pace? Huh? Is it the firing squad for old Oveson?"

I lurched out of my chair and walked over to the door and, as expected, Pace spoke up. "Where do you think you're going?"

"Are you planning to arrest me?" I asked.

"C'mon, Art, sit down," said Wit. "Let's talk some more, like civilized men."

"If I'm not under arrest, I'm leaving," I said.

Pace leaned toward Wit and spoke in a hushed tone. "Let's arrest him. An overnighter in a cell oughta set him straight."

Wit tilted closer to his partner and whispered, but I could still hear him. "We've got nothing on him, and he knows it. That malarkey about obstructing a homicide investigation won't stick. He can plead ignorance to her whereabouts, and no judge in his right mind is about to throw the book at a police detective for that."

"Tell you what, Pace," I taunted, "when your bite finally catches up with your bark, come back and pinch me. Until then, leave me alone, because I've had it with you." I gave a friendly nod to Wit. "You have a good evening, Wit."

"Yeah, you too, Art," he said, sighing.

Oddly enough, my comment made Pace laugh as he leaned back in his chair and knitted his fingers behind his head for support with elbows pointing outward. On my way out the door, I overheard him say, "*Pinch me.* This clown is on the radio once and he thinks he's Sam Spade."

The telephone rang in the middle of the night.

I switched on my bedside lamp and looked at the alarm clock: 2:41 A.M. I rubbed cinders out of my eyes, kicked my legs off the bed, and pushed my feet into my slippers. The shrill ring continued, coming from outside my door, and still in a daze, I crossed my room and stepped into the hallway. I picked up the candlestick telephone and raised the receiver out of the cradle, holding it up to my ear.

"Hello?"

"This is the operator," said a woman's voice. "I have a person-to-person collect call for Arthur Oveson from Mr. Orville Babcock."

I instantly recalled the frumpy man at the used car lot in the Dixieland outfit. I wondered for a silent second why on earth he would be calling me.

"I'm Arthur Oveson."

"Will you accept the charges?"

"Yes, ma'am."

There were a few clicks, followed by a lot of crackling and hissing.

"Hello?" I said.

The static continued. I stayed on the line, repeating "hello" several times. After two minutes of this, the line went dead. I gave the earpiece hook on the telephone a good shaking up and down and waited for the operator to return to the line.

"Operator, this is Arthur Oveson at Wasatch one-four-eight-four."

"This is the operator. Go ahead."

"Yes, a man named Orville Babcock just tried to call me a minute or two ago," I said. "Unfortunately, he didn't ever connect, and I'm wondering if there's any way of finding out where the phone call originated from?"

"Sorry, sir, but we have no way of determining that."

"Okay," I said, closing my burning dry eyes tightly and blinking a few times. "Thank you for your assistance."

"You're welcome."

She disconnected and I placed the earpiece in the cradle and lowered the telephone to its home on the little wooden table.

No use in going back to bed, I thought. *I'm awake now.* I sauntered into the kitchen, poured milk in a saucepan, and placed it on the stove. I turned on a simmering flame, went over to the table, and sat down on one of the chairs to wait for my milk to heat up.

The telephone rang again. I rushed over to the wall phone in the kitchen and raised the receiver to my ear. "Hello," I said eagerly into the transmitter horn.

"This is the operator," said a woman's voice, the same nasally voice as the one that had called earlier. "I have a person-to-person collect call for . . ."

"Go ahead and put Mr. Babcock through," I said. "I'm expecting his call."

A click sounded, and I waited for a few seconds, only to be greeted once again by the popping and a few ghostly, barely audible party lines.

"Hello," I said. Nothing. "Hello, this is Arthur Oveson. Who's there?"

The receiver emitted a sound like bacon fat crackling in the pan.

"Hello, is this Orville Babcock?" I asked. "This is Art Oveson. Can you hear me?"

The noise from the telephone was starting to hurt my ear, and once again, I pulled the earpiece away from me to hang it up. That's when I heard the desperate voice bursting through the wall of static.

"Hello! Oveson! Can you hear me now?"

I raised the telephone again. "Babcock? Is that you?"

His voice sounded distant, and it kept getting drowned out by the endless hissing and popping. I could make out only certain words before he'd get cut off, but then he would return again. This back and forth continued the entire time I had him on the line.

"Oveson . . . you?"

"Yeah, it's me! You're going to have to speak up, Babcock!"

Static, and then: ". . . call . . . night, but I couldn't . . ." Static.

"Babcock! Please, talk louder!"

". . . because he was my first cousin!"

"Who is your cousin?" I asked. "I didn't hear the first part!"

"Jeppson! He . . . cousin and closest friend . . . broken up about . . ."

His voice cut out again.

"Babcock, are you there?" I asked.

"Can you hear me now?"

"I can, yes," I said. "Go ahead. You were saying that Carl Jeppson was your cousin?"

"I never thought it'd come to this."

"I take it you've heard about what happened to him?"

"Yes. His wife, Arla Gwen, told me!"

"Where are you now?"

"What? Speak up?"

I yelled into the phone: "I said where are you now, Babcock?"

"I'm . . ." He cut out again. A few seconds later, he came back: ". . . kill me if they find . . ." Gone again. Then back: ". . . don't want to take that risk . . ."

"Is there somewhere we can meet?" I asked.

"If there's a way you . . ."

Static cut him off. Waiting for his return, my heart beat fiercely and my hands shook. I felt beads of sweat forming on my brow.

"I can't hear you," I finally said. "You're going to have to talk louder, Babcock!"

". . . the entire time, Carl was worried sick about the four banished boys! He helped . . . all kinds of ways, and right now they're holed up in . . ."

Babcock gone. Static back.

"Holed up where?" I asked. "Where are they?"

". . . Floyd!" he shouted. A moment later, his voice broke through the static again: "Fairfield."

"Floyd Fairfield?" I asked. "Hello? Hello? Babcock, can you hear me? Hello?"

The line went dead. Both the static and Babcock were gone.

I parked in front of Roscoe's apartment. The lights in the windows glowed orange behind pulled-down roller blinds. I shut off the engine and second-guessed myself once again, wondering whether I was doing the right thing. My first instinct was not to bother Roscoe, especially at this ungodly hour. Yet I knew him to be a night owl, a man every bit as plagued by insomnia as I'd been my whole life. I entered the building and went up a flight of stairs, taking a deep breath before knocking on his door. When I finally worked up the nerve, I gave three hard raps and waited. In the dimly lit hall, I wondered if Roscoe was scoping me through the little peephole. When he finally opened the door, he had on a familiar dark blue bathrobe that I'd seen him wearing on a few other occasions when I'd come to pick him up.

"Art," he said. "Hold on, will ya?"

"Sure."

The door slammed abruptly. I turned around and inspected the grimy walls, desperately in need of a fresh coat of paint. I stuck my hands in my pockets and whistled the theme song to *Footlight Parade*, still fresh in my mind. The door opened again, wider this time, and Roscoe stepped back and with a wave of his hand invited me in.

"I hope I'm not interrupting," I said, stepping inside.

"It ain't every day you show up at half past three in the morning," he said, closing the door. "But you're welcome here any old time. Make yourself at home."

I strolled into his living room and sat down on the sofa, and his two cats—the orange tabby Barney and the tortoiseshell Millicent—came charging out and the faster of the two, "Millie" (as Roscoe called her), leaped onto my lap, in pursuit of chin rubs and back scratches.

"Can I get you something to drink?" he asked. "I know you don't like the hard stuff, but I have . . . well . . . tap water."

"No thanks," I said.

Clopping high heels of women's shoes approached, and seconds later a striking-looking Chinese woman emerged from the darkened hallway wearing nothing but a garter belt, thigh-high hosiery, and exotic sparkling shoes. She froze when she saw me, and made no attempt to cover her breasts or the black bush between her legs. I dipped my head in embarrassment.

"Xing Li miss Roscoe," she said. "Come in. I tickle you more."

Roscoe situated himself between her and me. "Go back in the bedroom, my little Mandarin flower," he said. "Papa will join you soon. I want to talk to my friend first."

"Bye, friend!"

I looked up at Xing Li waving, and her little breasts jiggled along with her fingers. I waved while I blushed. Xing Li left, her footsteps echoing until the door closed, and Roscoe sat in a chair nearby.

"Sorry," he said. "Modesty has never been one of her strong suits."

"It looks to me like she doesn't have any suits, period," I said. "Friend of yours?"

"Yeah. I help her a little. She helps me. If you get my drift."

I nodded. "Drift gotten."

"You're as bald as I am. That's a nasty gash you got there. What the hell happened to your head?"

"Funny you should I ask," I said.

I spent the next hour filling Roscoe in on everything that had happened to me since we received our suspensions on Monday. He listened intently to my every word, letting me know from time to time that it was okay for me to push his cats off if they were bothering me. They weren't. I liked having Barney and Millicent around. I found their purring presence comforting, and I stroked them the entire time I talked to Roscoe. He grimaced when I told him about the photographs of Carl Jeppson falling out of the airplane, and he seemed troubled to hear about my late-night phone call from Orville Babcock. I also let Roscoe know that before coming over here tonight, I'd driven past Babcock's used-car lot, but the place was pitch-black, with no signs of life. Since Babcock wasn't listed in the city directory, I had no idea where he lived, which ruled out a late-night visit to his house.

"Listen, thanks for hearing me out," I said, toward the end of my long talk. "I guess I'm more tired than I thought. I haven't been sleeping well. I've got the jitters. These polygamists spook me. And I worry about Nelpha. I still don't know anything about her. It's like Wit said last night: Maybe she's the one who pulled the trigger on those two men."

"You've been through a lot, Art," said Roscoe. "Why don't you stay here? You can sleep on the couch. Xing Li and I will keep it down in the next room."

"That's a swell offer," I said. "But I won't stay. I just needed someone to talk to, after that creepy telephone call."

I stood up, and he got up and circled the chair to get to the front door. On my way out, I stopped at the table when I saw that picture of the dark-haired girl with the toothy smile. I found her cheery face comforting, a nice way to bring to a close such a troubling night. Roscoe noticed me looking at the picture, so I smiled at him and gave him a wink.

"Nona," I said. "Don't worry, I won't ask."

"She's my daughter," he said.

I wasn't expecting that. I swallowed hard and managed to say, "I didn't know . . ."

"It's a long story," he said. "Maybe some other time I'll tell it to you."

"Okay," I said, trying to hide my disappointment. I wanted to know now.

I squatted to pet his cats, and they both brushed up against my legs, purring like a couple of automobile engines. I reached for the knob to open the door, and as I did, Roscoe pointed to Barney and Millicent.

"Please don't let 'em out," he said. "Those two are all I've got."

I managed a smile. "They're not all you've got. Good night, Roscoe."

"Night, Art."

I closed the door behind me, and halfway down the stairs tears welled up in my eyes. I wasn't expecting to get choked up at four thirty in the morning, but there I was, getting in my car, and wiping my cheeks with the back of my hand.

Twenty-nine

Something quite unexpected yet welcome happened during my drive home: it began raining. And not the light sprinkle that typically passes for a rainstorm in Utah, either. No, these droplets turned into a downpour, sheets of rain, with the occasional lightning flash burning neon webs into my retinas. Motoring up L Street, the deluge became so blinding that my windshield wipers hardly helped me at all, even switched on high. Climbing up the steep road, I noticed in my mirror that the once mighty canyon blazes to the south had dimmed to a faint orange, like dying embers in the wee hours. The heavy rain lifted my spirits. Maybe this meant there was an end in sight to all of those destructive wildfires raging across our state. It so pleased me, in fact, that after I steered into my driveway, I shut off my car, got out, and stood in the showers until they soaked me to the marrow. Stepping up to the covered porch, dripping water everywhere, I fumbled for my keys, unlocked the door, and entered my darkened house. I patted the wall blindly until I found the button and pushed it, and the light fixture above my head went on.

Exhausted and dripping water, my head still throbbing from the injury, I went into the kitchen, opened a little brown bottle of morphine tablets that Dr. May had given me, and popped one in my mouth without even bothering to get a glass of water. Then I took off my wet clothes, stepped into the shower, and stood under the water awhile, letting it warm my body and spray my face. I scrubbed myself with a bar of soap and took my time rinsing off the lather. Afterward, I stepped out onto the tile, dried off, and used my towel to wipe steam off the mirror. I looked terrible. I had no hair and sported that ghoulish, stitched-up scar on the top of my noggin. Leaving the bathroom, my need for sleep trumped my grumbling stomach, and I donned my temple garments and a pair of flannel pajamas. I'm certain I fell asleep before my head even touched the pillow, and I plunged deep into slumber.

I slept fitfully. In my dreams, I wandered through crooked corridors, went up winding staircases, walked past outrageously shaped doors. One flew open and an engorged, slimy purple tentacle lunged out of the darkness and wrapped around my ankle, pulling me down a set of rickety wooden stairs. My chin bounced on each one—*thud-thud-thud*—until when I hit the cold floor, I dug my fingernails into the ground to try to stop the tentacle from pulling me inside a giant mouth full of razor-sharp teeth.

I opened my eyes and sat up. The clock said quarter to seven in the morning. I ran my hands over my face. My heart pounded something fierce. *What was the significance of a giant tentacle pulling me into a basement?* Then I remembered encountering

Nelpha as she came out of the basement right after she arrived here, and Clara witnessing the same thing while I was away in Dixie City. *Why was Nelpha so fixated on our basement?* I leaped to my feet, rushed into the hallway, and flung the basement door open and hurried down the steps. At the bottom of the stairs, I reached up and pulled the light's chain. The glowing bulb swung from the ceiling on a cord, throwing shadows all over.

I scanned the room and almost missed a large, rectangular box-shaped object in the dust-filled darkness, tucked away to the side of the boiler, adjacent to a shelf of jarred foods. I went over to it, crouched low, and removed a green wool blanket from it to reveal a steamer trunk, closed with fasteners, reinforced by buckled straps. I gripped one of the brown leather handles on the side and used all of my might to drag it out a few feet. I dropped to my knees before it, popped up the fasteners, unbuckled the straps, and lifted the lid. The swinging light above me slowed and cast a dull yellow glow on more money than I'd ever seen in my life. I lifted a stack of twenty-dollar bills held together by a currency strap. I pressed my thumb into the edge and began flipping bills until I reached the end, guessing I held a hundred twenties in my hand. I looked down at the trunk full of money. I must have been staring at a million dollars.

Then came the dull thud of the front door closing, followed by floorboards creaking above my head. I wasn't expecting Clara or anybody else who would let themselves in. I moved fast, closing the trunk, situating it back where I found it, covering it with the blanket. I reached up and turned the dangling light off, and I held the hot glass in my hand for a second to stop it from swinging. Though it was now pitch-black, I knew the layout of the basement, and I quickly sprang into a storage closet, where we kept boxes of winter clothes and various knickknacks. I

reached for the knob and pulled the door most of the way shut
behind me. This gave me an ideal view of the main basement
room, should whoever was upstairs come down here. I took a
deep breath and held it for a moment as two sets of footsteps
came down the stairs, and a few seconds later, a flashlight beam
danced around the room like a glowing sword. I watched intently through the narrow opening.

The light went on. Claudia Jeppson lowered her arm from
the chain and looked around the basement. The dim bulb illuminated her dark polka-dot dress, and even from here I could
see her trembling. A figure approached her from behind and
gave her a hard shove, sending her stumbling forward with a
fearful little squeal. She straightened and turned to face Ferron
Steed, whose wide-brimmed hat still dripped water from the
rainstorm outside. She said something to him, but I could not
hear her from where I was standing, so I inched forward and
moved my ear closer to the doorframe.

"Where is it?" asked Steed.

"It was dark when we brought it here! I need a second. . . ."

He hauled off and slapped her. The crack from it jarred me.
She fell to her hands and knees. She returned to her feet, stroking her cheek where he hit her.

"Quit stalling," he said. "Find it! Now!"

Claudia looked around for a few frantic seconds, eventually
spotting the trunk. I couldn't help but wonder how on earth she
had brought that hefty thing into my basement without any of us
noticing. She knelt in front of it, moved the blanket, and reached
for the fastener. Her hand froze before touching it, and I realized I'd forgotten to fasten the trunk closed after I opened it.
She looked over her shoulder, and I felt a strange sensation
that she knew I was hiding nearby. Steed walked up to her

and, still holding a gun, smacked the back of her head with his free palm.

"Stop hitting me!" she screamed, on the verge of tears.

He reached down and grabbed a clump of her hair and pulled her to her feet. She writhed in pain, and when standing, Steed pushed her out of the way and squatted near the open trunk, gun aimed at Claudia. He used his free hand to pick up a wad of bills, and nodded with approval when he inspected it in the dim yellow light. When she stepped out of my line of vision, I poked the door slightly, careful not to let the hinges squeak. She came into view again, standing by the boiler, wiping tears from her eyes.

More footsteps trod heavily down the stairs, and I craned my neck to get a look at who was coming. The brawny physiques of the Kunz brothers moved into the light, taking their places near Steed with revolvers drawn and aimed at Claudia. Steed tossed his stack of bills back into the trunk, closed the top, and snapped the fasteners shut. He shot up to his feet and turned to the Kunz brothers with a scowl on his homely face.

"Did you find her?" he asked.

"No," said Devlin with a headshake.

"We searched every room," said Dorland. "Place is empty."

"Where is Nelpha?" Steed asked Claudia.

She said something quietly. I think it was, "I don't know."

Whatever she said, it prompted Steed to slap her in the face again, and she yelped in pain. I coiled up in rage, wishing I could go out there and challenge Steed to a good old-fashioned fistfight. I had no illusions about my prospects of going up against that heavily armed trio. I stayed hidden in that stuffy little closet, however, trying my hardest to keep my anger in check. Somewhere in the back of my head was my father telling me to choose my battles wisely, and to know which hill is worth dying on.

"It'll displease the prophet if we go back without the girl," said Devlin. "He knows she was at the church that night. He thinks she saw everything."

"That scum Oveson has got her in hiding," said Dorland. "I tell you, I ain't gonna sleep easy at night until I take his head clean off."

"You'll get your chance," said Steed. "But we've got to focus on what's in front of us now. The prophet wants the girl and the money. Sooner or later, we'll have to find her."

"I say we hand her over to the prophet, too," said Dorland, gesturing to Claudia. "She was at the church when the killing happened. At least that's what her father blurted out, sometime after I sliced him up, but before we pushed him out of the airplane."

He chuckled, until Claudia smacked him in his nose. He bent over and howled in agony.

"You bitch!" he shrieked, flinging his head back, pointing his revolver at her, cocking the hammer. "Imma put a bullet in you right now!"

I backed up a step, knocking over a broom behind me. All faces turned in that direction.

"Did you hear that?" Steed whispered.

"It came from over there."

I crouched low, backed up, and ducked behind a big box of coats and snow boots. My feet were sticking out beyond the box's edge, so I pulled them in, and not a moment too soon. The light in the closet went on. I wasn't about to peek over the top to see who it was, and as long as I remained in the fetal position, I stood a chance of not being spotted.

"I don't see anything," said a voice belonging to Devlin Kunz. His shadow moved along the wall and I feared he was coming toward me, but the light went out and the door slammed closed. I was too frightened to move. A minute later, the familiar sound of footsteps on the main floor rumbled above me, and I took that as my cue. Gradually, I eased the closet door open until it became apparent that I was the only one in the basement. The steamer trunk was gone. I rushed up the stairs, slipped into the hallway, and cut over to the front door. Peering through a window in the door, I watched a black Model T truck pulling out of my driveway. Gears grinded when it was on the road, and it sped southward, followed by the Hudson belonging to the Kunz brothers, which had been parked by the curb. The roar of motors faded, and the only sound left was the patter of rain falling outside.

When I went back inside my house, the telephone was ringing. I hesitated to answer it. How much more could I take?

I raised the candlestick telephone and lifted the receiver to my ear.

I heard sobbing and shaky breathing on the other end. "Art?"

"Clara?" I asked. "What is it?"

"It's Nelpha," she said. "She's gone. Again."

Thirty

I stopped at a door with the brass numbers 308 nailed into the wood. I fished my little address book out of my pocket, flipped to the *W*s, and confirmed the address in my handwriting. *J. Weeks—Maryland Apts, 839 So. Temple.* I put the booklet away, gave a knock, waited, and heard footsteps on the other side. The knob turned, the door opened a few inches—secured by a chain—and Jared blinked at me through the space. He closed the door, the chain rattled, and he opened it, stepping back and signaling me with his hand to enter. We exchanged quiet hellos and I removed my hat as I entered his sparsely furnished apartment. It was bright and airy, with wooden floors and a balcony looking out over South Temple, one of Salt Lake City's main east-west thoroughfares.

He closed the door, and we left the front entrance hall for the living room. A table against the wall had been turned into a gun-cleaning station, with a cloth draped over it and covered with bottles of solvent and oil, an old toothbrush, pipe cleaners, and a cleaning rag. Two revolvers and a box of cartridges sat in the center of the table, right below a wall clock that said 7:20. The wind blew that beautiful clean smell of rain into the apartment.

"Have a seat," he said, tipping his head at a little green sofa.

I sat down. He plunged into a nearby chair and studied me for a while.

"It's all happened so fast," he said. "Carl is dead. They've taken Claudia."

"And Nelpha is gone," I added.

He went wide-eyed. "But I thought . . ."

"She was staying with my wife and kids at my sister-in-law's house," I said. "This morning she was gone. Clara doesn't know where she went. Clara's reached her breaking point. She can't take it anymore. Frankly, neither can I." I waited a beat for Jared to take that in before questioning him. "How did you know Claudia was gone?"

"Steed and the Kunz brothers took her at gunpoint," he said. "I was just over at Claudia's house. Several of the kids saw it happen in the early-morning hours. They're pretty shaken up about it, and they're even more frightened to call the police out of fear they'll be taken away and put in foster homes or sent back to Dixie City. I'm guessing Claudia is on her way down to Rulon's compound as we speak. That's where I'm headed. If you'll excuse me, there are few things I have to do before I go."

"That's a bad idea," I said. "You're going to be outgunned."

Jared got up and walked over to the table. He opened a box of cartridges. He snapped open the revolver's chamber and began loading bullets into his .38, one after another, and then closed it. He did the same thing with the other gun. He was being so methodical, despite the rage I saw in his eyes a moment ago when we were talking.

"Do you think they found Nelpha?" he asked.

"I don't know," I said. "There's nothing more I can do. I'm suspended. And even if I weren't off the job, I wouldn't think of going up against Steed and the Kunz brothers. Not in a million years."

"I won't ask you to come with me, boss," he said. "But I have to go. I've got no choice."

"Sure you do," I said. "Stay here. Look after those kids. They need an adult to take care of them. I bet they're scared out of their wits about what happened to Claudia. I'll call Sheriff Burke Colborne down in Kingman. I'll tell him about Claudia being taken down there against her will. We'll let the law handle it."

"A lot of good that'll do," said Jared. "Colborne doesn't even know where Rulon's compound is."

"That makes two of us," I said. "Shoot, I don't even know if it's in Utah or Arizona. Do you?"

"Do I what?" he asked, clearly preoccupied.

I stood up and walked over to him. "Do you know where Rulon's compound is?"

"I wouldn't be going there if I didn't," he said.

"Do you really think this will do any good?" I asked. "Taking the law into your own hands?"

"Look at all the harm they've done, and tell me something, boss," he said. "How many of the polygamists are actually serving time for the crimes they've committed? How many of them have ever known the consequences, or paid the price, for their actions? Not a single one."

"What's your plan?" I asked. "Are you just going to waltz right into the hornet's nest? So you can join Carl Jeppson in the cemetery? If you do that, then they've won again. Those poor kids will be on their own, left to fend for themselves. If they're lucky, the state will parcel them out to foster homes. Maybe some of them will get stuck in orphanages, or worse, in the state industrial school, which is just a glorified dungeon for unwanted children. Is that what you want?"

"No! Justice is what I want." Jared lifted one of his guns. "This is the only language those men understand, boss. And I aim to speak it louder than they do."

"Stay," I pleaded. "Help me build cases against them."

"How? Our squad is dead. Remember? What are we gonna do? Build cases in our spare time?"

"If we have to, yes!"

"We've been working at it full-time for months now, and we're no closer to putting any of those men behind bars than when we started. We don't stand a chance. They've got everything on their side—money, a high-priced attorney, and an entire town they control out in the middle of nowhere. Nobody dares touch them. They'll go on getting away with murder, and a lot worse, until someone works up the nerve to go down there and put a stop to it."

I was staring at a man with nothing to lose. If he were willing to put his life on the line to rescue Claudia Jeppson, then surely he would show that same loyalty in shielding a murderer who he cared about. It hit me right then that Jared probably knew who had shot and killed LeGrand Johnston and Volney Mason, that he was covering up for the person or persons, and it was somehow all connected to the money in my basement. Earlier this morning, when I saw Steed and the Kunz brothers roughing up Claudia for information, I began to suspect she might have been the shooter. Possibly she was. I knew Jared would do anything to protect her. He'd do the same for Nelpha, too. And he would go down fighting to safeguard the integrity of his own hallowed name—one he took from his deceased brother—in order to prevent it from being associated with the crime of murder. They were natural-born survivors, these young exiles from polygamy. They knew how to take care of one another, and they knew how to look after themselves.

"At least tell me this," I said. "Where did that money in my basement come from?"

The question caught him off guard. He considered his response for about half a minute. I could tell by his sigh and suddenly drooping shoulders that he had decided to tell me the truth.

"It came from a heist," he said. "The four missing boys—Boyd, Garth, Frank, and Chester—they pulled it off. Back in May. It happened on a remote stretch of highway in northern Arizona. The boys hijacked a truck, a Model T, carrying a trunk packed with cash. The money was being hauled from the bank in Dixie City to Rulon's compound. See, by this time, Rulon was the real head of the cult, the brains behind the operations. LeGrand Johnston was a prophet in *name* only. He wasn't running things at all. Everybody knew it. Rulon siphoned the money from the crooked dealings of his various front scams."

When Jared mentioned the Model T truck, I nearly told him about the one I saw in Claudia's detached garage. I was certain it was the vehicle used in the heist, and I was wondering if it was the same one I had seen at the Fundamentalist Church the night the double homicide occurred. To be certain, it was not the only Model T truck on the road. There were plenty of others. But what a striking coincidence that the truck used in the robbery was the same make as the one at the church that night.

I decided to postpone asking about the truck. Now was not the right time. That would come soon enough, I figured.

Instead I asked, "How did the boys find out about this big haul?"

"Before the heist, they all lived together, barely surviving out in the wilderness near Dixie City."

"I don't get it," I said. "Why not just come here? Surely they know about Claudia's place being a haven."

"Not everybody makes the Salt Lake pilgrimage," he said. "Some boys try to stick it out down there. Often, a sister wife or two will secretly pitch in and help out with food and clothing and whatnot. See, a lot of these boys regard that part of the world as their home. To them, Salt Lake City seems like a big, cold, indifferent metropolis. They opt for the devil they know."

"I see. You were saying these boys were barely getting by outside of Dixie City?"

"Yeah. And the only way they could've found out about that shipment of money is if somebody on the inside tipped them off."

"Inside?" I asked. "You mean Rulon's inner circle?"

"Yes."

"Got any ideas about the source of the leak?" I asked.

"The boys claim it came from Eldon Black," Jared said.

"Eldon?" I asked. "Not Rulon?"

"In case you haven't noticed, Eldon is Rulon's attack dog," Jared said. "He acts as his father's enforcer, so Rulon can continue living in seclusion. The boys told me that Eldon found out they were living in an abandoned prospector's shack about fifteen miles from Dixie City. They say he paid them a visit, told them about the money, and he coaxed them to steal it. In their version of events, he said he felt sorry for them, and they deserved the money for all the hardship they'd been through. He assured them it was insured and would be replaced at no cost to Rulon. He even provided the firearms. Eldon threatened the boys that if any of this ever got traced back to him, he'd kill them."

"What was Eldon's angle?" I asked.

"He wanted the boys do his dirty work. He arranged for the money to be shipped by a licensed transport company based out of Flagstaff, so the insurance would cover it if it was lost or stolen. Eldon's plan was to replace the money and then send his goons out to hunt down the boys, kill them, and take the stolen money back. Only the boys didn't know that at the time."

"How did they finally figure out that Eldon wanted his money back?"

"The boys brought the money up here and gave some of it to Claudia," he said. "At first they said nothing about the heist. One of the boys made up a lie about his father giving him some money. They told Claudia they wanted her to have it, to help her out. At first, she couldn't resist. She took some. She purchased things for her house—some new furniture, a radio, a lawnmower. But the boys kept giving her cash, see, and it didn't take her long to figure out the story of the father giving his son money was fishy." Jared paused to rub the bristles on his chin. "She pushed the boys and got the truth out of them, and realized they were in danger. She knew that sooner or later—probably sooner—Eldon's goons were going to come looking for the money. That's why she insisted on hiding the boys."

"How much money are we talking about exactly?"

"I don't know the precise amount," said Jared. "Hundreds of thousands, possibly close to a million. On the shipping forms, Rulon had it listed as a transfer of tithing funds."

"Does this have anything to do with why Nelpha came to Salt Lake City?" I asked.

Jared nodded. "Nelpha and Boyd are close. Real close. She came all the way up here to ask Johnston to have mercy on the boys."

"I don't get it," I said. "Why didn't she go straight to Rulon?"

"Rulon is a jealous man," said Jared. "Her bond with Boyd Johnston would've sent him into a fit of rage. Nelpha knew that."

"Did Rulon know about this heist?" I asked.

"I don't know," said Jared, with an edge of exasperation in his voice. "You're talking about one of the most secretive men in the world. We don't even have a picture of him. If you think about it, the only person who would know for sure is Eldon, and he's not about to go around spilling that information to a group of boys who his old man banished."

"So Nelpha decided to see Johnston?" I asked.

"Yes."

"Did Carl Jeppson set up a meeting between the two?"

"Yes."

"Who all was at that meeting?"

"Nelpha, Johnston, and Volney Mason. Claudia dropped Nelpha off at the fundamentalist church and left."

"What about you?" I asked.

"I only found out about it after it happened," Jared said. "In fact, I didn't know about any of this—the heist, the money, Nelpha coming here to plead with the prophet—until after the killings. Claudia explained it all to me, just before I took you out to see her the first time."

"Let's go back to the night of the meeting," I said. "What exactly was discussed before the shootings happened?"

"At Carl's urging, the boys had agreed to surrender the

money. Carl had discussed the matter with Uncle Grand—er, I mean Johnston—a few days before the main meeting, just the two of them. Johnston gave Carl his word that if the boys gave back the truck and the money and apologized for their actions, they wouldn't be harmed."

"So where had the boys been staying since the heist? With Claudia?"

"No. They were lying low, in a hiding place. Claudia worried that if they came to stay with her, it would endanger the other kids."

"Where's the hiding place?"

"I'd rather not say."

"Are they still alive?" I asked.

He nodded.

"I still don't understand something," I said. "Why would Carl Jeppson stick his neck out to arrange this meeting?"

"Carl wanted to help Nelpha and the boys. The man was dogged by remorse for his involvement in the rackets of the polygamists. He just wanted to make things right. His plan was to give the money back to Johnston and ask him to intercede on behalf of the boys."

"Would Rulon actually have those boys killed over this?"

"Absolutely," said Jared. "He's bloodthirsty."

"I see. The night of the murders . . ."

"Yes."

"Walk me through it. Claudia takes Nelpha to the church . . ."

"Yes."

". . . to meet with Johnston. . . ."

"Yes."

"The meeting has more or less been prearranged between Johnston and Jeppson. . . ."

"Yes."

"The plan is to give the money back."

"Yes."

"And what else?"

"Ask for Johnston's forgiveness."

"Okay. Where does it all go wrong?"

He was quiet for a while. Literally, this was his moment of truth. I watched him as he stared down at his guns on the table.

"Johnston got angry," Jared said.

"Why?"

"He said Carl Jeppson was supposed to bring the four boys to the meeting, to apologize in person," said Jared. "They'd made a verbal pact before the meeting, which Jeppson interpreted to mean that he could apologize on behalf of the boys. The night of the meeting, LeGrand flew into a rage because the boys weren't there. But I think that was a smokescreen. He'd planned to betray Carl all along. Johnston wanted the boys to come that night so he could telephone Eldon Black to come out and pick them up and take them to Rulon for punishment. Those boys would've suffered unspeakable horrors at the hands of those two."

"Why would Johnston do something like that?"

"He was terrified of Rulon and wanted to get on the man's good side. It was his way of pacifying the monster."

"How come Johnston was scared of Rulon?"

"How could he not be? Rulon and his goons are vicious killers. And, like I said earlier, Rulon was the real leader of the sect. Johnston was leader in name only."

"So when the boys didn't show up to the meeting . . ."

"He got cross, started yelling about how everything was all wrong, and then telephoned Eldon to come and pick up Nelpha.

But Nelpha had no intention of going back to Rulon. When LeGrand went to make the call, that's when shots were fired."

"Who fired them?"

"I don't know," said Jared. "The day after the murders, I examined the crime scene after the Homicide dicks left, to see it for myself. I think the shooter acted fast. Gun is drawn. Gun is fired. LeGrand is shot first, giving Mason time to reach for his gun. But the shooter turns on Mason. Mason fires off a shot, but it enters the wall. That tells me the exchange happened quickly. I don't think Carl was the shooter. He trusted LeGrand, which is why he agreed to the second meeting. Claudia doesn't own a gun."

"That leaves Nelpha," I said.

"Does it matter who pulled the trigger?" he asked. "Whether it was Carl or Claudia or Nelpha, the killer had no choice."

"I found Nelpha hiding in the closet on the second floor of the church," I said. "How do you suppose the gun ended up in the hedges outside?"

"The killer got sloppy, I guess," said Jared. "Tossed the gun out without thinking about it, then got out of there on the double."

"That's possible," I said. "How did the money end up in my basement?"

"When Nelpha ran away from your house last week, she found a way to get down to the hideaway where the boys are staying," said Jared. "She wanted to see Boyd. She stayed there for a couple of nights. That was where the truck and the money were being kept. Boyd gave Nelpha a ride back to your house on Saturday."

"But wouldn't Clara . . ."

"When they got there, nobody was home. Nelpha knew a way to get in, through a basement window with a loose latch.

You'd best get it fixed, boss. Anyway, when Boyd found out that was your house, and you're a policeman, he got the bright idea of hiding the money in your basement. He and Nelpha carried it down there. Your wife and children got home from the store right as Boyd was driving away. That's when your wife found Nelpha. Boyd told all of this to Claudia and she went through the roof. Hollered at him something terrible. She drove him back to . . . well, back to the hiding place. She kept the Model T truck, so Boyd wouldn't repeat any foolish stunts like that one again. It's parked in her garage."

A wave of relief swept over me, as if Jared had just opened the curtains on a panoramic window, and I now I got to see everything on the other side. But there was still a big pane of glass blocking my way, preventing me from entering that world.

"What do you think they're going to do to Claudia?" I asked.

"Same thing they did to Carl," Jared said. "Same thing they're gonna do to the boys, if they ever catch them. And unless they're stopped, they'll go right on destroying more innocent people."

Jared slipped his loaded guns into a holster belt he was wearing, and he reached for his olive green fedora and placed it on his head. He started to leave, but I stepped in his way.

"I'm afraid I can't let you go, Jared."

He dipped his head, giving me a prime view of the top of his hat.

"Step aside, boss."

"You're my subordinate until Monday morning," I said. "I'm ordering you not to go."

He glared at me. "I said move out of my way."

"Have you even thought through what you're going to do?" I asked. "What good is a pair of .38s in a situation like this?"

"I've got a whole arsenal packed into Claudia's Nash outside," he said. "And I'll use it, if need be. Now clear out of my way."

"No."

His body relaxed and he turned his back to me, as if prepared to give up.

I didn't expect him to hit me. He did, however. A second later, I was flat on my back, in a pained daze, only semiconscious, my face burning with searing white pain in the spot where his knuckles struck my skin, coupled with my head throbbing from my other fresh injury. He said something on his way out the door. In my current state, I could not be sure of his exact words, but the gist of it was, "I hated doing that."

Thirty-one

Although I knew I wasn't supposed to set foot in Public Safety during my suspension, I opened the door marked ANTI-POLYGAMY SQUAD and entered the familiar office with Roscoe tailing me. I'd been briefing him ever since I picked him up from his apartment, but I only had time to tell him a portion of everything I knew. When we walked into the office Myron looked shocked to see us. He dropped his fountain pen, swiveled toward us in his chair, and watched me go to the filing cabinet, where I opened a drawer and pulled out the dossier on Rulon Black. Roscoe sat down at his desk and opened a pouch of Red Man chewing tobacco while I went to work, flipping open the file and turning pages.

"Aren't you two suspended?" Myron asked.

"I've got a message for the higher-ups," said Roscoe, raising his middle finger.

"Charming, as always," said Myron.

"My way of saying thanks for the memories," said Roscoe, lowering his finger.

"Jared has gone off to Rulon Black's compound," I said, flipping through the file on my desk, searching for hints about the compound's location. "The son of a gun coldcocked me, so I can't be sure of precisely when he left. I think it was around eight."

I glanced up at the clock on the wall. It was nine fifteen.

Myron winced. "Why did he hit you?"

"I wouldn't get out of his way."

"Sorry to hear," said Myron. "But last I checked, you're not supposed to be here."

"Let them fire me," I said. "I need to find out where Rulon's place is."

"What are you going to do?" asked Myron.

"See if I can head off Jared," I said. "Otherwise it's certain suicide for him."

"Why not put in a call to the sheriff down there?" asked Myron.

"I telephoned Sheriff Colborne from Roscoe's apartment," I said. "He says he's putting his deputies on alert, but he doesn't actually know where the compound is, or how to find it."

"Notify the highway patrol," said Myron. "They'll issue an all-points for Jared's car."

"Good idea. He's driving a Nash Ajax belonging to Claudia Jeppson." I looked at Roscoe. "Will you do the honors?"

"Sure. Got a year and color?"

"Twenty-six," I said. "Green."

He got on the phone and rattled the earpiece cradle up and down. While he asked the operator to dial the UHP, Myron slid his chair closer to me.

"Should we go talk to Claudia Jeppson?" asked Myron. "Maybe she knows . . ."

"The polygs have got her," I said.

"Ask the mute girl, then," said Myron. "Possibly she can write it out."

"She's missing," I said. "A lot has happened since last night that you don't know about. I'm still trying to figure it all out. My head is spinning."

"Sounds like there isn't anything you can do," said Myron. "I can tell you right now there's nothing in that file that's going to help you."

Despite Myron's advice, I flipped my way through thin carbon sheets and news clippings that told me nothing about the location of Rulon Black's compound. I was wasting my time. I closed the file, slid it aside, and buried my face in my hands.

Roscoe lowered the telephone earpiece into the cradle. "That's done. They're going to broadcast a bulletin on Claudia's Nash. Hopefully they'll spot it."

The telephone on my desk rang. I lowered my hands. I almost answered it. Then I remembered my suspension. I looked at Myron. He nodded and came over to my desk.

He lifted the receiver to his ear the and transmitter to his mouth. "Anti-Polygamy Squad, Detective Adler here." He listened for several seconds. "Uh-huh." He went silent again. "Uh-huh. Okay. Thank you for telling me."

He placed the receiver in the cradle and set the telephone on the desk. Gazing at me from behind those thick glasses, he hesitated to tell me what he'd just heard.

"That was Wit," he said. "Orville Babcock is dead."

The announcement hit me hard. I instantly felt drained and defeated. I even broke out in a cold sweat. What more could happen? I thought about what Jared said about how the justice system couldn't stop the polygamists. Their reign of terror was all happening out of view of the police.

"The last time he was seen alive was in a telephone booth at an all-night diner up in Ogden early this morning," said Myron. "The waitress told police he was making a frantic telephone call to somebody, but apparently the operator couldn't establish a connection in the storm. Eyewitnesses saw him leaving. A few hours later, his automobile crashed into a ravine. Looks like it was forced off the road."

"Aw shit," said Roscoe. "I didn't like the shyster, and I didn't want him selling you one of his lemons, Art, but he didn't have that coming."

"No," I said. "He certainly didn't."

I suddenly remembered something Babcock had told me on the telephone, a fragment of what he said that I could actually hear through all the static. I snagged a city directory and began thumbing madly through it to the *F*s.

"What is it?" asked Myron, watching me with concern.

"That frantic call Babcock made was to me. He telephoned me in the middle of the night, before I went over to Roscoe's place," I said. "It was a bad connection. I only heard a bit of what he said. He mentioned somebody named Floyd Fairfield. I'm pretty sure he mentioned the man in reference to the four boys who stole the money. Maybe this Fairfield guy is somebody who lives in town, who was trying to help the—"

"He probably meant Camp Floyd," said Myron. "It's an abandoned army outpost, near a little village called Fairfield, about ninety minutes' drive southwest of here."

"I wonder if that's where the four boys are hiding," I said.

"How would Babcock know that?" asked Roscoe.

"He's Carl Jeppson's cousin," said Myron, with a pensive squint. "You know, it's got me wondering. Since Babcock already split with the fundamentalists, maybe he was helping Jeppson do the same. That's not so far-fetched, if you think about it. Jeppson might've been confiding in him before they were both killed. Babcock probably knew too much, and that's why they went after him."

Roscoe reared his head in amazement. "I'm still trying to figure out how in the hell you know they're related?"

"It's in Jeppson's file," said Myron. "Babcock used to be one of the apostles in the Fundamentalist Church of Saints before he got driven out. I found a picture of Babcock and Jeppson taken in happier days, in an old issue of *Truth*. The caption identified them as quote—proud cousins Carl Jeppson and Orville Babcock—unquote."

"How do you remember this shit?" asked Roscoe.

Myron tapped his temple. "Eidetic memory."

"Hell, there are times when I can't remember to buy toilet paper," said Roscoe. "I once had to rub the pages of a *Saturday Evening Post* together—"

"I don't want to hear that," interrupted Myron.

"I guess this means I'm going to Camp Floyd," I said.

"What on earth for?" Myron asked.

"On the off chance one of the boys will know where Rulon Black's compound is," I said.

"What good will that do?" pressed Myron. "You don't know what Jared's got planned."

"I've got a pretty good idea, with all of that firepower he's hauling," I said. "It's not going to end well for him, either. Not unless I try to stop him."

"I hate to have to agree with Adler on this one," said Roscoe.

"Even if you find Jared, he's chosen his fate. I don't see how we're going to stop him."

I smiled warmly at my old friend. "I'm not asking you to come with me," I said. "This is *my* squad. At the end of the day, I've got to be able to say I did everything possible to protect the men under my command."

"That's it?" asked Roscoe.

"Yeah."

He nodded. "I'm coming, then."

"It's up to you," I said.

"I'm sure as hell not gonna let you go alone, Art," said Roscoe.

"Count me out," said Myron. "When I applied for this job, nobody told me I'd have to be in the gunfight at the OK Corral."

"You'd be doing me a favor by staying here and watching over this place," I told Myron. "Until I get back."

Myron nodded. I checked the clock again: 9:34. I looked at Roscoe.

"Well?"

"My chariot awaits out back, sir," he said.

To get to Camp Floyd, I took U.S. Route 89, a highway built about eight years ago that connected Salt Lake Valley to its southern neighbor, Utah Valley. It was late morning, with pristine blue skies. For the first time in weeks, I could hardly see the dark plumes of smoke coming out of the mountain canyons. The rainstorm had worked its magic. It was one of the few good developments I could point to from the last twenty-four hours.

Much of our drive took us past either farms or uninhabited land, and sometimes we'd pass through a little town—Murray, Draper, Lehi—on our way. We exited 89 in the north end of the valley and headed west, along the shimmering tip of Utah Lake, a freshwater cousin of the Great Salt Lake. During the drive, I caught Roscoe up on everything I knew, and by the time we exited 89, I'd essentially gotten him up to speed on the situation, as I knew it. He kept quiet for most of the trip. With Fairfield coming up in a few miles, I couldn't resist asking him about something that had been vexing me.

"You told me she's your daughter," I said. "You had to know I'd ask about the girl in the picture."

I expected him to shake his head or roll his eyes or sigh—something to show his displeasure. He just looked over at me with sleepy eyes. "What do you want to know?"

"Well, for starters, what's her name?"

"Rose. Rose Chisholm."

"Not Rose Lund?"

"No."

"How old is she?"

"Fourteen."

"Where does she live?"

"Denver."

"Why Denver? Why not here?"

"After Rose was born, I left my wife, Catherine. She raised Rose on her own."

I kept driving in silence. What could I say? Eventually, Roscoe continued.

"I was young. I was a goddamned fool. The only things I was any good at in those days was getting drunk, getting laid, and beating up strikers. I ran out on my little family in the middle of the night, too cowardly to do it when the sun was up."

He took out his silvery flask, unscrewed the lid, and took two swallows. He capped it and put it away. I could see the torment in the lines on his face.

"I fooled myself into thinking that what I'd done wasn't all that bad. I mean, after all, I kept sending them money each month. I told myself they're better off without me. And then about, oh, four years ago, I heard Catherine died in a tuberculosis ward in Denver. Her parents took in Rose, let her live with them."

"So Chisholm is their last name?" I asked.

"Uh-huh."

"Do you regret it?" I asked.

He looked at me grimly. "Every single day of my life."

"It's not too late, you know," I said. "A girl never stops needing her father."

"I send her grandparents money each month," he said. "I ain't got the gumption to visit her. I'm sure she wouldn't want to have anything to do with me."

"Where did you get the picture of her in your apartment?" I asked.

"Last year, when I put some money in the mail, I included a letter, asking for a picture," he said. "I wasn't expecting to get one. But lo and behold, a few weeks later, it came in the mail. I cherish it. If that apartment building ever caught on fire and burned to the ground, it's the only thing I'd risk my life to save." He paused. "Well, that and my cats."

We passed through Fairfield, a cluster of houses and barns and trees and not much else. That meant we were coming up on Camp Floyd soon.

"It's never too late," I said.

Thirty-two

Roscoe and I arrived at Camp Floyd in the late morning, sometime around half past eleven. It consisted of a cemetery and a few pre–Civil War buildings now barely standing, a crumbling mess of nailed-together lumber and broken glass. Most of the structures had deteriorated into skeletons, thanks to a lack of upkeep and scavengers who'd stripped the place of anything of worth. When I was a little kid, teenagers from my hometown of American Fork would come back from late-night outings to this place with tales of disembodied whispers, glowing apparitions, and faraway screams. I never placed much stock in those tales. Then again, I had no plans to come out to this place to see what it held in store after sunset.

Back in the late 1850s and early 1860s, Camp Floyd had been a bustling U.S. Army post with thousands of residents, mostly military personnel. They served under the command of Colonel Albert Sidney Johnston, an ambitious officer sent out here in 1858 by then-president James Buchanan. In those days, war threatened to explode across the territory, pitting armed Mormon insurgents against federal troops occupying Utah. Ultimately, the conflict that everybody feared would happen never transpired, and the soldiers were eventually shipped back east, in response to the outbreak of hostilities between the North and South. Nowadays, the cemetery and few remaining buildings are the surviving remnants of that tense standoff. The cemetery they left behind served as a final resting place for scores of soldiers, most victims of diseases or natural causes. Rows of white headstones made a somber sight out here, in the middle of nowhere.

I parked in the shade of box elder trees and shut off the engine of the unmarked Ford Deluxe police sedan. It shocked Roscoe to see me unholstering my revolver. I handed him the gun, but he wouldn't take it at first.

"What the hell are you doing?" he asked.

"Hold on to it, will you?" I asked. His perplexed expression told me he wanted an explanation. "They're kids. They're scared. If I go in there armed, I'll frighten them."

"If you go unarmed, there's a chance one of those trigger-happy brats will fill you up with lead," said Roscoe, still refusing to take the gun out of my hands.

"There might not even be anyone in here," I said. "In which case, this is all for naught. I'll find out soon enough."

Roscoe scowled as he took my gun. I got out of the Ford, closed the door, and crossed a grassy field to get to the brooding commissary building. The abandoned installation had taken on a forlorn quality over the years, and I could not escape the thought of how awful it would be to be a teenager living on these desolate grounds. That is, *if* they lived here. I knew I was taking a risk by coming out here. I understood that this might be the end of the line in my search, and if so Jared's fate would be out of my hands.

I reached the commissary, the most intact of all the remains, and hence the most likely to provide a shelter from the elements. It seemed to me to be the ideal starting point. A two-story wooden structure with doors and windows and long railings on both levels, the commissary also boasted a pair of chimneys jutting out of a sloped roof. Towering trees on all sides shaded the building. Whitewashed walls had turned grimy with age, and when I lowered my foot onto one of the steps, it groaned and I thought the ancient wood might snap under my weight. On the porch, I looked in both directions, but saw no signs of life.

"My name is Detective Arthur Oveson, Salt Lake City Police Department," I called out loudly. "I've come unarmed. You're not in any trouble. I've come here to ask for your help. In return, I'll help you. Think of it as a bargain. I know none of you boys have had an easy go of it. You shouldn't have to live this way, hiding out in this isolated place. There's a better life waiting for you. I can take you there, if you can somehow find the guts to trust me." I raised my hands, to show I had no intention of harming anyone. "I'm entering the commissary building right now. The only thing I ask is that you come out here and talk to me. I promise I mean you no harm."

I opened the commissary door and stepped inside a darkened room. The windows on the first floor had all been boarded. A sign on the wall said DINING HALL, and it was a spacious, empty area with a counter running the length of one wall and a rectangular service window behind it opening up to a kitchen. I walked to the counter and was impressed by the shiny wooden surface. Not a speck of dust in sight. The room did not smell as musty as I expected. No, it had a lived-in feel about it. Someone had been here not long ago.

I found a doorway that opened up to a set of stairs. The passage was narrow and dark, and the stairs were rickety. I arrived at a door at the top of the stairs and nudged it open. The upstairs turned out to be much brighter than the first floor. A long corridor was lined with open doors and a tall window at either end. Signs on the doors announced who the occupants of each room had once been: CAPTAIN'S OFFICE, TELEGRAPH ROOM, QUARTERMASTER'S OFFICE, and COMMISSARY STAFF QUARTERS. I pushed open the door of the staff quarters and entered a room with four beds, each covered with bedclothes that appeared to be clean, although some were less tidy than others.

In the corner of the room, I happened upon what I guessed to be a little shrine of some sort. There were a few books—*A Little Boy Lost* by Dorothy Lathrop and *Peter and Wendy* by J. M. Barrie, two books that focused on lost boys—and several framed pictures on a small table, each showing little children standing side by side, smiling for the camera. Two of the photographs featured adults in them, but most showcased kids, the oldest of which couldn't have been more than eleven. I picked up one of the framed images, this one showing three children—a frecklyfaced boy and two girls, with smiles all around.

"Freeze!"

I put the picture back and stood still. My eyes wandered to the open window, with drapes blowing, which offered a prime view of the Ford parked under the trees in the distance.

"My name is . . ."

"I know what your name is! You don't need to tell it again! I heard you already!"

The voice belonged to a boy in the middle of puberty: deep, yet squeaky around the edges. Low enough to sing baritone, high enough to scream like a girl.

"Reach your hands up," he said. "Turn around."

I turned and faced a lad with a canvas flour bag over his head that had a pair of holes cut out for the eyes. The words LEHI ROLLER MILLS were stenciled on the bag. That meant it came from a big mill not far from here.

Of greater concern to me was the long revolver in his hand, aimed at me.

"What's to stop me from shooting you?" he asked.

"I'm a policeman," I said. "If you shoot me, there'll be lots of other policemen crawling all over this place by nightfall."

"Maybe I'll shoot you and bury you out there where nobody will find you," he said. "How does that strike you?"

"My partner is waiting outside, and he's got an itchy trigger finger. Don't give him a reason to use it, son."

"I ain't your son!"

"That thing can go off accidentally," I said. "If that happens, I'm dead, and you've committed a capital offense."

"I'm a kid," he said. "I won't get the firing squad."

"Do you really want to put your legal expertise to the test?" I asked. "Lay the gun down. Let's talk."

Without warning, three other boys with Lehi Roller Mills flour bags covering their heads came charging into the room, all carrying the same type of long revolvers as the first fellow on the scene. With four guns pointed at me, I can tell you right now that the old stomach started doing backflips. Any jittery fingers would have sent me off to the great glory beyond. They were as nervous as I was, staring out through those holes in the canvas. Each hand trembled, and that didn't make me feel any better about the spot I was in.

"Freeze!" shouted one.

"Hands in the air!" cried another.

The kid who arrived first on the scene shook his head. "He's doing it already! I gave the orders!"

"Oh."

"It doesn't hurt to say it twice."

"Keep your hands in the air!"

"I told him that!"

"Oh."

"What are we going to do with him?"

"I say we shoot him like the mangy varmint he is!"

"We can't," said the first one.

"Why?"

"Because he's a policeman," the first one explained. "If we shoot him, the police will come here and get us. We might even get executed."

"They can't do that to us. We're kids."

"I ain't gonna chance it," said the first one. "He says he wants to help us."

"And you're taking his word for it?"

"What choice do we have?"

"I say we shoot him in the balls!" hollered a masked kid in the back. "I can blow 'em clean off from here."

"I say we hear what he's got to say," reasoned the first one. "What've we got to lose?"

One of the boys standing off to the side, near a window, tossed his gun on the floor. "They ain't loaded, no how."

"You're not supposed to say that, Garth!" shouted the zealous one in back.

"Freeze!"

Roscoe stood behind the boys with my gun trained on them. "Drop 'em, fellas. Now!"

One by one, the other three boys began dropping their guns on the floor. Each revolver made loud clacking noises when hitting wood. The first lad in the room removed his mask. I recognized him as the boy I glimpsed for a fraction of a second at Claudia Jeppson's house. Wavy brown shoulder-length hair. Blue eyes. Maybe thirteen. He was the assailant who'd hit me in the head and knocked me out cold. I almost said something to him about it, but I left it alone. Seeing him in the light, I then connected his face to the photographs I'd seen of a young Boyd Johnston. I knew right then that I was face-to-face with Le-Grand Johnston's son.

"Is there somewhere we can talk?" I asked.

"Right this way," he said.

We'd all gathered around a long table in the commissary, with light spilling in through the open door. The other boys introduced themselves as Garth Christensen, a paunchy kid with tousled black hair and freckles; Franklin Boggs, a handsome boy with short brown hair, beady eyes, and a kind smile; and Chester Hammond, the tough talker from upstairs, a redhead, who turned out to be an awkward and shy young man without the mask on. Using big wooden spoons, we ate cans of beans they kept stored in the back room. The water we drank out of tin cups came from the pump out back and tasted metallic, but the boys assured me it was safe.

They were honest and open about the heist and filled Roscoe and me in on all of the details, right down to Ferron Steed supplying the guns, courtesy of Eldon Black, and showing Boyd how to drive a truck. The foursome had been hiding out here ever since the robbery, visited mostly by Claudia and Jared. One or the other of them—or both—would drop by once a week, occasionally more often, with supplies.

Boyd confirmed that Nelpha had visited here last week, which is where she was when I thought she had returned to Dixie City. He also apologized for putting the money in my basement. That wasn't his original plan, he insisted, but when he drove Nelpha back to my house and saw that nobody was home, the trunk that held the money was still in the back of the truck and it seemed like a good idea at the time.

When I told the boys about Claudia being abducted by the Kunz brothers and Ferron Steed, all four went wide-eyed and Chester began to wipe tears from his face. I informed them that Nelpha, too, was missing, which did not seem to carry quite the same weight as the news about Claudia.

"There's one other thing," I said, spooning the last of my beans into my mouth. "Jared Weeks is on his way down to Rulon Black's compound as we speak. He's got a lot of guns, and much blood will be spilled, including probably his, if we don't do something to stop him. Problem is, I don't know where Rulon's place is located. I need someone who knows the lay of the land to help me find it. I won't put any of you in harm's way. Whoever helps me will be kept a safe distance from Rulon's. Can any of you help me find it?"

"We all know where it is," said Franklin. "But there's only one of us that's actually been in it and knows where everything is."

"Frankie," said Boyd, shaking his head.

"We should tell him," said Franklin. "It'll make him feel better, knowing she's here."

"You talk too much, Frankie," said Boyd.

"Who's here?" I asked.

"I told you to stay put!" said Boyd.

I turned around in my chair to see Nelpha emerging from the kitchen, like a ghostly pioneer hovering across the battered wooden floor. She smiled when she saw me, and in her hand she carried a handheld chalkboard—black slate framed in oak— along with a piece of chalk and a strip of cloth. She came over to where I was sitting, wrote something down on the board, and showed it to me.

HELLO ART

"So you can write," I said.

She nodded and erased the words with her strip of cloth and began writing something else. She turned the board toward me.

SORRY IF I GAVE YOU A FRIGHT

"You scared Clara and me," I said. "We care about you—very much. We want you to be safe. That's all."

More erasing. More writing. She turned the slate my way.

SO SORRY

"How did you get down here anyway?"

Under *SO SORRY*, she wrote: *THUMBED IT.*

"You hitchhiked?" I asked, my voice full of disapproval. "That's not safe."

She wiped the board and wrote more.

I CAN SHOW YOU WHERE RULON LIVES

"I won't put you at risk," I said. "I was hoping one of the boys could show me."

"He's right," said Boyd, stepping out of the dimness. "I'll go."

She rubbed the cloth on the slate and the chalk moved quickly.

She showed me her message: *THEY DO NOT KNOW IT LIKE I KNOW IT.*

"It's no place for a girl," said Boyd. "Take me instead."

Another came seconds later.

PLEASE

She wiped that one and wrote a longer note.

JARED AND CLAUDIA ARE MY FAMILY—LET ME HELP YOU

I looked at Roscoe. He gave me a solitary nod. I turned back to Nelpha.

"I'm sure I'll regret this," I said. "All right, listen, when I give you orders, you mind me. Whatever you do, don't wander off. Understand?"

She pulled the chalk away from the board and showed me, smiling.

YES

Boyd approached her. They faced each other. "I won't let you do it."

She wrote something on the board and showed him. I couldn't see it, and I figured whatever it said, it was between the two of them.

I sensed Boyd getting choked up. "Then I want to go, too. I'm coming with!"

More clacking of chalk on slate. She held up the board.

"Okay," he said, with a solitary tear running down his cheek. "But please be careful."

I looked away while the two embraced.

"We best get going," said Roscoe.

We said our farewells after having spent a good hour at Camp Floyd. Outside, on our way across the grassy expanse to the Ford, the boys tagged along with Roscoe and Nelpha and me. It surprised all of us to come upon another car, identical to the one we drove here, parking alongside ours. The driver, topped with a black fedora, stepped out, slammed the door, and faced us. Myron Adler was his usual deadpan self, only this time he came prepared with a pair of loaded shoulder holsters.

"I thought I asked you to stay behind and hold the fort," I said.

"What are you going to do?" he asked. "Arrest me?"

Roscoe laughed heartily and turned to me.

"You know something?" he said. "I think I'm starting to like this guy."

Thirty-three

Around five o'clock, crossing rough desert terrain near Rulon Black's compound, we spotted a dusty green 1926 Nash Ajax parked in an arroyo. I pulled over, shut off the engine, and got out of the car for a closer look. I opened the passenger-side door. Registration in the glove box confirmed that the vehicle belonged to Claudia Jeppson. I swallowed hard at our find, and Nelpha sized up the car with a forlorn expression. I probed the interior thoroughly, but all I found was a lone, shiny cartridge that had rolled under the seat. Jared had been here. For all we knew, he'd breached the compound walls to exact his bloody vengeance. Behind me, Myron and Roscoe got out of their car and traversed the rocky surface to get down to this level ground, still muddy from a recent flood.

"Well?" asked Myron.

"He beat us here," I said.

"He had a hell of a head start," said Roscoe.

Myron said, "You don't think he'd be crazy enough to . . ."

"In his state of mind, I wouldn't put it past him," I said. "Let's go."

We got back in our cars and drove off. Nelpha guided me to a spot with a prime view of Rulon Black's compound. It made me feel uneasy being back here among the red cliffs and arid sweeps of southern Utah and northern Arizona. I couldn't even be sure which state we were in right then. When we reached our destination, sunlight still lit the sky, yet shadows were long. I parked away from the cliff, got out of the car, and asked Nelpha to stay put. She sat down on the running board while I retrieved my binoculars from the backseat. Myron and Roscoe arrived, joining me over to the escarpment's edge to survey the scene below.

The compound itself turned out to be more of a village than the solitary dwelling I was expecting. It was an orderly community of sapling-lined roads, houses, stables, a garage, a barn, and beyond those, an airstrip and a hangar. A paved road ran through the center of it, linked to a gated entrance. Enclosing the main grounds was a high brick wall topped with barbed wire. Beyond the walled city were grazing lands belonging to Rulon Black, fenced in by shorter wooden posts connected together by tight lines of barbed wire. What a relief to see living, breathing people outside, mostly women and children, going about their activities as afternoon turned to evening.

Roscoe appeared by my side, gazing below. I said, "Either he isn't there or . . ."

"We could speculate until the end of time," said Roscoe. "Got any bright ideas?"

"I've got to go in," I said. "Reason with Rulon."

"Do you hear what you're saying?" asked Roscoe. "You wanna try talking sense to an insane recluse who thinks God speaks to him? He'll probably order one of his thugs to cut your throat."

"I'm open to suggestions, if you've got any," I said.

"Let's go home. We tried to head Jared off at the pass. We failed. That's all there is to it."

"There are children down there," I said. "What if Jared shows up and there's shooting? One of those kids might get caught in the crossfire. I can't live with that."

"So you plan to go up to the front gate and ask to be let in?" asked Roscoe, making a face. "What'll you tell Rulon if they let you see him? 'Can't we all just put our differences aside and bury the hatchet?'"

"Have you got a better idea?" I asked.

Myron showed up by Roscoe's side after listening in on us. "He's right, Art. This isn't your responsibility anymore. It's out of your hands."

"I've got to try," I said. "I've got to be able to say I did everything I could."

"To whom?" asked Myron.

"I'm not asking either of you to risk your lives by coming with me," I said. "In fact, I'd prefer you stay here. Look after Nelpha."

"I won't let you do it," said Roscoe, shaking his head.

"Still got my sidearm?" I asked.

"In my suit coat, in the car," he said, jerking his head at the Ford. "What of it?"

"Give it to Nelpha," I said. "Tell her to stay put in my Olds. She can leave the windows down, but I don't want her wandering off."

"You're really going to do this, aren't you?" Roscoe gave me a hard stare with a raised eyebrow. I nodded. He sighed. "All right, I'm coming with you."

"Roscoe, I don't need you . . ."

"Oh for hell's sake," said Roscoe. "Let's get this over with."

Roscoe went off and retrieved my .38 from his jacket in the backseat of the Ford, then headed over to my Oldsmobile to deliver it to Nelpha. A minute later, she was running toward me, almost tripping, clinging to that little slate chalkboard of hers, with Roscoe in pursuit. When she got to me, she fumbled for her piece of chalk, frantically wrote something down, and held the board up for me to read.

IT IS TOO LATE! DO NOT GO! YOU CAN NOT SAVE JARED.

She was breathing hard, on the verge of tears, and her eyes were wide and penetrating.

"I'll be back," I said. "Then we can go home."

She turned the board toward her, wiped it off with the corner of her hand, and scribbled for a minute or so. Then she flipped it around.

SCARED OF YOU GETTING HURT. SORRY I SHOWED YOU THE WAY HERE.

"Do this one thing for me," I said. "Stay here, with Myron, until I return."

She lowered the board. Her shoulders sagged. She knew she couldn't change my mind. She returned to my Oldsmobile and sat down on the running board with her chalkboard and a morose expression.

Roscoe and I hiked to the bottom of the escarpment. Once at the base, we set off, journeying across that craggy landscape together without speaking most of the way. Being out here in this stark land of mesas rising hundreds of feet into the sky and all manner of unusual rock formations—the hoodoos and chimneys and deep slot canyons cut into the earth by thousands of years of erosion—it was hard not to become a little philosophical. Although this region was unsuitable for farming, it provided plenty of nourishment for thought. By coming here, I knew I was running the risk of robbing my children of a father. I thought about my own father, about how much I'd missed him over the years. I began to second-guess myself, wondering if I was doing the right thing. *It's not too late to turn around*, I told myself. But I didn't turn around. Neither did Roscoe. We kept going. Some deep inner compulsion kept me moving forward.

In a small wooden guard station in front of the compound wall, a pair of familiar hired muscles in suits, one swarthy and freshly shaven, the other with a beard that probably hadn't been trimmed since 1908, got up out of their chairs and came over to me, armed with Thompson submachine guns. I remembered the swarthy one went by the name Duke. They recognized us from our previous visit and shot each other glances on their way over.

I developed that nauseous feeling I sometimes get when I know I've committed myself to something big and I can't turn back. Duke aimed his weapon at me while his partner came over and frisked me. He did the same to Roscoe. Not finding a firearm on either of us, he turned to Duke and simply said, "Clean."

"How did you find this place?" asked Duke.

"It's big," I said. "Not like the proverbial needle in a haystack."

"Why are you here?" asked the bearded one.

"You fellows are just so scintillating, we couldn't stay away," said Roscoe.

The bearded guard raised his Thompson and advanced menacingly. I sidled between the two men and gave Roscoe a fleeting, over-the-shoulder *knock-it-off* glare. "We've come to speak to Rulon Black," I said. "We have reason to believe the inhabitants of this compound are in imminent danger. As you can see, we've come unarmed. Our sole purpose here is to protect lives."

"It's nothing these kittens can't fix," said Duke, patting his Tommy gun.

"If there's a way of stopping him peacefully, isn't that preferable?" I reasoned.

"Why don't I just put a bullet in your head and we'll forget you ever came," snarled the bearded one. He eyed Roscoe. "You first. It'll be a pleasure to take you out."

He chuckled in a sinister way. I grinned, to show I wasn't afraid, even though I secretly was. "That's one option," I said. "Not a good one, though. Even as we speak, there's a detective in our squad awaiting our return, and if we don't show up, he'll go round up the authorities. A lot of folks up in Salt Lake City know we're here, too. That includes my brother, who's an FBI agent. The feds are searching for a justification to drop the iron heel on the polygamists. Kill us and you'll be giving them an early Christmas present with a big red-and-green bow on top. When Rulon finds out you two are the reason he's getting a life sentence in a federal prison, I don't imagine the reprimand will be humane."

They eyed each other for a second. Duke walked over to a metal box attached to the compound wall and used a tiny key to open it, revealing a telephone. He lifted the earpiece, turned a crank, and waited for someone to answer. He turned away from me, as if to guard his conversation, but I could hear him from here. "Hello, Mr. Black, it's Duke." Pause. "Yes, we have a visitor at the front gate." Pause. "Detective Oveson, from Salt

Lake City." Pause. "He wishes to speak with the prophet, says it's urgent." Pause. "Yes, sir."

He hung up, shut and locked the box, and faced us. "He wants to see you."

"Lead the way," I said.

Roscoe and I followed the men into a compound that I can only describe as being frozen in time in the 1850s. A whitewashed one-room schoolhouse stood empty at this time of evening. We walked by several two-story wooden frame houses surrounded by picket fences. Children peeked out of windows and pointed fingers and their mouths moved, as if they were talking to one another. A young blacksmith bearing a striking resemblance to Eldon Black stopped what he was doing inside of his workshop to come over to the door and look out. Women in long dresses took a break from their chores in yards to watch us.

We rounded a corner and came upon the Victorian mansion that quite clearly stood at the epicenter of this desert utopia. An iron fence with spikes wrapped around it, and its lawn was a deep shade of emerald—as green as anything gets outside of Ireland. Flowers that I would have assumed could not grow in this desert environment flourished in beds, watered by a sophisticated irrigation system piped in here from elsewhere on the property, perhaps an underground spring.

The bodyguards escorted Roscoe and me up porch steps where a young man with peach-fuzz hair, dressed in a suit and tie—another younger, bucktoothed version of Eldon—stood by the door and greeted the bodyguards with a nod. He opened the door and we walked into a grand entrance hall filled with lots of natural light and a high ceiling that let you know right off the bat that you were inside of someplace huge. We continued down the hallway. With its tapestries and yellow walls, its shiny floors and marble columns, the interior reminded me of a museum.

Last time Roscoe and I were here, we'd agreed to wear blindfolds at Eldon's request. It was a disorienting experience, to say the least. The only part of the compound we'd gotten a good look at was the cold, dimly lit office where Rulon and Eldon Black conducted their business. That room had a distinctly subterranean feel to it, though I could not be certain of anything on that last visit. So this sumptuous feast for the eyes that was Rulon Black's mansion was new to me, as it was to Roscoe, yet it possessed a certain familiar quality that I could not quite pin down, like a place I'd been to in my dreams. Was I experiencing déjà vu, or had this place left a more potent stamp on me than I thought the last time I visited?

Roscoe and I followed them down a corridor with wood-paneled walls to an elevator, and the bearded one unlatched and opened an accordion gate, stepped aside, and gestured for me to enter. I stepped into the elevator, followed by Roscoe and the pair of bodyguards. One of them pulled the gate closed. The elevator trembled its way down. A moment later, the door opened, and I stepped into a familiar marble room, long and dark, with lights above us that gave off a soft glow, and that desk fit for a pharaoh at the end of the room. Once again, I puzzled over why there was a row of four theatrical spotlights attached to the ceiling above the desk.

Roscoe and I were shown to the two marble benches in front of the desk. My memory of that hard surface made my rump hurt before I even had a chance to sit down. They kept us waiting a long while. I checked my wristwatch by the low light a couple of times. Close to an hour had passed when Eldon Black emerged from a heavy steel door on the other side of the desk, and when he eased it closed, it groaned for more hinge oil.

Eldon walked over to us purposefully. His dark suit gave him the appearance of an undertaker. As he spoke, his stare shifted back and forth between Roscoe and me, as if he were observing a tennis match.

"The prophet wishes to have the lights in the room dimmed except for the high-powered ceiling beams above his desk, which will be switched on and aimed at you. I must warn you the lights will be bright. They may hurt your eyes at first. I advise you not to stare directly into them. It's like looking at the sun. I'm afraid this is a condition the prophet demands in order to safeguard his appearance in the presence of visitors. If you do not accept his terms, he will not come out and talk to you. Do you men agree to this arrangement?"

"Yes," I said.

"Sounds bats-in-the-belfry crazy, like most of the shit you people do," said Roscoe. "But go ahead and knock yourself out."

Eldon turned and walked away. The lights in the room suddenly went out. A few seconds of disorienting pitch-black transpired. Then a loud metallic sound echoed across the room and the spotlights flashed on. Oh heavens, they were bright, the brightest lights I'd ever seen.

Each time I closed my eyes, I saw four dots burned into my retinas. I shielded my brow with my hand, but it made no difference. Through the shine, I did manage to briefly glimpse the darkened silhouettes of Eldon pushing his father, Rulon, in a wheelchair. Rulon wore a wide-brimmed hat, I could see that much, and he appeared to be leaning forward. As they positioned themselves behind the desk, it became harder for me to make out their shapes through the veil of light.

When Rulon finally spoke, he did so in a guttural voice. Raspy. Low. It almost sounded as if he was growling his words. I wanted to see his face, but I could not.

"The prophet was foretold of this day," he said glumly. "A day of vengeance, when a man who was banished from his family as a youth would return to unleash his wrath upon those who cast him out. The prophet fears blood shall be shed today, and there will be a killing in Zion, maybe many killings, unless . . ." He coughed and cleared his throat. "Unless the virtuous slay the wicked wanderer first."

"Bloodshed is not inevitable today," I said. "*If* you are willing to help me."

I squinted in a futile attempt to see him in the shadows, but I could only barely make out the outline of his wide-brimmed hat and the lanky form of his son hovering behind his wheelchair.

"What do you want of the prophet?" he asked.

"Give me Claudia Jeppson," I said.

"Who?"

"I won't repeat her name because you know who I'm talking about," I said in frustration. "We're onto you. The crooked land-grabs, the shady investments and illegal business activities, the recruitment scheme that your son here ran out of room 308 at the Delphi Hotel. Your financial dealings have got blood smeared all over them. We've got the records to prove it."

"What records?" asked Rulon.

"Courtesy of Carl Jeppson before he slipped and fell out of your airplane," I said. Now I was bluffing. But it was for all the right reasons, which made me feel better about it. "An incident captured on film, by the way, by a CCC photographer in Kane

County. All we have to do is match the markings of the craft in the picture to your airplane parked in the hangar outside. I've got your wife Nelpha in protective custody, and there are four boys that took part in a heist that nabbed nearly a million dollars of yours in May so you could collect the insurance money. They're willing to testify that Eldon helped them in pulling it off."

I expected Eldon to deny the charges, but he said nothing. Tense silence followed. Burning-hot light made my eyes throb and bleached our faces. I straightened on the bench, licked my dry lips, and did my best to remain confident.

"I've got everything documented or backed up by folks willing to testify," I said. "I plan to share what I have with Harold O'Rourke, who's investigating the polygamists of Dixie City for the Federal Emergency Relief Administration. I'm no poker player, but if I were, I believe I'd be holding a royal flush right about now."

"All of which begs the question: Why are you here?" asked Rulon. "If you plan to act on this information of yours, then bring the other authorities with you. Bring the FBI. Bring the state troopers. Bring the county sheriff. Raid my compound. Arrest and incarcerate the prophet and his inner circle. Confiscate incriminating evidence for a trial at a future date. But when you come to this sanctuary and speak of card games, you merely amuse the prophet."

I caught a flash of movement in my peripheral vision. One of the Kunz brothers—I'm not sure if it was Dorland or Devlin, but he wore a big black Stetson—shot past us. I craned my neck, trying to see beyond the lights. I glimpsed Kunz's silhouette leaning in close to Eldon. Whispers hissed. The bodyguard left,

walking past us in the opposite direction, into the darkness.
Through the blinding glare, I saw Eldon's figure stooping to
whisper to his father. More uneasy silence followed.

"What are you proposing, Mr. Oveson?" Rulon finally asked.

"Give me Claudia Jeppson," I said.

"In exchange for?"

"I will act as an intermediary to stop Jared Weeks from at-
tacking you," I said.

"Is that what he goes by now?" asked Rulon. "He's taken his
mother's maiden name and his brother's Christian name. Not
wise choices, as they are both dead."

His comment caught me off guard. "Do you know him?"

Rulon let out a gravelly laugh.

"You really should not come here and talk of card games,
Mr. Oveson, until you learn how to play cards," he said.

A series of doors opened in the darkness—the entrance on
the other side of his desk, the elevator behind us. I kept squint-
ing, trying to see what was happening, but those lights were
so intense and jarring that I had no sense of what might be
unfolding in the dark.

Footsteps approached from behind, growing louder with
each one. A lineup formed behind us. The first in the light was
Claudia, blinking the brightness out of her eyes. A moment later,
Jared hobbled forward, hair messy, bruises and swelling on his
face, a tiny line of blood trickling down his chin, shirt untucked,
clearly roughed up.

Rulon said, "And the pièce de résistance . . ."

The final person to step into the light, Myron, approached
slowly and with a sheepish expression, unable to make eye
contact with me. I stared at him over my shoulder, and when he
finally looked down at me, I mouthed only one word. "How?"

He just shook his head, puffed his cheeks and blew air in apparent exasperation.

"What were you saying, Detective Oveson, when I so rudely cut you off?" asked Rulon from the darkness. "Something about cards, I believe it was."

Thirty-four

After our dismal conclave in Rulon Black's office, the Kunz brothers, in Stetsons and pointing .45s, escorted all five of us—Myron, Roscoe, Claudia, Jared, and me—to a small, low-ceilinged concrete room with no windows. When the heavy steel door clanged shut, the room went black. In that grim setting, deep under the ground, I found out how Rulon had gotten the best of us. All of the whispering back and forth brought clarity to the picture of what went wrong.

In Myron's case, one of Rulon's aerial patrols had spotted the cars parked on the escarpment, and Dorland Kunz was dispatched to nab him. Kunz thankfully missed Nelpha, due to her split-second decision to inchworm her way under my Oldsmobile. Myron wasn't so lucky.

Claudia recounted her ordeal of being abducted by Steed and the Kunz brothers in Salt Lake City, along with the trunk containing the stolen heist money. I left out my story about hiding in the basement, witnessing her with Steed and the Kunzes, fearing she wouldn't understand my paralysis at the sight of three armed men.

And Jared? Never stood a chance. Rulon's guards had seen him coming from a mile away. They intercepted him in a secret escape tunnel leading in and out of the compound. In a room like this one, he endured a terrible beating at the hands of the Kunz brothers.

It occurred to me, sitting in the dark and listening to all of these stories, that I'd grossly underestimated Rulon Black. Going into this case, I had regarded the polygamist leaders as sex-obsessed codgers who wanted to leave civilization behind to go live in the wilds and marry as many women as they pleased. It had occurred to me only recently that their choice of lifestyle might actually serve as a cover for all manner of crimes and bloodletting. My black-and-white thinking had steered me wrong. It also failed to make allowance for the few kind souls among them, like Carl Jeppson.

My inability to understand the polygamist mindset also prevented me from seeing Rulon Black for what he was: a tyrant, complete with his own cutthroat security forces. Over the years, he'd developed his own twisted vision of Zion, where obedience reigned supreme, and nobody dared question his authority, lest they end up dead. I had not realized till now just how ruthless he was.

While others whispered, I wondered about Nelpha. I hoped against hope that Rulon's men hadn't caught her. She had my gun, but I feared she would not be able to defend herself. In my eyes, she was a vulnerable girl, like my Sarah Jane, in need of protection and love.

Time passed, and I continued mulling over these matters. At some point, the heavy steel door moaned open, and light splashed in from the dim glow of dangling bulbs in the corridor.

Ferron Steed stood in the doorway. "Let's go."

With machine guns aimed at us, we left Rulon Black's house, venturing into the night. We boarded a motor coach bus with the words FUNDAMENTALIST CHURCH OF SAINTS CHOIR, DIXIE CITY, AZ on both sides. Duke walked up the steps, entering first, and went to the back of the bus, and we five captives filed on without a word of protest. Dorland Kunz took his place behind the wheel, turning the key in the ignition. Last aboard was the bearded man, who kept the bad end of his Thompson trained on us. Kunz shut the door and revved the engine.

"You each sit alone," said big beard. "So much as whisper to anyone, you're both dead—the whisperer and the listener."

I sat on a wooden seat as the motor coach lurched forward, taking the middle spot in a three-vehicle convoy that drove across the nighttime desert. In front of us was a limousine driven by Devlin Kunz, transporting Rulon and Eldon Black in the backseat. Behind us was the town marshal's dark blue Model A, with Ferron Steed behind the wheel.

With my window down a crack, I could hear the distinct howl of coyotes outside. I gazed up at the sky, splashed with stars. The full moon followed us, illuminating the landscape with a soft glow. We spent an hour on that rough road.

The vehicles reached a steep grade. The road narrowed and hugged the edge of a mesa. The climb made me woozy, on top of the dread I was already feeling. The moonlight shone bright enough that I could gaze out at the desert floor dropping away, until we were hundreds of feet above it. My fear of heights began to kick in as the bus rocked from side to side, hitting jarring bumps. I'm sure I would have been a lot worse off in the day, when I could see everything.

The cars and bus reached the mesa top and parked side by side a hundred feet or so from what appeared to be a deep fissure in the earth. When I stepped out of the bus, warm air fanned my brow. A symphony of nearby car doors slammed. All of the headlamps remained on, casting light on the opening in the ground. The men with guns—Duke and the bearded man, the Kunz brothers, and Ferron Steed—formed a phalanx behind Roscoe, Myron, Claudia, Jared, and me. They herded us forward, toward the gaping crevice. Behind the row of armed thugs, Eldon dutifully pushed his father's wheelchair. The only part of the prophet I could see from here was the dim outline of that wide-brimmed hat on his head.

The distant, muted voices of Rulon and Eldon conversed. Then Eldon came forward, stepping between the grim-faced men aiming guns, and his lanky scarecrow legs took him over to the edge of the opening. By the light of the bus and cars, he picked up a stone and tossed it into the void. It never made a sound.

Eldon looked at me and smiled. "No one knows how deep it is," he said.

I gazed into the yawning abyss. On either side of it were embankments dipping at about a forty-five-degree angle, and at the end of those, a sheer drop. A covering of loose rocks and pebbles on the embankments spelled doom for anyone unlucky enough to end up there.

"The prophet calls it the Den of the Transgressors," said Eldon. "He likes to imagine it has no floor, and God's punishment is to make the wicked spend an eternity falling in darkness."

"Too many people know we're here," I said. "They'll come looking for us."

Eldon picked the strangest time to showcase his big overbite with a smile, but that is what he did before walking away. He went over to Claudia, standing between Myron and Jared with her head dipped, staring at the ground.

"You can save yourself," he told her. "Tell me where the boys are."

"No."

"So be it." Eldon faced Devlin Kunz, who was watching intently, .45 in hand. "The task falls upon you," Eldon told him.

"Yes, sir."

Devlin strode forward, but Jared lunged in his way. Devlin swung his pistol into Jared's cheek. Jared grabbed at his bleeding wound with both hands and teetered backward. Devlin walked around him to Claudia, hooked his hand on her forearm, and gave her a powerful push. She almost fell over the chasm's edge, but she steadied herself inches away from it.

Out the corner of my eye, I saw the interior light of Steed's car flash on, and the passenger-side rear door opened and closed silently. The light went off again. The gunmen had their backs to the vehicles, so they missed it. Someone had been hiding in the back of the marshal's car. I wondered if it could be Nelpha.

I had to distract these men. I moved forward several steps. All guns turned on me. Never before had I had so many firearms aimed at me. Any one of them could have gone off right then and I'd be a dead man.

"You're about to make a big mistake," I said. "You can still turn back."

That set off Ferron Steed. With his revolver in his left hand, he came at me, stirring dust under his feet. He seized my shirt collar and forced me—tripping and stumbling—to the monster fissure. He glared at me with cold-blooded ferocity and raised his gun to my face.

"I've had it with you!" he shouted. "You're first!"

The force of the push made me yelp in terror. I hit the ground and rolled, and the earth went sideways, and I went over the edge, sliding down a pebbly slope. Claudia screamed. I would've plunged into the blackness had it not been for a patch of hardy desert scrub that I grabbed with my right hand and a protruding rock embedded in the sandstone that I clutched with my left. Flat on my stomach, on a slope steeper than the roof of my house, I clung for dear life. With my eyes surface-level, headlights and blurs of human shapes appeared in my line of vision. Yet gravity pulled mightily at me.

My heart thumped like one of those machine guns. Shoe soles crunched gravel nearby. I sensed a presence. Digging my fingernails deeper into the rock, squeezing the scrub near the roots, I raised my head.

Ferron Steed arched forward, blocking the stars. He aimed the revolver in his left hand and cocked the hammer.

Three gunshots went off, but they came from a distance. Steed jerked with each crack and then stiffened. Wide-eyed, he lowered his firearm. His jaw quivered. "I . . . someone . . . shot . . ."

He tipped over, chest striking the embankment, and plummeted like a log in a chute, face-first, off into the void. I cringed at the sound of his wailing. I never heard him hit bottom. I shifted my sights back to the surface.

What happened next was a blur. The bodyguards began firing their Tommy guns into the night to try and shoot the ambusher. Eldon bolted for cover, and though I couldn't see where he went beyond the glare of headlamps, I imagined he must have been wheeling his father to safety. Movement occurred all around. Roscoe dove at a distracted Dorland Kunz. The two men rolled on the ground, struggling for Kunz's pistol. It dropped out of his hand. Myron snatched the gun and took off running.

Closer to me, Devlin Kunz, ever the obedient follower, pushed Claudia in the small of her back. She tripped, fell onto the embankment, and slid past me. I let go of the scrub and flung my right hand down to grab her wrist. I stopped her from falling, but her weight almost took me with her.

"Oh God!" she screamed. "Please don't let go!"

"I won't!" I shouted. "It's not our turn today!"

There we were, two people dangling on the precipice. I can't speak for her, but I was offering a silent prayer to God that I'd be reunited with my family in this life.

"I'm not ready to die!" she cried.

I tightened my hold on her wrist. I was so focused on clutching that rock and hanging on to Claudia that I missed the clashes on level ground above us. The steady bursts of gunfire told me that chaos reigned. I adjusted upward to survey the situation as best I could, all the while gripping both Claudia and that protruding rock.

It dawned on the Thompson-toting guards that everything had unraveled. They returned, cradling their machine guns. Myron had taken cover off to the side of Rulon's limousine and squeezed off a round. A bullet struck Duke's knee. He fell, blasting his machine gun into the sky, hollering in agony. Roscoe and Dorland were on each other, rolling around, fighting over what appeared to be a knife in Dorland's hand. The bearded man aimed his Thompson at them, but he couldn't get off a shot because he might hit Kunz.

Nearer to the chasm, seemingly out of nowhere, Jared rushed Devlin Kunz, plowing into him. The men collapsed, wrestling for the gun. A shot startled me. Jared groaned and his resistance melted. Devlin pushed him off and staggered victoriously to his feet.

I felt Claudia slipping. Our mingling sweat made it harder to get a firm grip. I turned away from the violence up above and concentrated on pulling her and me to safety.

A heel came down hard on my hand that held the rock. Pain shot through my fingers, down my arm, reverberating through my body. I shrieked and almost let go of Claudia. Devlin appeared, kneeling over the edge, raising his boot to stomp again.

Deafening bursts filled the air. Machine gunfire came steady. A car engine roared with acceleration. Gears ground between bullets crackling. Devlin Kunz turned in time to get the wind knocked out of him by the grill of Steed's Model A. Devlin was briefly airborne before falling into the abyss. "Oh God," he cried. In the blink of an eye, Devlin Kunz no longer existed. The auto skidded to a halt, its front tires perilously close to the embankment, its engine hissing steam.

Myron appeared above me, taking shelter on the driver's side of the car as the Tommys blazed. Bullets pierced the passenger side, flattening tires, blowing up glass like crystal fireworks. Jared crawled to Myron during the maelstrom. Footsteps rapidly approached on the other side of the car. The bearded man popped up, probably standing on the passenger-side running board. He lifted his Thompson and a muzzle flash lit the area. Bullets tore up the ground, ripping a straight-line trench over to Claudia. She began convulsing as bloody holes exploded all over her body. Her wrist shook in my grip. Her body went limp.

"No!" Jared shouted.

He leaped over the hood of the Model A and tackled the bearded assailant. A scuffle erupted outside of my line of vision. The engine of the stopped car continued to blow steam as I worked up the nerve to look down. Claudia was dead. I would have gone down with her if I didn't let go of her to use my right hand to help me to the surface. "I'm sorry," I whispered. I released her. She disappeared into the earth. At least she was not alive to see it happen.

"Give me your hand!"

Myron was lying on his chest, reaching as far as he could. Our hands met and squeezed. I used my legs, my feet, and my free hand to try to climb up the steep embankment. With Myron pulling me, I could feel myself moving toward level ground. I grabbed ahold of the tangled scrub with my free left hand and threw my entire body into climbing. A moment later, I made it up to the surface and rolled on the ground to get away from the slope.

"You okay?" he asked.

"Been better," I said. "You?"

"I got hit in the shoulder," he said, pointing to a tear in his suit coat and shirt. "It hurts, but I'll live."

Myron slumped against the front tire to catch his breath. "Steed and Devlin Kunz are down," he said. "Eldon and Rulon took off. One of the bodyguards, the clean-shaven fellow, got shot in the leg and he's hiding. There's a fight between Dorland and Roscoe. And Jared is on the other side of this car with the other one."

"Do you have a gun?" I asked.

"Front seat," he said.

I opened the front driver's-side door, crawled across a bed of shattered glass on the seat, and fished a black .45 pistol out from under all of the shards. The passenger-side window had already been shot out. Gripping the gun, I popped over the edge like a jack-in-the-box, right as the bearded man was standing above Jared, raising his Thompson. He turned to me with a horrified expression. I squeezed off two rounds. They passed through his long beard. He dropped the Thompson on the ground and fell to one side. Streams of blood ran down his shirt. The spark of life vanished from his eyes.

He was the first man I'd ever shot and killed, and I didn't even know his name. The significance of that was not lost on me, but I had no time to dwell on it. Instead, I offered a fleeting silent prayer that he would be my last victim.

Pistol in hand, I opened the passenger-side door and cut myself in several places traversing the glass to get out of the car. Sprawled on the ground, Jared had a wound on his waist that he held tightly, and his face appeared pale.

I dropped to my knees to examine the hole at his waistline. I found an exit wound on the other side as well, and the bleeding was slow.

"Today's your lucky day," I said. "A few inches over could've been fatal."

He began to cry. I didn't have to ask why. Claudia was family to him. Nothing could bring her back.

I left him alone and crept to the rear of the Model A. On the mesa-top clearing, Dorland Kunz and Roscoe were still locked in a fight over a long-blade knife. Kunz gained the advantage and plunged the knife downward. Roscoe blocked it and the blade punctured the palm of his hand. His yell could have curdled blood. I sprinted to them, gripping that .45. A few yards away, I raised the gun and pulled the trigger. CLICK! I tried again. CLICK! Out of bullets.

Kunz looked back over his shoulder at me. Brimming with rage, he withdrew the knife from Roscoe's hand and charged at me. I swung the gun at his face but failed to connect. He slammed into me, pinning me down. I could not breathe or move under his weight. He raised the bloody knife into the light of the bus headlamps. Three gunshots rang out. He convulsed with each one. He fell to the ground, as limp and lifeless as a sack of potatoes. The moon glowed in his watery eyes.

Nelpha stood behind him. She lowered my .38. Her cheeks puffed and she blew out air.

A second later, Duke limped out from between the bus and the limousine, leveling his Thompson submachine gun. I pulled Nelpha by the arm to the ground and used my body to cover hers. The booming of automatic gunfire rolled around the top of the mesa.

I looked up in time to see Jared outflanking Duke, approaching from the rear, matching his firepower with the other Thompson. A loud volley sent Duke into a freakish marionette dance as bullets riddled his back. A second later, he was dead at Jared's feet, his gun still smoking. I eased off Nelpha and she stood up and helped me to my feet. I went over to Roscoe, who propped himself up in a sitting position and held a strip of shirt in his hand to absorb the blood.

"You okay?" I asked.

"I'll survive. But if you hadn't show up, he'd a turned me into a pin cushion."

"You hang in there, we'll get you to a doctor," I said.

"Boss," said Jared.

He was holding on to the Tommy gun with one hand, aiming it down at the ground.

"I think I know where Eldon and Rulon went," he said. "I'll show you the way."

Thirty-five

I followed Jared into the darkness, beyond the light from the headlamps, a ways farther down the mesa. I'd retrieved my .38 from Nelpha and I carried it in my right hand. Jared switched on a flashlight to help us find our way through that uneven terrain. We followed the chasm's edge until I caught sight of a pair of figures in the dark up ahead. As we drew closer, I picked up the pace, stumbling or losing my balance a few times in rocky spots. We closed in on the shapes of two men, one with a hat on and seated in a familiar wheelchair, the other standing over him with his back to us. As we got within fifty feet, Jared aimed his flashlight. Eldon peered over his shoulder into the glow, eyes wide with fear, mouth no longer smiling. He turned around and bent over his father's wheelchair, wrapping his arms around the old man. He lurched upward, putting all of his strength into lifting Rulon to his feet. Now twenty feet away, I raised my .38.

"Freeze, Eldon!" I shouted, taking aim at his back. "Put him down!"

"This is between my father and me!" he cried. "It always has been!"

"Let go of me," said Rulon in a throaty growl.

I said, "Do as he says, Eldon. There's been far too much bloodshed here!"

"I'm not going to let you do this to anyone else!" yelled Eldon.

"You haven't the gumption to throw me in there," said Rulon.

"I should've done this long ago," said Eldon.

"What are you doing? You're hurting me!" yelled Rulon.

"Stop right now, Eldon," I said.

Eldon gasped, maneuvering for a better position. He scooped Rulon by his armpits, raising him to his feet. With his son still using both arms to prop him up, Rulon struggled to stay standing on both feet.

"You're a vile old man," said Eldon. "This madness ends tonight."

"It's over, Eldon," I said, advancing toward him. "Let a judge and jury decide his fate. Testify against him in court. You've got the power to put him behind bars, maybe even in front of a firing squad."

"Get away from me, Oveson!" yelled Eldon, with another backward glance. "This has nothing to do with you!"

"Let's go somewhere and talk," I said, moving a few more steps. "That's all I ask. We'll work it all out."

"I said get away!"

Eldon dropped his father in the wheelchair and abruptly faced me. He reached his hand inside in his coat and withdrew a revolver. I opened fire. Two shots echoed across the desert. Eldon's gun slipped out of his grip and he stumbled backward, grabbing his father, launching him out of the wheelchair and down atop himself.

I hurried over to the two men. First I pocketed Eldon's handgun by glow of the flashlight, then I holstered my own firearm, reached down, and hooked my hand around Rulon's arm.

"Here, let me help you up."

"Stay away from him," gasped Eldon.

Rulon was lighter than I expected. As I lifted him into his wheelchair, his large black hat fell off. He was strangely silent. Had he been shot? Was he still conscious?

I said to Jared, "Give me that, please."

Jared passed me the flashlight. I shined it on Rulon. When I saw his face, every goose bump on me stood at attention. I tried never to use the Lord's name in vain, but this one time I let an involuntary "Oh God" slip out.

Rulon's face was frozen in a permanent leer, his lips mostly gone. The gleaming whiteness of his teeth contrasted sharply with his leathery brown skin, which was flaking off in areas. His nose had turned black and pug-like, pressed in against his face. His thick eyelids were open, but housed no eyeballs to speak of. The skin on his long forehead was lighter than the rest of his face, more yellowish, and he still had a head of unruly dark, wavy hair. His ears had deteriorated into shriveled prunes.

I looked down at Eldon. Still lying on the ground, he gripped wounds on his stomach and rib cage. His breathing had grown labored and crackly. "You weren't supposed to see him."

"How long has he been this way?" I asked.

"I found Perry Tindal's book on the desiccation methods of the Maori people most helpful," said Eldon, gasping for breath. "I also read a lot about how the British preserved the body of Jeremy Bentham. . . ." His body rocked as he coughed up blood.

When he caught his breath, he said, "The father of modern utilitarianism. His remains are perfectly preserved and on display at University College in London. Or so I've read."

"Rulon's a mummy?" I asked, in shock. "Since when?"

"I was waiting for him," said Eldon. "I used a shovel."

"You killed him?" I asked.

"He made promises to me," said Eldon bitterly. "I was his favorite son, you see. He told me so, over and over. The compound would go to me when he died, he told me. He had sons who were older than I was, but he banished them, in favor of me. I was to be his successor. You see, he loved my mother more than any of his other wives, and he always said I had a good head for business. Everything changed when I told him I fell in love with a girl I met at a dance. But when Rulon met her, he vowed to make her his eighth wife. He cited a revelation. Claimed God told him this was to be. Heavenly Father sent down word to banish me because my heart was evil. That's what Rulon said, anyhow. He commanded me to leave and never return. I tricked him into thinking I was going away. But I never left. I hid in the barn and . . ."

His words trailed off.

"That's when you hit him with the shovel," said Jared.

"Over and over and over. I had to use these special pins that I ordered out of a medical catalog to reconstruct his head. I think I did a good job, under the circumstances. Don't you?"

"I'm not following this at all," I said. His explanation astounded me. "How could you possibly fool all of those people—the wives, the apostles, the children—into thinking that Rulon was alive?"

"After I killed him, I invented a tale of him being attacked by an unknown assailant, probably a rival," said Eldon. "I got away with it because nobody knew that he banished me right before I killed him. All they knew was that I was his trusted son. Nobody ever questioned my role as his main caretaker. I told people the incident left my father horribly deformed and in need of a wheelchair to get around."

Eldon rolled over and moved into crawling position. I stood back, aiming the flashlight in front of him to show him the way. On his hands and knees, Eldon moved slowly over to the wheelchair. He scaled the apparatus, grabbing on to the armrests to help him up, and he moved in close to his mummified father, placing his head on the dead man's chest.

"You did everything in the dark," he said, stroking the dead man's dusty coat. "That's how you consummated your marriages. That's how you conducted business with the prophet and the apostles. That's how you ruled over an empire and put fear in the hearts of men and women. The shadows gave you power. I only provided the voice." He coughed again, and blood coated his lips and dripped down his chin. He now spoke in a near-whisper. "People fear most what they don't know. That's why they're afraid of the dark. Their imaginations run wild, and they fill the empty places with dread."

"Tell me one thing," said Jared. "Why did you help those boys steal your own money? Did you really want to collect the insurance on it? I mean, you've got more money than most people can imagine. What more could you possibly want?"

Eldon shook his head. "How can you be so naive? It wasn't about insurance money. Father was the next in line to be the prophet. I knew he terrified Uncle Grand. I arranged with those four boys to carry out the robbery. I sent Nelpha up to

Salt Lake City to murder the prophet. We had a deal, she and I. I even gave her the gun she used. In exchange for shooting him, she'd sign a confession to the police saying she murdered Grand to protect her one true love. No judge would throw the book at an innocent child bride who was defending herself. At most, she'd probably spend a few months in the reformatory. I promised her that once she was out, I'd . . ." Eldon erupted in another coughing fit.

Jared finished his sentence: "You promised her you'd leave her and Boyd Johnston alone after that. Then Rulon—really you—would become the next prophet of the Fundamentalist Church of Saints, meaning you'd preside over one of the richest empires in the western states. I'm sure you'd wipe out any potential foes—real or imagined—in your church while you were at it."

"You're not as naive as I thought," said Eldon, with a bloody grin. He caressed his father's football-like head. "Nelpha didn't hold up her end of the bargain. I knew that day you came to arrest me, Oveson. She betrayed me."

"That's because she didn't shoot Johnston," I said. "Someone else did it."

I stared meaningfully at Jared. Our eyes met. He confirmed with a single, solemn nod. A crackling gasp came from Eldon. When I looked down at him, I noticed he seemed awfully still. I moved the flashlight near his face. No need to check for a pulse. He was gone.

Jared said, "Is he . . ."

"Yeah."

After a long silence, Jared asked, "How did you know it was me?"

I reached into my pocket and fished out that rain-drenched speeding ticket I had found in the glove box of the Model T truck parked in Claudia's garage. I handed it to him, along with the flashlight. "I found this inside the Model T truck parked in Claudia's garage." Says you were going sixty-eight in a forty-five-mile-per-hour zone," I said. "You were driving a delivery truck owned by Columbia Transport out of Flagstaff. When the Utah Highway Patrol officer who wrote up that ticket saw that you were the one driving, he voided it, tore it out, and gave it to you."

"Maybe he just didn't want to ticket an out-of-state truck," said Jared.

"No, that's not it," I said. "You were in the motorcycle bureau long enough to know two things. One, there's a ticket-collection agreement in place between Utah and Arizona. Two, when you rode a police Harley, you befriended a lot of highway patrolmen, including the one who voided that ticket. I'm sure if he were subpoenaed, he'd confirm what I'm saying."

He gave me back the ticket. "That's all you've got? A speeding ticket?"

"Nope. A few other things gave you away. When you told me you sneaked into the crime scene the day after the murder, I knew you were lying. Two uniformed officers were assigned to guard the church full-time until the Homicide dicks wrapped up their investigation, and I'm sure they'd confirm my suspicions that you never showed up there on July the third. Oh, and the gun in the hedges? Nice touch, Jared. No homicide investigator in his right mind would ever assume that a detective bureau man would do something so sloppy. It worked. You threw off the bloodhounds. You were never even on Wit's long list. Too bad you didn't wipe the gun well enough before you tossed it. Some of Nelpha's prints are still on it. I'm sure you didn't intend for her to be a suspect."

"No," he said. "I didn't. After I shot Uncle Grand and Volney Mason, I turned around and she was gone. I had no idea where she went. I got panicky. I knew there was a chance you'd be watching the premises. So I fled, without looking for her. Had Claudia or Carl gone there with her that night, they might've done the same thing as me, but they wouldn't have been as mindful as I was about the need to clear out fast. I guess I threw a real scare into Nelpha, huh?"

"She was pretty shaken," I said. "One other thing gave you away."

"Yeah?"

"Yesterday, in your apartment, when I was questioning you, you knew too much," I said. "Only two of my questions failed to get a conclusive answer out of you. The first was when I asked if Rulon was in on the heist, and of course you had no way of knowing. So you passed that one. The other was my question about who might've pulled the trigger on Johnston and Mason. You didn't even offer a theory. And after you answered all of the other questions so smoothly, I knew you were protecting either the Jeppsons or yourself."

Jared let out a shaky sigh.

"Everything you say is right," he said. "When we get back to Salt Lake City, I'll voluntarily surrender. I'll sign a confession."

I shook my head. "There won't be any confessions."

Even in the darkness, I could see that Jared looked confused. "Why?"

"You did what you did for the noblest reason of all," I said. "To protect a frightened girl who was so tired of being abused that she was willing to consider murdering someone else to get out of it. That she couldn't bring herself to do it, but you could, doesn't make you a criminal. It makes you a man with a good heart who had no choice but to do something terrible."

He closed his eyes and I heard a forlorn sob in the darkness. I reached up and gently patted his shoulder.

"Let's go home," I said.

Thirty-six

Three weeks later, our third child, a daughter, was born.

She came into the world on the first day of August. She had a thin layer of golden brown hair. She weighed eight pounds, two ounces. And she was a kicker.

Good thing the LDS Hospital had such a big waiting room. Between Clara's sizable family and the massive Oveson clan, it looked like half of the state of Utah had invaded the place. Old and young, men and women, boys and girls had squeezed inside the area, packed in like sardines.

I sat on a hard wooden chair, sandwiched between Roscoe and Myron. Without changing his expression one iota, Myron handed me a little square box wrapped in silvery paper, topped with two bows, one pink, one blue.

"Open it."

I tore off the paper and lifted the lid. Inside, I found two pairs of knitted baby booties. Like the bows on the package, one pair was a deep pink and the other a shade of robin's egg blue.

I examined them with delight, holding them up for my various relations to see.

"Thank you, Myron," I said. "They're beautiful."

"Don't thank me," he said. "Hannah made them. Obviously, she wasn't sure if you were having a boy or a girl, so she erred on the side of caution."

"Well, I'll be sure to send her a thank-you card," I said. "In the meantime, maybe you could let her know how happy we were to get these. They're perfect."

Myron nodded. "I'll do that."

When the doctor burst out of the swinging doors, he froze in shock at the sight of the huge crowd. "Is the father here?" he called out.

"Look alive," said Roscoe, patting me on the back. "Time to meet the newest Oveson."

"Let him through, let him through!" hollered my brother John, herding the family apart to clear a pathway to the double doors.

The doctor led me to the hospital room at the end of the hall.

"Emily Margaret Oveson," said Clara, "I'd like to introduce you to your father."

I bowed low and Clara placed the baby into my arms. The blanket shadowed her sleeping round face, soft and pink, with puffy eyelids and little red lips that moved every so often. The nurse slid a chair near the bed and gestured for me to take a seat. I sat down, cradling my new daughter in my arms, feeling her gentle movements. I lost track of how long I sat there, holding her, rocking slowly, whispering to her about how proud I was to be her father.

I returned the baby to Clara. She told the doctor she wanted to take the baby out for all of our relatives to see. He hesitated, but finally agreed, and a nurse assisted Clara into a wheelchair. I pushed her while she held the baby in her arms. We went through the double doors into the sea of people out in the waiting room. Clara allowed only a select few people to hold the baby. "I don't want her catching anything from anybody," she said.

By the late afternoon, the crowd had cleared. Only Roscoe remained in a quiet corner of the waiting room, thumbing through a magazine. I motioned for him to come over. He tossed his magazine on the stack, got up, and ambled over.

"The proud papa," he said. "I suppose congratulations are in order."

Clara looked up at me with a smile that told me all I need to know. I delicately lifted Emily with both hands out of her arms and walked over to Roscoe.

"Here," I said. I leaned toward him with Emily.

He shook his head and flashed his palms. "No. I'd better not."

"No, seriously. Take her."

"I'm no good at this. . . ."

"C'mon," I said. "Here, hold out your arms. . . ."

"Shoot, Art. I don't know. . . ."

"You can do it."

Roscoe raised a skeptical eyebrow. "Yeah?"

"I insist. C'mon. You just have to support her head."

"Yeah, okay. Let me see. . . ."

He moved in with his arms spread like a forklift.

"Hold them closer together," I suggested. "Like a little cradle."

I passed the baby into Roscoe's big arms. He stood as stiff as a barbershop pole. He kept his hand behind her head at all times. He started to look panicky, like he was about to drop her. He eyed me to make sure I wasn't leaving. "She's a cute kid."

"I thought you'd like her," I said.

"What're you planning on calling her?"

"Emily," I said. "Emily, this is your uncle Roscoe."

"Hey, kid, you're cute as a button, but I'm gonna give you back to your old man before I die of heart failure."

Roscoe returned Emily to me and I gently handed her back to Clara. Straightening, I elbowed Roscoe and winked. "I think you're a natural at this."

"As long as we keep it to uncle," he said, "everything will be fine."

"You have one of your own," I said. "Rose."

His smile faded as he dipped his head and sighed. "Yep."

"It's not too late," I said. "A girl always needs her father."

He raised his head and his mouth formed a rueful grin, but it could not hide the pain I'm sure he felt inside.

The rest of the summer lives on as a series of fragments in my mind. We welcomed our newborn daughter to her home, but the place felt a little emptier without Nelpha. Not long after the incident at Rulon Black's compound, I persuaded Wit Dunaway to drop his investigation of Nelpha. I told him that Claudia Jeppson had confessed to pulling the trigger that night. Despite how much I hated lying, I knew what I was doing was for the best. Wit had no great passion to charge Nelpha with the crime. He admitted that she'd left only partial fingerprints on the gun. With no eyewitnesses, and a public that would be overwhelmingly sympathetic to Nelpha if she were ever put on trial, Wit declared the case closed. When the story broke, the press portrayed Claudia Jeppson as a heroine, a former polygamist wife who came to the defense of a helpless child bride, to prevent Nelpha from being sent back to a fate worse than death.

I thought of Nelpha often, but I faced my own challenges in the summer and fall. After Emily's birth, I spent endless weeks staying up late with her, thanks to a bout of colic and a tendency toward wakefulness on her part that made her every bit as much of a night owl as her father. I'd take her out for moonlit auto rides around the Avenues, and on certain nights, I'd park high on the hill and watch the glow from a distant wildfire.

By early August, overworked volunteer brigades had managed to contain most of the blazes, with only one or two of the most tenacious infernos still burning as of Labor Day. A few well-timed rainstorms helped. The fires of '34 had been catastrophic, scorching millions of acres across the western states. Fourteen men, ranging in age from nineteen to fifty-four, perished in the flames that summer. A memorial was later erected in Big Cottonwood Canyon to the men who died in the Fire Season of 1934. It is still there, shaded by aspen trees.

After the Anti-Polygamy Squad folded, Roscoe quit the police force to launch his own detective agency, Beehive Discreet Investigations. He ran it out of a little office in the Rio Grande Railroad Depot on the west side of town. To supplement his income, he worked as a railroad dick, patrolling the yard for intruders and tossing hoboes off boxcars. I put on a cheery face and wished Roscoe well, but inside I was sad to see my old friend go. Public Safety seemed like a less lively place without him.

I wound up back on the Morals Squad, under the command of laconic, sleepy-eyed Lieutenant Harman Grundvig. He launched a highly publicized crusade to drive every slot machine—or "one-armed bandit," as he called them—out of Salt Lake City.

With the press in tow, we raided downtown clubs and isolated roadhouses alike, occasionally smashing down doors with axes for a little added drama.

The shutterbugs snapped pictures as we loaded the gambling devices onto dollies and carted them out to waiting police vans. I hammed it up for show, whipping out my pistol for the cameras, wearing my hat low, playing up my Running Board Bandit credentials. But the reality was, I missed my old squad. I did not miss commanding it, or even necessarily what we did. No. It was the people I missed. Roscoe. Myron. Jared.

Myron had returned to the records division in the basement. We stayed in touch through our monthly lunches. During one particularly memorable noontime meal at the Chit Chat Luncheonette, he opened up about his own personal history, discussing his father, the retired former rabbi at the B'nai Israel Temple, and his mother, who escaped the pogroms in Russia. He showed me a picture of his wife, Hannah, and recounted what it was like to grow up Jewish in Salt Lake City. "It was pretty boring, when you get right down to it," he said. "But after everything my people have been through, I'll take boring any old day."

Jared, like Roscoe, resigned from the police department in the summer. He founded a new charity called Hospitality House to aid refugees of all ages fleeing polygamy. The press loved it, and his smiling mug appeared on A1 of all the local dailies. He refused to take a dime of the heist money, still packed away in a trunk down at Rulon Black's compound. Instead, he used the press as a bully pulpit to raise funds for his new undertaking. His success exceeded my highest expectations. Playing on the antagonism that most mainstream Mormons felt toward polygamy, he managed to raise enough money to renovate the house on B Street and purchase a second home next door, to make space for new arrivals. Donations poured in from concerned citizens, in Utah and across the country. Even in hard times, people sent what they could, and every little bit made a difference.

One day in fall, chilly and overcast, I was raking leaves in the front yard with the help of Hyrum and Sarah Jane. A car pulled up to the curb and who should get out of the passenger side but Nelpha. She looked beautiful with her hair freshly styled and a brown dress with white lace. I stuck my head in the house and called Clara, and she came outside with the baby in warm clothes and a coat. Jared had given her a ride that day, and he got out of the car to join the reunion. Hugs were exchanged all around, and we Ovesons took a break from raking to reminisce about Nelpha's time with us. Finally, she passed me a gift box and asked me to open it. I ripped the wrapping off, lifted the lid on the box, and looked down at a familiar needlepoint pillow that I once saw inside of the soiled little pillowcase that held all of her belongings. The big, block serif words on it said GOD BLESS OUR HOME.

"Thank you," I said, getting choked up. "We will cherish it."

I held out my hand to shake hers, but she did something that caught me off guard. She wrapped her arms around me and hugged me tightly. I leaned forward and kissed her on top of the head.

"We'll always be here," I said.

She pulled back and nodded, as if I was telling her something she already knew.

Jared walked up to me and shook my hand.

"You busy on Thanksgiving, boss?" he asked. "Because I got two dozen kids just itching to cook a dinner with all the fixins for you all."

I looked at Clara and she smiled and nodded her approval.

"We'd love to come," I told Jared.

"Fabulous! Why don't we say, oh, about five? I've invited My-ron and Hannah, and Roscoe, too. It'll be like having the old squad back."

I grinned warmly. "Thanks, Jared."

Nelpha climbed in the car and closed the door and Jared cir-cled to the other side. Before he opened the door, I called out to him. "Hey, Jared. You aren't my subordinate anymore. No need to call me boss."

He chuckled and winked. "I guess not. But, at this point, anything else just seems wrong."

With that, he got in the car and drove away.

The violence that plagued that dark summer of 1934 soon faded from the public's memory.

The homicides of Carl Jeppson and Orville Babcock were eventually declared unsolved in the respective jurisdictions where they occurred, and subsequently filed away. Down in Kingman, Arizona, Sheriff Burke Colborne accepted my fabri-cated version of events: that a bitter rivalry had developed be-tween Rulon Black and his son Eldon, leading to a bloody confrontation between rival factions at the Black compound. Ironically, I wasn't that far off.

The lackluster response of these investigators reflected a deeper, troubling reality of the times: Nobody wanted to touch the polygamists. I went to DAs, state attorneys, and judges, lug-ging around with me a box of evidence that shed light on the polygamists' criminal business enterprises. Among the docu-ments in my possession was a notarized statement from Carl Jeppson that one of his wives gave me after I returned from my brush with death down at that deep chasm. It detailed a variety of crooked practices, including the infamous Homestead land scheme. The district attorney in Salt Lake City apologized and informed me that none of it fell within his domain. An attorney with the state of Utah declared that he did not have the time, resources, or inclination to pursue the case. Federal judges in Arizona and Utah counseled me to drop the whole thing.

"You seem like a decent fellow," said the judge in Phoenix. "Mind if I give you some unsolicited advice, off the record and free of charge?"

"Please," I said. "Go right ahead."

"Go home to your family and forget about all of this." He shrugged. "So what if some guy marries a bunch of ladies? A quarter of my state is outta work, Oveson. Men that used to own respectable businesses are now out riding the rails, looking for work. Forgive my foul mouth—I know you're a Mormon and all—but they don't give a shit about polygamists and, frankly, neither do I. Let those fools marry as many women as they want. If they break the law, the justice system will have at 'em. Take your box, go back to Salt Lake City, and count your blessings that you've still got a job."

I followed his advice. Not because I agreed with him, but because what choice did I have? I carried my box to the depot, boarded the train bound for Salt Lake City, and found a comfortable seat in the observation car, where I watched the red-and-orange desert streak past me. When I got home, I found a spot on the highest shelf in my closet for that box, and I pushed the door closed on it.

I recalled Buddy's words. *"Don't let the polygamists become your white whale."*

And yet, my longstanding animosity toward the plural marriage racket ruled out any hope of following that advice. So it was with mixed feelings that I watched more and more local polygamists pack their belongings in the summer and fall of 1934, sell their property in town, and relocate to Dixie City. On the one hand, I wouldn't miss them. On the other, I knew they'd be impossible to bust once they retreated to that insular little community way out in the middle of nowhere.

The fundamentalists found a new prophet, Alma Covington, to head their church. He sold his house on Third Avenue and he and his many wives took up residence in Rulon Black's compound. I'm sure there was plenty of room in that grim behemoth of a dwelling for the whole lot of them, and his sizable printing press.

SATURDAY, DECEMBER 1, 1934

We sat in the idling car, parked alongside the curb, on a hill in a suburb of Denver. As the weather reports promised, the snow was falling sideways, blanketing everything in white. I kept the radio tuned to station KOA, which broadcast Paul Whiteman and his Orchestra performing Christmas music. Up and down the block, colored Christmas lights flashed on and off in living room windows.

Roscoe sat on the passenger side of the front seat, gripping a teddy bear and a bright bouquet for dear life, as if afraid they'd be snatched out of his clutches. He was freshly shaven, and he wore a fancy suit that he'd purchased for this very occasion. On the car floor, a festive green-and-red bag with handles on it held a bunch of gift-wrapped presents. The weight of my stare must've gotten to him, because he turned his head toward me and gave me the angry eye.

"What?"

"You look handsome."

He faced forward and took a deep breath. "I shoulda never let you talk me into this."

"You won't regret it."

"How do you know?"

The snow was falling harder now, covering everything in sight. I switched on the windshield wipers, and they squeaked back and forth, clearing the powder out of our way.

"A girl needs her father," I said.

"She's probably gonna tell me to go to hell," he said. "I wouldn't blame her if she did. My old man ditched my mom and me when I was a little kid. I never knew the prick. Shit, I don't even know what happened to him. If he ever came back, which I don't expect he'd ever do, but if he did, I'd tell him to go fuck himself."

"She needs you," I said. "You'll see."

A big black Packard rolled past us through the slush and snow and swerved into the driveway of the house across the street. An older man in a hat and overcoat got out of the front, stepping off the running board into the snow, and closed the door behind him. A woman with white curly hair and a long coat emerged from the passenger side. She opened the back door and a teenage girl with a green hat and a red coat climbed out of the car. The trio went inside.

"That's her," I said. I looked at Roscoe.

"I know! Christ, Art, you don't gotta tell me! I already know!" He licked his lips, and I noticed his hands trembling. "I don't think I can do it."

"Sure you can."

"What if she tells me she doesn't want to see me? All this time I haven't been in her life . . ."

I leaned over and patted him on the shoulder. "It's never too late."

He looked over at me and took another deep breath. "Yeah?"

I nodded.

He nodded, too. "All right. I'll give it a shot."

He opened the door and snow flurries blew inside the car. He maneuvered out onto the sidewalk, still holding the flowers and the teddy bear, and then he leaned inside the car and lifted the bag full of presents.

"Need some help?" I asked.

"Naw, I got it." He stopped and looked in at me. "Thanks."

He slammed the door and crossed the street, making his way carefully up the sidewalk and porch steps to the front door. I watched intently as he managed to balance everything in his arms and bang the knocker. He glanced back at me. I noticed the uncertainty stamped on his face before he turned around again. The door opened and the girl appeared. The two of them spent the next few minutes talking to each other. I wondered what they were saying. Why was it taking so long? What if Roscoe's worst fears came true and she told him to go? I bit my fingernails with nervousness. She reached out, squeezed his forearm, and tugged him inside. Roscoe gave me one last look, smiling, and he ventured into the house. The door closed.

Even though the temperature had plunged below zero outside, I felt warm all over with happiness for my best friend. So much so, I whispered the words one more time, to nobody in particular.

"It's never too late."